A Body to Die For

ALSO BY KATE WHITE

If Looks Could Kill

'Til Death Do Us Part

more . . .

A Body to Die For

KATE WHITE

WARNER
VISION
BOOKS

NEW YORK   BOSTON

Cover design Shasti O'Leary Soudant

WARNER BOOKS

Time Warner Book Group
1271 Avenue of the Americas, New York, NY 10020
Visit our Web site at www.twbookmark.com

Printed in the United States of America

Originally published in hardcover by Warner Books

First Paperback Printing: April 2004

10 9 8 7 6 5 4 3 2

To my fabulous brothers whom I adore:
Mike, Jim, Rick, Chuck, and Steve

ACKNOWLEDGMENTS

Thank you to those who so generously helped me with my research for the book: Paul Pagenelli, M.D., Chief of Emergency Medicine, Milton Hospital, Milton, MA; Barbara Butcher, director of investigations for the office of the chief medical examiner, New York City; Roger Rokicki, Chief Inspector, Westchester County Police; Sanjay Singh, New York City Police (Vice); psychotherapist Mark Howell; former FBI profiler Candace deLong; Erin Scanlon, partner, Deloitte & Touche; Kathy Beckett; and Mary Ewart.

I also want to say a special thank you to my fearless agent, Sandra Dijkstra, and to my awesome editor, Sara Ann Freed, who provided me with such wonderful guidance.

A Body to
Die For

CHAPTER 1

WHEN I THINK back on everything terrible that happened that autumn—the murders, the grim discovery I made, the danger I found myself in—I realize I probably could have avoided all of it if my love life hadn't been so sucky. Or let me rephrase that. Nonexistent. Late in the summer, I'd been kicked to the curb by a guy I was fairly gaga over, and though my heart no longer felt as raw as a rug burn, my misery had morphed into a sour, man-repellent mood. It was as if I had a sign over my head that said, "Step any closer and I'm gonna bitch-slap you."

So when I was invited to spend an early fall weekend free of charge at the Cedar Inn and Spa in Warren, Massachusetts, I grabbed the chance. Trust me, I wasn't expecting to meet anyone there—except maybe a few rich women in pastel sweat suits and fanny packs who thought having their bodies slathered in shea butter would miraculously vaporize their cellulite. I should also admit that I've generally found spa stuff pretty goofy. I once had a complimentary prune-and-pumpkin facial, and when it was over I kept thinking that I should be stationed on a sideboard between a roast turkey and cornbread stuffing.

But I do go nuts for a good massage, and I was hoping that a few of those and a change of scenery would improve my mood as well as jump-start my heart.

Unfortunately, soon after I arrived at the inn, all hell broke loose.

I pulled into Warren just before seven on Friday night. A reasonable arrival time, but three damn hours later than I'd originally planned. A combination of things had thrown my schedule into a tizzy. I'm a freelance journalist, specializing in human-interest and crime stories, and an interview that I was scheduled to do with a psychologist for an article on mass hysteria got pushed from morning to midafternoon. I would have liked to just blow it off entirely. But the piece was due at the end of the following week, and I was feeling under the gun. I didn't hit the road until three-thirty, guaranteeing that I'd have a good chance of getting caught in a rush-hour mess somewhere between Manhattan and Massachusetts—and I did. In addition, I was undone by a smoldering car fire on the southbound side of the New York State Thruway, which caused people on my side to practically crawl by on their haunches so they could get a better look. You would have thought the front half of the *Titanic* had been dredged and deposited along the side of the road.

If I'd arrived on schedule, I would have been welcomed by the owner of the inn, Danielle (aka Danny) Hubner. She was the one treating me to an all-expenses-paid weekend. An old college friend of my mother's, Danny had been pleading for me to visit the inn since she'd opened it three or four years ago. But I'd always been too crazed with work—or too caught up in the stages of grief that followed the demise two years ago of my flash fire of a marriage: heartache, healing, and manic horniness. This fall, because of my snarky mood, I'd finally said yes.

It would be great, I figured, to not only be pampered 24/7, but also to spend a nice chunk of time with Danny. She was really my friend, too, and she had a slightly off-beat personality that I found absolutely refreshing. I got the sense my visit would also prove beneficial to *her.* My mother had called right before she flew to Athens for a Mediterranean cruise to say that Danny had seemed in a bit of a slump lately, but she didn't know why. My mother was worried she might be having troubles with her second husband, George, whom I'd yet to meet—and whom my mother didn't seem wild about.

Since I arrived so late, I'd missed Danny. According to the desk clerk, she'd driven into town on business she could no longer put off, but she'd left word that she would check in with me later. I was given a brief tour before being shown to my room.

The inn, a rambling, clapboard building probably erected in the mid-1800s, was really quite smashing, even more so than in the pictures I'd seen. Instead of dripping with the cutesy country charm that you so often find at a restored inn, the decor was elegant, pared down—lots of beige and cream tones and brown-and-white-check fabric. And there wasn't a whirligig, weather vane, or wooden swan in sight.

Since I was late, I figured I'd blown any chance of getting a treatment that night, but my guide explained that Danny had arranged for me to be squeezed in for a massage at eight—before a late dinner. The inn's spa, which also operated as a day spa for the area, stayed open until ten.

I had about fifteen minutes to catch my breath before the massage. My room was maximum charming, a suite, actually, with a small living area. It also sported checks, but in red and white and paired with several quirky print fabrics. I unpacked the clothes most likely to wrinkle and hung them in the closet. (I'm a contributing writer for *Gloss* magazine, and I read in a recent issue that you should roll your clothes in tissue paper before packing them in order to prevent wrinkles, but I'd no sooner take the time to do that than I would to iron my underpants.) Next I took a very quick shower, letting the spray of hot water do a number on muscles achy from a long car ride.

I dried myself off with a thick Egyptian-cotton towel. Thanks to a towel warmer, it was as toasty as a baked potato. As I buffed my body with it, I noticed a small earthenware jar on the bathroom countertop. It was filled to the brim with amber-colored bath salts, and a little tag announced their availability for sale in the spa. They were a blend of sandalwood and sweet orange aromatics with a hint of frankincense, prepared, the tag said, so I could "surrender to a state of total enchantment and emerge with a primitive power." God, just what I needed. Was it actually suggesting I could get *both* in the same weekend? I glanced up, into the mirror above the sink. I'm five six, with short, brownish blond hair, and blue eyes, and I'm considered pretty in a slightly sporty way, but there was no denying that at this moment in time, I looked weary, even burned-out. It was going to take a helluva lot of bath salts to leave me feeling enchanted and empowered.

I arrived downstairs at the spa with just a few minutes to spare. It was actually a large addition to the inn, abutting the eastern edge of the building. The decor was Asian inspired: beige walls, cracked stone floors, bamboo plants in large putty-colored pots, and hallways lined with sheer beige curtains that poofed outward from the breeze that you created walking by them. It was very different from the decor of the inn, but because they both featured such muted tones, it all seemed to work together.

I undressed in a spacious dressing area and then waited for ten minutes in the so-called relaxation room. Haunting Asian music played in the background, water gurgled over stones in a small fountain, and the scent of green tea wafted from two flickering candles. I tried to let go and relish it, but I felt a little silly. It was as if I'd somehow stumbled into a scene from *Crouching Tiger, Hidden Dragon.*

Fortunately, it was only a few minutes before I was led to a treatment room. I could barely wait for my massage to start, for the chance to have those sore muscles unknotted. My only concern was that it had been so long since I'd had any physical contact with another member of my species that I might begin to whimper at the first touch—like a poor little pound puppy. Unfortunately, on a scale of one to ten, the massage was no more than a seven. My "therapist," a red-haired woman in her thirties, was skilled enough and had plenty of strength in her hands, but she seemed distracted, pausing at odd moments as she worked. It was enough to make me wonder if I had something weird happening on my butt—like a humongous boil—that was forcing her to stop and gape in horror. I was almost relieved when I was finally back in my suite and could totally veg.

After ordering a club sandwich and a glass of Merlot from room service, I unpacked most of the rest of the stuff from my bag, sticking my underwear and shirts in a dresser. In the early days that I'd traveled, I used to wonder who actually *used* hotel dressers, but lately, at the ripe old age of thirty-three, I'd come to discover that I prefer not having to forage through my suitcase each time I get dressed.

My food arrived within twenty minutes and, ravenous, I devoured it. Then, after opening the window a crack, I undressed and turned back the thick white duvet on the bed. I was looking forward to reading between sheets that felt as if they exceeded a three-hundred-thread count.

As I lay between said silky sheets, though, I could feel my mind itching to go places it shouldn't. In other words, it was dying to ruminate about my most recent love trouble. His name was Jack Herlihy, and he was a thirty-five-year-old professor of psychology from Washington, D.C., whom I'd met in May after he'd come up to teach a summer course in New York. At the time, Jack had come across like a breath of fresh air compared to most of the guys I'd been meeting. He was great looking, nice without being a wuss, and an amazing listener (well, he *was* a shrink), and he managed to be all of these things without ever showing up, like some New York men, with too much product in his hair. He seemed like a straight shooter, not the kind of guy who promises to call the next day but doesn't for weeks, giving you reason to believe that he calculates his time in dog years. Jack didn't like games—or at least that's what I assumed before he started playing them.

Most of my Jack ruminations generally involved trying to figure out how I'd blown things. Admittedly, our romance had gotten off to a slow start, but he'd seemed okay with the pace, and it was certainly fine with me. I'd been fairly skittish since my ex-husband—the attorney-at-law and gambler-at-large—had fled the scene. Jack and I had some fun nights in the Village (he was hoping to eventually relocate to New York), one glorious day on the beach on Fire Island, and a night of half-naked groping in his apartment, during which I explained I wanted to wait a little longer for the full-frontal variety.

Then, in the beginning of July, Jack announced that his younger sister had meningitis and he was going to be going home to Pittsburgh each weekend to help his family. Since his life was about to become insane, he wanted to put our relationship on hold for the next few weeks—until he and his family were through the worst. I promised to be there when his life returned to normal.

We'd stayed in phone contact through July and the first week of August, and then suddenly I stopped hearing from him. I told myself to be patient, that he was caught up in the crisis. But after several weeks had gone by and he was still incommunicado, I started to panic. Since I didn't have any reason to believe he'd entered the Federal Witness Protection Program, I suspected that I'd been given the boot.

But wait, things get worse. Just before Labor Day, as I was cruising the Village in search of fall shoes, I spotted him from a distance with a couple of cute female student types—he seemed talky, flirtatious, Mister Not-a-Friggin'-Care-in-the-World. As I'd ducked on wobbly legs into a store to avoid being seen, it was finally clear that it was o-v-e-r.

The only question left in my mind was *why?* Had he not been that interested in me to begin with and his sister's illness had become a good excuse to put distance between us? Had he met someone else in the weeks we'd been apart? Had my request to take the sexual part of the relationship slowly discouraged him despite the fact that he had sounded okay with it?

Just as I was about to travel this tiresome ground in my mind for the millionth time, the phone rang.

"Bailey, it's Danny. I didn't wake you, did I?"

As she spoke, I could see her in my mind's eye. She was in her early sixties, pretty, or rather handsome, I'd say, with blondish gray hair lightly curled. And she was *tiny*—only about five feet tall and as slim as a candlewick.

"No, no, I'm just lying in bed with a book," I said. "Danny, your inn is absolutely gorgeous. You've done an *amazing* job with it."

"Thank you so much, dearest. How has your evening been?"

Well, for the last twenty minutes I'd been tapping a

freshly scabbed emotional bruise, seeing if I could make myself squeal—but I spared her that sordid detail.

"Terrific. I had a lovely massage and then a light dinner up here in my room—or should I say my suite fit for a princess."

"Who was your massage therapist, do you recall?"

"A woman. Redhead. Name started with a P, I think."

"Piper. She has wonderful hands, don't you think?"

"Yes, definitely." I wasn't going to get Piper in any kind of trouble by saying her heart hadn't been totally into her work tonight.

"By the way, I've set up a meeting for you and Josh, the spa manager, at four tomorrow—if that's still okay with you."

I write a few travel articles each year—it's a free way to see the world and also a nice break from the crime grind—and Danny was hoping that while I was ensconced at the inn I could provide some ideas on how to better pitch her place to editors and travel writers.

"Of course," I said. "But when do I get to see *you?*"

"How about breakfast together tomorrow morning?" Danny asked. "Would nine work for you?"

"Absolutely, though I still may be in a stupor from my massage."

She laughed lightly, like someone jangling her keys. "Well, you know what I always say—too much of a good thing is wonderful. Just wait till you have some of the other treatments I've got booked for you. Have you ever had a massage with hot stones before?"

"No—but I'm game for anything as long as it doesn't involve colonics."

"Oh, Bailey, you always make me laugh," she said.

"Well, I'm going to turn in now because my head is throbbing for some reason. I'm staying here at the inn tonight, by the way, in case you need to reach me."

"Do you do that to see things from the guests' perspective?"

"Partly. But also George is out of town and I hate staying alone. Our house isn't far from here, but it's very secluded. Shall we meet in the lobby, then?"

"See you then. I can't wait."

And I meant it. I felt a tremendous debt to Danny. She had been so good to me when my father died the year I was twelve, taking me on all sorts of little adventures and day trips at a time when my mother was struggling so much that it was hard for her to comfort me. Danny must have sensed early on my fascination for the macabre, because one of our excursions had been to Salem, to learn more about the witch trials. My mother had looked slightly agog at both of us when she'd learned where we'd ended up that day, but it had been pure heaven for me.

My family eventually lost touch with Danny, during a period when she'd lived out west in a bad marriage. But after she moved back to Massachusetts (with a new husband) to open the inn, she and my mother had reconnected. Though I was only now paying a visit to the inn, Danny and I had spoken a few times on the phone, and I'd had lunch with her once in New York when she'd come to the city on business.

The call from Danny had managed to take my mind off Jack, and I picked up the book I'd taken into bed with me. It was of all things a decorating book. Lately I'd been feeling in desperate need of a change in my

Greenwich Village apartment. After my divorce, I'd jettisoned all the modern stuff my ex had encouraged us to buy and introduced a Sante Fe feeling—with the help of cinnamon-colored walls and some cheap baskets. But it was suddenly boring me, adding to my burned-out feeling. Last week I'd asked the *Gloss* decorating editor for some guidance and had been forced to watch him recoil in horror as I described my place to him. You would have thought I'd announced I'd just installed wall-to-wall shag carpet.

"Sante Fe is totally stupid to do east of the Mississippi," he'd said. "The light is all wrong for it. Besides, who wants to see another turquoise coyote with a kerchief around its neck."

He'd suggested I go "minimal" and had pulled a book from his shelf for me to consult.

I'd gone through four or five chapters, covering everything from the value of white space to the pure evil of tchotchkes, when I instinctively glanced at my wrist to check the time. My watch wasn't there.

I felt a tiny swell of panic. It had been my father's watch, an old stainless-steel Rolex I'd started wearing shortly after he died. My mind raced, trying to recall where I'd left it. It had been on my wrist during the drive to Massachusetts because I recalled checking it. Since it was waterproof, I never took it off when I showered. The *massage*. Rather than leave it in the locker, I'd worn it into the treatment room and placed it on a small stool in the corner. I would never fall asleep if I didn't retrieve it.

I dialed the spa number, which was listed on a panel on the phone. As I counted the rings, I leaned out of bed and glanced at the digital clock on the bedside table: 10:25. I wasn't surprised when no one picked up.

Plan B. I'd just head down there. There might still be someone on-site, cleaning up and not bothering to answer the phone.

I threw off the covers and dressed in the same clothes I'd worn earlier. My room was on the second floor of the inn, not far from a back staircase that ended near a side entrance to the spa. Hurrying along the corridor, I was surprised at how deadly quiet it was—no murmur of voices, no hum of TVs, and definitely no headboard banging. Guests here obviously preferred getting loofahed to getting laid.

The door to the spa was solid glass, and I could look directly into the small reception area that was reserved for the use of the inn's guests. It was dark, except for a backlight in a case of spa products. I tapped on the door and then tried to open it. No luck. As I turned away, though, I thought I heard a sound, something thudlike that I couldn't identify, from deep within the spa.

It sounded as if someone *might* still be there, but I was going to have to try the main reception area, which could be reached only from the outside. Walking along the ground-floor corridor, I found an emergency exit and let myself out. I was on the edge of the parking lot, dark except for a few perimeter security lights and a big puddle of moonlight. I headed around the edge of the building toward the main entrance of the spa.

I was surprised at how cool the night was. The early October temperature had hovered around seventy earlier in the day, almost balmy, but it had dropped at least twenty degrees. There was a stiff, choppy wind, making the tree branches shake. This was one of those nights that told you that if you'd been hoping the summery weather would last forever, you were a fool.

Before I even reached the door of the spa, I could see I'd wasted my time. There was a narrow window alongside each side of the front door, and it was dark inside. There were no cars at this end, not a soul in sight. It was totally silent, too, except for the wind and the faint yawning of cars speeding along a far-off highway. I felt nervous all of a sudden, standing out there in the darkness all by myself.

I quickly broke into a jog and crossed the distance of the parking lot to the front of the inn. There were about twenty cars at this end, obviously belonging to guests. The front door was open and I walked into the reception area, where a girl of no more than twenty-five was sitting at the front desk, staring at a terminal screen. Like my massage therapist, she had bright red hair, held off her face with a tiny blue clip. Without giving her time to inquire if she could help me, I explained the situation to her and asked if she could open up the spa.

"I'm sorry, I'm not allowed to let anyone into the spa," she said. "But they open at seven. I can leave a note under the door asking them to look for your watch as soon as they get in. Who was your therapist?"

"Piper."

"Oh, I'm sure she saw it and put it up someplace. There's no need to worry."

"You're probably right, but I can't help it," I told her. "The watch has incredible sentimental value to me. Who *can* let me in?"

"Well, Danielle could, but—"

"I don't want to wake her. Is there someone else?"

She thought for a second, her blue eyes raised to the ceiling.

"Well, the manager had the day off. But I guess I could call Piper. She's an assistant manager, and she's got a key."

"But then she'd have to drive all the way back here."

"No, she wouldn't—she lives right here. There's a building out back where some of the staff stay. I don't think she'd mind coming over."

Natalie—that's what it said on her nametag— glanced at a phone sheet on her desk and placed the call. A machine obviously picked up after five or six rings because she left a message, detailing what had happened and asking Piper to call.

"She must have gone into town for dinner," she said, setting the phone back down. "I doubt she'll be gone long. There's another assistant manager, Anna. . . ."

She let her voice trail off without asking if I wanted to track down *her*, obviously hoping I wasn't going to push the issue even more.

"I can wait till Piper gets back," I said.

Once back in my room, I alternated between reading my book and fretting. I had just glanced at the digital clock for about the four hundredth time—11:13—when the phone rang. It was Piper.

"Hi, Miss Weggins? Natalie said you left your watch in the treatment room."

"Yeah, I'm pretty sure it's on the little stool in the corner. You didn't see it?"

"No, but then I don't recall looking over there." She

hesitated a second. "Why don't I run over and check—I'm just behind the inn."

There was something about her tone—resigned politeness—that told me she was doing it not out of any inborn generosity, but because the inn encouraged staff to bend over backward for the guests.

"God, I hate to put you out, but I'd die if something happened to that watch. Should I meet you down there?"

"I'd be happy to drop it off in your room—but actually maybe it's best for you to show me exactly where you think you left it."

She said we should meet by the inn entrance to the spa. I'd kept my clothes on, so it took me less than two minutes to get down there. I had a five-minute wait, though, before Piper strode down the corridor from the front of the inn. It was funny how different she looked out of "uniform." Instead of a beige T-shirt and baggy beige pants, she was wearing jeans and a long-sleeved green jersey shirt, low-cut with a ruffle. Her shoulder-length red hair, which had been tied back earlier, was spread around her shoulders like a brush fire.

She was courteous enough when she greeted me, but it seemed like that kind of phony politeness she'd displayed on the phone. She already had her keys out, and she unlocked the door, lifting the handle slightly as she pulled it forward, obviously familiar with the door's quirkiness.

She flipped on a light in the reception area, and I followed her down one of the corridors. The scent of green tea still hung in the air, and something else, maybe jasmine. The only sound was our footsteps on the stone floor. It felt kind of creepy to be here alone, after hours.

I wouldn't have been able to recall which room we'd been in, but she seemed sure of it. As we reached the open doorway, she froze suddenly, like a gazelle picking up the scent of something possibly predatory.

"What is it?" I asked.

"There's a light on," Piper said in a hushed tone, using her chin to point down the hall ahead of us. I glanced in that direction and saw a chink of light coming from beneath a doorway.

"Is someone here?" I asked, my voice as quiet as hers.

"No. It's just funny. I swear I turned off the light and left the door open. Why don't you look for your watch and I'll check."

She flicked on the light for me, and as she walked off down the hall, I made a beeline for the stool. I mouthed a big "Thank you" to the gods when I spotted the Rolex lying there, all by its lonesome. As I slid it onto my wrist, I heard a scream.

With my heart thumping, I stumbled out into the hall. Piper was standing paralyzed in the doorway of the room down the corridor, half in the room, half out.

"What's the matter?" I yelled.

She turned to me with a look of absolute horror on her face, unable to form even a single word. I rushed down the hall, pushing past her into the room. It was another massage room, though slightly larger than the one I'd been in. The lights were dim, and at first nothing seemed amiss. Then my eyes fell to the floor.

Lying on the stone floor, absolutely still, was a body,

or at least what I thought must be a body. Every inch of it was wrapped up in some kind of silver paper. I could see the outlines of the limbs and the torso and the head, and the outline too of the nose, protruding from the face. It looked like some kind of mummy. Like some horrible mummy from outer space.

CHAPTER 2

I FROZE, JUST like Piper. It felt as if I were in one of those dreams where you think you're awake and you try to move, but every inch of you, even your eyelids, is paralyzed.

"Is—is it a customer?" I asked stupidly, stumbling over my words. For a split second I actually wondered if someone had been wrapped up like that for a type of spa treatment and accidentally left behind at the end of the day. But of course it couldn't have been a type of treatment. There was no way to breathe.

"I don't know who it is," Piper said hoarsely. "I can't tell."

I forced myself toward the body and, leaning down, lightly laid my palm on it. Warmish. Like something that had been taken from the oven and covered with aluminum foil. I patted a larger area with my hand, feeling for movement or breathing. I couldn't detect anything.

But since there was warmth, it meant whoever was inside *might* still be alive.

"Is there a phone in here?" I snapped, turning back to Piper.

She seemed dazed, as if she'd been kicked in the head by a horse. "Uh, no, not in here," she said, aimlessly swinging her eyes around the room.

"Okay, run down to the reception area and call 911," I told her. I looked right into her eyes as I spoke, attempting to keep her focused. "Can you do that?"

"What do I tell them?"

"To send an ambulance—and the police. That it's a life-and-death matter. Then come right back and help me. And—and bring scissors. Hurry. Go."

As she blundered out of the room, I knelt next to the body. Based on the size and the length, I was pretty sure it had to be a woman. Frantically I ran my hands over the surface of the head, hunting for where the silver paper ended. I knew better than to tamper with a crime scene, but if someone was alive in there, I had to take action. I quickly realized that the paper had been secured in place by gray duct tape, which I hadn't noticed earlier in the dimness of the room. Even through the tape, though, I could feel the outline of the face, and my stomach turned over as my hand found the nose and mouth.

I took a deep breath, willing myself to stay calm and my hands to stop trembling. Slowly and carefully, as if I were reading Braille, I fingered the surface of the tape, searching for the end piece. It wasn't until I'd lifted the head and let my fingers explore in the back that I found it. Holding the head up, I began to unwrap the tape, wadding it up as I worked. There were three revolutions' worth, and as I yanked it away, section by section, it made a sound like someone laying rubber on the road with their car. Once it was off, all balled up in my hand, there was still the silver paper to contend with. It appeared as if it had been wrapped around the head several times and then continued around the body. Unwrapping it, I realized, would take forever. It might be smarter to try to create a hole where the nose and mouth were.

"Hurry, hurry!" I yelled to Piper, hearing her footsteps in the corridor. As she stumbled into the room, I felt a rush of relief seeing that she'd remembered to bring the scissors.

"How long, did they say?" I asked anxiously, reaching for the scissors.

"No, I don't know. They wanted me to stay on the line but I couldn't bring the phone down here."

With the scissors opened in a V, I tried to wedge one of the blades under the edge of the silver paper, but I could see there was a danger I'd cut the person inside.

So instead I began gently scraping the blade back and forth over the material in the spot where the mouth should be. I made a small hole finally, not much bigger than the kind you get when you use a pen to stab at the seal on a bottle of painkillers. But it was a start. I then alternated between making tiny cuts with the scissors and using my fingers to peel back the paper. At last I could see flesh—part of the lips. I made my fingers go even faster, peeling back more of the paper until most of the mouth was exposed.

I lowered my ear to it, listening for a breath. There

wasn't a sound, though my heart was beating so loudly, it was hard to tell.

I attacked the material again, trying to peel away the area around the nostrils. For a second I glanced back at Piper. She was just standing there, mouth agape, watching and running her hands up and down her arms.

"You gotta help me, okay?" I told her. "There's tape around the body. See here? Get down and try to unwrap it. If you run your fingers around it, you can feel where the tape ends."

She still had that stupefied look on her face, as if she hadn't heard a word I said, but before I could repeat myself, she knelt down and began to tap around the torso area, as if she were testing to see if a plate was hot. I couldn't take the time to help her do it any better.

I returned to my work, cutting and peeling. Soon I had a big enough flap of material to hang on to and slit it like a piece of fabric. As I cut away, the nostrils appeared, then the rest of the nose, and the left eye, which was closed. Behind me Piper moaned, but I didn't take time to turn around. I turned my ear to the face again, listening for a sound. Nothing. I took a breath and began mouth-to-mouth resuscitation. The lips were cool, like night crawlers fresh from the ground on a rainy evening, and my stomach somersaulted as I realized that she had to be dead. But I tried anyway, forcing breaths into her mouth. There was no response. After around twenty breaths, I gave up.

"She's dead," I said, light-headed, glancing toward Piper. She was leaning back on her heels, wide-eyed, mouth slack.

"Oh God," was all she could manage.

"Do you know who it is?" I asked.

"I think—I think it's Anna Cole."

"She works here?" I remembered that the desk clerk had mentioned someone named Anna.

"Yes, she's a therapist."

"Was she here when you left tonight?"

"Yes. I left after I finished with you, but Anna and this other therapist—they both had nine o'clocks. Anna was supposed to lock up—at the end of the night. Oh God, how could anyone *do* this to her?"

"I don't know, but we need to get out of here. We should go to the reception area and wait for the police."

She looked confused but followed my instructions. She lumbered out of the room first, heading down the hallway in the opposite direction from where we'd come in, toward the main reception area. I was at her heels providing momentum, like a border collie.

The reception area was all lit up. Piper had obviously flicked on the lights when she made the 911 call.

"Is it safe here?" Piper asked in a desperate whisper. I was wondering the same thing, of course. Whoever was responsible was probably gone, but I couldn't be certain. I listened for a second, for any sound deep within the spa, but the only thing I could hear was Piper's anxious breathing.

"I think we'll be okay if we stay right here, in reception," I said.

"God, I think I'm going to be sick," she announced suddenly. Her face was a ghastly white.

I took her arm and led her to one of the khaki-colored armchairs, forcing her to sit.

"Put your head between your legs and just let it hang there for a minute," I told her.

As I stood there with my hand resting gently on her back, my eyes roamed the room. There didn't seem to be any signs of a break-in. I kept listening, too—making sure there were no sounds coming from anywhere in the spa.

Her breathing quieted after a minute, and that gave me a chance to call Danny. After explaining it was an emergency, I asked the desk clerk to put me through to the room she was staying in. Danny answered groggily, and there was no doubt I'd roused her from a deep sleep.

"Danny, it's Bailey. I'm sorry to wake you like this, but there's an emergency down at the spa." I spoke slowly, trying to give her a chance to fully awaken.

"What's the matter? Are you okay?"

"I came down to the spa with Piper. We found a dead body down here. Someone all wrapped up in silver paper."

"Mylar," Piper interjected, raising her head. "It's Mylar paper." I ignored her for now.

"Omigod—who *is* it?" Danny asked.

"We're not a hundred percent sure. Piper thinks it may be Anna Cole."

I explained that we had already phoned the police and that we were in the main reception area. She said she would be right down, and I urged her to use the main entranceway.

"What were you saying?" I asked Piper as soon as I'd hung up.

"I said it's Mylar. It's used with the mud wrap. First

they rub this stuff over you, and then they wrap a piece of Mylar around you."

"Do they ever put the Mylar around the face like that—I mean, with openings left to breathe?"

"No, no. It would be awful. The mud gets hot and starts to bubble."

"Was Anna doing a wrap tonight?" I knew I shouldn't be questioning Piper—that was for the police to do—but I felt overwhelmed by the need to know what had happened to the woman I had fruitlessly tried to save.

"No, the wraps are usually done by these two European women. And we don't schedule wraps at night."

"Was Anna's client—"

There was a pounding then on the door, and we spun around in unison. Through a front window we could see Danny. Piper jumped up, but before she could reach the door, Danny had pushed it open. A gust of wind burst with her into the reception area.

"Did you just use your key?" I asked hurriedly.

"Yes, the door was locked—why?" she demanded. Her short blond gray hair was frizzy from having been slept on, almost as if it had been teased. She was still wearing her pajamas, though she'd thrown a quilted pale blue coat over them.

"I'm wondering how the person who did this got in."

"Where *is* she?" Danny asked desperately. "Where's Anna?" As she spoke, I detected the scent of sandalwood wafting from her. It seemed incongruous that she could smell so good at a time like this.

"I'm not sure it's her, Danny," Piper said. "I couldn't see her whole face."

"The body's in one of the massage rooms," I explained, "but you can't go back there now. We should wait for the police."

"Then—then at least explain to me what's going on here," she said. "What are you two doing in the spa at this hour? And Bailey, for goodness' sake, why are *you* here?"

I took her quickly through the story. Just as I was finishing, a police car pulled up outside, its blue lights dancing a jig on top of the car. Two uniformed cops jumped out, sprinted up the front steps, and pushed open the door.

One, a baby-faced guy of no more than twenty who had obviously graduated from the police academy earlier that morning, had a bug-eyed expression on his face that suggested he'd been told by the dispatcher to respond to a possible alien spacecraft landing. His partner was a woman at least ten years older, pretty, but tough looking, with her hair all tucked under her cap.

"What have we got here?" she asked tersely.

Danny took over, introducing herself and recapping what I had told her. As the two cops then strode down the hallway toward the room with the body, the female cop barked into her radio. Calling for backup. If the town was big enough, the police force would have detectives who would handle the case. If not, the state police would be called in.

The next few minutes were a whir of chaotic activity. The paramedics arrived fairly quickly. A few minutes later, two guys who were obviously plainclothes detectives showed up, snapping on latex gloves as they hurried down the hall. My guess was that the most exciting thing that generally happened in Warren on a Friday night was a barroom fistfight between two guys with mullets. This was going to be a big, big deal.

Through all of the commotion, the three of us just sat there sadly in the reception armchairs, with the junior patrol cop as our baby-sitter. Danny looked worried as hell, Piper looked as if she'd had most of the blood drained from her veins. I spent the time thinking of nothing but Anna—or whoever it was—wrapped up in the other room. Had she been killed first? Or wrapped up alive so that she'd suffocated to death?

When the two detectives emerged from the crime scene about ten minutes later, they asked for our names and a brief account of the night. Then they told us they wanted us to wait back in the inn until someone had a chance to interview us.

The young cop was given the job of escorting us, and we were instructed not to discuss the situation among ourselves. As we left the spa, the female patrol officer was beginning to wrap yellow crime scene tape around the front.

When we'd dragged ourselves halfway down the parking lot, a black car drove by us, and I turned to see it jerk to a stop next to the ambulance. The driver was obviously middle-aged, because as he climbed out of the front seat, his silvery gray hair glinted in the light from the spa. He paused for a second, appearing to take a mental picture of the front of the building.

Piper had fallen aimlessly in step with the cop, and Danny and I walked behind them. I cupped her elbow in a supportive gesture, realizing that we had never even had a chance to say hello to each other.

"Oh, Bailey . . ." She sighed. "I'm so sorry you got caught in the middle of this."

"Don't worry about me," I said. "I'm glad I can be here to help. You've just got to let me know if I can *do* anything for you."

Dry, crackly leaves charged across the parking lot in our path, like a stampede of wildebeests. From behind us I could hear the voices of the cops and the paramedics and the bursts of static from their radios. The noises must have flipped a switch in my brain, because suddenly I recalled the thud I'd heard when I'd first gone looking for my watch. Had it been the sound of a struggle, I wondered, of someone holding the dead woman down as he tried to wrap the paper around her? Or was it her flopping on the floor, trying to free herself after he'd fled? I felt a wave of guilt roll over me. At the time, I'd told myself the thud might be from someone cleaning up—but then I'd discovered that the spa was empty. If only the sound had raised more of an alarm in me, if only I'd informed the front desk about it. If I'd *done* something, the woman in the massage room might still be alive.

CHAPTER 3

DANNY UNLOCKED THE front door of the inn with a key from the pocket of her jacket. As soon as we stepped inside, Natalie hopped up from the desk, sending her chair rolling into the hallway behind her. She'd put through my urgent call to Danny, she'd probably seen the police cars and ambulance go by, and now she was wide-eyed with expectancy.

"What's the matter?" she blurted out.

"Dear, there's been a death in the spa," Danny said. "We're not actually certain who it is. The police are here, and they're taking care of things. Are there any guests who are still out tonight?"

"Uhh, gosh, I don't think so. Let me see." She fumbled nervously around on the desk until she located a sheet of paper that appeared to be a guest log. "No, everybody's in," she said, sweeping her eyes over it.

"You'd better give that to me," the young cop said,

holding out his hand for the sheet of paper. "The detectives will want to see it." It was the most I'd heard him say all night.

Danny suggested that Natalie join us and then led the group of us behind the front desk to a suite of several small offices. There was also a sitting room with a love seat and a small round conference table. She told Piper to try to rest on the love seat. Natalie volunteered to sit with her and also to listen for any guests who might come downstairs because of the commotion.

The rest of us traipsed into Danny's office. As I settled in a small armchair, Danny announced that she was going to make tea in the kitchenette across from the office. The young cop parked himself by the door. He'd clearly been instructed to keep an eye on us and make certain we didn't discuss the case or make phone calls.

Tucking my legs underneath me, I began replaying in my mind everything that had happened from the moment I'd left my room. I didn't want to be fumbling for the info when I finally talked to the police. Two things made me nervous. First, the whole deal with my watch. I was sure the police would view it as odd that I'd insisted on retrieving it. Cops take an immediate dislike to stuff that sounds illogical or out of the ordinary—and making someone open a spa in the middle of the night fell into that category. Second, they were going to be extremely unhappy about how much I had disturbed the evidence. If there'd been fingerprints on the Mylar paper or tape, I'd surely smeared them—and by removing and handling the tape, I might have mucked up their chances of tracing the roll it came from.

But I couldn't fault myself for unwrapping the body.

The foil was still warm when I'd touched it, and as far as I knew at the time, the person inside might have been alive. I did the math in my head: The spa supposedly had closed around ten. Piper and I had discovered the body just before eleven-thirty. I'd heard the thud at around ten-thirty. That meant it easily could have been the sound of someone being overpowered or perhaps struggling to free herself.

The question, of course, was who could have committed such a gruesome crime. There hadn't been any sign of a break-in; plus, why would a burglar go to the trouble of wrapping the body? Most likely someone had gone to the spa intending to kill the woman inside the Mylar. It might have been a stranger, some sort of psychopath who'd been stalking her. But an enraged and/or jilted lover was the strongest possibility. Whoever he was, he certainly hadn't been expecting anyone to come barging into the spa after hours. I felt a chill as I considered how close I'd come to bumping into him as I'd headed across the parking lot earlier that night.

Danny returned, carrying a tray with cups and a teapot. She had made some lemony kind of thing that I knew didn't have a single molecule of caffeine in it, but I accepted a cup anyway just to give myself something to do. The cop declined. He looked more like a Dr Pepper man.

Danny parked herself at the desk and announced she was going to check out the spa's schedule for the night.

"We had only two nine o'clock appointments tonight," she said after she'd turned on the computer and found the place. "Both were female clients. Anna was scheduled to do one. A therapist named Eric had the other."

"Were the women guests at the inn?"

"Yes. We don't take day spa guests after seven."

The cop shot us a look that said we shouldn't be gabbing with one another about the case. I went back to my thoughts, replaying the evening over and over in my mind. A half hour had passed and there was no sign of anyone coming to talk to us. I fought off the growing urge to doze and closed my eyes just to rest them. The next thing I knew, I was being roused from sleep.

A strange man stood over me, saying my name. He was about five ten, trim, in his mid-thirties, I guessed, though his hair was nearly all gray—as if it belonged on someone in his forties or fifties.

"I'm sorry I startled you," he said. "I'm Detective Supervisor Beck. I'd like to ask you a few questions now." He was dressed in gray pants, a gray wool crewneck sweater over a white shirt, and a brown suede jacket, a little bit dressy, suggesting that he'd been off duty tonight and called to the scene. I realized suddenly that he was probably the guy I'd noticed earlier climbing out of the car in the parking lot. At the time, I'd assumed, because of the hair, that he was middle-aged.

"Of course," I said, pushing myself to a sitting position as I tried to unstick my eyes. "Where is everybody, anyway?" Neither Danny nor the uniformed cop was in the room.

"Everyone but Mrs. Hubner has been escorted home. She's lying down next door. She wanted to wait for you."

"Gosh, I must have been out to the world."

"Do you need a minute?" he asked, though he didn't sound as though he cared to wait that long.

"No, no. I'm fine."

"Let's get started, then," he said crisply. "You're a guest here?" He pulled a straight-backed chair from against the wall to the area in front of me and sat down, making me feel like a shrinking Alice in Wonderland in the armchair.

I explained my friendship with Danny and the reason for my trip up from Manhattan. As I spoke, he pulled a notepad from the pocket of his leather jacket. The jacket lifted slightly, and I noticed that when he'd belted his pants, he'd missed a loop. Maybe he'd actually been in bed when he got the call about the murder.

"So what were you doing in the spa at eleven-thirty at night?"

I knew he'd gone through all of this with Piper, but he wasn't going to let on to me that he knew anything. He would want to hear my own version of events, step by step. I told him about my massage, missing my watch, talking to Natalie, her calling Piper, and Piper coming over to let me into the spa.

"And this couldn't wait till morning?"

Okay, here we go, I thought, just as I'd expected. I took a breath and urged myself not to overexplain.

"Well, it's a watch with a great deal of sentimental value," I said, "and I knew I couldn't sleep until I found it."

"So take me through what happened in the spa—from the beginning. Did you and Piper go in together?"

"Yes, we went in the side entrance, the one in the inn. But actually, that's not really the beginning."

He'd been taking notes, and he looked up, surprised. "Yes?"

"I need to explain something," I said. "Before I even called the front desk to see if anyone could let me in, I ran downstairs to double-check whether the spa might still be open."

He didn't say anything. Just stared, with eyes the dark blue shade of wet slate. The gray hair had thrown me off so much initially, I hadn't noticed how staggeringly good-looking he was.

"And?" he said finally. There was a slight edge to his voice, as if I had begun to try his patience.

"It wasn't. Open. It was dark inside. I tried the door, and it was locked. But I heard something that might be significant."

Pause.

"And what was that?" he asked. Boy, his interviewing style was making me squirm. There was a chance that by the end of the night, *I'd* confess to the friggin' murder.

"I heard a thud," I explained. "I can't describe it any more specifically than that. Just a thud. Now I'm wondering if it was the woman who died moving around on the floor."

"At what time was this?"

"Around ten-thirty."

He flipped back through his notes and reread something I'd said. "And when you heard the sound, did you do anything?"

"Well, no," I said defensively. "At the time, I didn't think the noise was any cause for alarm—if that's what you mean. I just thought it meant someone might still be in the spa. I went out the side door of the inn and over to the front of the spa."

He offered no reaction, but I noticed his eyes widen at this new detail.

"Keep going," was all he said.

I described crossing the parking lot in the dark, seeing the spa locked up for the night, turning around, and going back into the inn.

"This is very important," he said, his voice as flat as lake water on a windless day. "Did you notice any movement inside or out, anything at all suspicious?"

"I didn't see anything worth reporting."

"Let me decide what's worth reporting. Tell me everything you saw."

"There was no sign of *anyone,* anywhere," I insisted, annoyed at the brusque tone he'd used. Apparently satisfied that I wasn't keeping some monumental detail to myself, he directed me back to where I'd left off. I described walking down the corridor, Piper seeing the light, finding the body.

"Whose idea was it to take off the paper?"

Okay, here we go again.

"It was mine. Totally mine," I revealed. "I should also tell you that I performed CPR on her—so you're going to find my saliva in her mouth."

"You thought there was a chance you could resuscitate her?" he asked, apparently incredulous.

"No, I just thought it would be fun to go around saying, 'I kiss dead people.'"

I shouldn't have said it, but I couldn't help myself. The guy was seriously annoying me with his no-nonsense, borderline-grouchy interrogation style. I half expected him to slap some cuffs on me as a result of my insubordination, or at the very least say he was going to revoke my Red Cross lifesaving certification, but instead he looked slightly—and I mean slightly—bemused.

"Look, I know in hindsight it was a bad idea," I told him, not giving him a chance to say anything. "But the foil was warm, and as far as I knew, she might still be alive."

Really big pause this time. More staring with those dark blue eyes.

"You did the right thing, of course," he said finally. "There are plenty of people who would never have been as quick thinking in a crisis—or as competent."

I felt relieved. I also felt stupid because I'd experienced a kind of goofy rush when he'd complimented me.

He still had a few questions left, stuff like what I'd touched in the room other than the body, what I'd handled in the reception area, a few questions, too, about doors and lights. He also asked for my address and phone number in New York. Then he told me that I'd need to come down to police headquarters the next day and make a formal statement. He drew a brown leather wallet from his back pants pocket, pulled out a business card, and, before handing it to me, scribbled his cell phone number on it.

"Call me if you think of anything else," he said, suddenly warmer. "I believe the sound you heard is significant. I want to know if you recall *anything* else, even the most minor detail. Is that clear?"

"It is. And I will. But I don't want to get your hopes up. I didn't see anything."

"You'd be surprised at what comes to people."

He rose from his seat, and I pushed myself awkwardly out of the armchair.

"I have a question," I said as he turned to go. "Was—was she alive when she was wrapped up in that paper?"

"That's our concern, not yours." I don't think he meant for it to come out as curtly as it did, so he softened the impact with a small smile. "Look, we're going to do our best to find the person responsible. Why don't you get some rest now? You've had a long night."

It *is* my concern, was all I could think as he left the room. I could still feel Anna's cool lips on mine. She was a total stranger to me, yet there'd been a moment in which I'd thought I could save her life. Now I was overwhelmed with a need to know how she'd died—and who had killed her.

I walked next door to find Danny curled on the love seat, asleep, a frown on her face. I flashed back suddenly to a moment the two of us had shared years ago. She had taken me to get my first manicure and pedicure. I was only twelve, and the pedicure had tickled so much that I'd kept balling my foot up reflexively. Danny had nearly doubled over in laughter. It seemed strange to have the roles reversed, to feel the need to comfort *her.*

I gently jostled her shoulder and called her name a few times. As she woke, focusing on my face, she moaned softly.

"I thought for a moment that it was just a nightmare," she said. "But it's not, is it?"

"No, it's not. The detective's gone now, Danny. We can go to our rooms."

"All right. Though I can't imagine how I'll ever fall back to sleep."

"Would you like to talk for a while? I know I'll never get back to sleep, either."

"Yes, I'd like that, actually. I've got so many questions. Why don't we go into the lounge."

She stood up from the couch, still in her jacket and PJs, and led me down the corridor to the lobby. The inn was absolutely silent.

"Did any guests come down tonight?" I asked.

"A few did. They could see the madhouse from their windows, and they seemed totally distressed. I know this sounds so selfish of me to say with someone lying dead on the premises. But I keep thinking about the inn. I've worked so hard the last few years. And now it's in danger of being ruined."

"That's not true. You'll get through this—and the inn will survive."

"You don't understand," she whispered. "I don't see how we can survive now. This isn't the first death we've had here."

CHAPTER 4

I CAUGHT MY breath. "What?" I exclaimed. "Who? When?"

"Let's not talk about it here," Danny said softly. "I don't want anyone to hear me."

She led me out into the lobby and across to the lounge on the far side. The front door of the inn was partially open, and I caught a glimpse of two cops standing on the front step talking, their faces illuminated by the lantern lights on the front of the inn. Once Danny and I were inside the lounge, she slid the wooden pocket doors partially closed. She lit two table lamps and used a remote control to ignite the gas flame in the fireplace.

"Okay, so tell me about this other death," I urged as we both sank into the sofa.

"It happened this past July," she said, her voice laden with discouragement. "A man who'd come for a massage died of a heart attack in the men's locker room."

"Was there something suspicious about his death?"

"No, no. I didn't mean to imply that," she said. "He was in his late sixties, and the autopsy showed that he had a weak heart valve, one of those things that had never been diagnosed. But to have two deaths here . . . The next thing you know, people will be saying the inn is *cursed*."

"Did the police get involved?"

"Yes, actually Detective Beck. The man who died—William Litchauer—was fairly prominent, and his wife and son were all up in arms. They threatened to sue, but there were absolutely no grounds. Everyone who has a treatment here signs a waiver that stipulates we aren't liable in these matters—unless of course there's negligence on our part. And the police found nothing."

"What's your impression of this Beck guy?" I asked. My voice sounded oddly bright as I spoke.

"He can be brusque, but he was also very thorough. He interviewed a number of people at the spa and seemed to give the case his full attention."

"On the surface, the two cases certainly don't *sound* connected," I said. "We're not even sure whose body was lying there tonight."

"I'm almost positive it's Anna," she said mournfully. "Detective Beck asked me for her emergency contact number because they found her purse in the employee locker room—and besides, there's no sign of her in her room."

"You said earlier that Anna had a nine o'clock appointment. Was she in charge of locking up the spa tonight?"

"Yes. Josh, the manager, usually leaves about six, and either Piper or Anna closes up. This was supposed to be Piper's night, but Anna apparently switched with her earlier in the week."

"Have you called Josh?"

"No, I couldn't with that policeman sitting there. I'll try him first thing in the morning. He's going to be as devastated by this as I am."

"I wonder if he'll have any ideas on who might have done it."

"Are you thinking it might be someone who works at the *spa?*" she asked, clearly distressed.

"I feel it's got to be someone who either works at the spa or is *familiar* with it. Like someone in Anna's personal life—or even a client. Because how else would the person have known about the Mylar paper?"

Danny pressed her hands tightly to her face, her eyes closed. When she opened them, she looked at me pleadingly.

"Bailey, you've got to help me. Please."

"Of course I will, Danny. You know you can lean on me."

"No, I mean you have to help figure out who did this. Your mother told me how you solved that murder last spring—of your boss's nanny. If the police don't find Anna's killer, it will hang like a pall over the inn and the spa."

She was right, of course. If the murderer wasn't apprehended quickly, the spa's business could suffer. One death was bad enough, but now there were two. And though one had been an accident and the other a homicide, people would connect them in their minds, assuming that there really *was* something cursed about the inn and the spa—kind of The Golden Door meets *The Shining*. My mother's final onshore request suddenly rang in my ears over the sound of the crackling gas fire: "Keep an eye on Danny. I'm worried about her."

"I'll do whatever I can, Danny," I said.

"Oh, Bailey, thank you," she said, squeezing my arm.

"Look, I'm not sure how much I can accomplish between now and Monday, but since I'm staying right here in the inn, I may be able to learn a few things. People might be more comfortable talking to me than to the cops. We just have to be careful not to interfere with their investigation. And I wouldn't let this Beck guy know I'm asking questions. Trust me, he'll be less than thrilled."

"Fine. And since I'd planned for you to talk to Josh, why don't we just proceed with that. I'll tell him that we're going ahead since you've made the trip."

"Good idea. Now tell me about security at the spa. What's the general procedure when it comes to locking up?"

"The back door of the spa is *always* locked—or at least it's supposed to be," she explained. "The front door is locked after the last local guest arrives, and the door that goes directly to the inn gets locked last, usually after the last inn guest arrives."

"Who has keys?"

"I have a set, and so does George. Josh. Piper and Anna, since they're assistant managers. And the manager of the inn has one—he's out of town this weekend for a wedding, by the way."

I stood up from the couch and walked the short distance toward the fireplace. I wanted to feel the warmth of it on my body, but the gas flame gave off so little heat, it was like holding a votive candle to my butt.

"Of course, the killer didn't necessarily have a key," I said. "Anna could have let him in after all the guests had gone. What do you know about her as a person?"

It turned out not to be a great deal. Anna, Danny reported, had been in her late thirties, attractive, single, and extremely aloof. Like Piper, she lived on-site. She had moved here a year ago from Manhattan, where she'd done her massage training, and prior to that she had lived all over. Her file had listed one emergency contact: a sister in Florida.

While I waited, Danny went back to her office and returned with a group shot that included Anna. She was not only attractive, but there was something tantalizingly sexy about her. Dark eyes and dark hair—worn short and provocatively shaggy—and she stared at the camera as if she had decided to seduce the person taking the picture. She was about five four or five five, I guessed, from eyeballing the various people in the picture. Her body was curvy and sensuous. A killer body, I thought as I stared at her image, and then groaned to myself over the words I'd chosen.

"Did she have a boyfriend?"

"A while back something was apparently going on with her and Eric, the therapist, but it supposedly fizzled. He's second-generation Indian and fairly quiet. It's hard to imagine him holding his own against Anna."

"Oh boy, the police are going to focus on him bigtime since he was there on duty with her tonight. Anyone new on the scene?"

"We got a new tennis pro this past summer and lately I've noticed him buzzing around her a bit, but I have no idea if there was anything going on between them. You know me, I like to reach out to people, but Anna was not receptive to that. She liked to keep to herself."

I asked if that was fairly typical of women in her line of work, and Danny explained that in her experience, massage attracted several different kinds of women. There were the earth mothers, for whom massage was just another way to connect with people. There were what she called the yoga types, free spirits who were into taking care of their bodies and couldn't bear to set foot in an office or be pinned down in any way. And there were the odd birds, women searching for something, anything, to make them happy. Anna, she felt, had been sort of a combination of the last two.

"How did she get along with the people she worked with at the spa?"

"I know most people found her distant, too. She made one friend when she first came here, but that woman moved last winter—she left the field entirely. There was—No, that's meaningless."

"Tell me."

"Well, it's just there was a little rivalry among the female therapists over the number of clients they each had. Anna—and Piper, too—got more repeat business than the other girls, and there was some resentment, especially about Anna, because she'd been here for just a year. It's partly because of all her business that Josh made her an assistant manager after just nine months."

"Anyone more resentful than others?"

"Cordelia," she said after a pause. "She's one of the girls who's been with me the longest, and she's very, very good. She's an earth mother type, strong as an ox. But, you know, it's not always strength that matters. Sometimes a therapist has something else—a hypnotic technique, for instance—that people love even more than powerful hands. I suspect too that Cordelia may be a bit chatty, and most people can't bear that."

As I listened to her, I saw that she looked exhausted, even tinier than usual, and it was clear she needed sleep. I suggested that we turn in and talk again first thing in the morning. She agreed, suddenly seeming distracted.

"Danny, what is it?" I asked. "Is there something you aren't telling me?"

She looked at me, her brow furrowed in confusion.

"Yes and no," she said finally. "Something *is* bothering me, but the reason I'm not telling you is that I don't know what it is. For the past few months, I've felt as if something odd is going on at the spa. I've tried to spend more time over there, but I haven't come up with anything concrete."

Ah, so this was what my mother had tuned into when she'd sensed distress on Danny's part.

"Can you be more specific?" I asked.

"Mainly it's this vibe I started picking up. From Josh, but also from a few of the others, including Piper and Anna and this other girl Lauren, though she moved to Hawaii in August. I've caught them shooting glances at each other when I'm over there, as if they had some secret they're keeping. If I offer to help in any way, they discourage me from staying."

"Did you mention this to the police?"

"No, because what could I *say*—that I had a bad feeling?"

"How's the spa business?"

"It's excellent. And that's why I haven't said anything to Josh about this. He's been here just two years, and he's made the spa a huge success, especially this past year since we redid some of the interiors. So there's no question of them slacking off or not doing their work correctly. Josh is very prickly, and I'm afraid he'll be furious if I accuse him of something so vague."

"I wonder if they're skimming money? Do you review the bills and paperwork?"

She said she did, but not nearly as closely as she should. I told her that one of the first things I'd do tomorrow was take a look at the financial records and see if anything odd popped out. It would give me something concrete I could attack immediately.

"When does George get back, by the way?" I asked as she switched off lights.

"Tomorrow. I tried to reach him on his cell phone tonight, but he's obviously turned it off for the night."

The room Danny had taken for herself was on the first floor. After waiting for the door to close behind her, I hurried down the corridor and up the front staircase to the second floor. Though the lights were on along my corridor, the far end was thick with shadows, and I unlocked my door quickly, slammed it behind me, and turned the dead bolt.

As soon as I had the door to my room locked behind me, I kicked off my shoes, tore off my clothes, and flung myself onto the end of the bed. I felt overwhelmed with so many emotions, it was hard to tell which ones were dominant and which had just decided to home in on the action. The alpha feeling was clearly the distress and *guilt* I was experiencing about Anna's death. If I'd only reported the thud. It might not have saved her life, but her killer might have been apprehended. I was also highly distressed about Danny. If the police didn't arrest someone soon, this event really *could* end up harming her business. I wanted to do everything in my power to help her.

And it wasn't just for Danny's sake. It was because of my mother, too. What can I say? She'd asked me to help, and I have an endless need to please her. It's not that she's ever pressured me to be the dutiful daughter, but in the early years after my father died, she was often reserved and detached, and I worked like a little beaver to maker her happy. Old habits die hard.

I was also experiencing some déjà vu. Five months ago, I'd set out to help my boss at *Gloss,* Cat Jones, when her nanny had been poisoned to death. My life had ended up in jeopardy, and I knew that playing detective in Danny's situation could put me in danger as well. But if there was something I could do, I knew I had to make the attempt—for Danny's sake, and Anna's, too.

As I lay on the bed like a big blob, I began to detect yet another feeling: a swelling of self-pity. I'd come to the spa to be pampered, to take my mind off my love woes and my pathetic social life, and now I felt lonelier than when I'd left Manhattan. How nice it would have been to have a man to call right now for comfort.

Specifically Jack Herlihy. He had that shrink gift of being a great listener, someone who could drag every sorry feeling out of you into the light of day, where you could then watch it shrivel to the size of a chickpea. He wouldn't have minded being awakened at two A.M. and listening to the whole terrible tale.

Instantly I kicked myself for even thinking of Jack, and worse for trying to romanticize him. The man had dumped me, and done it as rudely as possible. I'd read once in *Gloss* that if you find yourself yearning for an ex, you can drive away the feeling by imagining him in a humiliating moment. I pictured Jack walking down the streets of Georgetown in his perfectly pressed tan gabardine pants and a passing FedEx truck spattering every inch of those pants in wet mud. Unfortunately, in my current state of fatigue and despair, that was the best I could do.

I dragged myself, sea otter–like, to the top of the bed, wiggled under the covers, and hit the off button on the base of the lamp. I was torn between my need to sleep so I could start the next day at full throttle and my desire to plot out what I would do tomorrow. I was anxious to look at Danny's financial records, and there were people I wanted to talk to. I just had to be careful not to tip off Detective Beck that I was going to be his secret junior partner on the case.

As I lay in the dark, a question suddenly formed in my mind. I'd dropped Danny off only ten minutes ago, so I doubted she'd be asleep yet. I hauled myself up in bed, picked up the phone, and hit seven plus her room number.

"It's Bailey," I said. "So sorry to disturb you, but I had a quick question."

"Yes, dear."

"The heart attack victim. What masseuse had he gone to?"

"Actually," she said, "it was Anna."

CHAPTER 5

SATURDAY MORNING ARRIVED as cheerful as a sledge-hammer. I woke to the patter of rain on the roof and the kind of throbbing headache you get when you're a caffeine addict like me and are forced to temporarily subsist on lukewarm lemony water.

I heaved myself out of bed with one thrust. As soon as I had both feet on the ground, memories of the night before stampeded through my brain. I groaned out loud. My trip to the Cedar Inn could easily turn out to be the most *un*rejuvenating spa weekend in recorded history.

After a fast shower, I fished Detective Beck's business card out of my purse. My priority this morning was helping Danny figure out if something fishy had been going on at the spa, but I wanted to get my trip to police headquarters out of the way. A woman answered the phone, and after putting me on hold for more than a minute, she informed me that I should plan to be there at eleven-thirty. It sounded closer to a command than a request. I wondered if the person she'd consulted was Detective Beck himself.

After throwing on tan pants and a black turtleneck sweater, I headed downstairs. The lobby was bustling, mostly with rich-looking women over forty and a few tottering husbands whose millions had not been able to keep the liver spots at bay. There was a hyper hum in the air, which suggested people knew something big and bad had happened. Yet no one was charging out of the building with bulging suitcases, looking indignant and demanding a refund.

I asked the morning desk clerk, a guy this time, where I could find Danny, and he reported that she was off-site somewhere but would return shortly. This, I decided, would be my opportunity to grab breakfast. First, however, I wanted to check out what was happening at the spa. I walked outside and headed around the east side of the building. The rain had tapered off, but it was damp and raw out. As I crossed the parking lot, I saw that the police zone had been broadened to include a much larger area. Cops were walking along the perimeter of the parking lot, obviously using the daylight to scour for evidence, and through the spa window I could detect movement inside. No sign, however, of the dashing Detective Beck.

Back inside the inn, I followed a long corridor toward the dining room. Like the rest of the inn, the decor was charming but not cutesy—more brown-and-white check as well as brown-and-white toile, and along the walls there were a dozen framed prints of leaves. I was shown to a window table with mismatched antique wooden chairs. Though the room was only half-filled with diners, there was a nervous hum here, too. People were clearly buzzing about the murder but weren't sure what to *do*.

Fifteen minutes later, after wolfing down a blueberry muffin and a cup of coffee, I hurried back to the lobby, where the desk clerk revealed that Danny was back. As I walked toward her office, I saw that a dark-haired guy in his thirties was standing just inside the doorway, obviously on his way out. I stepped into the office, and before I could even say hello, Danny introduced us. It was Josh, the spa manager.

"I'm so sorry to meet you under such terrible circumstances," I said, holding out my hand. His handshake turned out to be more of a hard squeeze than a grasp, like someone using a grip strengthener.

"Likewise," he said, cocking his head. He was extremely hunky looking and buff, with dark brown eyes and pale, almost milky skin that was in sharp contrast with his nearly black hair. He had a thin, jaggedy scar running along the lower right side of his jaw, which elevated his face from merely a model of perfect bone structure to something more intriguing.

"Danny was hoping we could still meet later, though," I said. "If it's all right with you."

"Of course," he said evenly. "The show must go on. Now if you'll excuse me, I have plenty of fires to put out."

As he strode out of the room, I turned my attention to Danny. Her face was saggy with fatigue, but she'd applied lipstick and a smear of pink on each cheek, clearly attempting to appear pulled together and in control. As we hugged, I caught the scent of sandalwood again and other smells that suggested far-off places, even other centuries.

"You holding up okay?" I asked.

"More or less," she said with a deep sigh. "I'm so grateful you're here, Bailey."

"What's the latest?"

"I don't know where to begin. I went to the morgue this morning and confirmed that it was Anna. It was heartbreaking to see her. Her body was mostly covered, but I could see these awful bruises along the top of her neck."

"Then she must have been strangled or bludgeoned somehow. I wonder why the killer wrapped her in the Mylar. Maybe he wanted to be absolutely certain she was dead."

"I can't bear to even think about it. The police called her sister, and she's flying up from Florida at some point this week."

"Have the police let anything slip about what happened?

"Nothing. They had me walk through the spa with Josh this morning, and there's no sign of anything missing. Apparently Eric got quite the grilling, just as you said he would. I spoke to him this morning and he says that he left the spa at ten and let his client out with him because she wasn't going to bother changing out of her robe. He last saw Anna in the corridor, waiting for her client to come out of the treatment room. From the spa he went directly to a birthday party in town."

"So he's got an alibi of sorts. What about things here at the inn? Have you lost any business because of what's going on?"

"No—not yet, anyway. Josh and I have decided that we're going to use the beauty salon to do treatments."

She explained that the staff was currently in the process of setting up the waxing and facial rooms to handle massages and that they would also offer them in guest rooms. The spa was going to be off-limits for several days, at least, but fortunately they had extra massage tables and equipment stored in one of the outbuildings.

"I know things are going to be crazy," I said, "but I'd like you to have Josh try to squeeze me in for a few treatments. Ideally, I'd like to have some contact with Eric—and with Cordelia, too, since she's a chatterbox."

"I'm sure that can be arranged," she said.

I also asked that she book me a lesson with the tennis pro, the one who'd been seen buzzing around Anna. His name was Rich Wyler, she said, and he worked on a freelance basis. The inn wasn't big enough to require a full-time teaching pro, so they used a floater, someone who gave lessons at half a dozen hotels in the area. Part of his deal included free massages at the spa. Danny said she'd have Natalie track him down and schedule something, probably for tomorrow.

"One more thing," I told her. "I want to chat with Anna's last client. Are you okay with me popping by her room? I thought I could tell a little white lie and say I handle PR for you—and that you wanted me to make sure she was okay."

"Actually that's not a bad idea. Her name is Babs Hollingswood, and she and her husband are in room seventeen, on your floor. I was hoping to contact her myself, but things have been insane."

"Is George back yet, by the way?"

She pursed her lips, looking perplexed. "He's not due back from his trip for a few hours," she said. "I'm a little concerned because I haven't been able to reach him on his cell phone. He obviously has it turned off."

"What kind of work is he involved in these days?" I asked.

She explained that George was now working with *her*, helping her expand the business. He'd gone to Boston to talk to someone about promoting the inn and spa for business retreats. He had phoned her yesterday in the early evening, and the plan was for him to have dinner in Boston at seven with a potential client, spend the night in a motel just outside the city, and be home by lunch today.

Oh God, I thought. I was in no position to criticize, having been married to a man who'd blown fifty grand on football pools and pawned the jewelry he'd given me to prevent our apartment from being torched. But I didn't like what I'd just heard from Danny. Guys who glommed on to their wives' businesses always gave me the creeps. Ditto for guys who went out of town, stayed in motels, and failed to phone home.

Rather than add to her troubles, though, I assured her that everything was most likely fine. I'd have to see how I felt about George when I finally met him.

"Now let's talk financial records," I said. "Have you got things computerized?"

"Yes, it's all on a Quicken program."

My volunteering to go through Danny's financial records was on a par with my suggesting I should perform laparoscopic surgery on someone's knee, but I had a plan in my mind for how I was going to pull it off. Danny and I agreed that we would tackle the project right after lunch. She was about to hold a meeting for the staff to explain to everyone what was going on. And I, of course, had my appointment with Beck—he of the blistering stare.

As I came out from behind the front desk I saw hotel personnel moving along the corridor toward the dining room, obviously assembling for the meeting with Danny. Spa staffers were recognizable in their khaki-colored T-shirts and matching drawstring pants. I spotted a young Indian guy and figured that must be Eric. There was also a buxom blonde, very much an earth mother type. That had to be Cordelia.

On the way to my room, I knocked on the door to room 17, but there was no answer. Babs Hollingswood, I realized, might be down at police headquarters this morning, making a formal statement.

Back in my room, I dug through my purse for my PalmPilot and, after finding his number, placed a call to Bud Patterson, a forensic accountant. I'd interviewed him two years ago when I was writing an article on a woman whose husband had bludgeoned her to death with a golf trophy after she'd discovered he was draining gobs of money from their business and funneling it into a secret offshore account. As a forensic accountant, Bud approached a bank statement as a possible crime scene. But instead of searching for fingerprints or clumps of hair, he scoured for signs of money in motion when it shouldn't be. I knew he'd be able to tell me how to spot any funny business in Danny's records.

He answered right away, sounding bright eyed and

bushy tailed for a Saturday morning. Not bothering to get into the murder, I explained Danny's concern about the spa staff and asked how I could help.

"Follow the cash," he said without hesitation. "That's always the first rule." I heard him take a swig of a drink.

"But it's not a cash business," I told him.

"I don't mean literally," he said. "You want to look at what's coming in each month and what's going out. See if all the bills are paid up. When people siphon off money, the bills often get ignored."

"But how do you siphon off money when it's not a cash business? You can't just write checks to yourself."

"Well, actually, that's exactly how people do it. They create a fictitious vendor—or vendors. It's a spa, you say? If I'm the bad guy, I might make up a vendor called Super Smooth Massage Oils. I send in invoices for them and make sure those invoices are paid and sent to an address I have access to. Then I cash the checks. Top management isn't close enough to the operation to notice we never *use* Super Smooth Massage Oils."

Before signing off to head for his in-laws, he gave me a couple of other tips that I jotted down.

At eleven I was on my way to the police station, allowing plenty of time in case I got lost. Though the inn's setting had an out-of-the-way, almost rural feel to it—in part because of its abutment to a nature reserve—it was actually just at the edge of town. I drove down several quiet roads, which after a few minutes gave way to suburbanlike streets and then, as I got closer to the center of the town, to older streets lined with clapboard houses. In their front yards sat glistening wet piles of raked leaves, waiting to be bagged. I was only a few hours north of New York City, yet autumn was far more entrenched here.

The building was a nondescript, one-story affair on a lot that years before had once probably held something more historic, like the old New England–style buildings surrounding it. There was no receptionist at the desk in the lobby, but a patrol cop was holding up the wall while drinking coffee from a Styrofoam cup, and he said he'd let Beck know I'd arrived.

It was ten minutes before he emerged, and he was accompanied by a couple in their mid- to late sixties. I overheard Beck thank them for all their help, and I suspected that the woman might be either Babs or the other nine o'clock client. Beck nodded at me, said good-bye to the couple, and then told me to follow him.

He was wearing brown pants, a white dress shirt, and a tweed blazer. Natty, like last night. He led me to a large open room with about ten metal desks, some but not all with computers. There was only one other cop at a desk, though I noticed five or six others standing around a table in a glassed-in conference room. Anybody who'd had Saturday off had probably been called in because of the murder.

"I appreciate your doing this twice," he said, indicating with an outstretched hand that I should take a seat in a plastic stack chair next to his desk.

"No problem," I said, though I was looking forward to it with the same enthusiasm I reserved for a leg wax. As I sat, my eyes scanned the desktop area. There were a bunch of files, one stuck with a Post-it note with the words *Det. Jeffrey Beck* written on it (so *that* was his first name), a walkie-talkie, a green mug filled with pencils. No photos, no knickknacks, nothing personal at all—unless you could count a schedule of Boston Patriot games taped to the desk lamp. He lowered himself into his swivel chair and leaned back in it, making it groan. I noticed that in the bright light of day, his eyes really were the darkest blue I'd ever seen. They looked as blue as the part of a map that shows where the ocean is deepest.

"You feeling okay?" he asked. "You had a pretty rough time last night."

To my utter surprise and horror, I felt myself blush.

"I'm okay," I said. "Thanks. It was all such a shock. I'd come up here from New York City expecting to discover the benefits and joys of reflexology, and the next thing I know I'm giving mouth-to-mouth to a mummy." Shut up, Bailey, I told myself. You are talking way too much.

He took me in deeply with his eyes, a slightly puzzled expression on his face. Maybe he was wondering what reflexology was.

"Let me get you out of here as quick as possible, then," he said, tapping a few keys on his computer. "Here's what's gonna happen. We'll run through the same questions I asked you last night. Once I print out your statement, you'll sign it. After that I need to take your fingerprints so we can tell which are yours at the crime scene. I also need a piece of your hair. That way we eliminate your hair and DNA from any we discover on the body."

"Fine—will it hurt?" Oh God, why was I trying to be cute?

"Will what hurt?" He looked at me seriously.

"The hair removal."

He allowed himself a small grin. "Only momentarily."

He started the questioning, traveling basically the same ground he had the night before. As I answered, he typed quickly and confidently, barely looking at the keys. Once or twice he glanced at the written notes he'd taken the night before. Mostly, he kept his eyes on me.

His manner was a notch warmer than it had been last night, yet I felt nervous, as if someone were tossing my stomach up and down like a tennis ball. Why was I feeling so discombobulated? It must be because of the way he held on to my eyes, I thought. And because he was so darn attractive. Those eyes. That gray hair. His soft, full mouth. And whereas some of the cops I'd spotted in the conference room looked as though they'd had Butterball turkeys stuffed under their shirts, Beck was taut, clearly in terrific shape.

By the end of twenty-five minutes, I'd shared everything I could possibly think of. But he had one more question.

"Have you had a chance to think about what we discussed last night?" he asked solemnly. My heart took off like a startled titmouse. I had no idea what he meant.

"I—I'm sorry, I'm not following," I said.

He sighed lightly in a way that suggested he was summoning a wee bit of patience. "I asked you last night to think about whether you may have noticed anything suspicious in the parking lot when you walked back there. As you can probably deduce from the timeline, you were clearly at the scene around the same time the murderer was. Are you absolutely certain you didn't observe anything?"

I paused a minute before answering, not because I needed the time to think, but because I wanted to offer the impression I was doing just that.

"No, nothing," I said finally, forming an expression on my face that I hoped suggested I had racked my brain so hard, I was in danger of blowing a fuse. "In fact, I remember noticing how absolutely quiet it was back there. There were no cars in the parking lot at that end, by the way. The killer was either gone or had parked the car someplace else. Or, of course, if it was someone who worked at the inn, he didn't need a car."

He stared at me, expressionless. "Why do you say 'he'?" he asked finally.

"Oh, just using the universal pronoun," I explained. "Though clearly the body was wrapped up by someone awfully strong. Do you have any theories yet?"

I hadn't expected an answer, of course, but I thought I might get a bemused smile for my gumption. But no. Just more of that staring thing. Burning a hole through my head.

"I'll tell you what," he said wryly. "You're a writer. In fact, from what I hear, you write crime stories. When we catch the killer, we'll give you the exclusive."

Before I could summon a flip comment, he rose from his seat and nodded his head toward the far end of the room.

"Let's get those fingerprints taken care of."

I trailed behind him toward an alcove. A few of the cops in the conference room paused in their conversation and checked me out. It appeared as if the force were large enough to handle the case themselves without having to play second fiddle to the state police.

Inside the alcove, a technician was waiting. He drew a pair of latex gloves out of a box, and stretched them onto his hands. I nearly jumped when one of them made a hard snapping sound against the back of his hand. I had no idea why I felt so jittery. Next he picked up a small set of scissors from the drawer, lifted one strand of hair from my head, snipped it, and sealed it in a plastic bag.

Once the technician was done, it was Beck's turn. From the top of the counter he picked up an inkpad and a white card. After flicking off the top of the inkpad, he set it closer to me.

"Let's start with your right hand," he said. "Your thumb first and then the other four digits."

I moved my hand over the pad, then hesitated.

"Here, I can help you."

He took my right hand in his and pressed my thumb onto the squishy pad, lifted it, then moved it onto the card and pressed again. He repeated the same procedure with each finger.

"Is everything okay?" he asked. Was he inquiring, I wondered, because my hand was as limp as an overcooked fettuccine noodle and he was being forced to guide me, or because I wasn't lobbing any cute remarks during the process?

"Yeah, fine," I said.

When he was done, he handed me a tissue to wipe off the tips of my fingers. He glanced at his watch, turned, and strode back across the room toward the lobby, clearly expecting me to follow.

"You're just here for the weekend?" he asked as he held the door for me.

"Yes. Why? Will you need to talk to me again?"

"Possibly. Depending on how things develop. Thanks for coming down."

The street was bustling outside, people finally out of bed and running their Saturday errands. I hurried along the sidewalk to the Jeep and threw myself inside. And I just sat there, trying to get a handle on what had happened. There was no denying it: When Beck had held my hand and pressed my fingers onto the inkpad, I had felt the hottest jolt of lust I'd experienced in months.

CHAPTER 6

WAS I OUT of my mind? was all I could think as I fired up the engine. The guy was a too intense, apparently humorless, small-city cop. I couldn't believe he was making my heart pound so hard. This is what happens, I thought, when you go for months without physical contact. You look at men who are total strangers and feel the urge to tear their boxer shorts off with your teeth. You become attracted to a guy who probably bowls every Tuesday night and has a best friend named Choppy.

I pushed the thought of Beck from my mind, deciding it was a complete aberration—like one of those blinding pains you get in your temple one day that convinces you you have a brain tumor the size of a beefsteak tomato but then never occurs again—and attempted to find my way back to the inn. I got lost twice, once so badly that I was forced to stop and ask directions. When I drove through the gate fifteen minutes later, I saw two TV vans parked on the road outside and an array of police vehicles still in the parking lot.

I was so absolutely zonked from the night before, I had to fight off the urge to return to my room and crawl into bed. But if I was going to learn anything between now and Monday morning, I'd have to use every minute I had. The first thing I wanted to do before meeting up with Danny was check out the back door to the spa. Since the parking lot was taped off, I walked around the west side of the inn, following a path that bordered the gardens.

Once I was behind the inn, I saw that the area directly in back of the spa was taped off as well, though I could see the rear door from the small incline that rose behind the building. There was a fir tree near the door, and several birches, and it would certainly have been easy for someone with a key to slip in without being noticed. It was impossible for me to tell from my vantage point whether the lock had been broken.

Following the yellow police tape, which flapped with a snapping sound in the autumn breeze, I continued walking east until I could see the parking lot and the main entrance of the spa. I gazed at the spot where I had stood in the darkness last night. Despite what Beck had said, I had no recollection of having seen anything suspicious—no movement inside, no movement in the parking lot.

The next thing to check out was the converted barn. It loomed at the top of the incline amid a cluster of smaller outbuildings, and I found a path that took me right to the front. It was a bark-colored, weathered structure that looked as old as the inn, though it now sported a dozen windows and a large glass door. Through the door I could see a small vestibule and staircase. As I paused on the path, scanning the building, a person came tripping down the staircase, very much in a hurry, and pushed open the door. It was Piper.

She was wearing a limp, puckered brown leather coat over her uniform, and she had pulled her mass of red hair back in a low ponytail. She still looked shaken. When I called out her name, she jumped about a foot.

"Sorry, I didn't mean to scare you," I said. "How are you doing? I was hoping to get a chance to talk to you today."

"Lousy," she said, advancing toward me. "And I can't believe they expect me to work today."

"That's got to be tough," I said. "Have the police been over here? To Anna's room?"

"Yeah, they've got it all taped off." She glanced over my right shoulder toward the back of the inn, as if something had caught her eye, and I turned instinctively to follow her glance. But there was no one there.

"Have you been to the police station to give a formal statement yet?" I asked.

"First thing this morning," she said. "That guy needs to take a chill pill, if you ask me."

"Could you tell from his questions what angle they're pursuing—do they think it could be someone who works at the spa?"

"They didn't tell me *anything,*" she said, shaking her head.

"The room we found Anna in. You mentioned that you'd turned the light off in that room before you left last night. So that wasn't the room Anna did her last massage in?"

"No," she said distractedly. "She was scheduled to use another room."

"When you left last night, were all the doors locked?"

"Yes, yes. I told the police that. I would never be careless about something like that."

"Danny told me that you were originally supposed to work last night, but Anna agreed to switch nights with you."

"And your point is?"

"I'm not being accusatory. I'm just curious about what Anna's plans might have been."

"She'd told me she was planning on staying in Friday night. That's why she was willing to switch nights with me."

"I'd heard she'd been dating another therapist— Eric."

"What? Oh, that was over weeks ago."

"Was she seeing anyone new?"

"I have no idea," she answered quickly. "We weren't what you'd call buddy-buddy. In fact, I hardly knew her."

Another glance over my shoulder. This time I didn't turn to follow it. In the flat light of the day, I could see that her white skin was marred slightly by tiny acne scars.

"You seem worried, Piper," I said. "Do you think that the killer is someone who works here?"

She didn't answer, just pulled a long breath and let it out anxiously in a gust.

"Can I help in any way, Piper?"

"No, no," she said irritatedly. "There's nothing anyone can do that will make it any better. Look, I've got to get over there. I've got a client in a few minutes."

I watched her head down the path to the inn, her ponytail swishing like a horse's as she walked. What had caught her eye a few minutes ago? I wondered. I remembered suddenly how she had frozen when she had seen the wedge of light under the door to the treatment room last night. In some regards she had seemed more startled than you might expect over what could easily have been nothing more than an act of forgetfulness. I flashed back too on how distracted she'd seemed when she'd massaged me—pausing at odd moments. It was as if she'd been anticipating something, not danger necessarily, but *something*. Had Piper expected some kind of trouble last night?

I hurried back to the inn myself, keeping a distance from her. The lobby was empty, though a few people sat in the lounge, chatting in hushed tones before the fire. As I approached Danny's office, I caught the sound of her voice, raised slightly, agitated. I picked up my pace, worried something was wrong. Not bothering to knock, I shoved open the half-shut door.

I knew instantly that the man Danny was talking to— or *had* been talking to, since she stopped in midsentence as I burst through the door—was George. At about six feet two, he towered over Danny as she sat at her desk chair. He was fairly slim, though soft looking, and his face was jowly. He wore dark green pants, a beige Banlon golf shirt, and dated, dark-framed glasses, kind of Austin Powers style. The one thing he'd done to beat back the clock was dye his hair jet black.

"Sorry," I blurted out. "I just wanted to be sure everything was okay."

"Oh, Bailey, yes. Uh, everything is fine," Danny said, fumbling. "We were just rehashing everything that's happened. This is George. George, this is Bailey, who I've told you so much about."

"Of course," he said, all debonair as he stepped out from behind the desk to take my hand. "I'm so sorry we have to meet this way."

His handshake was strong but clammy, as if his sweat glands had been keeping busy this morning. He also gave off a slightly smarmy vibe. I had the distinct impression that if I didn't keep my guard up, I'd end up buying a Honda from him or a time-share for a south Florida condo with walls made of two-inch-thick particleboard. Danny had raved about George at our lunch in New York, but my instant take on him wasn't positive.

"Well, I'd better go over to the salon and see what I can do to help," George volunteered. "I hope I get a chance to talk to you later, Bailey."

"Oh, I'm sure you will," I said. "I'm here till Monday."

He pecked Danny on the cheek before he left, but she stood there motionless, as though she were playing a game of freeze tag. As soon as I heard George's footsteps at the far end of the corridor, I asked her gently if everything was okay.

"I don't want to burden you, Bailey," she said. "You've been dragged into this mess enough."

"It's not a burden, Danny. Please."

"It's just . . . well, George didn't stay near Boston last night. He drove back and spent the night at *our* house. He was there during this whole terrible mess. After you left this morning, I called the house to leave a message for him, and I almost died when he picked up the phone."

"Why did he change his plans?" I asked evenly, trying not to reveal that the hairs on the back of my neck were now standing at attention.

"Apparently dinner fell through at the last minute, and he decided to just get in the car and drive straight back. He got in around eleven, and he says that since I'd told him I had the start of a headache and was going to turn in early, he was afraid to call and wake me. I know he was simply thinking of me, but the whole thing just upsets me."

I didn't like what I was hearing. For starters, I'd learned the hard way to react with alarm whenever a man overexplains or uses the expression "I was afraid to. . . ." George's rationalizations might bug me even on an ordinary day, but this was no ordinary day. A woman had been murdered last night, and George had been missing in action. Yet I didn't want to say anything that would freak out Danny. I'd have to keep my eye on George and let my gut guide me.

"You're going to need George big-time over the next

weeks," I offered. "Why don't you just chalk up last night to crossed signals and move on?"

My words of semi-reassurance appeared to calm her instantly, and she relaxed back in her chair. I asked her if she was up for digging into the financial records. She insisted that she was, and I went through what Bud had told me, suggesting that we start by looking at all the vendors used by the spa. If we saw anything suspicious, we'd pull out the actual bills.

While she accessed the computer files we needed, I pushed the office door shut and dragged an extra chair back around next to hers. For the next half hour, we reviewed the list of all the vendors used by the spa and how much they'd been paid. There were suppliers of everything from massage tables and oils to candles and heating pads, and Danny was familiar with many of them because she'd been intimately involved in the initial setup of the spa. I asked her how the billing process worked, and she explained that when an invoice came in for something used exclusively by the spa, it was given to Josh for his authorization and then initialed by the business manager.

"It sounds to me like you're pretty on top of this," I said.

"Yes and no," she replied. "I'm a good businesswoman. But I've gotten sloppy looking at things related to the spa because Josh has done such a great job. I used to initial the bills, but I don't anymore."

In the end we spotted no red flags. There were at least a dozen vendors Danny *didn't* recognize, but she said it was perfectly reasonable that Josh would have added new vendors over time, based on the needs of the spa. And as she pointed out, none of the checks cut to the new vendors were for an excessive amount.

"It's still worth investigating," I said. "Is it possible for you to glance at these bills today and see if they look kosher?"

"The business manager is off Saturdays, but I can go through the bills in his office. It's all pretty organized."

What *I* wanted to do, I told her, was go through the files of all spa employees.

"There's not much in them," she said. "Just their application, reference letters, some insurance stuff."

"That's okay. You never know what might jump out. By the way, this accountant source of mine said we should consider if anyone on staff has had a big improvement in lifestyle lately. Are you aware of anything like that?"

She shook her head. "As I mentioned before, a lot of the spa staff live in the barn," she said. "Josh lives in a town house—rented—not far from here. He's been living a *bit* more extravagantly lately—he just bought a new car—but then I'm paying him more."

"Because he's doing such a good job?" I asked.

"Well, he works partly on a bonus basis. And since he's done such a marvelous job of growing the business, his bonuses have been very nice."

She spent the next few minutes gathering files for me, during which time she mentioned that she'd arranged for me to have a hot stone massage with Cordelia at six-thirty. She'd also set up a tennis lesson for me with Rich at eleven tomorrow. As for Eric, she was still working on it—he'd had nothing free, and she was afraid if she asked Josh to rearrange his schedule, it might look suspicious. My meeting with Josh would be at four in the solarium.

Since it was almost two and I hadn't eaten, I stopped off at the restaurant for a salad. The whole time I ate, I thought of Beck. I've met plenty of cops reporting the kinds of stories I do, and I'd found some of them hunky. But I'd never had one send me into a tizzy like this. I was feeling that ridiculous urge I used to get in high school when I was infatuated with someone—I wanted to get in my car and drive by his house four or five hundred times or call him on the phone and hang up after he answered. Maybe my crazy feelings had to do with the intensity of the situation in which I'd met him. Dead body, over-the-top lust. It could be a bizarre permutation of the Stockholm syndrome—in which hostages bond with their captors.

Back in my room, I spread Danny's folders on my desk. There weren't many. I knew from previous conversations with Danny that the core staff of the spa numbered about twenty: Josh, about a dozen full-time therapists, three receptionists to cover every hour of the week, two women who did the wraps and baths, and several coordinators who showed people to their rooms and kept the place tidy as appointments came and went. During the summer and over the holidays, the spa beefed up with a handful of freelancers.

Danny was right. The folders for each staff member held next to nothing: an employment application, a résumé, and, in some cases, reference letters. A few contained a sheet on some issue that had arisen at work. One therapist, for instance, had accused a desk clerk last year of stealing tips.

There was nothing of significance in Piper's file, or in Josh's, though I was intrigued to learn that prior to getting into the spa scene five years ago, he'd been working in Los Angeles as a so-called model/actor.

Finally I got to Anna's file. As Danny had pointed out, she'd lived all over the place, trying her hand at a variety of different jobs, including tour guide, restaurant hostess, and real estate agent. Until she'd landed in the world of massage, she'd averaged about a year's stay in each job. There were small gaps in the résumé, and a line at the bottom attempted to explain them by stating that she had taken time off here and there to travel. I wouldn't have been surprised to discover that many of those gaps reflected jobs of even shorter duration.

In New York City, she had been employed at the Paradise Spa, no address given. The name didn't ring a bell with me. It's not that I had the money to drop regularly at day spas around Manhattan, but my boss at *Gloss*, Cat Jones, did. She preferred not to let a week go by without having some portion of her body scrubbed with sea salt or blasted with oxygen, and I'd heard the names of most of the trendy places from her.

Anna's letter of reference had come from a woman named Nina Lyle, manager of the Paradise Spa, and it was glowing, praising Anna's skills and professionalism. Knowing that the police might confiscate these files at some point, I jotted down Nina Lyle's phone number, which had been scribbled at the bottom of the letter. I glanced then at the application form. Filled out just over a year ago. My eyes ran down the page, past the section on allergies (none) and health ailments (none). On the line that inquired whom the applicant had been referred by, a small surprise awaited me. It said Piper Allyson. Piper, who had told me, quote, she barely knew Anna.

CHAPTER 7

I PICKED UP the phone and called Danny in her office. I mentioned what I'd discovered on Anna's application and asked if Piper had played a role in securing Anna the job.

"She might have," she said. "I just don't know—Josh does all the hiring for the spa. *Why?*"

"Piper told me earlier today that she barely knew Anna. And then lo and behold, I see her name on Anna's application."

"Perhaps the two of them worked together once but weren't necessarily friends," Danny suggested. "You don't have to like a person or think of them as a friend to consider them a good therapist. Why would it matter, anyway?"

"I'm just following up on what seems like an odd discrepancy," I said. "If Anna and Piper were in cahoots with Josh on some bad business in the spa, they might have chosen to play down how well they knew each other."

After I signed off, I pulled down Piper's folder from the pile again and slid out the résumé, laying it next to Anna's. I couldn't see where the two of them could have met. At no point, at least according to their résumés, had they ever worked together, nor had they even lived in the same city. Piper's massage experience, all seven years of it, was concentrated mostly in hotels in Los Angeles and Lake Tahoe and at a spa in New Jersey, whereas Anna's only experience had been in New York City. The only thing worth noting was that part of the year Anna had been in New York, Piper had been working in New Jersey.

I jumped from the bed and pulled a black-and-white composition book out of my tote bag. Whenever I take on an article assignment, I use a composition book to scribble notes and questions to myself. Though I always write the actual article on my computer, there's something about putting down my initial impressions in a composition book with a number two pencil that jumpstarts my thinking and helps me develop an angle. I intended to use the same approach with the case. I cracked the spine and jotted down notes about the murder, Bud's insights, my brief conversation on the path with Piper, the small discovery I'd made about Anna and Piper's connection, plus various questions that had formed in my mind about the murder. I didn't end up with any brilliant insights, but at least felt I was doing *something*.

It wasn't quite time yet to meet with Josh, but I wanted to try room 17 again. I strode down the hall and rapped on the door.

This time a woman called out, "Who is it?" in a voice that suggested a trace of anxiety.

"It's Bailey Weggins," I said as the door opened a crack, the chain still on. "I work with Danielle Hubner, the owner of the inn, and I was anxious to see how you were doing."

She swung the door open, and with the kind of haughty smile she might offer a salesgirl at Louis Vuitton, she motioned for me to enter the living area of the suite.

It was the woman I'd seen earlier with Beck. She was about sixty, handsome looking, with hair the same shade as one of those blond ranch minks women wore in fifties' movies. Her skin was beautiful, almost porcelain-like, but she'd already had a face-lift or two, and her eyes were slanted upward slightly and pulled back too far. If she kept going under the knife, she'd end up looking just *like* a mink, with an eye on each side of her head.

"As you've probably heard," she said, pulling off a pair of reading glasses that had been perched midway down her nose, "we're checking out as soon as the police tell us it's fine to leave. I certainly don't expect to have any trouble getting our deposit back."

"None whatsoever," I said. "We're so terribly sorry you had to find yourself in the middle of this. How did everything go with the police?"

"You were there, too, weren't you? I saw you when Walter and I were coming out."

"That's right," I said. She took a seat in one of the armchairs, and I perched on the edge of the couch. "I had to give a statement myself. One of the other therapists and I found the body."

"My goodness, how *dreadful*," she exclaimed. "Do you know how she died? The police wouldn't tell us a thing."

"I'm not sure. Just that it must have happened shortly after you went back to your room. There wasn't anyone still in the spa when you left, was there?"

"Not that I was aware of. There was one other appointment at the same time as mine—I saw the woman earlier in that waiting room with the dripping water— but it appeared she left ahead of me. Some women will go upstairs wearing just a robe, but I *refuse* to do that. I'd sooner be caught dead than sashay around a hotel in nothing more than a housecoat—though I suppose that's a terrible thing to say right now."

"Did you see Anna again before you left?"

"Anna?"

"The one who was murdered."

"Yes, she let me out. And you know what's strange? Right before I went upstairs, I suddenly felt nervous down there."

"How do you mean?" I asked. In a split second I was back in the spa that night—the dark, silent halls, the faint hint of green tea, the ominous chink of light in the hallway.

"After I finished dressing in the changing room, I went looking for the girl—this Anna—because the door to the inn was locked and I wasn't sure how to turn the bolt. She wasn't in the main reception area or anywhere else I looked. Most of the lights were off, and it seemed *spooky* to me. Finally I went back to the changing room, and that's where she was—sitting at the counter. She was out of her uniform and into her street clothes, and I didn't recognize her at first. She nearly gave me a stroke when I saw her. Generally at a spa you don't find the employees hanging around the guest locker room."

"Maybe she was waiting for you," I suggested.

"No, because she apologized when she saw me. She said she assumed that the other therapist had already let me out. She walked me to the door, unlocked it, and said good-bye. That was the last I saw of her. You know, Walter and I just spent two weeks in South Africa, and I was a nervous wreck the whole time—needlessly, as it turns out—and then we come here and *this* happens. Who would have imagined."

"What about the other therapist—the one who'd worked on the other nine o'clock appointment? Did you see him around?"

"I didn't see any sign of him after I got dressed. I assumed he was gone. As I said, it was all very quiet and spooky down there."

"Did Anna appear apprehensive in any way?"

"Well, I don't go around calibrating the mood of my masseuse, but she certainly didn't seem like someone who was contemplating being murdered. I must admit she wasn't the most pleasant person in the world, and I've certainly had better massages."

She pressed me then for what I knew about the murder, and I gave her a brief, very incomplete version of the story and then rose to leave. I apologized again on behalf of the inn.

As I walked downstairs to the main floor, I considered what I'd just learned. Anna had been a dutiful assistant manager on Friday night. She'd made sure that the side door to the inn had been locked at some point during the evening. So, chances were she'd checked the back door, too. I considered all the possible scenarios: The killer could have broken in, or forced his way in, or been let in by Anna willingly, unaware that her life was in danger. Or he could have slipped in using a key. I shuddered as I imagined such a scene in my mind. Anna turning off the lights one by one and suddenly a man appearing from the shadows. Her relief, perhaps, when she recognized him. Her terror when she realized that he intended to harm her.

There was something else Babs had said that intrigued me. The part about Anna sitting at the counter in the locker room. It *did* seem odd. On the occasions when I'd had massages in spas, I'd noticed how the therapists were generally careful not to overstep the boundary between themselves and the clients. They never got too friendly, never ventured into the clients' space. So what was Anna doing in the clients' changing area? I knew she didn't store her things there because I remembered Danny saying that Anna's purse had been found in the employee locker room.

It took me longer than I'd expected to find the solarium. It was at the west end of the inn, diametrically opposite to the spa, tucked away at the end of a maze of rambling corridors. As I passed several guests along the way, I tried to measure their mood. They seemed subdued, some almost somber. Clearly everyone knew about the murder, and people were feeling less than blissed out. When I finally found the solarium, I discovered that I had it all to myself.

I took a seat on the black wicker sofa and put my feet up on a large ottoman. Because of the drab weather, the room hardly lived up to its name today. But I could imagine how inviting it would be on a sunny day. The large windows overlooked the gardens and, at the far end, the beginning of the nature reserve. I pulled out a notebook from my bag and waited.

I felt a little bit more anxious than I liked. Theoretically, I was here just to talk about the spa. But if something fishy was going on there, Josh might very well be in the thick of it, and I was going to have to test the waters carefully.

Josh strode into the solarium twelve minutes after four, just as I was wondering if one of us had our signals crossed. He certainly hadn't gotten less good-looking in the hours since I'd seen him last.

"How's it going?" I asked.

"Needless to say, not great," he replied, pleasant but cool. "But then this can't be much fun for you, either." He chose the armchair directly across from me. He had a real smoothness to him, though I could picture him arrogant and smug when it served his purposes.

"No, not much fun," I said. "But Danny was hoping I could forge ahead as planned."

"And tell me what that plan is again?" he asked, holding my eyes.

"I write a few travel articles every year, and Danny wanted my insight on how she could do a stronger pitch to travel editors. I know business is good, but she'd love more coverage for both the inn and the spa. I've reported on a few spas and have colleagues who've visited lots of them."

"Let's get started, then."

"Great. Danny tells me you've done a fabulous job of revitalizing the spa and introducing some amazing services. I'd love to hear about some of them."

I thought that having the chance to talk about his business might warm him up, but it didn't. He sat toward the edge of the chair, one leg crossed tightly over the other and his hands locked over his knees. They were long, slim hands, as pale as his face—and deceptive. Based on his handshake from earlier, they were far stronger than they looked.

"When I got here two years ago, the spa was a *mess*," he said. "It offered a total mishmash of new age stuff. It was my idea to go the Zen route. I sensed that the Asian thing was going to take off big-time, and it did. We renovated the interiors and then planned out a new range of treatments—Shirodhara massage, different types of wraps, *sento* baths."

"*Sento* baths. Are they . . . ?"

"They're Japanese in origin. You sit on a wooden stool and have buckets of water poured over you. Then you're scrubbed in total silence with a cloth called a *goshi goshi.*"

Goshi goshi. It sounded more like a type of lapdog, the kind that fits into a purse and yaps at the sight of a dustball blowing across the floor.

"Is it because of all these new treatments that the spa's really taken off?"

"First and foremost, I'm running the spa far more efficiently today than it was run when I got here," he declared. "I won't bore you with what a disaster Danny's first manager was. But yes, the Zen decor and treatments have played a major role in the success. People love it. It's exotic, a taste of a world they might never experience. I'm sure, since you've covered spas, you've seen what a big draw the Asian influence has been at other places."

He made it sound like a rhetorical question, yet I could sense he was curious about what I knew.

"Sure," I said. I was going to leave it at that, but suddenly I wanted to see what would happen if I dinged that slick exterior just a little.

"Though there are actually a few big trends," I continued. "There's Asian or Zen or however you want to refer to it. Then there's the indigenous stuff—treatments that reflect the locale where the spa is. If the location is Colorado, for instance, the treatments could include things like . . . well, I'm making this up, but something like *alpine exfoliation.* But I've started to hear more and more about places offering a combination of Zen *and* indigenous treatments. People say it's good because it leaves the spa with someplace to go if the Asian stuff starts to lose its magic."

"Based on the business *we've* been doing, I hardly see it peaking anytime soon," Josh said, narrowing his eyes.

Ah, so he did bristle if you hit the right button.

"I'm sure you're right," I said. "You obviously know what you're doing. I guess you must have a terrific staff to have grown the business the way you have." I was sidling over into new territory, hoping I wasn't being obvious.

"I do—or at least I did," he replied. "Who knows how many of them are going to bolt because of what happened." There wasn't a soupçon of remorse in his voice.

I glanced around the room, gathering my thoughts. I needed to know if Danny's vibe about the spa was right. Was it only her imagination, or did Josh have something to hide? Getting close to the answer would require stronger button pushing on my part.

"By the way," I announced, "I'm planning to come back in a couple of weeks for another chance to see the spa. I'd love to spend some time over there—as an observer."

He stared at me poker-faced, without emotion. But his scar wiggled like a water snake, so I knew he was grinding his jaw. Obviously my little suggestion hadn't pleased him.

"We'd be happy to arrange as many treatments as you'd like," he said after a moment, forcing a tight smile. "But unfortunately, playing the observer is *not* an option. Our clients take part in the treatments in order to get *away* from people. We'd never do anything to upset the equilibrium we've tried so hard to establish."

"I wasn't suggesting I stand around *during* the treatments. I'd love to just sit at the front desk, watch the ebb and flow."

"And the reason for that would be?" he asked.

"Just to form impressions. Get a feel for the spa so I could offer Danny ideas."

"Unfortunately, that's not a possibility," he said, his voice as hard as the edge of a steel door. "As you might imagine, we'll be lucky to get the spa up and running again over the next weeks." He glanced at his watch. "I hope you don't mind, but I really do have to get moving."

I indicated I was finished for now and thanked him for his time.

"What a strange convergence of events," he said as he rose from his chair. "I mean, you and Piper going into the spa on the night that there just happens to be a dead body there. What was it that you left in the spa?"

"My watch."

"Oh, right," he said dryly. "I guess you'll have to be more careful in the future."

I was struggling to figure out just how loaded his comment had been when the door pushed open. It was the therapist I'd seen earlier, who I assumed must be Eric.

"Josh, we need you," he said. "We've got some major scheduling problems." His voice and demeanor were almost preternaturally calm, as if he'd really announced that tea and scones were about to be served in the lounge.

"Where's Piper? Isn't she sorting it out?"

"She's . . ." He glanced over in my direction. "She's a little overwhelmed right now."

"All right, I'll take care of it." He strode quickly out of the room, offering me a cool good-bye as he left.

"You're Eric, right?" I asked as he too turned to go, his eyes downcast. He was totally exotic and mysterious looking—skin the color of coffee and eyes so deep brown they were really almost black. Yet he had failed in the end to light Anna's fire.

"Yes," he replied. His face registered nothing.

"I'm Bailey Weggins, a friend of Danny's. I was supposed to help her on a project with the spa this weekend."

He shook my hand, smiling politely.

"I'm sorry for your loss, by the way."

"I'm not sure what you mean," he said. He had closed the smile down so slowly and imperceptibly that it was hard to remember it being on his face.

"I was told you were very close to Anna."

"No, not at all."

With that he turned and left the room.

I remained by myself in the solarium, replaying my conversation with Josh and my even briefer one with Eric. I'd hit a nerve with Josh, that was for sure. Just as Danny had said, he *was* territorial about the spa. But why? Eric's comments were also curious. He'd reportedly dated Anna, but now he was playing it down.

As I stood there, my eyes were drawn to the gardens and then beyond that to the woods. I wasn't certain how big the area was or how far the trails went. But I found myself suddenly intrigued—and in need of a way to clear my head. After returning to my room to change into hiking shoes and my jeans jacket, I set out. I had an hour before I needed to be back for my massage.

The skies were now clear, though the ground was soggy, heaped with shiny wet leaves—mostly yellow and ocher and burnt sienna—that had been stripped from the trees by the rain earlier. Digging my sunglasses out of my jacket pocket, I walked briskly through the empty formal gardens, following the small gray signs that indicated the way to the nature reserve. Most of the flowers were gone now, though there were still a few dead heads on stalks and two rows of purple mums in full festive bloom, like guests who'd showed at a party after everyone else had gone home.

The garden ended, but the path continued through a cluster of large fir trees. Two middle-aged women, obviously inn guests and both in spandex leggings and fanny packs, emerged from the grove of trees just as I entered it and acknowledged me with nods, expressionless.

I followed the path through the trees to a heavily forested area of mostly hardwoods—maples and oaks. The leaves were yellow and orange, with just a hint of red. There was a small bridge ahead of me, over a narrow stream, and as I reached it I saw a sign that announced that I was entering the nature reserve. I took off my sunglasses and stuck them in my jacket pocket. Worn trails led off in several directions, and I chose the one that said "Juniper" and began to follow it.

For the first time since last night, I felt my body start to relax. The air was heavy with that nutty, mossy, mushroomy aroma that woods always release after a rainfall. And it was absolutely quiet, except for the sound of my shoes trampling the leaves and a few birds whistling to one another at the very tops of the trees. I walked for ten minutes or so along the same path, wondering exactly where it would take me and how far the woods extended.

Suddenly, I heard the tread of a boot that wasn't my own. I stopped in my tracks and listened. Nothing. Craning my neck, I peered into the woods ahead of me, but no one was visible.

Had I been stupid, I suddenly thought, to have traipsed out here on my own? I turned and looked behind me in the direction I'd come. The path I'd walked along disappeared quickly, and then there was nothing but trees and blankets of leaves. I turned back and stared ahead of me.

Suddenly, without a sound, Detective Jeffrey Beck emerged from the thicket. For a second it seemed as if he'd been conjured up out of nowhere, like a black hound or a stallion in a fantasy story. My heart lurched and I felt that same rush of lust I'd had when he'd held my fingers in his hand.

CHAPTER 8

BECK LOOKED AS startled by the sight of me as I was by him. He was wearing the suede jacket he'd had on Friday night, a pair of corduroy pants, and hiking boots. My first thought was that he was out searching for evidence. But why so far from the spa?

"So what are you doing sneaking around in the woods, Miss Weggins?" he asked, stepping closer to me. I felt the slightest, weirdest trace of fear. I was all alone in the woods with this man. I had to remind myself that he was a cop.

"I'm not sneaking," I said, more defensively than I'd intended. "I'm just getting some exercise."

"Is that so?"

"Yes. Is that what *you're* doing—getting some exercise? Or are you looking for evidence?"

"Evidence?" he asked, feigning ignorance.

"Yes. Clues about the murder."

"My, aren't we curious?" He gazed at me intently, and in the darkness of the woods, his eyes seemed more gray than blue today. His face was ruddy, as if he'd been walking briskly. "I hope you won't let that curiosity get the better of you. I wouldn't like to think you'd go poking into something you shouldn't."

"You don't have to be so mean to me," I said. "I was just making conversation. I'm sure you're used to that. Girls trying to chat you up."

I couldn't believe I'd said that, but I knew why I'd done it. The man filled me with the urge to rattle his hunky but hard-assed cop exterior to see if there was anything human underneath. He actually smiled slightly, pulling his mouth to one side.

"Forgive me if I sounded mean," he said, softening by a centimeter. "That wasn't my desire."

What *is* your desire? I wanted to ask.

"Well, I'd better be going," I said instead. "If I don't get some oxygen in my bloodstream, I may pass out." I knew I needed to be on the move before I said or did anything else borderline ridiculous.

"Wait just a second," he said.

"Sorry to see me go?" For God's sake, Bailey, put a gag on it, I pleaded with myself.

Without warning, Beck leaned forward and reached with one hand toward my face. I pulled back, startled.

"You've got a twig in your hair," he said, drawing it out slowly. As his fingers brushed my scalp, I felt as if my hair might ignite, like dry sagebrush from the sun.

"Thanks," I said. "There's not a bird in there, too, is there?"

He smiled, really smiled, this time.

"Have a good walk," he said. "And remember, just because you're a writer, don't go butting into anything that's not your business."

I mumbled a quick good-bye and tramped off in the direction he had come. My cheeks felt hot. Had the twig thing been a flirtatious gesture? And what had he been up to out here in the wilderness? His presence, I realized, must have something to do with the murder. *Was* he looking for evidence? A weapon, perhaps? I still wasn't certain how Anna had died, but if the murderer had used an object to strangle or bludgeon her, then he may have tried to dispose of it in the woods. Except if the weapon was missing, wouldn't there be a whole team of police out here scouring for it? I trudged along for five more minutes until the trail forked in two directions with a small sign by each new path. One read "The Marsh," the other read "Durham Road." There was no way of knowing which direction Beck had come from, but the notion of a road nearby intrigued me and I struck off that way.

The woods grew denser, and then, after ten minutes of walking, they began to thin out again. I realized that I might be coming to the other side of the reserve. I saw a clearing ahead and also a gate running parallel to a road. I stopped and looked around. A small sign by the gate announced that the main entrance to the reserve was one mile down the road. But next to the gate was a dirt shoulder, roomy enough for a single car to park there.

Something told me that this was what Beck had come to investigate. He may have been considering whether the killer had parked his car here, snuck through the reserve to the inn, and then slipped back into the woods after he had finished his deadly business. It was certainly a possibility. Unless the killer worked at the inn or was a guest there, he would have had to drive to the inn that night. But if he'd parked in the parking lot, someone might have spotted him or at the very least remembered his car. Slipping through the woods would have guaranteed that there was little chance of being noticed, especially if he had used the back door of the spa. Of course, it would have been extremely tricky moving through the nature reserve at night, but the trails were clearly defined, and with a good flashlight and moonlight, it would have been doable. That would mean, however, that the killer had to be someone *very* familiar with the area.

I started back in the direction I'd come. Light was falling, and the wind had picked up the slightest bit since I'd first entered the woods. The tops of the trees swished, making that sea sound you hear when you hold a conch shell to your ear. I had walked for about five minutes when I heard a twig snap hard behind me. I turned my whole body around, facing backward, but there was nothing there—just trees and an endless carpet of soggy orange and umber leaves. It may have been a branch snapping or a deer or squirrel making its way through the woods. I started walking again, this time faster, my shoes tramping firmly along the path. I heard it again—the snapping—but this time it was softer, almost cautious, and it was followed by what sounded like the slide of shoes on leaves. As my heart hurled itself forward in my chest, I spun around again. The sound stopped as soon as I faced the direction behind me.

"Who's there?" I called out. "Is that you, Beck?"

No answer. Just absolute stillness. Someone was out there, following me, and they weren't announcing themselves, and that meant they didn't want to be seen. With fear beginning to pump through my body, I turned around again and began to move, faster this time, gathering speed until I was running. I thought I could hear footsteps behind me, but I wasn't sure because the sound of my shoes tearing through the leaves carried in all directions. I craned my neck around two or three times as I ran, but I could see no one behind me.

"I'm right here, Beck," I yelled. "I'm coming." I wanted whoever was behind me to know that we weren't alone out here. I was in the thickest part of the woods now, where the trees seemed to huddle together, and I was scared as hell that I would lose my way. I watched the path as I ran, being careful not to step off it. Suddenly I was at the fork, with one sign pointing to the marsh and the other to the Cedar Inn. The sound seemed to have retreated, back into the woods. I kept running, though, until the woods grew thinner. A stitch began to throb in my side. I slowed my pace just a little and craned my neck around again. There was nothing. And the only sound was the shrill call of a bird, high in the branches.

By now my lungs felt as if they would burst, and I slowed down even more, into a jog. Finally I burst out of the woods into the garden of the inn. I leaned forward, hands on knees, trying to pull in a breath but all the time watching the border of the woods. It wasn't my imagination. Someone had chased me and tried to scare me and possibly wanted to harm me. He'd succeeded in scaring me. He had also made me mad.

I stood in the garden until my breath slowed to normal and the stitch was gone from my side. After letting my eyes sweep one more time across the trees, I nearly stumbled back to the inn.

It was almost time for my massage, and I wondered whether I should just chuck it. I felt too rattled to lie on a table and vegetate. But I would simply have to force myself to let go, I decided. I didn't want to pass up the chance to have a conversation with the chatty Cordelia.

The salon turned out to be a small space at the back of the inn. A girl at the desk was explaining in patronizing tones to a tubby woman in a rayon warm-up suit that they had left a message for her this morning, canceling her appointment, and they were terribly sorry she had never received it. What about tomorrow morning at eight? She grudgingly agreed, then stormed off. Josh, I noticed, was nowhere in sight.

Considering what a mess everything was, I expected a delay, but there wasn't one. As soon as I offered my name, I was ushered to a small dressing room and given a robe and terrycloth slippers. Cordelia was waiting for me right outside the changing room. She was the same blonde I'd spotted heading for the meeting this morning. Up close, I could see that her face was pretty and soft, with light blue eyes, almost transparent. Her boobs were humongous—there was no other word for them— and she was probably twenty or thirty pounds overweight. But being large boned, she wore it well, kind of Rubenesque. She led me down the corridor to the far end of the salon, and we entered a small room with a massage table. She told me that she'd wait outside while I disrobed and made myself comfortable on the table.

It appeared as if I were in a space ordinarily used for storage. In its present incarnation, however, boxes had been shoved up against the walls to allow for a massage table. The lights in the room were as low as they could go, obviously to draw attention away from the clutter. I laid my robe—with my watch in the pocket this time—over a stool and wiggled down between the two sheets on the massage table. The muscles in my neck were hard and tight, but my legs still trembled slightly from my frantic run. I let my head sink into the head cradle at the end of the table and tried to relax a little.

"Comfortable?" Cordelia asked as she stepped back into the room. Her voice was deep and soothing, like a late night DJ's.

"Yes," I muttered to the floor. "Does this work pretty much like a regular massage?" I wanted to signal to her that I was open to chitchat.

"It's similar, yes," she said, lowering the sheet to expose my naked back. "Except instead of my hands I use natural river stones that I've heated. They feel amazing on the body."

She stepped over to the side of the room, and I could hear her hands swishing in a tub of water.

"It must be tough with the spa closed," I said. "I mean—having to work in a makeshift setup like this."

"Not really," she replied. "You can work with these stones anywhere. Just let me know if they're too hot. By the way, I'll be using an oil that's scented with lemongrass. It's a wonderful stress reliever."

"Just what I need," I said. "Though I'm sure with

everything that's happened, you must feel as stressed as I do."

"I'm fine, actually." So much for her being a talker. Maybe finding out one of her colleagues had been murdered on-site had robbed her of the gift of gab.

Before she began the massage, she set two large stones in the palms of my hands, almost like ballast. I felt kind of silly, like a piece of tarp being used to cover a hole in the ground. But then she started her magic. The stones she used for the massage were warm and smooth and lightly slicked with oil. She moved them over my back and neck in strong, hypnotic strokes, and before long I felt my muscles let go, totally seduced. I lay there like a big blob, savoring every minute of it. There was no music being piped in—obviously this room wasn't set up for it—and the only sound I could hear as she worked was her breathing. Shallow, from being overweight perhaps. I felt myself start to drift off, and I opened my eyes, forcing myself to stay awake. Through the circular hole in the head cradle, I stared at the tiles on the floor. I was startled when one of Cordelia's tiny feet came into view. It was like catching a glimpse of something I wasn't supposed to see.

When she was done with side one, Cordelia removed the face cradle and held a towel between us as I flipped over. Before she began on my legs, she placed small, slim stones between my toes. It was borderline erotic, almost as good as having my toes sucked by a guy. I couldn't understand why Cordelia wasn't considered one of the spa superstars.

Despite her talent, once I was on my back, the switch in my mind flicked on again. I kept seeing myself thrashing through the woods like a deer on the run from a hunter. Who had been following me? Was it *Josh?* He hadn't liked my suggestion about camping out in the spa. After reporting to the salon, he might have doubled back to the solarium and seen me heading for the reserve.

"That was terrific," I managed to say when Cordelia finished my massage by misting my feet with scented water. "You must have quite the following."

"I'm glad you liked it. Why don't you take a minute to relax before getting up, and I'll meet you outside."

She had about as much interest in chatting today as a highway toll taker.

When I slipped out of the room a moment later, I spotted her down the corridor. She was leaning against the wall, talking to Eric, who apparently was also waiting for a client to emerge. I couldn't hear what she was saying, but her body was in a flirty pose. He watched her intently, his face expressionless. When she noticed me, she sprang away from the wall and, turning all professional again, escorted me to the reception area. He ignored me completely.

There were no showers in the salon, so I snuck upstairs wearing a robe, my clothes bunched under my arm. I noticed the light on the phone blinking as soon as I walked in my room. It was a message from Danny. Though she planned to stay at the inn tonight, she was heading to her house for a few hours. She suggested that we meet for breakfast at eight-thirty and catch up. She'd gone through the invoices and found two that she was concerned about. She would bring them to breakfast to show me.

I blew off the idea of dinner in the dining room. Not only did I feel oily from the massage, but I was also too wrung out from my *Blair Witch* chase in the woods. After ordering from room service, I pulled out my composition book and jotted down notes and impressions from my conversation with Josh. I was eager to know what Danny had turned up.

I also couldn't help but wonder where Beck was. He hadn't worn a wedding ring, so perhaps he was still single—or divorced. Maybe he was spending his Saturday night at Chuck E. Cheese, doing the divorced dad thing amid a million screeching kids. Though chances were that because of the murder, the only thing he was doing tonight was working on the case.

I hoped that because I was totally exhausted I'd be able to fall asleep easily, but within minutes of being between the sheets I could tell my brain wasn't going to cooperate. Last month I'd gone to see a hypnotist, part of my endless and apparently hopeless quest to deal with my insomnia. He'd told me that I should lie in bed and pretend I was riding down an escalator, getting sleepier with each floor. I tried it now, but it made me hyper and anxious. I felt as though I were trapped between floors at Bloomingdales.

So instead I just let my mind run wild. As the wind moaned outside my window, I replayed the same old questions. Who had chased me through the woods? What had Josh been up to at the spa? Who had killed Anna? I thought, too, of Beck's insistent question: Could I have seen something significant last night and not remembered it? I climbed out of bed to check that the door was locked.

As I tested the dead bolt, another question suddenly formed in my mind, one that hadn't wormed its way into my thoughts until this point. Could the killer have seen *me* that night? The lights in the spa had been off when I'd scurried across the parking lot, but someone might have been standing inside the dark, preparing to sneak away—and watching me from the window. Did he, like Beck, think that I'd seen something? Was *he* the one who had chased me through the woods today?

CHAPTER 9

THE DINING ROOM was nearly empty when I arrived at eight-twenty on Sunday morning, though Danny was already there, staring forlornly into a cup of green tea. She was wearing a pretty ice blue blouse, and though she generally looked great in pastels, today the lack of color emphasized how drawn and pale she was.

"Oh, Danny," I said as I slid into a chair across from her. "Tell me how I can cheer you up." I'd already made a decision *not* to tell her about being chased in the woods. I was afraid if I did, she'd be reluctant to let me help anymore.

"It's not as bad as it looks," she said, flashing a pale imitation of her usual cheery smile. "I was just taking a minute to try to gain some clarity."

"How's business?" I asked.

"The cancellations have begun—as well as some early checkouts," she said, sighing. "It's partly because of the murder and partly because the spa schedule is so messed up. We've had to shift people around and cancel appointments, and folks aren't happy."

"I'm sure it's just a temporary thing. You'll have the spa back open in just a few days."

"Thank you, Bailey. You know, one of my favorite affirmations is 'I look to the future because that's where I plan to spend my life.' I just keep repeating that to myself."

God, I thought, I wish affirmations worked for me. The only thing I ever repeated to myself on a regular basis was, Bailey, just don't fuck up.

The waitress arrived for my order, and once she was out of earshot I asked Danny if there was anything new on the case. She reported that the police had shared practically nothing with her, though she'd heard through the grapevine that Josh didn't have an alibi—he was supposedly home watching a ball game on Friday night—and though people apparently saw Eric at the birthday party, he didn't show until after eleven. She also revealed that Detective Beck had called late in the afternoon yesterday, asking for her to put together a list of Anna's regular clients.

"Ahh, interesting," I said. "I wondered myself if a male client could have developed some weird fixation on her. I take it you keep track of all the clients and what therapist works on them each time."

"Yes, it's all in the computer. That way, if a client forgets the name of a therapist, we've got a record of it. We have all sorts of ways to cross-check information."

"Now tell me about the two bills you mentioned last night. They looked funny to you?"

"False alarm," she announced. "I tracked down the business manager at home last night and he explained them to me. They were totally on the up-and-up."

"Okay, so it's not looking like a money thing. But after my talk with Josh yesterday, I really do sense something's going on over there. He seemed very protective of his turf. Let me ask you a question. Are you certain the weird behavior began in the spring and not later, around the time this guy Litchauer had his heart attack? I wonder if they could be covering up something about his death."

"Dear goodness," she said, clearly perturbed at the notion of that. "Well, like I said, he died in July. I feel as if I picked up the vibe earlier—but maybe I'm confused. Maybe it all happened around the same time."

"You said that Anna was his therapist the night he died. Had he ever been to the spa before?"

"Oh yes. He had a standing weekly appointment with her. But Bailey, you're not suggesting Anna or someone at the spa *caused* his death, are you?"

"No, not intentionally. But maybe something happened there. Like he reacted poorly to one of the massage techniques."

"Wouldn't the coroner have discovered any irregularities?" she asked, her voice growing higher with anxiety.

"Maybe, maybe not," I said. "Danny, I can see you're getting alarmed by this, but I'm not headed in any clear direction with it. I'm just trying to turn over every stone. This son you mentioned—does he live around here? Maybe I could talk to him."

"Yes, he's around here. Matt Litchauer. He's about

thirty-five, I'd say. He runs a pub in town called the Bridge Street Tavern. But I don't think you want to talk to him. He's a very, very unpleasant man."

Unpleasant enough to kill Anna, I wondered, if he suspected that she was responsible for his father's death?

"I'd also love to talk to more people who work at the spa," I told her, "but I'm afraid of setting off alarms. You mentioned Friday night that Anna had a friend who moved away. Is that the therapist who left for Hawaii?"

"No, Anna's friend was Eve. She moved to Rhinebeck, New York, to work as a weaver. Oh dear, I should probably contact her and let her know what's happened."

I suggested that since Eve was no longer in the thick of things at the spa, she might be a good source for me. I asked Danny if she could arrange for me to talk to her either on the phone or in person on my drive back to New York, since I knew that Rhinebeck was off the New York State Thruway. Just as I was about to ask her how things were with George, he came barreling into the dining room, with our table in his sights. Danny glanced over and offered him a warm smile.

"Darling, I hate to interrupt, but we desperately need you up front," he announced. "Good morning, Bailey. How are you holding up?" He gave my hand an obnoxious squeeze, just long enough for me to notice that the sweatiness was gone, so it obviously wasn't a 24/7 condition.

"Perfectly fine, thanks," I said. I was having a tough time generating any warmth for him.

He smiled that ingratiating smile of his, but I could see his eyes taking me in, trying to get a bead on me.

"What is it, George?" Danny asked anxiously.

"We're having a *towel* crisis. We don't have access to the spa towels, of course, and Josh is just helping himself to anything he can find at the inn."

She excused herself, and I watched them leave, George with his hand on Danny's back, guiding her along as if he were afraid she'd go off course. He hadn't done one thing to offend me, but my dislike for him had already hardened like a stone.

Back in my room, the first thing I did was get the number of the Bridge Street Tavern from directory assistance and phone there, hoping to find they were open on Sunday. There was no answer, but then it was only ten o'clock.

Next I called Paul Petrocelli, a young ER doctor I'd once interviewed for an article and who now allowed me to pester him with the odd medical question from time to time. When I need answers involving a particular field or specialty, I track down an expert, but if I want just basic background info or someone to point me in the right direction, I start with Paul. Since he'd told me a month ago he was going to be working on Sundays, I tried the hospital first. The person who answered put me on hold for five minutes, and then finally Paul picked up.

"Working Sunday?" he said in that husky voice of his. I had never met him in person, but I pictured him dark and handsome. "Must be a big story."

"Pretty big. I'm not interrupting a code blue, am I?"

"No, I was just suturing a gash in someone's fore-head."

"Okay, so here's my question. A guy dies of a heart attack in the locker room of a spa. He's in his sixties. Apparently his heart wasn't in the best of shape to begin with, but I'm wondering if there's any way the heart attack could have been triggered during the massage he had—like maybe the masseuse used pressure on the wrong spots."

"Not likely," he said, "unless it was shiatsu and the masseuse used karate chops."

"Very funny."

"There *are* things at a spa that could create problems for someone with heart disease. At a spa or anywhere else, for that matter."

"Like what?"

"The thing that jumps to mind first is some kind of heat-related problem," he said. "Saunas, steamrooms—they obviously get very warm, and that can cause trouble. When a person is overheated, the body redirects blood to the surface of the skin so that some of the heat can be released through perspiration. The downside is that the organs that need blood flow the most—like the lungs and the brain—aren't getting as much. The heart starts to beat faster to accommodate the situation. For someone with a healthy heart, that's not a big problem, but an unhealthy heart doesn't *like* to beat faster. It can ultimately lead to a heart attack."

"So perhaps he took a sauna or steam after his mas-sage and the heat triggered a heart attack?"

"Could be," he said. "But bear in mind that if his heart was in bad shape, it wouldn't necessarily have taken heat to make it fail. It might just be a coincidence that it happened then and there."

I heard someone call his name, so I signed off, promising to buy him a beer if I was ever in his part of the world.

After a bottle of water from the mini bar fridge, I began to pace the suite, trying to conjure up possible scenarios involving William Litchauer's death, scenarios that would have left the staff with something to hide. Maybe Litchauer had indulged in a sauna or steam after his massage, passed out, and not been noticed until much later. Some staff members might have carried the body to the locker room so they wouldn't be accused of negligence. That was the only one I could think of, and it didn't seem all that plausible. I phoned the Bridge Street Tavern again.

This time someone answered. Yes, they were open today, a sleepy-voiced woman said, both for lunch and for dinner. Dinner, I decided, was my best bet. You always found out more at night, when the booze was flowing. I'd decided that rather than try to confront Matt Litchauer directly, I'd see if I could get someone else talking and find out just how mad he'd been.

It was finally time for my tennis lesson, and though I was anxious to check out this Rich dude, I wasn't looking forward to running around the court. Volleyball was the only net sport I'd ever mastered in school.

The tennis court, I was informed at the reception desk, was behind the barn, and as I came around the building in my sneakers and khaki shorts (the closest things in my overnight bag to tennis wear), I could see a man I assumed to be Rich already on the court, picking through a grocery cart of tennis balls. He was tall, maybe six three, totally bald, and dressed in white shorts that hugged his butt too tightly for a guy over forty. Based on what I knew of Anna, he didn't look like her type. When I entered his peripheral vision, he glanced over toward me, and I could tell by the movement of his head that he was running his eyes up and down my body, checking out my makeshift tennis outfit. I felt as though I'd walked onto the court wearing my jammies.

"You on vacation?" he asked after we'd introduced ourselves. He had large green eyes, kind of roundish, that dominated his face, but he barely took me in with them now that I was up close.

"Yup, just for a few days, though."

"Okay, so let's see what we can accomplish in an hour. Where's your tennis these days?"

"Where *is* it?" I said. "To be honest, it isn't anywhere. I only played twice this past summer, and it's been years since I had a lesson." I shot him a flirty grin, but it seemed to bounce off him, like a robin against a plate-glass window. Maybe he was having a hard time getting past the khaki shorts.

"Then I won't have to undo any bad teaching. Why don't you go to the baseline? I'll feed you some balls and we'll loosen up."

For about fifteen minutes he fed me a constant stream of balls, alternating between my forehand and my backhand. He appeared to be in awesome physical shape, and no matter where my balls landed, he never seemed to have to lunge for them. Only occasionally would he offer some kind of comment, like "Relax" and

"Easy does it—you don't have to kill the ball." It all seemed to be part of a long established patter.

"All right," he said finally. "You're obviously feeling a little more fluid. Come on over here and we'll talk for a minute."

He had an obnoxiously patronizing style, and just to get even I felt tempted to whip out my lip gloss and apply it using his bald head for reflection. But I behaved myself. I smiled politely and met him at the net. He suggested we concentrate for the rest of the session on my forehand and backhand.

For the next fifty minutes he ran me ragged, forcing me from one side of the court to the next. I'm pretty religious about going to the gym, but before long I was huffing and puffing. He gave me a few tennis tips, like remembering to touch my shoulder at the end of every forehand, but for the most part he seemed to be operating on automatic pilot. I wondered what he had on his mind.

"I saw an improvement in your forehand, didn't you?" he said when we'd finished. He'd seemed so disinterested in me, it was hard to imagine he'd noticed *anything,* but he was too smug not to give himself a pat on the back.

"Yeah, I think so. Any suggestions about what I should be concentrating on?"

"You need to move more," he said, zipping up his racket in its case. "It's not just about hitting the ball. Tennis is a moving game." It was his sweet way of saying that I'd looked like a slug and that Serena Williams had no reason to worry.

"Well, thanks," I said, forcing a smile. He seemed

itchy to go. I needed to get busy and see how well he'd known Anna. "I'm glad you could fit me into your schedule—what with everything that's happened here."

"It's not something that impacts directly on me."

"But you knew her, right? The girl who was killed?"

"I knew her in passing," he said slowly, beginning to pick up the scattered balls with a tennis hopper. "I'm not full-time here. I work at a lot of different places."

"Just in passing? Someone told me they thought you knew her pretty well."

He stopped in his tracks and looked at me. It was the first time since we'd started that he seemed to actually register my face, to register *me*.

"Hardly," he said testily, his eyes locking with mine. "Who told you *that?*"

"Just someone talking. I don't recall."

"Well, if you think of the person, please *correct* them."

He seemed defensive, but I didn't know why. Maybe he'd buzzed around Anna, as Danny had said, and she'd blown him off. Maybe he'd taken her out once and bored her to tears. Maybe he'd killed her. I couldn't possibly tell, and it was clear he wasn't going to share anything with me.

I said good-bye and thanks, which he acknowledged with a hard, phony smile. Once I was off the court and onto the path to the inn, I glanced back. He was just standing there, leaning on the ball hopper and staring at me.

For the rest of the afternoon, I hung in my room. I made some notes in my composition book, looked through the employee folders again, and replayed all the questions about the case over and over in my head. I didn't have a single clue or theory. I threw down the composition book and called the cell phone number of Parker Lyle, a criminal profiler I often interviewed. Maybe she could offer some insight, but I got only her voice mail.

Tomorrow morning I was going to have to get in my Jeep and drive back to New York. I didn't have a choice. My mass hysteria piece was due at the end of the week, and all my files were in Manhattan. Plus I had a meeting at *Gloss* early Tuesday morning.

Around five, Danny called to suggest that we meet again tomorrow for breakfast and to inform me that Anna's friend Eve had agreed to see me on my trip back to New York. All I could hope was that she had some piece of information that would prove valuable—or that I might stumble on something during my excursion to the Bridge Street Tavern.

At six-thirty, dressed in jeans and a sweater, I set out for the evening, stopping to get directions from Natalie in the empty lobby. The tavern turned out to be in historic downtown Warren, not far, actually, from the police station. Just thinking of that made my heart go up and down like a pogo stick.

There were only about a dozen cars in the tavern's parking lot, and I pulled into a spot midway down the building. Stepping inside, I was hit by a wave of nostalgia. The Bridge Street Tavern was like so many other old bars and taverns I'd been to in my life, especially the ones I'd hung out in during college in Providence. The air was smoky, the wood tables and booths were carved with initials, and from the jukebox came the mournful sound of the Zombies singing "She's Not There."

There were pegs in the entranceway for coats, and I took my time pulling off my jeans jacket so I could gauge the best spot to sit. Grabbing a stool at the bar would guarantee conversation with the bartender, but there were too many townies there tonight, and they'd all be sure to eavesdrop. A table was a safer bet. As I lingered by the entrance, a young waitress in her mid-twenties strutted over, brandishing a nametag that said "Stacey." She'd pulled the very top part of her long strawberry blond hair into a tiny ponytail, making her look like a Yorky.

"How many?" she asked perkily.

"Just one."

"Nothing wrong with that," she said, pulling a menu from a wooden slot and leading me across the dining room.

"What can I get you to drink?" she asked as I slid into the booth.

"Have you got Cabernet?"

"Uh-huh. But it's room temp, not chilled, if that's okay."

"That's perfect," I said.

"Lemme get that for you and give you a sec to look at the menu. There's only one special tonight. It's pot roast. It comes with mashed potatoes and it's real, real good. If you prefer somethin' a little less fatty, we've got a nice roast chicken. It comes with mashed potatoes, too, or I can substitute wild rice."

As she spoke, she leaned closer, pointing to the spot on the menu where I could find the chicken. She was wearing an open-neck white shirt, and at closer range I saw that she had a hickey on her neck the shape of Texas and just about as big. I wasn't going to hold that against her. I was just grateful she was the friendly, chatty type.

"Great," I said. "I'll take a look."

While she sashayed off to place my drink order, her butt twitching, I checked out the room. It was only a quarter full, reflecting the fact that it was Sunday night or still early or both. Though redneck types seemed to dominate the bar and the alcove with the pool table, most of the people who were eating looked like middle-class locals, maybe even a few tourists. There was no sign of anyone who might be William Litchauer's son. The people waiting on tables were all women, and the bartender appeared to be under thirty.

"You decide what you'd like?" Stacey asked, setting down my wineglass.

"I'm leaning toward the chicken. It's good, huh?"

"Oh yeah. Everything's good here."

"How long has this place been here? George Washington didn't eat here, did he?"

She laughed. "Maybe. The tavern's been here forever, though it changes owners every once in a while. You visiting the area?"

"Yeah, I'm just up for the weekend. I'm staying at the Cedar Inn. I didn't feel like eating there tonight, though—what with everything that's happened."

"Omigod, you're *staying* there?" She swung her eyes once around the room, making certain none of her customers looked impatient, and then back to me. "I just can't believe someone was *murdered* there."

"You didn't know her, did you?" I asked, keeping my tone easy.

"No. Those folks never come in here. I heard that the police don't have any idea who killed her."

"I don't think they do," I said. "I mean, they're not telling *me* anything, but they haven't arrested anyone yet as far as I know."

"I bet the boyfriend did it," she said, shaking her head in disgust. "Anyway, you said the chicken. Mashed potatoes okay?"

"That's fine. *Was* there a boyfriend? Is that what you'd heard?"

"No, just assuming. Isn't it always the creepy boyfriend? Lemme put this in for you."

Go easy, I told myself as she wiggled off again. If I acted too eager beavery, she was going to suspect I was up to something.

I had nothing to do while I waited for my order but observe the scene and listen to the old music—Bonnie Tyler was now singing "Total Eclipse of the Heart." The townie types in the alcove finally pushed off from the walls and started a pool game. A table of diners paid their bill and departed, but two more groups came in, including four people arguing about a movie they'd just seen. Other diners raised their voices to compete with the crack of billiard balls and the new conversation, and in an instant the noise level of the room went up two notches. My waitress and two others bustled around like real pros, chatting, busing their own tables, never looking frazzled. As they moved back and forth from the kitchen, pushing through a swinging door, I caught sight of a tubby short-order cook. Could *that* be

Litchauer? I wondered. Doubtful, I decided as quickly as I'd asked myself the question.

I'd waited about ten minutes for my meal when Stacey suddenly rocketed out of the kitchen, the swinging door flapping behind her. This time I got a surprise. Talking on a wall phone was a hefty guy in a plaid sports jacket. That, I realized, could very well be Litchauer.

"Here ya go, hon," Stacey said, setting down a half chicken the size of a pterodactyl. "Careful, the plate's real hot."

I was hoping she'd stay to chitchat, but another diner flagged her down just then. My last chance was going to come when I finished the meal. I ate slowly, trying to look as if I had all the time in the world. Twenty minutes later, as I was pushing a pile of bird bones around on my plate, Stacey sidled up to my booth again.

"How'd you like it?"

"It was wonderful," I said. "I wish I'd known about this place earlier—I would have come last night, too. Anything to get away from that inn."

"It's givin' you the heebie-jeebies, huh?"

"Yeah, that's for sure. And I heard this afternoon that someone else died there this past July."

She surveyed the room for potential eavesdroppers and then turned back to me. "That was my boss's *father*," she said sotto-voce. "He wasn't staying there. He was at that day spa they run."

"And he was *murdered?*"

"Well, no. He had a heart attack. But there was something weird about the whole thing. You've got a guy who's fit as can be, goes in for a massage, and then boom—he drops dead. Tell me that ain't funny."

"The police have any ideas?"

"Matt told me they couldn't be bothered," she said, rolling her eyes.

"Well, what do *you* think was going on?"

It was no sooner out of my mouth than I realized I'd asked it too fast and too eagerly. Her eyes widened slightly, and I could see her brain go on alert. Shit, I'd spooked her.

"Who knows?" she said quickly. "You want any dessert? We've got ice cream, cheesecake, and apple pie."

"Sure," I said, desperately trying to sound breezy. "Why don't I try the pie?"

I had as much interest in pie as I had in slow dancing with one of the mulleted morons playing pool, but I was hoping maybe she'd give me a second chance. No such luck. Stacey never came back, other than to slide my pie across the table and hand me my bill. And when she did, she barely made eye contact with me.

By the time I called it a night, the room was half-full and thick with smoke and there was a large, raucous crowd around the pool table. I'd come hoping for info, and I was leaving with nothing. Unless you counted the tidbit about Matt being upset with the police—and the carbo load I had from the potatoes and pie. I pulled on my jacket and slipped outside.

The moon was riding on the crest of a large cluster of clouds, augmenting the security lights on the wall of the tavern. As I hurried across the parking lot, now crowded with cars, I couldn't help but think back to the night of the murder, of me scurrying across the parking lot of the inn. Had the murderer watched me from the spa, I wondered, or from behind the trees? As I approached the Jeep, I realized that I'd stupidly forgotten to dig out my car keys beforehand, and now I had to riffle through my purse for them. Behind me, suddenly, I heard the sound of crunching gravel.

"Who the hell are *you?*" someone said through the darkness.

CHAPTER 10

I JUMPED A foot and spun around. The man in the plaid coat was standing just a few feet behind me. He looked as big as a water buffalo and as mean as one, too.

"*Excuse me?*" I said with what I hoped sounded like indignation. My legs were feeling floppy, but I knew it was essential to keep my cool.

"You come into my establishment and start asking lots of questions. I want to know who you are."

"Is that what the waitress told you?"

"Yeah, that's right," he snapped. As Danny had mentioned, he was probably in his mid-thirties, but his ruddy, thick-skinned face belonged to someone who'd packed a lot of booze and bad behavior into those years.

"I think she's got it backward. *She* was the one who started asking *me* questions—about what it was like staying at the Cedar Inn since the murder. It just evolved into a conversation from there."

"That right? She said you seemed awfully nosy about my situation."

"So *you're* the one whose father died?" I said, playing dumb.

"Yeah, and what makes you so damn curious about it?" He took a step closer, and I caught a whiff of his breath—a mix of bourbon, garlic, and swamp gas.

"Okay, I'll be honest," I said. "I'm up here on vacation, but I'm a writer, and when the waitress mentioned that there might be something odd about your father's death, I wondered if there was a story in what was going on at the inn. If you *are* suspicious, maybe I can be of some help."

"Prove it to me," he said.

"Prove what?" I asked.

"That you're a writer."

I yanked open my purse and fished around quickly for the little leather case that I carry my business cards in. As I drew out a card, I couldn't see in the dark if it was the one I use that says "freelance writer" or the other kind with "contributing writer, *Gloss* magazine" on it. He practically tore two of my fingers from their sockets as he grabbed the card from my hand.

"*Gloss* magazine?" he read sarcastically, holding it up so the light from the tavern caught it. "What do you write? Articles on how to pop a zit?"

"Actually, I write true crime stories for them. That's why your story caught my interest. If you think something was covered up, I'd love to know. I could help investigate."

"What makes you think something was covered up?"

"That's what your waitress implied. That you

thought there was something *off* about the situation, but the police didn't seem to care."

A door slammed at that moment, followed by the refrains of a Journey song and the sound of people making their way toward the parking lot. Litchauer relaxed his stance. He obviously didn't want anyone to observe him threatening me.

"The police didn't do jack shit," he said quickly. "They wouldn't even take my calls. But I don't need any help from you or your candy-ass magazine. Do you hear me?"

"Loud and clear," I said. The other customers were approaching, chattering loudly. If I was going to escape, this was the moment. I turned on my heels, hit my key case to unlock the door, and then threw myself into the Jeep, locking the door behind me.

As I peeled out of my parking spot, spraying gravel, Litchauer stayed right where I'd left him, legs astride and welded to the ground, doing an imitation of the Colossus at Rhodes. I didn't give him the satisfaction of glancing over in his direction, but out of the corner of my eye I could see him glaring at me.

As I drove quickly through the empty streets of town, I checked my rearview mirror every three seconds, making sure Litchauer hadn't hopped into the Death Star and taken off after me. But there was nothing behind me other than blackness. This was a town that shut down on a Sunday night. I'd driven for about ten minutes when I realized I'd made a wrong turn. I can get from Great Jones Street to Jane Street with my eyes closed, but outside of the Village my sense of direction is abysmal. I drove around for a few minutes with my heart going skippity skip, until suddenly out of nowhere a sign for the Cedar Inn appeared. Five minutes later I pulled into the driveway.

An older guy I hadn't seen before was on duty at the reception desk, leafing through a copy of *Yankee* magazine with a slightly wigged-out look on his face, but otherwise the lobby was empty. The only sound coming from the lounge was the hum of the gas fire in the hearth. I walked down the corridor to the dining room to pick up a glass of wine, and that room was empty too, except for one couple sitting at the tiny bar. As I accepted my glass of Cabernet, I noticed that my hand trembled slightly. That obnoxious asshole Litchauer had rattled me more than I'd realized.

Back in my room, I drew a hot bath, not bothering with the bath salts that promised enchantment and empowerment. At this point, that seemed way too much to hope for. After stripping off my clothes, I sank into the tub, wineglass in hand. As I lay there, I replayed my conversations with Stacey, the stoolie slut, and Litchauer, the host from hell. That guy needed to be checked for rabies. If he was convinced there was something suspicious about his father's death, why not take me up on my offer to help? Perhaps he simply preferred being an independent operative. Or perhaps he'd already taken matters into his own hands, so to speak.

I wondered suddenly if Litchauer's name had darted across Beck's radar screen yet or if he was too busy concentrating on people at the spa. What Litchauer had said about the police intrigued me—that in his view they hadn't given a damn about his father's death. Danny had articulated just the opposite from her vantage point—

that Beck had been extremely thorough. Based on the little evidence I had, I was tempted to buy Danny's assessment of Beck. Matt Litchauer seemed to have a giant chip on his shoulder. And I couldn't deny it—I wanted to think good things about Beck.

After half an hour of soaking, I hauled myself out of the tub and dried off with one of the big Egyptian towels. Then I slid into a robe. Still sipping my wine, I yanked my clothes off hangers and out of drawers and tossed them all into my bag, making sure the dirty things were separated into a plastic laundry bag swiped from the back of the closet. My plan was to be on the road right after breakfast tomorrow.

A part of me longed to be home again, away from this mess. The weekend ranked up there with my all-time worst, even more horrible than the time at Brown when I'd gone to a bed-and-breakfast in Newport with a guy I was smitten with. When we fell into bed for the first time, I found to my horror that he liked to refer to his penis as if it were a person: "He likes it." "He wants more." I faked a urinary tract infection for the next forty-eight hours.

But the other part of me hated having to bail on Danny. I was extremely worried for her—and not only because of the possible fallout to the inn. If something ulterior was happening at the spa, she could actually be in danger. I had spent two days trying to help her and failed to come up with a single thing. If only I didn't have the mass hysteria article hanging over my head, I could stay longer.

The phone rang, startling me. It was almost ten. I picked up the one on the end table next to the couch, expecting it to be Danny. But when I said hello, there was only silence.

I tried hello again. This time I got a reply.

"Bailey Weggins?" It was Beck's voice.

"Speaking," I said, feeling all nervous, as if Brad Pitt had just announced he was on the line.

"This is Detective Inspector Beck. I'm sorry if I woke you."

"You didn't. Despite the fact you had to rouse me from a nap the other night, I'm not much of a sleeper."

"No?"

"No. I don't do very well in bed." Oh God, what kind of bozo was I? "What I mean is, I'm sort of a hopeless insomniac. Are you still working? It sounds awfully quiet there."

"No, actually, I'm calling from home. . . . I live alone."

There was complete silence as his remark hung between us like a piece of paper that's been lifted by the wind but hovers motionless before the current shifts. He lived alone. He had no wife or live-in girlfriend and he wanted me to know it.

"Anyway," he continued, "I realized that I had your New York number, but you never said whether you were going directly back there tomorrow."

"I am. I mean, yes, that's where I'm headed," I sputtered.

"So if we need to get hold of you about the case in the next few days, that's where we should call?"

"Has there been some new development?"

"I'm not at liberty to say."

"Of course not," I said. "But why would you need to

talk to me again, anyway? I mean, like I said before, I've racked my brain and I don't remember anything more than I've already told you."

"I understand that. But we might need to clarify or review your statement with you at some point."

"Well, I'll be in New York all week if you need me."

"Do you still have my number—in case you have to reach me?"

"Yes, don't worry. I've been guarding it with my life."

He actually laughed a little on the other end.

"Good. If something occurs to you—"

"But—"

"I said *if*, okay?"

"All right, all right."

"Good night. Sorry to disturb you."

"No problem."

I hung up the phone and stretched out my body with my head against the arm of the sofa. What had that been about? On the surface it was straightforward enough. Because of my movements Friday night, I'd enabled the police to pretty much pinpoint the time of the murder. I was important to the case, and he *did* need to know where to reach me. But there was a possibility that he had used the case as an excuse to call me. Had the "Where should we call?" and "Do you still have my number?" remarks been code for "I want to stay in touch with you"? Was he hoping I'd give him a sign that it was fine to get more personal? Was that even ethical—since I was a witness in the case? I tried to picture what he looked like right now. Was he sitting on a stool in his kitchen, one hand on a beer? Lying on his sofa in a pair of boxer briefs? Or in bed naked? I imagined him naked. I imagined what it would be like to kiss him, to touch him. I couldn't believe I was so infatuated with him. At least it meant I wasn't pining for Jack Herlihy anymore.

That turned out to be the high point of the evening. Shaking off my X-rated fantasy, I reached for the TV remote and discovered to my chagrin that there was something woefully wrong with the reception. I cursed and picked up the decorating book, but my eyes began to glaze over from looking at pages of rooms with barely any furniture. I rang my next-door neighbor and friend, Landon, in New York but ended up with his voice mail. I left a message saying I was looking forward to the dinner we had planned for Monday night.

Finally, I decided to take my chances in bed. I flailed around for an hour, and when I finally did fall asleep, I found myself in one of those dreams that's as monotonous as painting a wall, in which you repeat the same movements over and over again. I was staying at an inn or hotel of some kind, but not the Cedar Inn. Dressed in an evening gown, I walked down a corridor, tapping quietly on one door after another. No one ever answered, and after waiting for an inordinate amount of time by each door, I would finally move to the next. After a while I could feel the part of me that observed the dream growing frustrated, wanting to encourage the Bailey *in* the dream to tap louder. My knocking was too soft; no one could hear it. I woke suddenly and bolted up in bed. The tapping, I realized, was coming from someplace other than my dream. Someone was at my door.

I switched on the bedside lamp and let my eyes race

around the room. I couldn't tell whether I'd actually heard a sound—or the dream had played a trick on my mind. I slid out of bed and made my way to the door.

"Who is it?" I called out softly when I was two feet away.

Utter silence.

I undid the dead bolt and eased the door open, the chain still on. There was nothing in the hallway, just the shadows cast from the sconces along the wall.

It took me over an hour to fall back asleep again. I woke at eight, ragged, almost hung over. I wiggled into my jeans and a long-sleeved T-shirt, threw on some lip gloss and concealer for my undereye circles (which appeared to have a landmass rivaling Central Park), and zipped up my bag. Rather than wait for a bellboy, I lugged the bag downstairs myself.

"You okay?" I asked with a wan smile when I found Danny sitting at breakfast.

"Yes, I'm better today," she said. "Though I'm sad to see you go, Bailey. You've been a rock for me."

"I just wish that I could have *discovered* something," I said.

"I've got some news, by the way. It turns out Anna really *was* strangled."

"Strangled? Did Beck tell you?"

"No, it was in the paper today."

I pressed Danny for more details, but that was all the paper had revealed. I fessed up then about my visit to the Bridge Street Tavern and my snarky encounter with Matt. There was a chance there might be some repercussions, and Danny needed to be in the loop.

"He wasn't interested in sharing anything with me,

that's for sure," I said. "I'm just hoping I might learn something from Eve."

Danny explained that Eve was going to be home all day and was expecting me. All she'd asked was that I call from the road a few minutes before my arrival so she would have some warning. From the pocket of her pale green sweater, Danny pulled a piece of paper with the phone number and directions to Eve's house.

I ordered eggs for breakfast, fortification for my journey. But when they arrived I realized I had little appetite and pushed them listlessly around my plate.

When it was finally time to go, Danny walked me to the parking lot and we hugged each other tightly. I felt awful leaving her like this. I once again heard my mother's words in my mind: "Keep an eye on Danny. I'm worried about her."

"I'll call you tomorrow night," I said, "and if I can get my assignment in on time and things are still crazy here, I'll come back next week, okay?"

The tears that welled in her gray eyes indicated she wasn't going to resist my offer.

Fifteen minutes later I was on the Massachusetts Turnpike, headed west to pick up the New York State Thruway. I felt a little like Sigourney Weaver in *Alien,* after she's ejected the ugliest creature in the history of the universe from her spacecraft while wearing only panties and an undershirt and finally climbs into her capsule. In other words, I felt safe. There would be no more chases in the woods, no more middle of the night awakenings wondering if someone was tapping at my door. Yet another part of me wished I could turn the Jeep around and go back.

I'd already programmed Eve's number onto my cell, so a mile from the exit on the thruway I hit the send button. She spoke in a monotone, like someone who'd recently popped a Xanax. I explained that I should be at her place in a matter of minutes, and she said dully to come ahead, she was expecting me. I'd talked to hotel room service operators who were more excited to hear from me.

Ten minutes later I was in downtown Rhinebeck, a quaint town not far from the Hudson River. When Eve opened the door to greet me, she appeared as somber as she'd sounded on the phone. She wore no makeup, and though she was fairly attractive, her skin was heavily wrinkled from the sun. Her brown hair, cut into a mid-length shag, looked as if it had been finger-combed four or five days ago and not since. She was wearing an over-size chambray shirt and jeans.

"Eve?" I said, half question, half statement.

"Yes, come in," she replied without smiling.

The house was a surprise. At some point there must have been a series of rooms on the ground floor, but walls had been knocked down and now there was only a small kitchen, which I glimpsed in the back, and one big space up front, almost like a studio. At the far end was a loom, and there were bundles and bags of yarn everywhere.

"So you're a weaver now?" I asked moronically.

"That's right," she said, leading me to a dark green sofa. "Do you want tea? I was just about to fix some for myself, so it's not a problem."

"Sure, that would be great. If it's possible, I'd love the kind with caffeine." Based on the back-to-nature feel of her home, I was fearful of getting something like the lemony stuff that Danny had forced on me—or, worse, something made with raspberries.

"I think I can manage that," she said, disappearing into the kitchen.

As I listened to the sound of the kettle scraping against the stove and the clank of cups, my eyes surveyed the room. Despite the studiolike setup, there was an oppressive, closed-in feeling to the space, maybe because of all that yarn. It appeared she worked mainly with jewel tones, and though the finished pieces she had strewn about were accomplished, they were also dark and brooding.

She emerged from the kitchen a few minutes later, carrying a wooden tray with two steaming mugs. I could tell by the first whiff that the tea was Lapsang Souchong, a strong, smoky blend that always made me gag. I lifted a mug from the tray, took a teeny teeny sip, and smiled with all the graciousness I could summon. I wondered if she had made such a weird choice as a passive-aggressive gesture.

"Your weaving is really wonderful," I said as she took a seat across from me. "Obviously it's not something you took up a couple of months ago."

"I started doing it in college," she said after drawing a long sip from her mug. "I never had the space for a loom or, frankly, the kind of money I needed to start it up as a business. But my mother died last year and left me this place."

"I'm sorry to hear about your loss. And I'm sorry about Anna, by the way," I said. "It must be very hard losing both a friend and your mother in such a short time."

She pursed her lips, not saying anything for a few seconds. She set her tea on a side table, kicked off her clogs, and tucked her legs under her.

"Actually," she said, "Anna and I hadn't been friends in some time. Yes, her death is very upsetting, but she's been out of my life for a while now."

"Did you lose touch after you moved?"

"No—our friendship was over before I ever left Massachusetts."

"Was there some kind of falling-out?" I asked, trying not to do that pouncy thing of mine.

"Tell you what," she said. "Since you've come all this way, I'm going to be perfectly honest with you. I wanted a different *kind* of relationship with Anna—a romantic one. She blew my mind, she really did. Initially I thought I saw something receptive in her. There was one very nice kiss that I thought was leading someplace else, but I was wrong. After that, she rebuffed me. It was quite clear I gave her the creeps and she wanted nothing more to do with me."

What did that kiss suggest about Anna? I wondered. That she'd tried something new just to see if she liked it?

"I appreciate your being honest," I said. "So I'll be straightforward with you, too. The reason I'm here doesn't have as much to do with Anna as it does with the spa in general. Danny has a sense that something funny might be going on at the spa. People have been acting very secretively when she goes over there. She doesn't know if it's related to Anna's death, but she wants to get to the bottom of it. Did you ever pick up any weird vibe when you were there?"

She laughed, the kind of forced, barklike laugh that people use to make a point.

"I picked up some weird vibes all right," she said bitterly. "But they were generally being directed by Josh toward *me*. That man just seemed to despise me."

"Why?"

"Why? Because I wouldn't twitch my fanny when he gave an order. Because I didn't look at him as if he were the most brilliant thing alive. Because he could tell I knew he was gay, but he didn't want anyone at the spa to know."

So how do you *really* feel about him? I was tempted to ask.

"But what about anything *dishonest?*" I asked instead. "Do you think a small group over there could have been skimming money?"

She took a long sip of her tea, obviously not minding that it tasted like fried bologna. Setting down the mug, she shook her head with her lips pursed.

"No, I never saw signs of anything like that," she said. "There *was* this very tight clique, though, kind of a members only thing."

"Who was in it?" I asked.

"Anna, unfortunately. Piper the Viper—"

"Why do you call her that?"

"Because she likes to eat men alive. This other therapist was in it, too. Lauren. She moved to Hawaii, I hear. That's all I can think of."

"What about Eric? What do you know about him?"

"I heard he and Anna had this little fling. She apparently bruised his heart big-time, but then Anna was the type of person who liked the heady, early days of a relationship. Once she got in the thick of it, she was ready to bolt. Anna, you see, could really be quite maddening."

"So maddening that a man would want to kill her?"

She shifted in her chair, rearranging her legs. Took another sip of the fried bologna broth. "You mean Eric?"

"Eric—or someone else in Warren. A guy she'd dated and rejected. Or someone she didn't even give a chance to."

"That's the obvious conclusion," she said. "I'm sure that's what the police assume. But if they do, I think they've got it all wrong."

CHAPTER 11

I SAT FORWARD in my chair, startled.

"What do you mean?" I asked. "What *should* the police be focusing on?"

"Anna's *past*," she said indignantly, as if she were ticked because she had a piece of valuable info and no one had bothered to check in with her.

"Where, when?" I blurted out. "Is there someone who once threatened her?"

"I don't know anything specifically," she said. "I just know that she was extremely troubled by her past. Something bad happened to her once. And I think she was afraid it would come back to haunt her."

"What exactly did she tell you?"

"It's not what she *said*, actually. Are you aware that the body is capable of recalling emotional pain?"

Oh boy, I was about to hop a train to kookyville. "No," I said. "I didn't know that."

"Well, it is. Pain can be released during certain types of massage. Memories come to the surface."

"Can you explain that better?"

"When someone gets through a traumatic event in their life, they experience the pain of it in their body. The body holds that information below the conscious level. It's a protective mechanism. The body remembers. It remembers everything."

"And this information is released somehow during the massage?" I asked, trying to hide my skepticism.

"Yes, the massage reactivates the physical responses that occurred with the trauma. The person experiences a flashback, both physically and emotionally."

"And what does this have to do with Anna?"

"One day, when Anna and I were friends," she explained, "I used this special type of massage technique on her. I'd offered to give her a massage that day—and since I'd been studying it, I decided to experiment on her. It triggered something very deep and very disturbing."

"What do you mean? How did she respond?"

"She started sobbing. It was clear something traumatic had happened, but she didn't want to discuss it."

"Do you think she'd been abused?"

"Not necessarily," Eve said, shaking her head. "It doesn't have to be about something that *happened* to your body. It can be about how your body felt when you were suffering from some kind of emotional pain that occurred in your life."

"How far back in her past do you think this experience occurred?"

"I'm not sure. But it seemed deep. Like something that had happened a long time ago."

"Do you know where Anna was from?"

"Her sister lived in Florida. I assumed that's where she was from. But she never talked about her past."

"Did she ever—"

"Look," she said, suddenly impatient. "Like I said, I know something bad had happened, but I have no idea what it was. There's nothing more I can tell you, and I really need to get back to my work."

I wasn't sure why she was shutting down the discussion, but it was clear I was being scooted out.

I apologized for taking up so much of her time and set my mug, still full, onto a chipped table next to my chair.

As I stood to leave, I heard the floor above me creak. Someone was moving around up there in one of the bedrooms. Eve's eyes shifted toward the stairs. It was probably a lover, a woman who hadn't spurned her as Anna had. Or an overnight guest. Or the ghost of her mother. I didn't really care. All I knew was that I'd come hoping to find out what was going on at the spa—and hadn't learned a thing.

I said good-bye, shook hands with her, and nearly tripped down the steps of the front porch. Before getting back on the thruway, I found a small café in town and bought a large cup of coffee that I hoped would burn all memory of the Lapsang Souchong from my taste buds.

The trip back to the city was uneventful. Traffic was heavy, but never bumper-to-bumper. As I drove I considered what Eve had revealed—not only about the massage, but about the kiss. Regardless of Eve's theories, Anna *did* seem like someone on the lam from her past: the restlessness, the moving from city to city, the fickleness in love, the experimentation. I ran through anything I could think of that had the power to haunt someone: physical abuse, sexual abuse, emotional cruelty, rejection, betrayal, illness, an accident, a death. There were so many possibilities, it was hard to imagine what might have troubled Anna.

I always get slightly giddy when I drive under the overhanging sign on the thruway that says "Now Entering New York City," but not today. I felt too ambivalent about being back. Even though I was looking forward to sleeping (or at least attempting to sleep) in my own bed, having dinner with Landon, and pitching ideas for my next article, I was leaving lots of unfinished business in Warren. I couldn't help but feel I'd failed Danny—and failed my mother.

As I exited onto the FDR Drive on the East Side of Manhattan, I rolled down the window. For an October day, it was almost balmy outside. The East River gleamed in the sunlight.

I parked my Jeep in the garage just before one o'clock and hauled my bags the block home. I live on 9th Street and Broadway, smack on the border between Greenwich Village and the East Village in a fairly modern fourteen-story building. My one-bedroom apartment is a gem and a steal, the one thing I have left from my marriage, and that's only because it's a rental and my ex was unable to find a way to use it to cover his gambling debts. In addition to having a walk-in closet large enough to be a tiny office, there are two drop-dead features.

First, there's the view. It's to the west, featuring a
skyline of sand- and brick-colored apartment buildings
and nineteen wood-shingled water tanks. It looks, especially at night when the sky is inky blue, like the backdrop for a Broadway play.

And then there's the terrace, right off my living
room. As big as a room itself, it's the perfect place for
contemplating that view, including sunsets that some
nights seem to have set half the sky on fire.

I said hi to the day doorman, picked up my mail and
newspapers, and rode the elevator upstairs. For some reason, my key fought with the lower lock, and by the time
I'd managed to undo both locks I was so anxious to get
inside that I kicked open the door. I wasn't expecting a
twenty-one-gun salute upon my arrival, but all the furniture seemed to sit there sullen and aloof in the dusty air.
The *Gloss* decorating editor was right. Santa Fe style
looked ludicrous in Manhattan. But it wasn't my fault
that I had no decorating skills. I come from a line of
WASP women who adhered to two basic rules for pulling
a room together: Use tons of chintz, and push all the furniture back against the walls.

I set down my bag and leafed through the mail. It
was pathetic—several catalogs filled with Santa dish
towels and a wedding invitation for two people whom I
couldn't recall ever having met. When I turned over the
envelope, I realized it had been delivered to the wrong
mailbox.

Without bothering to unpack, I made a cheese omelet
and took it into my office. I had a ton of work ahead of
me, and I could tell already that it was going to be hard

to get a foothold on a day that was half over—it felt like trying to jump on a moving train.

My number one priority was tackling my piece on mass hysteria. It was due at the end of the week, and at this point I was beginning to seriously regret ever taking it on. The case wasn't nearly as tantalizing as I'd thought when I'd accepted the assignment, and to make matters worse, my research was feeling thin.

I dug out my tape of the interview I'd conducted with the shrink on Friday, as well as the notes I'd jotted down that day. I always take written notes as backup—ever since, that is, I had the horrifying experience of replaying an interview I'd done with a murder victim's husband and hearing ninety minutes of what sounded like a Delta Airbus starting its engines.

The interview with the shrink turned out to be a dud. At the time, I thought he'd make a few decent observations, but as I listened to it as an outsider, I realized it was about as fascinating as a Senate hearing on C-SPAN. He hadn't been able to say anything of interest about the case because the case just wasn't interesting.

I was in a code blue situation, and though I'd been in them before with deadlines and had managed to survive, they were never any fun.

I decided that my only recourse was to call Don, a writer I'd met at a party last Thursday who claimed to have an old file on the subject of mass hysteria, a file he said he'd be willing to leave with his doorman if I needed it. He lived only two blocks away on University Place, and it would be a cinch to lay my hands on the stuff.

I ended up with his machine and left a message, but

I'd barely hung up the phone when it rang and Don was on the other end.

"Sorry," he said, "I was just getting out of the shower. So you *do* need the file? I thought you might."

"I'm pretty set on the piece, actually," I lied. "I just thought it would be good to have whatever backup I can. If you could leave it with your doorman like you said, I can swing by and get it."

"I've got an even better idea," he told me, sounding a hundred percent certain of the fact that he did. "Why don't you pop by my place later for a drink and I can explain some of it to you. If you're looking at it cold, it might not make much sense."

Oh, beautiful, I thought in exasperation. So the discussion the other night wasn't about one freelance journalist helping another. He'd been hitting on me. I tried to conjure him in my mind: frizzy reddish blond hair, a long, angular face. And he'd had this irksome habit of punctuating his comments to me with the word *lady:* "Lucky lady," he'd said when I told him about my gig with *Gloss.* "Funny lady," he'd said when I'd told the story of the *Gloss* fashion editor talking about the duplicity of a designer's approach when she'd meant duality.

"That's so nice of you," I said, squelching my annoyance. "My problem is that I'm kind of pressed for time. I have dinner plans tonight. Maybe I could just grab the stuff from the doorman tonight, look through it, and then get together with you later in the week if I need to."

"It's not gonna make much sense without me explaining it," he said peevishly. I knew for sure then that

I'd never lay my hands on it unless I gave him face time. What a jerk. But I was desperate for the information.

"I could stop by on my *way* to dinner," I said. "About six o'clock. I don't have to be at the restaurant till eight."

I was making him think I had more time than I did. Then I could stage an early escape once I got there.

"Yeah, I guess that's okay," he said, sounding slightly pissed that his bribery wasn't producing the results he'd hoped. "You know the building, right?"

I had planned to walk over to dinner with Landon, but that was out of the question now. I left a message for him saying that I would meet him at the restaurant at seven.

As I put down the phone, feeling pissy, I realized I hadn't checked my messages from the weekend. There were two from friends on Friday calling to see if I wanted to do dinner over the weekend, friends who hadn't known I'd had plans to be totally rejuvenated at a fabulous spa and then return to New York ready to hook up with dozens of hot, available hombres. The final call was from Parker Lyle, the criminal profiler I'd tried to contact from Warren. Though I'd left her my cell number, she had mistakenly called me at home. I grabbed the phone and punched in her number.

She picked up on the first ring, and by the background noise I could tell she was in an airport. I cut to the chase with her because that was the approach she preferred. I described the crime scene, the Mylar paper, and what I knew of the actual murder.

"Was she assaulted sexually?" she asked, cutting me off in the middle of a sentence.

"Don't know," I said. "The cops aren't saying, and there was no sign of it at the scene because she was all wrapped up. Is there any chance that it was a stranger? Or is it someone she knew?"

"Well, strangers do strangle, of course," she said. "But it's also the method of choice for men who have a lot of rage against a particular woman. My guess—and of course it can only be a guess with so little info—is that he knew her and was very angry at her."

"It's definitely a man, then?"

"That's just an intuitive response. It could be a woman. But strangulation generally is a guy thing."

"What about the Mylar paper? What do you think that was all about?"

"Was it available right there, on the premises?"

"Yeah, but the killer had to go to a closet to get it."

I lost her for a second as she turned her attention elsewhere. "Sorry, but I've gotta board my plane now. Mylar paper—that's the name right? That sounds awfully complicated. I'd say it *meant* something to him— but I'm not sure what."

I leaned back in my living room chair and massaged my head. I could feel a headache starting to gain momentum, one of those vise grip–like ones that make you want to squeal. What could the Mylar mean? It had to be symbolic in some way. Perhaps, as Eve had suggested, it was all tied in somehow to Anna's past. I would have loved to be at the spa when it reopened so I could check out the closet where the Mylar was stored and examine a roll of it. Right now I felt so far away from everything. It was as if I had imagined the whole experience.

The rest of the afternoon was a bust. I unpacked, realized I didn't have time for the gym, did a load of laundry, and confirmed an appointment I had at *Gloss* the next day to pitch story ideas to Cat Jones. I never managed to get any traction on the day.

When it came time to dress for dinner, I went to little effort. The restaurant was casual, Provence-style, plus I didn't want to do anything to stoke the flames Don apparently had flickering in his loins. I chose a knee-length black skirt, short-sleeved black sweater, and last year's short black boots, probably now a no-no according to *Gloss*. For makeup I did only blush and lip gloss. At 5:47, I threw my denim jacket over my shoulders and flew out my apartment door.

The Indian summer quality of the day had vanished by the time I hurried down 9th Street toward University Place. With the sun almost down, it was cool out now, fall-like. The flower beds along my block were bursting with purple and yellow mums, which made me think instantly of the garden at Cedar Inn, and Anna, and my frantic run through the woods, and Detective Beck, whom I might never see again.

I reached Don's building in less than five minutes. I gave my name to the doorman, and while he was ringing the apartment on the intercom, he looked at me with what I could have sworn was pity—as if I had come for a tax audit. Don, on the other hand, swung open the door of his apartment with a grin on his face that suggested *he* thought I had just become the luckiest girl alive.

He was wearing black denim pants and a mustard-colored flannel shirt, and his frizzy hair appeared to have grown like a Chia Pet in the several days since I'd seen him.

His apartment turned out to be typical generic guy space, with wall-to-wall carpeting, vertical blinds, a brown leather couch, and a smaller, puffy brown leather thing across from it that was either a matching chair or the world's largest baseball mitt. There were movie posters on the wall for *Chinatown, Giant,* and *The Apartment,* and I vaguely remembered Don telling me the other night that he used to review movies. The living room was L-shaped, and at the short end of the L there was a pass-through to the kitchen and a counter with a couple of bar chairs. He immediately headed off in that direction, with an air that suggested I should be following.

"Let me get you a drink," he said. "I make a mean sour apple martini."

"Oh, no, really, no," I said, trailing behind him.

"That's right—you're a beer drinker. I've got Corona or Amstel Light."

"Thanks, but I don't need anything," I said. "Like I mentioned, I've got this dinner to go to."

"You're not going to make me drink alone, are you?" he said, stepping into the kitchenette and popping back out with two Coronas. "Freelancers have to be there for each other."

Yeah, but let's not, I thought.

He set the beers onto the counter, flipped off the tops with a bottle opener, and dragged over a bar stool for me to sit on. I had no choice but to plop myself down. He'd

set out some food for us to eat on the counter: a paper
plate stacked with slimy orange buffalo chicken wings,
a plastic container of blue cheese dressing, and a half
dozen celery stalks with leafy tops that he'd laid on a
beige washcloth, obviously due to a shortage of plates.
It looked like celery people having a day at the beach.
At the far end of the counter was a manila envelope that
I suspected contained the clips I'd come for. Make nice,
I told myself, and in just a few minutes you can walk
out of here alive—with the prize.

"I guess a few sips won't hurt," I said, smiling.

"So what did you think of that party the other night?"
he asked. "I'd heard they were supposed to be getting
divorced, and then they throw a shindig like that. So
maybe not."

"I don't know them all that well," I said. "I worked
at the same newspaper with him once, but I haven't seen
them in years. We just bumped into each other recently
in New York."

He paused, his bottle midway to his mouth. "I
thought you'd always been in magazines. What paper?"

"The *Albany Times Union*. I worked there for a while
after college."

"You know, I regret not doing that. I have this fantasy
of one day taking a job on some paper and becoming the
oldest rookie reporter they've ever had."

"And then you create the TV series."

"I'm not following."

"The series about the old rookie who helps the young
reporters with their stories."

"Oh, clever lady," he said slyly. He set down his beer
and picked out a chicken wing from the plate. "You

gotta try one of these," he suggested as he tore a piece of skin from the bone like a bobcat. "They're the best in town."

"I'd love to, Don, really, but I've got to get moving. I've got this dinner at seven."

"I thought you said *eight*."

"No, seven. That's why I'm in such a rush."

He sighed with annoyance, as if I'd just turned his night into a train wreck. But without further delay he reached across me and grabbed the manila envelope. He turned it upside down and slid the contents out onto the counter. I spotted one article that I already had in my possession, but there were others I didn't have. I also noticed an interview transcript.

"Okay, here's the reason I wanted to go over the package with you," he said, picking up the transcript. "This is an interview I did with a psychologist who was considered one of the top experts on the subject. He's dead now, though. But there's a lot of great stuff in here."

Holding a wing in his left hand, he flipped through the thick transcript with his right, reading several quotes out loud. I could have figured it all out on my own, of course, but that wouldn't have allowed Don the opportunity to strut his stuff.

"This is terrific," I managed to interject.

"Yeah, I thought so," he said.

"When do you need it back?"

"You can keep the clips for a while, but I want the transcript back ASAP."

He dropped the wing bone, wiped off his hands with a napkin, and scooted all the material back into the manila envelope. I had to fight off the urge to grab it and flee.

"I'll get it back to you tomorrow," I said, beginning the slide from my chair. "Sorry I have to rush. I wish I could have changed my dinner plans, but they were made weeks ago."

"Sounds like you've got a pretty full plate," he said, handing the envelope to me and sliding off his bar chair.

"Yeah, right now I do. I've got a few assignments I'm real backed up on." Even as I spoke, I knew my comments about being in a crunch wouldn't discourage him from asking me out. Guys like him rarely took a hint because they always assumed they were the exception to any rule.

"I realize you're busy, but I've got a little proposition for you," he said as we both came to a stop by the front door. I bet he was going to suggest a jazz club, as early as Thursday night. "You got thirty more seconds?"

"Um, sure," I said, mentally scrolling down a list of possible excuses he might buy: gotta boyfriend; leaving town; scheduled to have gum surgery; recovering from trauma of finding a mummy in a spa . . .

"I like the sound of this gig you have," he said. "You know—the contributing editor thing at *Gloss.* I used to have a contract with *Parade,* but I let that die two years ago when I was trying to do a screenplay. I'm ready for another regular deal now—you know, a guarantee for a certain number of pieces a year. I was hoping you could help me out."

I could barely open my mouth, I was so stunned. So what he *really* wanted was a contract with *Gloss.*

"So what are you asking?" I said. "Do you want to

know if they're offering the same arrangement to other writers?"

"Yeah—and who do I talk to? I know it's only a woman's magazine, but I could do some seriously good stuff for them. I'd like to speak to that chick in charge—Cat Jones."

"Sure," I said, forcing a smile. "Let me find out if she's open to it. Look, I've really got to run, but I'll call you."

I had ten minutes to get to the restaurant, and I decided the fastest way would be on foot rather than by taxi. I took off south, past Washington Square Park and then down MacDougal, half walking, half trotting, and cursing Don the whole way. How dumb could I be? Maybe I'd also been wrong when I'd sensed attraction on Beck's part.

As I approached the restaurant, I could see Landon through the window, or rather the top of his head, with its cropped silver hair, as he sat reading at the table. He was seventy, about thirty to forty years older than most of my friends, but we had great chemistry, and after my divorce it had been so much easier to hang with him than some of my friends. Since he lived next door, I only had to drag myself five feet to get to his place. And since he hadn't known me during my marriage—at least no more than to say hello to—I didn't feel any embarrassment around him. As supportive as my friends were, I couldn't help but imagine what they said behind my back: "Didn't she *know* he gambled?" or, "God, I spent two hundred dollars on Simon Pearce barware and the marriage only lasted eighteen months!"

As soon as Landon spotted me, he dropped what he'd

been reading, pulled off his glasses, and rose to greet me. He looked dapper in a navy jacket, blue-and-white-striped shirt, and yellow tie. I hugged him, complimented the tie. Throwing myself into the chair across from him, I noticed that he'd been reading a catalog of lighting fixtures. Work related, obviously—he designed lobbies for a living.

"How's the Sixty-eighth Street project going?" I asked.

"Better now that I've diagnosed the client," he said.

"Is she ill?"

"No, she's *insane*," he said. "I think she has borderline personality disorder. I looked it up, and it's characterized by alternating extremes of idealization and devaluation. I guess if someone says you're brilliant one minute and the next accuses you of creating a lobby that looks like the Paramus, New Jersey, bus terminal, that would fit the description."

I asked him for an update on his love life. As a seventy-year-old gay man, it was more off than on, a source of constant consternation for him. Right now there wasn't even a flicker of hope.

"What about you, dear?" he asked. "You looked frazzled when you first came in."

I offered a quick rundown of cocktails with Don and how I'd been lured to his apartment not because he'd seen me as a babe, but because he wanted me to be a conduit to my boss, Cat Jones.

"Here I was," I said, "racking my brain for the perfect way to blow him off, and he's got nada interest in me. Do you think I really could be doing something these days to *repel* men?"

He took way too long to consider my question.

"You're actually pondering it, for God's sake," I exclaimed. "So you think I could be?"

"No, no, I was just recalling a comment my sister used to make about our cousin Ruth. She said she gave off skunk around men."

"And you think I do that? Give off skunk?"

Before he could answer, the waiter appeared for my drink order. I asked for a glass of Cabernet.

"Of course you don't give off skunk," Landon said once the waiter disappeared. "At least, not *usually*. But your heart's preoccupied these days, I'd say. I think you're sending off some kind of vibe that says, Don't bother me. How was the spa, by the way? I thought you were going to use that as a way to clear your head."

"Well, fasten your seat belt. If you think I seem frazzled tonight, you should have seen me this weekend. I've got a story—a big, huge, god-awful story. But maybe we should order first."

After we lassoed the waiter again, I launched in. Landon was one of those people who loved every detail of a tale, so I took him through what had happened blow by blow. The only thing I left out was my soft-porn fantasies about Detective Beck. By the time I wrapped up, Landon and I were done with our salads and well into our main course.

"How shocking and absolutely horrible," Landon said. "And she was entirely wrapped up in this silver paper? You mean like a loaf of garlic bread?"

"Well, I hadn't thought of it quite that way, but yes, that's right."

"Well, I'm just glad you're back in New York. I

know how you like to stick that sweet nose of yours into this sort of stuff."

What I didn't tell him was that I was deliberating going back up there as soon as I had my mass hysteria piece out of the way.

Over a shared plate of profiteroles, we discussed our super's new toupee and Landon's plans to visit Australia with his nephew.

"That's what *you* need, Bailey—a really good trip. And I don't mean to someplace where they kill off the staff. Aren't you due for a nice long adventure?"

"I know I should do something like that," I said. "And generally I don't mind traveling alone. But these days I'm just not feeling up for a solo excursion."

"What about all those old friends of yours from Brown? Can't you find one of them to travel with?"

"They're all married—with kids. They either don't go anywhere or they go only to those family resorts where the pool is half water, half pee. Hey, you wanna come back to my place for a margarita? I believe I have reached complete perfection with my recipe."

"Oh, Bailey, I feel awful. I promised my friend Thomas I'd stop by after dinner. He lives near here, and he wanted me to look at a presentation he's doing. If I'd known you were going to need me, I wouldn't have done that."

"No problem," I said, though I suddenly felt the oddest urge to cry.

"I'd cancel in a heartbeat, but there's a lot at stake for him."

"No, no, don't worry," I said. "I should do some work anyway."

We hugged good-bye and I slumped off, feeling horrible. Was it a hangover from everything awful that had happened during the weekend, compounded by my weirdly truncated day? Was it from coming up empty-handed in my quest to help Danny? Was it from talking to Landon and realizing how undefined my future seemed?

I walked all the way home, pulling my jeans jacket tight against the nippy air. As I drew close to my apartment building, I noticed someone out front, leaning against the wall of the building. To my utter astonishment, it was Jack Herlihy.

CHAPTER 12

I FROZE ON the sidewalk, panic-stricken. Last spring I'd spotted a guy I was seeing out on a date with another woman, and with that humiliating memory still hogging space at the front of my brain, my very first thought was that Jack must be dating someone in my building. Before I could figure out what to do, he turned his head and spotted me. He smiled and relaxed his body, and I knew then that he'd been standing there waiting for me.

I walked toward him, my heart thumping. Okay, I thought, he's here to see me, but what the hell for? His smile broadened and he took a few steps toward me. He was wearing black slacks, a white dress shirt open at the neck, and a sports jacket in a small black-and-tan plaid. Kind of dressy, as if he'd been out for dinner north of 14th Street.

"Hi," he said as he reached me. Leaning toward me, he brushed his lips lightly across my cheek. He smelled good, but it was a simple smell, maybe just soap and talc rather than cologne. Out of nowhere I felt an ache of longing.

"Fancy meeting you here," I said. That's why I write crime stories for *Gloss.* I'd never be allowed within ten feet of topics like "Clever Remarks to Make When You Run into Your Ex so That He Rues the Day He Ever Dumped You," because I'm such a miserable failure at moments like this.

"I came up this afternoon for a meeting," he said. "I walked by earlier tonight on the off chance you'd be here, and the doorman told me you'd gone out to dinner with Landon. So I got a cup of coffee around the block and came back."

"Maybe I should deduct ten dollars from the doorman's Christmas tip this year."

"Oh, don't do that. Look, would you be up for grabbing a drink someplace?"

What was this all *about?* He was a shrink. Maybe he'd decided he couldn't escape the need for *closure.*

"Why don't you just come up?" I suggested. I wanted to know why he'd landed on my doorstep, but if it *was* closure he was after, I didn't have the slightest interest in being on the negative end of it in a crowded bar. "I've got beer and wine and other stuff."

"Sure, that'd be great."

We walked the few steps back to my building and through the lobby, making clunky small talk. I was eager to learn his sister's status, but the lobby wasn't the place to pursue it. Instead I asked about the classes he was teaching this semester. So far, so good, he said. He asked where Landon was, and I explained. We rode the elevator side by side, only half turned toward each other, but I had a good enough view of him. I'd always been struck by the whole-is-greater-than-the-sum-of-the-parts quality to Jack's looks. There was no single drop-dead feature. His eyes were a nice medium blue. The nose was straight, the mouth full. But all together it could make your knees wobble. And that's what mine were doing just then. But I could also sense something else: Now that I was over the surprise of seeing him, my resentment toward Jack was starting to swell, like a hand that had been slammed in a door.

It was stuffy and dark inside my apartment, and I quickly turned on lamps and opened the door to the terrace. I considered lighting a few candles, but I realized how silly and possibly desperate that would look, me buzzing around the room like a bee with a box of Blue Point kitchen matches.

"So what would you like to drink?" I asked, opening the cabinet where I keep a few bottles of booze. "Like I said, I have beer and wine, or I could make you a gin and tonic. There's brandy here, too. And Marsala cooking wine. That would be nice if you're looking for something very, very sweet." I meant to make the last line light, kind of a little joke, but it came out sounding borderline sarcastic.

"Brandy's good. What are you going to have?"

"I'll have some brandy, too," I said. For one brief moment I'd considered playing it safe and going for a club soda. I'd already had half a bottle of wine at the restaurant, and a brandy topper might make me say something stupid or do something I'd regret—like bull-whip him with the strap of my purse. But if I was about to be "officially" dumped, I wanted brandy. Isn't that what they gave Civil War soldiers before they amputated their limbs?

I poured each of us a shot of Rémy-Martin into crystal brandy snifters, part of a set of eight I'd received as a wedding gift. I handed one to Jack as he sat on the sofa. I took the armchair directly across from him, rather than the couch. He slipped off his sports jacket, folded it in half lengthwise, and laid it on the couch next to him.

"It's really great to see you, Bailey," he said.

"Thanks," I said. It was sort of a dumb reply, but what *should* I have said—"It's great to see you, *too*"? Seeing him made me feel sad and mad. Plus I had no idea what bomb he was about to drop. Maybe he *wasn't* here to officially dump me. Maybe he figured we were long past that and he'd come for something else, like a favor. Maybe he was still planning to move to the city and wanted me to suggest a freakin' real estate agent or a decorator.

"Tell me about your sister," I added, though what I wanted to say was, "Tell me about those twenty-something brats I saw fawning over you like you were the next Dr. Phil."

"It looks like she's totally out of the woods," he said after a swig of brandy. "She still has some physical therapy ahead of her, but she's going back to work in a few weeks."

I threw out questions about her treatment, some of them borderline inane because I was stalling, dreading wherever the conversation was headed. I was just about to inquire about the dependability of her insurance carrier when I had the good sense to make myself shut up and meet my fate.

"I'm sure you're wondering why I was lurking outside your building," Jack said finally, setting his brandy snifter on my all-wrong-for-Manhattan pine coffee table and leaning forward, hands on knees. "Though maybe not. Guys probably do that on a regular basis to you. But there *is* something I wanted to talk about."

"Okay," I said. But inside all I was thinking was *not okay.* There was nothing okay about any of it.

"I know I haven't stayed in touch the way I promised I would," Jack said. "And I'm really sorry about that. But this thing with my sister was a lot tougher than I imagined it would be. I haven't felt I had my head above water until now."

"Look, Jack, you don't need to say anything else." I could have called him on the bullshit right then, but what was the point? I just wanted to get the whole thing over with.

"Do you mind if I do, though?" he asked.

I shrugged. He ran his hand through his hair, something he did when he was nervous.

"My life finally feels normal again," he said. "and I've realized that I miss you. A lot. I know it's tricky with me being back in Washington, but I was hoping we could pick up where we left off."

It took me about thirty seconds to absorb the gist of his words—and once I did, I felt totally flummoxed.

"You're not saying anything," he said as I just sat there. "I can't tell whether that's good or bad."

"It's just not what I was expecting at all," I said, fumbling. "I'd figured you'd just totally lost interest in me."

He shifted his position on the couch. "But I always said it might not be till the end of the summer that things got back to normal for me," he said with a trace of impatience in his voice. "You knew the situation."

"I know," I said. "But Jack, I haven't even *heard* from you since the middle of August."

"Late August is when things got the craziest for me."

I didn't say anything, just sipped my brandy.

"Tell me," he urged. "You've got something on your mind, Bailey."

"I saw you one day, Jack," I blurted out. "You were walking around the Village with a couple of girls. Happy-go-lucky. I hadn't heard from you, but there you were, relishing the day. Obviously you weren't too busy or too overwhelmed to flirt with a few coeds."

He furrowed his brow, thinking, perhaps trying to recall the incident—or perhaps he was disconcerted by the Yes, Bailey *Can* Be a Bitch moment.

"I'm sure I was simply headed in the same direction with people who had been in my class," he said. "You know, Bailey, it's interesting that you never bothered to call *me* during all that time. It would have been good to hear from you—and know that you cared about what I was going through."

"I—I didn't call because we'd left the ball in your court," I said, not containing my anger. "You said you'd call when you could. And until mid-August you did— every week. And then something changed."

He leaned all the way back against the couch and lifted his head toward the ceiling, as if something were written there that would help him know what to say next. When he lowered his head again, I could see in his eyes that something more was coming.

"Look, Bailey," he said suddenly, "I'm going to be honest with you about something."

"Nothing good ever follows a sentence like that."

"Maybe. Maybe I'm about to shoot myself in the foot. But I feel my chances with you will be better if I don't try to bullshit you. There was someone in Pittsburgh. Someone I was seeing for a very short while."

I felt the blood rush to my face and neck, as if I were being dressed down by a boss in front of thirty or forty co-workers.

"Seeing or *sleeping with?*" I asked. It was one of those questions that my pride should have prevented me from asking, but my need to know overrode all that.

He picked up his brandy and took another swig. "Sleeping with," he said. "It was an old girlfriend, actually. She'd stayed close to my parents, and she came back to Pittsburgh a couple of times this summer to be with my family during this whole crisis. Initially I tried to discourage her from coming, but I could tell my mother really wanted it. One night it just happened."

It had been weeks since I'd seen Jack, but I was surprised at how much his betrayal stung.

"Well, I'm so pleased you could find someone to help you through a tough time," I said sarcastically.

"Bailey, I hope you can understand that it really was a terrible time for me. I would have turned to *you* then—but I never sensed you wanted me to."

"You mean because I didn't sleep with you?" I asked, still angry. "You always indicated that you were okay with the fact that I wanted to take it slow."

"No, not because of that. You just never seemed a hundred percent gung ho."

I stared at him across the short distance between couch and armchair. He was right. I'd been smitten with him, but at the same time I'd felt gun-shy. I'd done things to drag down the pace of the relationship—and not just physically. I'd told him—and myself—that it had to do with being in a tailspin from the murder case I'd been involved in, but the idea of a full commitment to Jack had made me nervous. It had been almost two years since my divorce, but I still didn't know if I was really ready for something serious with another man.

"Jack, you're being honest with me, so I'll be the same with you," I said, calmer now. "You've thrown me for a total loop. Maybe I didn't have both feet in the water with you, but on the other hand I was pretty crazy about you. I've spent the last weeks doing my best not to even think about you. And I'm not sure how I'm feeling at this exact moment."

"So are you seeing someone?" he asked, probably more urgently than he wished.

"I've been dating," I said. It wasn't true, of course, but I felt if I admitted that I hadn't been, then *that* would be dishonest. Because there were those wild, crazy feelings I'd been experiencing for Beck. "A bit here and there. It's not that so much as, well—this is all coming out of left field for me."

Jack set down his brandy snifter and rose slowly from the couch. His crisp white shirt pulled against him, and I could see the rough outline of his smooth, broad chest. What was he doing? I wondered. He leaned over and picked up his jacket from the couch and laid it over his arm. He was on the move.

"It was pretty stupid of me to come here tonight and just surprise you with all of this," he said. "I'm sorry about that. As I said, I wish we could see each other again—but maybe the timing isn't ever going to be right for us."

"Jack," I said, getting out of my armchair, nervous suddenly about his departure. "I'm not sorry you came here tonight. I wish I knew exactly what was in my heart right now, but I don't. But I also know that I don't like the thought of never seeing you again. Would you—when are you coming up from Washington again?"

"Why?"

"What if we had dinner? Or dinners. We could spend some time together and see what happens. I'd be game for that if you would."

"Yes, I'm game," he said, smiling. "What about Saturday night? I'm going to be up most weekends. I've got this project I'm involved in. I ended up taking a sublet."

"You're going to keep a place in New York?" I said, surprised.

"I am. I still have every intention of living here."

"Well, Saturday's good," I said. I took a few steps toward him, planning to walk him to the door, but he didn't move.

"That's great."

"You know," I said, "maybe if I had slept with you that night at your place, none of this would have happened. There would have been a stronger connection between us."

"Well, let's promise not to make another mistake like that if the moment ever occurs again."

He leaned forward then and kissed me on the mouth. It was a soft kiss, a good-bye kiss for the night, nothing more, because it wouldn't be like Jack to push the situation. Yet when I tasted his mouth I felt a big, fast rush of desire going through me from tip to toe. I kissed him back harder, leaning into him, and then his tongue was in my mouth and mine was in his.

There was just one brief second when I thought, Shit, I knew I shouldn't have had that brandy, but then I wasn't thinking anything at all, just feeling his mouth and how good he tasted and how good he smelled. He slid his hand behind my neck and kissed me harder, deeper. I murmured in pleasure. He pressed closer, and when I felt his erection I pressed back hard. His hand slid from my neck to my right breast, fondling it, finding the nipple with the tips of his fingers.

"Do you want to stay, Jack?" I asked. Was I insane? I wondered as soon as the words were out of my mouth, but I didn't take it back. Admittedly, I was hampered by near toxic levels of horniness, but I didn't just want sex, I realized—I wanted sex with Jack. Perhaps I should have played hard to get, made him practically beg for it over the next weeks like a dog for a piece of bacon, but if I was ever going to find out whether it could work with Jack, I'd have to make both a physical and an emotional leap. If I decided to wait until this weekend—or some later date—to do it, I could easily lose my nerve.

"Yes," he said, "as long as I still get the dinner Saturday night."

He tossed his jacket onto an armchair and kissed me

again, more urgently. As I ran my hands across the front of his crisp white shirt, he reached for the edges of my sweater and pulled it over my head, taking his mouth off mine for only the second it required to get the sweater off. He fondled my breasts through my bra, gently, and when I moaned he reached behind and unsnapped my bra, dragging it to my waist. My whole body ached with lust. As far as I knew, half the West Village was watching us through my window, so I muttered a suggestion that we retreat to the bedroom.

I'd always had a hunch what kind of lover Jack would be, and I was right. He was generous, one of those guys with a slow, sure hand who seems to find pleasing you the most erotic thing in the world. We made love once, for what seemed like an hour, and then again later, after I had drifted off to sleep and woken to his fingers in me, moving, softly at first, then harder and deeper. There was one last time in the morning, fast and furious at six, before he left to catch an early shuttle back to Washington.

I took a long hot shower right after he'd gone, trying to rouse myself by using one of those pink nubby exfoliating gloves I'd scarfed up at a *Gloss* beauty department giveaway. My head was a big jumble of thoughts, all at cross-purposes with one another—I was glad I had finally taken the plunge with Jack; I was sorry I'd done it without being sure of what I wanted in the end; I was happy I was alone so I could sort out my feelings; I wished Jack were here.

After dressing, I stuck a bagel in the toaster, made coffee, and ate my breakfast standing up while scanning the *Times*. At nine-fifteen I was out the door, headed for the subway and for *Gloss*. As the train tore through the tunnel, I realized that in the heat, so to speak, of the moment last night, I'd never called Danny as I'd planned. Jack had taken my mind temporarily off the murder, but I was eager for an update. I would try to reach her after my appointment with Cat.

Typically, things at *Gloss* don't get humming until ten, so when I stepped off the elevator at nine-fifty, I wasn't surprised to hear only a faint murmur of activity. I strode down the white corridor toward my office, glimpsing a few early bird editors as they slipped out of coats or pretended to enjoy their Zone power bars. After tossing my stuff onto the straight-backed chair against the wall and checking my mail from the previous week, I poured myself a cup of coffee at the small food station. Then I headed directly to Cat's office.

Her assistant was nowhere in sight, but I spotted Cat through the glass wall of her office, perched on the front of her desk and talking animatedly on the phone. She was dressed all in black, in a long full skirt, high-necked blouse, cropped jacket, and tight, pointy boots—sort of *Horses and Hounds Monthly* meets Bram Stoker's *Dracula*. Her long blond hair was pulled back into the sloppy style that *Gloss* had dubbed "the après-booty bun."

She spotted me and indicated with her index finger that she would be just one minute. The person on the other end of the phone must be someone she wanted something from—her boss, perhaps, or a celeb publicist—because even through the glass I could tell the Cat Jones charm was working at full throttle. Cat exerted a force field—positive or negative, depending on the situation. If she was pleased with you she could make you feel like God's gift to the universe. If you'd pissed her off, you had better adhere to the advice offered for an encounter with a wild animal: Back away slowly and betray no fear.

I turned away so I wasn't staring at her, but I didn't move from my spot. Someone could easily usurp my place if I wasn't careful. And sure enough, within two minutes *Gloss*'s new entertainment editor, whose name I had yet to commit to memory, came strutting over. She glanced determinedly into Cat's office and then looked at me.

"Are you waiting to see her?" she asked impatiently.

"Yeah, I have an appointment," I said.

She let out a big sigh, as if I'd just told her she'd have to fly coach instead of business.

"I'd appreciate it if you gave her an important message for me, then," she said. "You won't know what this means, but tell her the Reese Witherspoon movie is going *wide* in February. Okay? It's important that she know that."

As soon as she strolled away, Cat was waving me in.

"Sit," she said, pointing to the brown Ultrasuede love seat. "I feel like I haven't seen you in ages."

I was there to pitch story ideas, but first she wanted to know what I'd been up to. Though Cat was my boss, the one who'd created the great gig for me at *Gloss,* she was also my friend in a weird sort of way and had been for seven years, since we'd met while working on a small magazine downtown. I ran through an abbreviated version of finding Anna dead in the Mylar paper.

"God, and I thought bikini waxes were a bitch," Cat said. "Is there an article in it?"

"N-o," I exclaimed. "I could never do that to Danny. It would really bury her business."

"Just let me know if you change your mind. And in the meantime, please be careful, will you? I pulled your hide out of the fire once this year. I may not be there to do it again."

I knew her morning was probably jammed, but I wanted to bounce the Jack episode off her. Cat was a master when it came to men. I described Jack's visit, his confession about the former girlfriend, and without mentioning the carnal coupling portion of the evening, I asked her advice on the whole business.

"How do you really feel about him?" she asked bluntly.

"I'm very attracted to him. But I think I also feel some resentment."

She sighed. "This may not be what you want to hear. And it almost sounds like I'm comparing this Jack guy to a pair of last year's Jimmy Choo shoes. But I've never been big on looking back, on focusing on something from the past, no matter how wonderful it might have been at the time. I always want to be in forward motion."

I nodded, as if impressed by her wisdom, but inside I felt sorry I'd asked. I think I'd been hoping she'd tell me to go for it. I quickly ran through my story ideas, and she okayed two out of three. As we were wrapping up, her assistant stuck her head through the door to announce a scheduled phone call and I said a fast goodbye. As I hurried back to my office, I realized I'd forgotten to give her the entertainment editor's message about Reese Witherspoon's movie. Oops.

There was no other reason to hang at *Gloss* today, and I was anxious to split for home, where I would first call Danny and then attempt to wrestle my article to the ground once and for all. As I grabbed my tote bag and jacket from the side chair, I noticed that the mail guy had stopped by when I'd been ensconced in Cat's office. There were two letters on my desk, sitting on top of a package. I tossed the letters to the side and picked up the package, curious as to who would be sending me something at *Gloss*. It was a cardboard box, about two feet long and secured with tan masking tape. I gave a start when I saw that the postmark read "Warren, Massachusetts," but then I noticed that Danny's home address was in the upper-left-hand corner.

It wasn't Danny's handwriting, though.

Using scissors, I cut open the end of the package and slid the contents onto my desk. It was a brown paper bag with something inside. It felt soft and squishy when I touched it, and poking out from the opening was the edge of one of those plastic freezer bags with the zippered tops. Holding the top of the plastic bag, I yanked it out. When I saw what was inside, I threw it on my desk and screamed. It was a dead mouse, wrapped in Mylar paper with its snout and pale gray tail sticking out at the ends.

CHAPTER 13

"ARE YOU ALL right?"

One of the junior fashion assistants who worked across the hall was standing in the doorway, bug-eyed. I rolled my chair slightly to the right so I blocked her view of the rotting vermin on my desk.

"Uh, yeah. I thought I saw a mouse."

"A *mouse*? Omigod—should I get someone?"

"No, no. It was just my imagination."

As soon as she'd trounced back to her office, I shoved the door shut and forced myself to look at the mouse again. My stomach turned over, and I had to fight off the urge to hurl my breakfast. Whoever had sent it to me had wanted to freak me out, and they'd succeeded. Was it the person who had followed me in the woods that day? Was it the killer, warning me away? Was it someone involved in the dirty deeds at the spa who wanted to make sure I stopped poking around? Were they all one and the same? Holding the brown paper bag upside down with a tissue from my drawer, I shook it to see if a note of some kind was stuffed at the bottom. But there was nothing else inside—or in the box either. I glanced at the date on the postmark. The package had been mailed from Warren yesterday.

Squeamishly, I picked up the freezer bag with the tissue, dropped it back in the paper bag, and shoved that into the box. Then I called Danny. The phone rang five times and was finally answered by someone announcing, "Cedar Inn." It sounded like Natalie.

"This is Bailey Weggins calling for Danny," I said. "Is she there?"

"Oh yes. She said to put your call through right away."

It sounded as if there might be a new development. Five seconds later, Danny picked up.

"I'm so glad you got my message, Bailey," she said, her voice quivering. "I wasn't sure where you'd be today."

"I didn't get a message. I'm at work. What happened?"

"It's George. The police think—I can't even get the words out. The police are questioning him about Anna's death."

I let out a small gasp. True, I hadn't liked George, and the fact that he'd been missing in action on Friday night had concerned me, but I'd never seriously considered him as Anna's murderer.

"Has he been arrested?" I asked.

"No, but he was brought down there first thing this morning for questioning."

"Why? What have they got?"

"I wasn't allowed in the room with him, but he told me they'd questioned him about phone calls he'd made to Anna—to her phone in the barn and her cell phone. Our lawyer told me later that they seemed highly suspicious about the calls, but they don't appear to have anything else. Of course, George has no alibi. He says he got back from Boston at around eleven that night and went to bed."

"So what is George's explanation for the phone calls—and how many were there?"

She let out a ragged sigh. "He said they were work related. And that there weren't that many."

"Does that make sense to you?" I asked.

"Yes. No. I'm so frightened, I don't know what to think. George says he'd been talking to Anna a little bit about these business retreats he wants to do here. I vaguely remember him telling me he was going to do that. Do you know what I think? I think the police are going to zero in now on George because it's *easy*. They're not having any luck solving the crime, and they're under lots of pressure."

"Are you talking about Beck specifically?" I asked. As I spoke his name, I saw him in my mind—the gray hair, the deep blue eyes.

"Well, he's the one leading the investigation."

"Oh, Danny, I wish I were there with you. And I'm sure this is all going to be sorted out. As far as you know, is there anyone else the police seem to be look-

ing at? Have you been able to get a hint of any other theories they may have?"

"No. But I did learn one thing important. There was
no break-in. Anna either let the person in or he had a
key."

"The police told you that?" I said.

"Yes, after I'd pestered them to death. We're due to
reopen the spa on Thursday, and I needed to know if I
had to repair the back door. It turns out it was perfectly
fine. Though I'm having all the locks changed."

"Look, Danny, I'm coming back up there. You need
me."

"But don't you have work to do in New York?"

"I think I've figured out a way to finish up my article pretty quickly. I probably can leave around midday
tomorrow."

"Oh, Bailey, I'd be so grateful if you could. You've
got to help prove that George didn't do it. By the way,
Anna's sister is flying in tomorrow, so that will give
you the chance to meet her."

"Great. One question before I let you go. You didn't
mail a package to me in New York, did you?" I certainly
didn't think Danny had sent me the mouse, but I wondered if someone had substituted the mouse for something that she'd mailed me.

"No. Why?"

"I'll explain when I get there." She had enough on
her mind at the moment.

I told her to expect me between four and five and to
call me if anything new developed between now and
then.

Carefully I wedged the mouse package into my tote

bag and flew out of the *Gloss* offices, grabbing a cab on Seventh Avenue to my apartment. I placed the package in a small cooler I kept for picnics, along with some cold packs. I would give it to Beck when I returned to Warren. I felt a small flash of guilt. Last night I'd been busy lighting the mattress on fire with Jack, and now I was conjuring up thoughts of Beck.

If I was going to leave for Warren tomorrow, I would have to have my hysteria piece out of the way. The thought of writing an 1,800-word piece in a day might have made *me* hysterical, but on the subway ride to *Gloss* that morning, I'd glanced through Don's files and a rescue plan had come to me. Rather than attempt to make the miserable little incident I was supposed to write about any more interesting than it actually was, I'd use it as a backdrop to discuss the whole phenomenon of mass hysteria.

First I ordered a BLT from the coffee shop in my building. When I'm under the gun, something about mayo and bacon kicks my brain into high gear without turning me into a madwoman. I read through the transcript of Don's interview with the dead dude, made a bunch of calls, talked to new people, and found some fascinating cases on the Internet. By four o'clock I'd put together a new outline and written a lead. During the next two hours, I raced through a pretty clean first draft. It was at times like this that I was grateful for my years grinding out newspaper copy.

At around six I shut down my computer and took my composition book and a cup of coffee out to the terrace. It was cool enough out to need a fleece jacket, but the setting sun felt good on my face. I peeked through the stockade fence between my terrace and Landon's to see if he might be puttering out there, but there was no sign of him.

I found a clean page in my notebook, and the first thing I wrote was George's name with a big question mark. If he had killed Anna, it would most certainly be because of some romantic-sexual factor. Maybe he'd had an affair with Anna and was then rejected by her, or else she'd threatened to reveal all to Danny. I had a hard time, however, imagining Anna falling for a geezer like George. A more likely scenario was that he'd become obsessed with her and then been snubbed. I considered what Parker had said about the Mylar paper. It *meant* something to the killer. George certainly knew where it was stored, and wrapping her up in it could easily reflect his anger at having been spurned.

As much as George made my skin crawl, I prayed he hadn't done it. But if he hadn't, who had? There was Eric, the eerily calm ex, and possibly Rich, if he'd ever hooked up with Anna—or had desperately wanted to. The tavern owner was another suspect. He apparently blamed the spa for his father's death, and Anna had done the massage. And Josh, of course, should be on the list as well. If he was possibly up to something shady at the spa and in cahoots with some of his employees, things may have soured, leading to a conflict. Anna may have wanted out and threatened to tell.

The last thing that I added to my list was an X. The killer could easily be someone I'd never met or *had* met but wouldn't know to suspect. Someone, as Parker had said, who knew Anna and was filled with rage. It might be an obsessed client. Or a totally new lover of Anna's, a man whose attraction to her had morphed into a deadly hatred or jealousy.

There was one last possibility I couldn't ignore. Eve had told me that Anna was haunted by something in her past. Could that have somehow led to her death? Maybe a former boyfriend had been stalking her, threatening her, and had finally killed her. Perhaps that was the reason she had left New York City. I remembered suddenly that I'd made a note of the manager at the Manhattan spa who had given Anna her reference. It was a long shot, but I decided to call her.

First, though, I needed a game plan. What I was hoping to discover was anything pertinent about Anna's background, anything that might suggest that one day she'd become a target for a murder. For instance, *was* there a disgruntled ex in the picture? But how much the manager revealed or let slip would depend on my tack. If I called her and announced that Anna had been murdered, she might clam up. A better approach might be for me to play dumb about the situation and offer another reason for the call. Of course, she might know about the murder already, but there was a bigger chance she wouldn't, especially if she was only a former colleague of Anna's and not a friend. A strategy formed in my mind, though it wasn't a very nice one.

I thumbed through my composition book to the page where I'd made the notation. Nina Hayes, the Paradise Spa, and a phone number. I was struck again by the fact that the name of the spa didn't seem familiar. Hopefully the place wasn't out of business now.

After locking the door to my terrace, I placed the call. A woman answered on the third ring, her voice so still and quiet that I thought for a second an answering machine had picked up.

"Ms. Hayes?" I asked.

There was a few seconds' hesitation before she spoke.

"Yes?"

"My name's Bailey Weggins. Anna Cole gave me your name. I've just moved to the city, and Anna thought you might be able to help me get a job—doing massage. I was hoping I could get together with you and talk."

She hesitated again, this time for so many seconds that I thought she might no longer be on the line.

"Are you—"

"How do you know Anna?" she asked finally. She spoke slowly and deliberately, as if she were weighing her words first. It was clear from her tone that she hadn't heard the news of Anna's death.

"I met her in Massachusetts," I said. "We have a very good mutual friend."

"How's she doing?"

"Good, I guess. It's been a few months since I've bumped into her. But like I said, she gave me your number, and I held on to it because I knew I'd be coming to New York."

"Anna's still working up there?"

"As far as I know. She was working at an inn—somewhere in the Berkshires."

"And she told you to give me a call?"

I was tempted to scream, "*Duh*, that's what I've said about forty times," but I kept up the little dance with her. She was clearly doing an assessment of me as we spoke.

"Yeah," I said. "She told me you might be able to help me find something. The two of you worked together, right?"

She did that maddening pause again.

"Actually, there might be something available in another week or two," she said. "You've got experience, right?"

"Yes, I've been working for several years—in the Boston area."

"You have a massage license?"

"Yes," I answered, hoping she wasn't going to quiz me on my knowledge of anatomy or the difference between Swedish and shiatsu.

"And I trust Anna told you we're not full service."

"She did," I said, though for the life of me I couldn't tell what that meant. Maybe they didn't get into all the kooky stuff, the way the Cedar Inn and Spa did.

"Why don't we meet for coffee?" she said. "We can discuss it all in person."

"Great. Did you want to meet tomorrow?"

"Friday's better for me."

"I have to go back up to Boston this weekend, to pick up a few things. Is there any chance you could squeeze it in tomorrow?"

She didn't answer right away, natch, but I could hear the shuffle of paper, as if she were checking a calendar.

"The only time I could do it is ten," she said.

"That's fine with me."

"Okay, there's a coffee shop on the northeast corner

of Third Avenue and Thirty-sixth Street. We'll meet there at ten. What do you look like, by the way?"

"I'm five six, with short, brownish blond hair," I said. "How will I know *you?*"

"What I meant is, you're attractive, right?"

Such an odd question. Did that mean if you were butt ugly, you couldn't get a job at her spa?

"Uh, yes," I said. "That's been the consensus of a few people, I guess."

"Good, then I'll see you at ten. You've got the address, right?"

"Yes. Is the spa nearby?"

Pause. "Yes. Yes, it is."

Sheez, how absolutely weird, I thought as I set the phone down. She'd answered with just a hello, so I'd obviously gotten her home phone or a private line in her office. I tried directory assistance and asked for the Paradise Spa. No listing. Maybe it had folded and Nina had moved on to someplace else. I wondered briefly if she wasn't a spa manager after all, but rather someone who had agreed to fake a reference for Anna. But then why agree to meet me? Then there was that strange question about me being attractive. Perhaps it would all fall together when I met her tomorrow.

That night I had long-standing plans to meet a friend for drinks. I was tempted to bag it but decided in the end it would be good to go out and clear my head. I needed, as Danny had said, clarity on the situation. I also needed to drop off the transcript with Don's doorman. And last but not least, I needed to get that disgusto mouse out of my thoughts.

But drinks proved to be a dud. The friend was someone I got together with twice a year, and it was becoming increasingly clear that just because we'd shared a cubby at *Get* magazine five years ago, we weren't destined to be lifelong pals. She was a professional event planner now, and after spending thirty minutes talking about gobo lights and giftie bags, she announced that she was involved with her married boss—and completely obsessed with him.

"I've Googled his wife," she confessed. "I even made photocopies of his kids' pictures. I'm terrified I'm going to turn into a bunny killer."

After two beers I feigned exhaustion and fled. There was a call on my answering machine from Jack, wishing me good night. I was happy he had phoned, but no less confused about what I wanted.

I could tell as soon as I crawled in bed that sleep was going to pull yet another elusive act. I tried another technique the hypnotist had suggested—counting backward and imagining the numbers written on black velvet. But I kept seeing black paintings instead—the kind with portraits of clowns and tigers and Elvis. The only decent night's rest I'd had lately was last night with Jack. Between all the sex, I'd fallen asleep easily—and slept deeply.

The next day I was up by six. I worked for two straight hours editing the draft of my article. It wasn't going to win any prizes, but it was finally done.

At nine-thirty I headed toward Murray Hill, where the coffee shop was located. The conversation was going to be tricky. I would have to discuss the possibility of a job with Nina, then work my way over to the topic of Anna. I would confide to her that Anna seemed troubled by things in her past and see what Nina coughed up. Since it was clear from our conversation that she was never going to win the Chick Chatter of the Year Award, I wasn't too hopeful about what I'd come away with.

The restaurant turned out to be a weird cross between a coffee shop, a Tex-Mex restaurant, and *Blade Runner*. There was a stainless-steel counter and futuristic lights and then these turquoise-and-pink booths with cactus plants all over. Since Nina had never given me a description of what she looked like, I was going to have to wait for her to pick me out. I was the only person alone in the place, so it was obvious she wasn't there yet. But then it was just three minutes to ten.

The waitress showed me to a booth and handed me one of those menus you get in New York coffee shops that lists at least four hundred dishes and tempts you to order the sole Veronique just to see if they can really turn it out. I asked for coffee and opened my *New York Times*. When I finished a story and checked the clock, I was startled to see it was 10:12. I glanced around the diner, just to make sure I hadn't missed her. There were no solo women in the restaurant other than myself.

I knew at that moment that she wasn't just late. She wasn't going to show. There had been that weirdness on the phone. Something wasn't right about the whole thing. I gave it another twenty minutes and paid the bill. On the way out, I asked the man at the cash register if he had ever heard of the Paradise Spa or any day spa in the area. Negative.

I wasn't sure what to think, but I found myself leaning toward the idea that had crossed my mind yesterday.

Nina had been a fake reference for Anna. Maybe she'd lured me out to the coffee shop just to make herself laugh. But wouldn't she wonder why Anna had given me her number in the first place?

I took the IRT home and put myself in high gear. I looked over my piece one more time, tweaking it here and there. Then I e-mailed it to my editor.

I'd planned to be on the road by two, but I was ahead of schedule. I called the garage, said I'd be picking up the Jeep earlier than originally planned, and took my trash down to the incinerator. On the way back I bumped into Landon coming off the elevator.

"Got time for a cup of coffee?" he asked.

"A fast one," I said. "Don't shoot me, but I'm headed back to the Dead Body Spa."

"Oh dear, *why?*"

I followed him into his apartment, my trash basket under my arm. His place was gorgeous—pale gray furniture, pickled floors, and dark antique pieces. While he made coffee I took him through the most recent developments. I also quickly updated him on the situation with Jack's visit, since he'd been stuck listening to me moan about my broken heart most of the summer.

"You're out of my sight for twenty minutes and look what happens," he said.

"See, you should never have left me stranded on MacDougal Street," I said.

"Well, I'm happy about the Jack thing—if *you* are."

"Yes, I'm happy," I said.

"You don't sound it. In fact, you sound like someone whose new puppy's been run over by a parade float."

"It's more that I'm confused. Everything seemed good

last night, but right now my heart is overwhelmed by an urge to flee. Let's talk about something else before I have a panic attack."

I related the strange conversation with Nina and her failure to show for our coffee klatch. Landon listened pensively.

"She asked what you *looked* like?" he said when I'd finished.

"Yeah, odd, huh? Do you think some spas really discriminate against ugly therapists?"

"Or maybe it's not a spa at all," Landon said.

"What do you mean?" I asked.

"Sounds more like a brothel, for God's sake."

"A *brothel?*" But even as I was manifesting my surprise, my mind was ticking off all the reasons he was absolutely right: The spa hadn't been listed; Nina had been so circumspect on the phone; she hadn't wanted to meet me at the spa. I'd naively asked at the end of the conversation if the spa was near the coffee shop. That had been the tip-off to her that I didn't know what I was talking about.

Nina could very well be a hooker. And Anna had worked for her. Had I just discovered the naughty business that was being conducted at the Cedar Inn?

CHAPTER 14

"You're not saying anything," Landon remarked. "Do you think I'm totally off base?"

"No, I'm speechless because I think you may be *right*," I confessed. "This Nina chick was so close-mouthed on the phone, so secretive, really. I feel stupid for not getting it."

I stood up from the table and began circling his living room, as if being in motion could help me think faster.

"It's not so obvious if you're set up to view it totally differently," Landon said. "You're told it's a spa, you know that someone who worked at a spa used to work there. It's not as if the word *brothel* should flash in your brain."

"You're nice to try to make me feel less like an idiot. It's clear I should be demoted to writing items for *Gloss* on things like how to remove a toe beard."

"What's a toe beard?"

"I'll tell you another time," I said. "So does this mean that this Nina is simply a high-class call girl working out of an apartment and the spa is a sham, or is there actually some massage component to all of this?"

"Well, I don't know about *this* case, but I believe some massage parlors include sex *and* massage," he said. "It's possible she's running some kind of X-rated spa."

"Oh God, I just remembered," I said, throwing my hands up. "She even used this one expression—'We're not full service.' I thought she meant they didn't do extra stuff, but it's obviously some hooker talk. I wonder what it means. That they don't do blow jobs?"

"Maybe it's the kinky stuff they don't get into. If you want a spanking or feel an urge to be peed on, you have to go someplace else."

"The bigger question, of course, is what does this mean about the Cedar Inn?" I said, still pacing. "If Nina's a hooker and she gave Anna a recommendation, does that mean Anna was a hooker as well? And since Anna was referred there by Piper, does that mean Piper's one? And does that mean they were working girls at the Cedar Inn?"

"Do you have any reason to suspect that this kind of thing *has* been going on there?"

"You mean other than the fact that Anna—*and* Piper—had a line of regular clients wrapping around the block? And neither apparently was brilliant at massage? That sort of points to something, wouldn't you say?"

"Your poor friend Danny," Landon said, shaking his head.

"Oh, I know. This could totally wreck her business, couldn't it?"

"Yes. If it got out."

I sat back down, considering his remark. "It doesn't seem possible, but I wonder if I'm the only one who *knows*. The police haven't given any indication that they're aware of this."

"My guess would be that if they *are* aware of it, they wouldn't share it with you."

"But it might turn up in the kinds of questions they've been asking Danny. Right now, they seem to have their eye on George."

"So what are you going to do with the information?" he asked. "You've got to report it to the police, right?" He took a sip of coffee, peering at me over the rim of his coffee cup.

"I'm not sure," I said. "For the time being, I think I'm going to keep my mouth shut."

"But Bail—"

"Hear me out for a sec," I said. "I have absolutely no proof this has been going on at the Cedar Inn. In fact, I have no proof that it was even going on at the Paradise Spa. Until I *get* proof, I can't take a chance of wrecking Danny's business, and maybe her life, by running to the police with this. Besides, even if it *is* going on, it might not have anything whatsoever to do with the murder. Once I have proof, I'd want to tell Danny so she can give the boot to Josh and Piper and whoever else is involved, but it might not be necessary to let the police in on things."

"I know you love to make my heart stop, so I'm a little afraid to ask this—but how do you intend to *get* proof?"

"Don't worry." I laughed. "I'm going to start by looking through some files at the inn. I'm *not* going undercover as a hooker, if that's what you're thinking. Though if I hadn't finally had sex this week, I might have considered it."

I glanced at my watch. It was just after noon. "Oh, gosh, it's later than I thought. I'd better split."

I pecked him on the cheek as he began to clear the coffee stuff from the table and hurried out of his apartment, taking my empty trash basket with me. Before I locked up, I spent five minutes digging out my pre-PalmPilot Rolodex to find the number of a vice cop I'd once interviewed. Because what I wanted to do, even before going through the list of spa clients in Danny's computer, was to try to confirm if Landon's theory about the Paradise Spa was actually right.

I'd talked to this cop only once, and that was over a year ago—he was the brother of a homicide detective I knew fairly well—but he'd been generous with his time, and I was hoping that he'd be that way again. I was also praying that the number still worked for him. Because he was the only vice cop I knew in all of New York City.

Ten minutes later I was in my Jeep, along with my overnight bag and my little Playmate cooler, packed with the day's specialty: mice on ice. At the first red light I hit, I put on my headset and placed the call. I was in luck—the message said, "This is Barry, leave a number and I'll call you back." I left a message reminding him who I was and said that I was anxious to ask him a few questions.

The trip this time was far less of a hassle than it had been last Friday. No smoldering car fires, no major traffic jams. But my mood couldn't have been more different. Though I had felt slightly frazzled last Friday, I knew that at the end of the line someone was going to press their fingers into my rock-hard muscles and make me moan with pleasure. This time I knew that nothing good awaited me at the end of the line. I felt again a little bit like Sigourney Weaver, but this time in *Aliens,* the sequel, returning to that big, bad planet and knowing that whatever was in store would surely be worse than some oversize glowworm with bad teeth gnawing its way out of people's tummies. There was a murderer up there, and quite possibly it was someone who worked at the inn, maybe even Danny's husband. Add to that the fact that the Cedar Inn might very well be the House of the Rising Sun. It could only get uglier if I discovered people up there were practicing witchcraft and using the hot tub to boil wool of bat and tongue of dog.

When my mind wasn't roiling with thoughts of the Cedar Inn, it was all churned up over Jack—and Detective Jeffrey Beck. I couldn't deny that I was intrigued about the idea of possibly bumping into Beck again. So what did that say about my feelings for Jack? My night with Jack had been nice, very nice, in fact, but I was still feeling ambivalent. The bottom line was that I was attracted to Jack, I'd enjoyed having sex with him, and I wanted to see him again—but I didn't totally trust him. He'd disappeared this summer without a trace, only to reappear with a confession that he'd banged an old girl-friend just because he'd had the blues. Maybe I *had* acted ambivalently toward Jack at times, but I didn't deserve all the blame. I wondered if Cat had been right: The past belongs in the past.

As for Beck, that seemed like mostly a physical thing on my part: that hair, those eyes, that body.

I'd driven for two hours when I tried Barry, the vice cop, again. Still his voice mail. I hated to be a pest, but I couldn't put a stopper on my need to know. As I pulled off the Massachusetts Turnpike at just after three, I made one more attempt. This time he picked up.

"Sorry to be hounding you," I said. "I'm pursuing a lead, and I could really use some information. I thought you'd be able to help."

"I can try. I had a guy in custody before, so I couldn't talk."

I ran through my phone conversation with Nina, asking if he thought it sounded suspicious.

"Sounds like a prostitute definitely," he said. His voice was smooth and easy. "The fact that she said she didn't do full service—that's the sure tip-off."

"What does that mean, exactly?" I asked.

"It means that the place where she works just does manual release. A hand job, if you'll excuse the expression, and that's it."

"You mean, kind of prostitution lite?" I asked. "And men go for it?"

"Yeah, it's a whole industry," he explained. "It's called release massage. Or happy ending massage. Guys love it because they have a full body massage and then they get the happy ending as a bonus. Plus, they tell themselves they're not really going to a whore or cheating on their wives. To them, it's just an extension of a massage—stress relief taken one step further."

"Where do the women work?"

"Generally out of an apartment. I saw one situation where they used a duplex with an entrance on each floor. The upstairs one was for new clients and the downstairs one was for old so that in case one of the new clients turned out to be a cop, they could shut off access to the other women and clients."

"They work in groups?"

"A lot of them do, yeah. For security reasons."

"So the women are basically prostitutes."

He snorted. "They don't see it that way. In their minds they're just housewives or actresses or teachers trying to make some extra money. But it still comes down to providing sexual gratification for a fee."

"Are any of them actual massage therapists?"

"Sure, some of them are."

My mind was in overdrive, and though I could sense he was anxious to hang up, I didn't want to let him go.

"Just one more question," I said. "Have you ever heard of a legitimate massage place doing this?"

"Oh yeah," he said. "In fact, we busted a place a year ago. It was a pretty decent day spa that was leasing space from a hotel on the West Side. Two or three girls were offering happy endings—and the management had no idea. The whole spa ended up being shut down because of it."

"If management isn't in on it," I said, "how do the girls get the word out?"

He chuckled. "It's all done real nice and subtle in

the beginning. The girl gets a little suggestive during the massage, letting her breasts touch the client, letting her hand get a little close to the action. The guy might end up suggesting the finish. And she says something like 'Well, since you're a special client . . .' From there, it's word of mouth. He tells a friend, and then the friend tells a friend. Look, I'm gonna have to wrap this up."

"Just one more question, I swear. What kind of money are we talking about? I mean, in the case of a legitimate spa, how much extra could a girl ask for?"

"For each session? A girl might ask for anywhere from fifty to a hundred dollars more—on top of her tip. That can mean hundreds more a week."

He signed off then. Which was a good thing, because I'd been so bowled over by what he'd been saying, I almost missed my last turn before the Cedar Inn.

The foliage around Warren was even more spectacular than when I'd been there on the weekend. In the two days since I'd departed, the oranges and yellows had intensified, and the reds had burst forth almost like little explosions everywhere. When I rolled down my window to check the temperature, I discovered that I was driving through one of those clear, crisp fall days that fill you with an urge to put on a pair of tartan shorts and head for a football game.

Yet it was hard to appreciate the autumnal splendor. I was too busy working over what Barry had revealed. Release massage. Happy endings. This *must* be what had been going on at the Cedar Inn and Spa. This was the reason they didn't like it when Danny popped over there. The massage therapists who were in on it (Anna and Piper, most likely, but maybe others) pulled in hundreds of extra dollars each week for their efforts. If Josh was involved—and based on Danny's description of his defensive behavior, I suspected he might be—he was probably benefiting in a big way, too. He most likely received a kickback for each client, but since he also earned a bonus from Danny on overall profits, he got a double hit. Now I knew why the spa business had exploded in the last year or so.

And this could shed new light on William Litchauer's death. He'd been a regular client, and he may have requested the special finish at his weekly appointments. And maybe one night it was all too much for his impaired ticker, and he'd ended up with the biggest special finish of all. It could be that he'd even died on the massage table and been moved—though wouldn't that have turned up in the ME's report?

The next question was whether all this nasty business had led to Anna's death. Maybe she'd been murdered by a freaky client. Or if Josh *was* involved, maybe he'd killed her over a dispute regarding the business.

I was in the midst of thinking bad thoughts about Josh when I nearly bumped smack into him—as I stepped out of my Jeep in the inn parking lot. The look on his pale, handsome face indicated he was totally surprised to see me—and not overjoyed.

"Hello, Josh," I said.

"I thought you'd gone back to New York," he said icily. He was wearing slim black slacks today and a black leather jacket. Very L.A. for the Berkshires.

"I did. But then my schedule loosened up again, so I

decided to come back and lend a hand to Danny—what with everything that's happened."

"Isn't she lucky? Are you going to stack towels in the linen closet—or just be an arm to cling to?"

"Maybe both," I said, ignoring his sarcasm. "I heard the spa is opening back up tomorrow. You must be relieved."

"Very. Now if you'll excuse me, I've got some business to take care of."

He brushed past me, his arm knocking against mine in a way that suggested it had been intentional. I felt a little trickle of fear. Was *he* the sender of the mouse? I wondered. Had he suspected I was investigating the spa and decided to warn me away from Warren? He certainly wouldn't be happy to have me back. I watched him climb into a silver Saab convertible and drive off.

The lobby was deserted, except for Natalie puttering at the front desk and the faint strains of something Chopin-like being piped from a nearby speaker. Someone had obviously put on a CD to add life to the place, but it was a sad, mournful piece that made the lobby even more forlorn.

Natalie informed me that I'd find Danny in the gardens. I left my bag and cooler behind the desk and headed for the garden, where Danny, dressed in a lavender wool poncho, strolled with her head down. We hugged, and as I pulled away, I saw that her gray eyes were troubled.

"So give me the latest," I said, taking her small, slender arm. We started to stroll slowly along the path.

"There's not much new to report," Danny said.

"Which is awful in its own way because you keep anticipating the worst. We found a criminal lawyer to switch over to. George is meeting with him today."

"How's George handling all of this?"

"He's—I . . ."

"What?"

"He's been acting strange to me ever since this happened."

"In what sense? *Guilty?*"

"No," she said, shaking her head. "But on the edge of his seat, wired. I can't tell if it's because he's got something to hide or because he's just so anxious about everything that's happened."

"Have you ever suspected him of being unfaithful?" I felt awful asking it, but it was a question that couldn't be ignored.

"No," she said almost curtly—in fact, practically before I had the words out of my mouth.

"Well, then he's probably just upset about being interrogated by the police," I said. "Hopefully they'll drop it since they don't seem to have much to go on."

I told Danny that there were a few things I needed her help with. First I wanted access to the computer files on which she kept a record of regular clients and their appointments. She gave no indication that she thought there was anything odd about the request. I said that I wanted her to give me a private tour of the spa as soon as it was reopened. And since I wanted to spend more time with Eric, I needed her to arrange for me to interview him as part of my "spa research."

"I also want to talk to Piper again, but I'll just pop in on her. I'd rather catch her off guard."

"You'd better do it soon. She resigned. And she's planning to be gone by this weekend."

"Interesting," I said—and I meant it. Piper might be simply wigged out by the murder, but in light of what I now knew about the spa, she might be scared for her life.

"What about Anna's sister?" I asked. "Is she here yet?"

"She arrived late this morning. She went through Anna's things and arranged for her body to be flown back to Florida. Now she's in town talking to the police. But she's coming back here shortly for us to discuss what to do with the things of Anna's she doesn't want."

"I'd really like to join you when you talk to her," I said. "Eve told me that Anna was disturbed by something in her past, and I'd like to see if her sister knows something about it. You can just say I'm a colleague. Is she staying at the inn?"

"No, she said she couldn't bear to. She's driving back to Albany tonight and will fly out of there in the morning."

We had reached the far end of the garden, near what appeared to be a large area for herbs. The only one I recognized was basil. There was row after row of it, but the leaves were shaggy and bruised from the colder weather.

We circled around, back in the direction we came. It was then that I told Danny about the mouse. She stopped in her tracks and gaped in horror.

"That's perfectly dreadful," she said. "And how scary for you."

"Do you have traps at the inn? I'm wondering where the sender could have gotten a dead mouse."

"Yes, we have traps set up in the basement. This is the time of year the mice start to come indoors."

"Could you ask your janitor if he's missing a trap?"

"Of course. Is this why you asked me yesterday if I'd sent you a package?"

I explained that her address had been on the package and asked if she had any thoughts on why someone would use it. All she could think of is what had occurred to me: that it was to guarantee that I would open it.

The sun was now low in the sky, and we quickened our pace. Ten minutes later I was ensconced in Danny's office in front of her computer.

It was all very simple, just as Danny had said it was the other day. The computer listed each of the spa's therapists with the name of every client they'd ever had—including the types of treatments they'd booked and the dates on which they'd had them. Danny pointed out the symbol that indicated which clients were guests of the inn rather than just visitors to the day spa. All of this information was available from the flip side, too—clients were listed in alphabetical order, and you could click to view the dates on which a person had had appointments and the therapist who'd performed each service.

I was glad Danny had decided not to sit in the office with me. Ever since I'd been in her presence at the inn, I'd felt guilty and awkward about withholding what I'd learned regarding Anna's background. It was one of those secrets that kept threatening to leap Linda Blair style from my mouth, and I was fearful that at some moment when I intended to make a benign comment like "Just lean on me, Danny," I'd end up blurting out, "Your spa is really a whorehouse!"

I scrolled down to Anna's name on the list and examined her record. Last year at this time, just after she'd started, she'd had a wide variety of clients and most of them were inn guests. Since she was new, she was obviously given clients who didn't request a particular therapist by name, which of course most inn guests wouldn't do. But as the months went by, not only had her business picked up in volume, but she had quickly developed a loyal band of day spa clients—almost all male. In the last seven months, she'd had at least eight or nine male clients with weekly appointments, a couple of semiregular female clients, and a hodgepodge of inn guests. In late July, she'd given a massage to the tennis pro, Rich, apparently part of the barter arrangement that Danny had mentioned to me.

Next I checked out Piper's track record. Her male fan club seemed to be about as big as Anna's. One by one, I went through the rest of the therapists—males as well as females. Four or five of them, including Cordelia, did appear to have fairly strong followings, but no one had as many regular appointments as Piper or Anna, and none of the women therapists had as many male clients as they did. Except for one—Lauren, the therapist who'd reportedly moved to Hawaii. Her last client had been on August 17.

It wasn't a big leap to conclude that three, then two, therapists had been offering relief massage at the Cedar Inn. According to the information Barry had shared with me, they probably had been pulling in as much as eight or nine hundred extra dollars a week—some of which would have gone to Josh if he was involved.

I wondered suddenly what had happened when Lauren had moved to Hawaii. Had Anna and Piper absorbed her clients? I scrolled down the list of clients under Lauren's name and on a scrap of paper jotted down the names of men with regular weekly appointments. Then I went to their names in the client file. A few of them had continued to visit the spa sporadically since mid-August, but going to a variety of therapists—not just Anna and Piper. The others had stopped coming altogether.

Just then Danny appeared in the doorway, announcing that the inn manager had phoned to say he was on his way back with Anna's sister.

"I thought I'd meet with her in the solarium," Danny said. "Why don't you join us there in a couple of minutes. Oh, and by the way, I arranged for you to have a massage with Eric tomorrow at eleven, and he knows you want to talk to him afterward. I told him you'd want to discuss the treatment."

I closed down the files I'd been working on, used the rest room off the lobby, and then found my way to the solarium. Danny was sitting on the couch, and Anna's sister had taken one of the black wicker armchairs. On the coffee table was a small tray with a plate of short-bread cookies, cups, and a silver pot. Though Danny rose to greet me, Anna's sister sat motionless in the chair.

"Connie Green, this is one of my, uh, colleagues, Bailey Weggins," Danny announced. "She's helping me right now—through all of this." Danny had lied badly, but Connie didn't seem to care that I was there. She leaned forward slightly in her chair and shook my hand limply.

She wasn't at all what I had expected. She appeared to be at least ten years older than Anna and on the heavy side. Her thick dark hair, streaked with gray, was tied back with a black ribbon. She was wearing a plain rayony blue suit, more appropriate for Florida weather than here, over a white blouse, and her shoes were the kind of comfy pumps that are supposed to energize your feet as you wear them. As for the grief factor, she had deep circles under her eyes, though she looked more dazed than distraught.

"I'm so sorry for your loss," I said, joining Danny on the sofa. I noticed that coffee had been poured into two cups, but neither Danny nor Connie appeared to be drinking it. "Is Green your married name?"

"Yes. My maiden name's Gianelli."

"So Anna . . . ?"

"Was married once. Just for a few years. But she kept that name. She always hated the Italian."

"Connie was just telling me about her visit with the police," Danny said, interjecting. "It was very trying."

"You met with Detective Beck?" I asked.

"No, with another man," she said somberly. "But his name came up. Apparently he wasn't available."

Where was he? I wondered.

"Did the police give you any sense of how the investigation is going?" I asked. I doubted they would have told her much, but they might have indicated whether an arrest was imminent.

"They say they're working very hard on it, but they

don't seem to know anything," Connie said. She shook her head in frustration and despair. "I should have known something like this might happen."

"What do you mean?" I asked, surprised. "Had someone threatened Anna?"

"Not threatened," she said, locking eyes with me for the first time. They were almost black, just like Anna's had been. "But like I told the police, several months ago Anna said she thought she was being watched."

"Watched?" Danny exclaimed, straightening in her seat. "This is the first I've ever heard of this."

"She got the feeling someone was looking in her window at night," Connie said. "And once she had the sensation someone was following her car."

"When did this happen?" Danny asked. "And I wonder why she didn't tell us about it."

"This past summer—in July, I think." Connie massaged her forehead with her fingers as if she had the headache from hell. "I told her back then that she should contact the police, but Anna didn't like to be told what to do. It only lasted a few days, and once it stopped, she just dismissed the whole thing."

I flashed immediately on Matt Litchauer. It was the time his father had died at the spa. He would have learned that Anna was his father's massage therapist and he may have tried to check her out.

"You and Anna kept in touch regularly?" I asked.

Connie shook her head, her face pinched. "We never used to," she said. "I'm much older than Anna, and we weren't close growing up. But we had started to talk a bit more after our mother died last year."

The sun had set since we'd been in the room, and it

had grown dark quickly. Danny stood and walked around the room, switching on lamps. The light was cast downward, and it made the circles under Connie's eyes even deeper.

"Do you know if Anna was dating anyone new?" I asked, hoping I wasn't making her too uncomfortable with my questions.

"Not that I know of," she said, sighing. "There was someone a while back—from the spa. That was over, though."

"Does the name Rich Wyler ring a bell?" I pressed. "He's the tennis pro here, and there was some talk she might have been dating him."

"No, it's not a name I've heard before."

"And what about Anna's husband?" I asked. "Was there any resentment on his part? Is there any chance he could be responsible for this?"

"I can't imagine that. He was someone she met years ago—in her last year of high school. I doubt she'd talked to him in years. No, it's got to be some kind of monster."

Connie lowered her face, holding her head with her fingertips. She was losing focus, and I knew I wouldn't have much more time with her.

"Where did you and Anna grow up?" I asked.

She lifted her face, hesitating a second before answering. "Wallingford. Wallingford, Connecticut."

"Goodness," Danny said, "that's just a few hours from here."

"Anything from that period worth noting?" I asked. "I mean, is there anything significant in Anna's past that could have caught up with her?" Her hesitation had reminded me of what Eve had said about old pain, buried deep.

"No, there's nothing in her past worth mentioning," Connie said. She rolled her lips in and pressed them tightly together.

I knew she was lying.

CHAPTER 15

BUT THERE WAS nothing I could do about it. Her sister was dead, and it would be wrong to prod Connie or challenge her or beg her to tell me what she knew. Instead, I was going to have to uncover the truth on my own.

Connie glanced at her watch and looked startled by the time—or maybe it was just a ruse to force the conversation away from where I'd dragged it. She announced that she wanted to be on her way back to Albany. She was exhausted, and she had an early plane to catch tomorrow.

She rose to leave, and Danny said she would accompany her to the front of the inn in order to make certain the driver was ready. I hung behind, shooting Danny a look that indicated I would catch up with her later.

For the next few minutes, I sat alone on the couch in the solarium, staring out the windows into the darkness and yet seeing nothing in the glass but myself staring back. With time to reflect, I was certain that Connie had information she wasn't willing to divulge. I'd read enough articles on body language and conducted enough interviews to know that when people lie, they often touch their mouth with their hand as they're speaking or pinch it shut afterward—it's as if their subconscious is trying to prevent them from prevaricating anymore. Of course, Connie didn't owe me anything, but if there *was* a traumatic incident in Anna's past, it might have played a role in her death—and I needed to know what it was.

One of the problems with this case, I realized, was that there were so many possible areas the murderer could have come from. I had Anna's love life to consider, as well as her sideline business, and then there was her past, which might hold some ugly secret. Tomorrow morning, first thing, I would pay a visit to Piper to learn what I could about the most recent days and nights of Anna Cole. As for Anna's past, it looked as though I might have to do a road trip to Wallingford— and see what was buried there.

After ten minutes of pondering in total solitude, I made my way back toward the front of the inn, down several long, dark corridors. I passed no one except a frowning chambermaid hugging the walls. In the lobby, I discovered the front door open, and Danny, wearing her poncho, stood outside on the top step, holding a set of car keys and peering into the cool autumn night.

"She's gone?" I asked, joining her.

"Yes, she just drove off."

I glanced back inside the inn to make sure no one

was within earshot. Natalie was at the desk but appeared engrossed in a phone conversation.

"The story she told us about Anna thinking she was being watched—you'd never heard anything about that?"

"No, not a word."

"I wonder if it could have been that brutish Matt Litchauer," I said. "He may have been checking her out after he'd heard she was the one who'd massaged his father the night he died. I'm glad to hear she told the police. This may take their mind off George."

"Dear, I hope so. Speaking of which, I need to get back to the house. I want to be there to hear how George's visit with the lawyer went. I hate to abandon you like this, Bailey. If it were any other time, I'd invite you to dinner. You haven't even seen my home yet."

"Don't worry," I told her. "I'll grab dinner in the dining room."

"Well, that's part of the reason I feel so guilty," she said. "It's not open for dinner during the week. I could have the kitchen make you something and send it to your room."

"I actually wouldn't mind going out for dinner. Is there any place around? Other than the Bridge Street Tavern, that is?"

She named two decent restaurants on Route 11, the road off the turnpike. She said she'd be coming back to the inn later and to leave a message if I needed anything. Lowering her voice, she confided that in addition to guest cancellations, several people who worked at the inn had resigned and they were slightly short staffed.

Since there was no bellboy in sight, I picked up my

bag and cooler from behind the front desk, took my room key, and headed upstairs. I was in the same suite I'd been in over the weekend, though as I trudged up the front stairway, everything about the inn felt different. It had been bustling with guests on the weekend, but now the halls were deserted. And while the old rooms had looked so charming several nights ago, they now seemed somber, almost spooky.

I knew I would have to watch my back over the next few days. The mouse I was hauling in my cooler like a ham-and-cheese hero had been a warning. I didn't know if it had to do with the murder or the dirty dealings at the spa or both. But its message was clear: stay away. With so few people around the inn, and so little activity, I needed to be very cautious.

The second-floor corridor was empty, and I looked up and down it as I unlocked my door. I switched on one light so I could see and then put both the dead bolt and the chain on the door. My stomach was growling, but I took a few minutes to unpack my bag and, feeling grungy from the long car ride, indulge in a quick shower. The soap of the day was citrus spice. As I lathered my body with it, I could smell orange and clove and what might be anise. For a moment I imagined being in a place far away, somewhere exotic and warm, and standing on a terrace lit with strands of lantern lights.

After throwing on black pants, a white T-shirt, and my black cashmere V-neck, I hurried downstairs, my jeans jacket over my shoulder. I knew I needed to skedaddle, because in a town this size they liked to serve their last Salisbury steak no later than nine. I said good night to Natalie and stepped outside onto the stoop, pausing while my eyes adjusted to the darkness. As I stood there, a black car pulled up right in front of the inn. Two seconds later, Detective Beck stepped out of the far side, zipping up his brown suede jacket. My heart jerked. It was as if I had conjured him up again, just as I had that day in the woods.

He didn't bother to disguise his surprise when he saw me.

"You didn't leave?" he asked bluntly.

"I did, sort of," I said, my heart at a canter, "but then Danny told me about George. She asked me to spend a few more days here." I climbed down the steps until I was standing near him in the driveway.

"Is Mrs. Hubner here now?" he asked.

"She's gone home. Why? What's going on?"

"She'd had some questions earlier in the week about security measures for when the spa reopened. I thought I'd stop by after work and discuss it with her. And where do you think you're going at this hour?"

"I'm in search of an Italian restaurant on Route 11. Leo's, I believe it's called."

"You're going alone?"

"Yes. Is that against the law in Warren?"

"No, but it might be a first at Leo's," he said, smirking. "Why don't I escort you there? It'll keep you out of trouble. Here, get in."

He opened the passenger door, clearly not expecting me to decline. What did this all mean, exactly? Was he actually going to sit there and have a meal with me? Did he want to pump me for information about Danny and George? Or had I piqued his interest as he had mine?

"I don't bite," he said as I hesitated for a second.

"Okay, fine," I said. "But I've got something I need to show you. Can you wait a minute?"

I raced back upstairs to my room to retrieve the cooler. On the way back down again, I passed a couple in their thirties on the stairs, and I felt relieved to know that the inn clearly wasn't at zero percent occupancy.

Beck was already back in the car, but he pushed open the passenger door for me again. His car smelled of leather and coffee.

"You're taking me on a picnic?" he asked as he eyed the cooler.

"No. And there's not a donor kidney in here, either."

I took a breath and slowly explained about the package. I told him I'd handled it with a tissue and had been as careful as possible. There was a chance that he'd be miffed—because if someone had sent me a warning, it indicated that I'd been poking my nose into things I shouldn't have. But the look on Beck's face registered mostly surprise.

"Was there a note?" he asked.

"No, nothing."

"Who do you think sent it to you—and why?"

Careful, Bailey, I told myself.

"Well, I found the body. Maybe the murderer sent this. Maybe he thinks I saw something or know something and he wanted to threaten me."

He thought for a second, giving nothing away by his expression.

"I want to drop this off at the station before we have dinner," he said. "There's a very good chance it *was* from the murderer. And you, miss, need to be very careful."

"How fortunate, then, that I have a police escort for the night."

He looked mildly bemused by my comment. I knew, of course, that the mouse *might* be from the murderer, but there was another possibility, one that I couldn't share with him. The mouse might be a warning from someone involved in release massage at the spa.

I fastened my seat belt and noticed that Beck didn't bother with his. Maybe that was why I liked him. Even though he was a cop, I suspected he had a renegade side—and I'd always been a sucker for that. With my infatuation for Jack, I'd hoped I'd finally burned off the last of my bad boy fascination, but maybe I really hadn't.

Beck had no apparent interest in making small talk during the ride, and that was okay with me. My wise-ass comments were going to be boring even me before long, but I wasn't sure how else to play it. Shutting up seemed to be the best strategy. We rode in silence, with me glancing from time to time surreptitiously in his direction. It was hard to see much in the green glow from the dashboard.

The stop at the station took about fifteen minutes. He left me in the car with the heat running and the radio on. I started to relax a bit, to feel less nervous about the notion of being with him. The minute he slid back into the car, however, my heart took off at a reckless gallop again.

Leo's turned out to be one of those old-style Italian places with red-and-white-checked tablecloths and a poorly painted mural of Venice on the wall. It was half-filled with diners, though most of them seemed to be in the final stages of their meals. The owner greeted Beck with a nod of recognition and led us to a table at the far back, with empty tables on either side.

I ordered a glass of Chianti, and Beck did as well. He was off duty, he'd said. I guessed he must have still been wearing his holster and gun, however, because he hadn't taken off his suede jacket.

"Do you come here a lot?" I asked, switching from cocky comebacks to hackneyed clichés.

"From time to time," he said. "The food is decent. And it's close. So what's the deal with you and Mrs. Hubner? I thought you were only doing some kind of work project for her?"

"Well, I am. But we're also old family friends—she and my mother go way back. I thought I could be someone for her to lean on this week. And besides, I needed to be sure you saw the mouse."

He gazed at me with his deep blue eyes slightly squinted, as if he were calculating how much truth there was to what I said.

"She's lucky to have you as a friend," he said. His face was inscrutable.

"I've been lucky to know *her,*" I said. "I have to say, I was pretty shocked to hear that you'd been questioning George. What would his motive be?"

I knew he wouldn't offer anything up, but I was interested in seeing how he'd go about shutting me down.

"You know I can't discuss the case with you."

"So you brought me here just for the pleasure of my company, then?"

"Like I told you, I wanted to keep you out of trouble," he said with half a smile. "That's my job." He took a long sip of his wine, watching me all the time over the rim of his glass.

"All right, fine, I won't try to discuss the case with you. There's just one thing I think is important for me to mention. William Litchauer's son, Matt? I had the unfortunate experience of meeting him, and he's a very angry man. Anna's sister told Danny and me that Anna thought she was being followed last summer, right around the time Litchauer's father died at the spa. Shouldn't he be considered a suspect? Maybe he wanted to avenge his father's death."

Beck's eyebrows had risen a millimeter as I spoke, and I was sure I was about to get a lecture on the value of minding my own business. But I didn't.

"I'll tell you what," he said, straightening his knife on the table. "Since you've been so nice to do some thinking on behalf of the police department, I'm going to share one fact about the case with you. And then we're going to order dinner and not talk about it anymore. Mr. Litchauer has a rock-solid alibi. He was in his bar that night and never left the premises according to the twenty people we interviewed."

I wanted to press for more details, but Beck had said all he was going to—and I didn't want to annoy him.

The waiter returned, and without having glanced at the menu, Beck asked for a veal chop. I ordered the chicken with white wine and mushrooms.

"How come you're able to get away from your job so easily?" Beck asked, pushing his chair back from the table as if the space constricted him.

"I'm a freelancer," I said. "I write for a bunch of different places, and I do most of it out of my apartment. One magazine has me under contract for six or so articles a year, and I have a tiny office there. But I can come and go as I please."

He asked about the types of articles I did, and I described a few stories I'd worked on, intentionally picking some human-interest ones. Beck wasn't stupid. He knew I wrote crime stories and that I was intrigued with Anna's death. But if I rattled on about my crime pieces, he might begin to suspect just how much I liked detective work—and the real reason I'd come back to the Cedar Inn.

"What about you?" I asked. "How did you end up becoming a cop? You're not from one of those cop families, are you?"

"No," he said with a wry smile. "My father, believe it or not, is a retired banker. My parents were horrified when I decided to do this."

"Where are you from?"

"Chicago."

"Right in the city?"

"Suburbs, actually."

"So then how did a banker's son go into law enforcement?" I asked.

"I had planned to go to law school after college and become a trial lawyer, but I spent a summer as an intern in a law firm and I hated it. I started questioning what had made me want to go down that road to begin with. And I realized that it was law enforcement that fascinated me."

He'd been to college and considered law school. My assessment of him required some revision.

"So how did you end up in this area?" I asked.

"I'd spent some vacation time in the Berkshires. The town's a decent size. Not so quiet that the only thing you ever do on Saturday night is throw guys in the drunk tank. But on the other hand, you're not dealing with crackheads and gang shootings. Plus, there's an interesting mix of people. You've got the locals with their basic issues, but also the tourists. They're always full of surprises."

"Are you including me in that mix?"

"I guess I'd say you're a tourist. And you are definitely full of surprises."

"So are you."

"Is that right? How so?"

"For one thing, you live alone. I would expect a guy like you to be married by now."

"A guy like me?" he asked.

"Successful, attractive."

"I could say the same about you."

"I was married once. It was a disaster. Have you ever tried it—marriage, I mean?"

"No, never. I'd like to, I think. Someday. I just haven't been ready."

So he was gun-shy, like me. An image of Jack came unbidden to my mind, accompanied by a side order of guilt. I pushed it away. After all, it wasn't as if I was out on a date with Beck.

Our dinner came and Beck ordered a second glass of wine. I didn't because I already felt a buzz from nerves. I sensed that he didn't want to linger on the personal stuff, so while we ate I asked him what kinds of murder cases turned up in this area. And though he flashed me a look that seemed to say, Don't even *think* about luring me back to a discussion of Anna Cole's murder, he described several cases he'd overseen, including one in which a nineteen-year-old girl had chopped off her mother's head. It was clear he liked talking about his work, and for the first time since I'd met him, he seemed to relax. I listened with my head lowered just a bit because I couldn't bear to look at him straight on. It felt too intense, a little dangerous, like staring at someone on the New York City subway. Earlier I'd thought my attraction to him was just a physical thing, but tonight I could see that he was smart and intriguing.

Before our coffee came, I excused myself to go to the ladies' room. In the mirror I noticed that my face was flushed. Nothing serious, just the same degree of red you'd see on someone who'd been scorched by a blowtorch or was in the throes of scarlet fever. Though how I felt was obvious, what *wasn't* clear was where this was headed. There was a chance that he'd taken me out tonight just to figure out what my agenda was. Yet never once in the evening had he pumped me—about Danny or George or the case. But even if he truly was attracted to me, dating might very well be against the rules. And that might be a good thing. Not only was I supposedly trying to rekindle my romance with Jack (and burning a hole in the bed in the process), but there was an even bigger geography issue with Beck than with Jack. Did I really want to start something with a guy who was a three and a half hour drive away? There was the fling option, of course. Would that be so terrible?

Once I was back at the table, he allowed me two sips of my coffee before he glanced at his scuffed leather watch.

"I better get you back to the inn or they'll call the police," he said. I offered to pay half the check, but he shook his head as if I were being silly.

We drove the whole way back in silence. I felt nervous suddenly, as if I were a high school sophomore on my first date with someone.

"I'll wait till you get inside," he said as we pulled up in front of the inn.

"Thanks," I said. "And thanks for dinner."

"See," he said. "I don't bite."

"That's too bad." God, one glass of wine and I'd thrown all caution to the wind.

He leaned over, reached behind the back of my neck with his hand, and pulled me toward him, kissing me hard on the mouth. I could taste the wine on his breath. His tongue found its way into my mouth for just a second, and then he pulled away.

"Good night," he said, his voice deeper than usual.

I said nothing, just looked briefly into his eyes and slid out of the car. He had said he'd wait to leave until I was safely inside, and it wasn't until I shut the door that I heard him gun the engine and take off. The older dude was at the reception desk, talking on the telephone. Otherwise the place was empty. I raced up the stairs two at a time, my key already in my hand, and hurried down the hall to my suite. The floor made a creaking sound and I turned quickly to check behind me, but there was nothing there.

Once I was in my room, I slammed the door behind

me, bolted it, and leaned against it, breathless. I felt like someone who had just shoplifted a pair of diamond stud earrings: guilty and deliriously giddy at the same time.

Giddy because I had liked that kiss, reckless as it had seemed. And guilty because of Jack. I'd offered to give things a go with him, thrashed around in the sack with him, promised to see him Saturday night, and now I was considering a fling with Beck. Yet at this point I hardly owed Jack my fidelity. He'd bolted this summer, and as far as I knew, he could do it again.

I kicked off my shoes, stripped off my clothes, and padded across the room in my underwear to get a nightshirt from my bag. Earlier I'd unpacked just the stuff that could wrinkle. My hand stopped as it reached for the nightshirt. The three pairs of socks that I had last seen balled together at the edge of the bag were now scattered apart. My mind raced replaying the moments when I'd dressed for dinner earlier. I was positive they'd been in one particular location, because I remembered noting that I hadn't brought my warm ones. Someone had searched through my things.

CHAPTER 16

I SWUNG MY head around toward the bed to see if the chambermaid had turned down my sheets. No. Taking a deep breath, I searched through my bag to see if anything was missing. There wasn't. Next I checked the closet. Everything looked normal, though the flap on a jacket pocket was oddly askew and I didn't think it had been that way before. As rattled as I felt, I was relieved I'd stuck my composition book in my purse before going out.

Sitting on the edge of the bed, I thought back to when I'd retrieved the cooler from my suite. I'd been in a hurry, anxious to be back with Beck, but I'd made sure the door had closed firmly behind me. I was watching my back, after all. That meant the snoop must have had access to room keys. Josh sprang to mind. He could have laid his hands on keys easily. So could Eric. And George. In fact, anyone who worked at the inn probably could have. The one person on my suspect list who wouldn't have had entry was Matt Litchauer, who was looking less and less like a valid suspect.

I dragged a small rattan side table in front of the door. I knew no one could get in with both the dead bolt and chain on, but I needed it for my peace of mind. Outside, the wind howled and rattled the windows. It felt more like November weather than October. I dressed for bed slowly, letting my eyes scan the room for anything else that seemed odd or out of place, but there was nothing. I turned off the lamp in the living area, but left the bathroom light on. Once in bed, I pulled the duvet cover up to my chin. I lay there forever, thinking of Beck and the kiss and the mouse and everything.

By eight the next morning I was on my way out of the inn, ready to pay Piper a visit. As I'd stared at the ceiling through the darkness the night before, I'd worked out my strategy: 1) I needed to strike early before she had a chance to leave her room and disappear into the day; 2) I had to convince her that if she told me the truth, I wouldn't betray her confidence.

It was freezing outside, and a light puff of smoke appeared each time I exhaled. The dead-headed flowers in the garden were covered with a film of crystallized frost. Had it been this chilly when I'd been with Beck last night? I had no recollection. I'd been in such an infatuated stupor, my body had been immune to cold.

As I circled the back side of the building, my eye caught the silhouette of a man walking quickly toward the rear door of the inn, his hands stuffed into his tan jacket pockets. It took me a second to realize it was George.

He stopped abruptly when he saw me, started to lift his hand in a wave, and instead hurried across the grass in my direction. As he strode closer to me, I could see that he looked drawn and pale, as if he'd just slept off a three-day bender. But his fake black hair gleamed brightly in the hard sunlight.

"Good morning," he said, pulling his hand from his pocket to shake mine. It was sweaty again, despite the chill in the air. "Danny told me you'd come back to help her."

"Yes, I came back as soon as I could. This must be a very tough time for you."

"The police have this all wrong, you know—though I shouldn't be talking about it. My lawyer *insists* that I not say word one about it." His eyes, magnified by the lenses in his glasses, were doing a little jig as he talked, like two butterflies attempting to mate.

"I can understand that," I said.

"You can also probably imagine what a strain this is putting on Danny and me," he said.

Strain was not a word Danny had used.

"I got the feeling Danny was being very supportive," I said.

"Of course, Danny's always—I—I'm not sure what you know, but Danny and I have had our ups and downs. There was one very poor indiscretion on my part. But I assured Danny it would never happen again, and I'm a man of my word. You have to help convince her of that. I've done nothing wrong."

I was flabbergasted by his revelation but fought not to show it.

"That's really not my role, George."

"You can't find it in you to help me?" he asked almost frantically, grabbing my arm. "Danny trusts you."

"You need to talk to her yourself about this."

"*When?* She's avoiding me."

A door slammed in the direction of the outbuildings and George whipped his head around, looking for the source. His hand was still gripping my arm, and I tugged it away.

"You don't like me, do you," he said. "It's like you're jealous of me, because I'm closer to Danny than you are."

Before I could answer, he hurried off toward the back entrance of the inn and, using a key, let himself in.

I was so discombobulated that I stood for a few moments on the path, rolling over in my mind what had just happened. His agitation, his comment about my being jealous—he seemed like a guy who was about to lose it. And then there was his confession. When guys of his generation used the word *indiscretion,* it didn't mean they'd divulged their salary to a colleague or broken a confidence. It meant they'd been humping some honey who wasn't their wife.

I started up the path again and made my way to the barn. It looked as deadly quiet in there as it did in the inn these days. In the vestibule, I found Piper's name next to one of the buzzers on the panel and pressed. I waited. Nothing. I tried again. This time a sleepy, sullen voice asked, "What is it?"

"Piper, it's Bailey Weggins. I need to talk to you. It's pretty important."

"It can't wait? I'm not even dressed yet."

"No, it can't wait."

The buzzer that released the door sounded as annoyed as she had. I realized as I walked through into the ground floor that I had no idea where her room was, though I remembered that last weekend I'd seen her coming down the flight of stairs. I climbed the stairs and discovered five doors along the corridor on the second floor. I'd stood there stupidly for a minute before she quietly opened one of the doors, wearing a red kimono.

Her room was slightly larger than a dorm room, with a single bed, dresser, small table and chair, sink, hot plate, and compact fridge. On nearly every foot of the floor were messy piles of clothes with wire hangers poking out of them and scattered books and papers. Two empty duffel bags gaped open on the bed, indicating that the packing process was soon to begin.

"I take it this has something to do with Anna," Piper said without even so much as a good morning to me.

"Yes, it does," I said. "I'm sorry to disturb you so early, but it's urgent."

Before I could say another word, she crossed to the table and hit the button on a blender, pulverizing what appeared to be a fruit, yogurt, and ice. When she'd finished she poured the pink contents into a glass and took a large swallow.

"Well, what is it?" she asked, licking the foam from the drink off the top of her lip.

"I figured out what was going on at the spa," I said.

"Excuse me?"

I could tell from her insolent tone that she didn't suspect what was coming next.

"I said I figured out what you were doing at the

spa—you and Anna and the other therapist, the one who apparently left in search of the world's biggest wave."

Now I had her attention.

"I have no idea what—"

"I'm talking about the release massage. I know you've been doing it here. But I also have no intention of reporting this to the police."

"No?" she said, looking half-angry, half-freaked. "Why not?"

"Because it could destroy everything for Danny if the police came in here and busted everyone. And I don't even want *Danny* to know—at least right now. What I want to do is help Danny and figure out who killed Anna. I'm wondering if one of Anna's *special* clients might have done it."

She sighed and pressed in the sides of her temples with her palms as if trying to relieve pressure on her brain.

"I don't think it was anyone like that," she said, releasing her hands and plopping onto the bed.

"Why not?"

"Because there was never any sign of trouble. Nothing seemed odd. There were no weird guys."

"Did Anna have any brand-new clients recently?" I asked.

"No. She hadn't taken anyone new in weeks."

"What about Josh? Were there any problems with him lately? He wasn't demanding a bigger cut and she resisted or anything like that?"

She looked startled, but I wasn't sure why.

"*Was* there a problem with Josh?" I urged.

"Josh wasn't in on this," she said.

"Josh didn't *know?*" I exclaimed.

"Oh, he knows *now,*" she said with an ugly smile. "He found out about two months ago. And needless to say, he's been in a rage over it."

"I'm finding this very hard to believe," I said. "How could Josh not have been in on it—or at the least not known it was going on?"

Piper rose from the bed and picked her way through the piles of junk on the floor toward the table, refilling her glass with the sluggish remains of her smoothie. She took a sip and, uninterested, set the glass back on the table.

"Josh has been preoccupied this year," she said. "He's been in a tizzy about getting a line of Cedar Inn and Spa products developed, and he's in and out all the time. Besides, it's not like this has been going on forever."

"When did it start up?"

"Look, how do I know I can trust you?"

"Because if I were going to tell the police, they'd be here talking to you right now instead of me."

"Okay, it started after Anna came," she said wearily. "She'd done it before and suggested it as a way to make extra money. I'd met her when I was living in New Jersey and doing some freelance work in Manhattan. At first I thought it was a bad idea to get started up here with it, but we get paid next to nothing. Besides, what's the real harm in it? In some foreign countries it's standard to do this as part of a massage."

"Weren't you ever afraid of getting caught?"

"Well, Anna certainly wasn't," she said with a smirk. "She seemed to enjoy life most when she was living on the edge of it. *I* worried about it—sometimes. But we were discreet. It was just the three of us. And we kept our business small."

"How did Josh find out, then?"

"He started going through the records this past summer—looking at what clients went to what therapists and when. He put two and two together."

"Was this after William Litchauer died?"

She hesitated, sweeping her fingers through her thick red hair. "Yeah," she said finally, sitting on the straight-backed chair next to the table. "Anna had given that lard-ass his massage. After he died and the police started snooping around, she got jittery. Josh could smell something fishy. When he went through the records and saw how many regular male clients she had, it all finally came together for him."

So to speak, I was tempted to say.

"What *about* Litchauer?" I asked. "Was he here for release massage?"

"Yes—but he wasn't even in the massage room when he had the heart attack. He was in the men's locker room. The guy was a walking time bomb, and if he hadn't died there, he would have died the next day mowing his lawn."

"Get back to Josh, then," I told her. "You said he was in a rage when he found out."

"Yeah, that's a word that sums it up nicely. Don't get me wrong—there was no *moral* outrage on his part. I've got the feeling Josh has spent his fair share of time on the dark side."

"But you'd put his business in potential jeopardy,

and that's what angered him so much," I said, urging her on.

"Bingo. Though he'd been happy as a clam when the bucks were rolling in and he could buy his new convertible."

"I can guess why he didn't go to the police. But why didn't he just fire the three of you?"

"That would have drawn too much attention," she said. "Everyone at the inn would have been curious about why all three of us were out on our asses or were suddenly quitting. And even if Josh made up some decent-sounding story, Danny might have started snooping."

"Did he just tell you to cool it?" I was leading the witness too much, but I was impatient about the pace she was moving at.

"No, he came up with a plan he called gradual withdrawal—which is kind of cute, all things considered," she added sarcastically. "We were each going to hand in our resignations a few months apart. He said that if we left any sooner, he'd report us to the police."

"And Lauren was first? That's why she moved to Hawaii?"

"Yes. Anna was supposed to go later this month, and me in December. Though a couple of weeks ago she'd asked if I could switch with her. She said she needed more time to try to find another gig."

"Do you think there's any chance Josh killed Anna?"

"That's the main reason I'm blabbing to you about all of this. If something happens to me in the next forty-eight hours, you can tell them about this whole Josh business. I've been scared to death of him ever since

Anna died. But then when I think about it, I can't figure out the reason he'd kill her. He'd know it would draw even *more* attention to the spa—and that's what he was trying to avoid. Unless he's some Jekyll and Hyde type. Which wouldn't surprise me in the least."

"The night of the murder, you seemed distracted when you gave me my massage. What was up with that?"

"*What?* I don't know. I've just been jittery since Josh figured it all out."

"Is there a chance anyone else knew about this?"

"No, of course not. Do you think we'd still be here if Danny knew? Cordelia told me once, about five or six months ago, that a guy had made a suggestion to her that she 'finish' the massage, and she asked me how I handled situations like that. I looked horrified and told her I would just act indignant with any dude who did that and tell him not to show his face again."

"I guess I was thinking more of Eric. He cared about Anna. What if he'd found out she was involved in something like this?"

She scrunched up her mouth on one side. "I never thought of that. I don't know. We were discreet. Unless Josh told him. They were sort of friendly."

"Why did Anna and Eric stop seeing each other?"

"Anna was never seriously interested in Eric," she said with a dismissive wave of her hand. "Like I said, she liked things edgy. She liked *men* with an edge. I think in the beginning she thought there was something exotic about Eric, because of the way he looks. But he was too much of a nice guy for her. He's kind of old-fashioned, actually."

"So he would really have freaked if he knew?" I said.

"Maybe."

"Was he still pining for her?"

"I think so. He's had a sick puppy dog look on his face for the last six weeks or so—ever since she lowered the boom. Cordelia has been trying to distract him with her mega tits, but he wisely hasn't turned his attention toward her."

"And what about the tennis pro? I heard he'd been buzzing around Anna."

"*Him?* That guy's a jerk."

"But could Anna have been dating him?"

"I doubt it. She didn't like him. He got massages as part of his barter, and I heard Anna tell the receptionist that she never wanted to work with him again."

"Did Anna ever mix business with pleasure? She never messed around with Josh, did she?" I was inclined to agree with what Eve had assessed about his sexuality, but I wasn't a hundred percent sure.

"Oh, please," she said. "I'm sure he plays for the other team—though he keeps his private life very private."

"And what about George, Danny's husband?"

"*George?* You think Anna would have dated *him?* Look, I know you only saw her when she was lying there dead, but she was a very attractive chick. She wouldn't have looked twice at him if she didn't have to. He called her a few times about some project he was working on and it drove her nuts."

"And as far as you knew, she wasn't dating anyone new?" I asked.

"I don't think so. What I told you the other day was

true. Anna and I weren't buddy-buddy. If she had some big new relationship happening, I probably would have gotten wind of it. But it's not like she'd confide intimate details to me. Look, I've got to get going. I want to be out of here by tomorrow."

"Where are you going?" I asked.

"As far away from here as possible."

She rose again, to encourage my departure. I said good-bye, and she watched sullenly as I stepped over a mound of bras and underpants and let myself out.

I walked back toward the inn slowly, a million thoughts bounding around in my brain. Piper had confirmed what I had suspected. The spa had indeed been used by some of the therapists for release massage. The mere thought of it made me cringe. But there was another revelation that had interested me almost as much: Anna had been eager to change her departure date. Maybe she'd called Josh's bluff, announcing suddenly that she wasn't leaving after all because she knew that if he reported her, he'd bring the spa down, too. And he'd killed her because of that. But as Piper had pointed out, murdering Anna would only make things worse for Josh in the long run. Or maybe her murder had nothing whatsoever to do with the release massage business. Eric had apparently still been stewing over his rejection. And there was still George to consider, of course—though nothing Piper had said made him any more of a suspect.

Regardless of who had killed Anna, sooner or later I was going to have to fess up to Danny about the spa. I should also tell the police. But that would be disastrous for Danny, and at this point there didn't seem to be any clear reason to. The murder might *not* have anything to do with the X-rated spa options. I wanted to continue my research until I had something concrete. Besides, the police were working the case, and there was every chance they'd stumble on it themselves as they went through Anna's client list.

Thinking of Danny stirred something in me. Ever since George had confessed his indiscretion on the path to the barn, my mind had been working over that information—and now a weird feeling gnawed at my stomach like a gypsy moth. It wasn't simply due to the fact that Danny's second husband, the man she'd forged a new beginning with, had been unfaithful to her fairly soon into the marriage. I felt weird because Danny hadn't been forthcoming with me. When I'd asked her yesterday if she'd ever had any reason not to trust George, she'd quickly cut me off with an emphatic no. Maybe she was just embarrassed to admit that her husband had strayed. But the bottom line was that for some reason, she'd chosen to mislead me. And I needed to know why.

CHAPTER 17

My FIRST STOP was Danny's office—but she wasn't there. The desk clerk, the guy who seemed to work early mornings, lifted his head up long enough from the morning paper to announce that he had no idea where she was.

My talk with her would have to wait. I announced that I was going to use Danny's office, and the clerk distractedly nodded his approval. The first thing I did was go on the Internet and call up a map that showed the best route to Wallingford, Connecticut, from Warren. The trip from Warren would take about two and a half hours. Not bad, but still longer than I'd hoped. I'd more or less decided that I'd go tomorrow, setting out early so that I'd be back by midafternoon.

The greater challenge would be digging up the information I needed. Anna's family was long gone from Wallingford, and there was no easy way to find out where she'd lived so I could connect with her former neighbors. There was a chance that the traumatic event in Anna's past—if there actually was one—had been covered by the local newspaper. But since I didn't know when it had occurred, researching it that way would entail spending three days looking at microfilm and ending up with a headache that throbbed more than a stereo speaker. Police records were also out. If Anna had done anything illegal back then, she'd been underage and the records would have been sealed.

The most logical place to begin, then, was the school. According to Danny, Anna had been in her late thirties, and I'd have to find someone to talk to who'd been at the school for over twenty years. And I was going to have to make my inquiry sound as innocuous as possible or I'd find myself being passed up the chain of command.

I started with a call to City Hall to inquire if there was a Catholic school in Wallingford. Anna was from an Italian family, and there was a chance she'd gone to parochial school rather than public. There was none, and I decided to bet on the fact that she hadn't taken a bus to another town. Then I called the public high school. A woman answered, friendly, but no-nonsense sounding. I figured that I'd probably reached a principal's assistant.

"Hi, my name is Bailey Weggins, and I'm with the *Connecticut Teachers Association* magazine," I said. "We're doing a story on teacher commitment and we're profiling teachers who've been with a particular school system for over twenty years. I'd love to include a teacher from your school. Is there anyone there who's been at the school for that long?"

"Oh, we've got a bunch," she said.

"Wonderful. I'm especially looking for . . . how should I say this? People who are very positive about their experience and very committed to what they do. Could you suggest anyone?"

"Could you hold for a sec?"

Damn, I thought, she was going to clear it with someone higher up, but then she was back in a second.

"I'm sorry about that—someone needed a pass. Well, Anne Haggerty, our math teacher. She's won all sorts of awards. And Don Schwenk. He's history and very articulate." She went through a roll call of names, admitting that there were a few people she wasn't sure were over twenty years or just shy of it. I jotted down all the names, along with the subjects each taught.

"How about the guidance counselor?" I asked. They tended to be easier to track down during the day because they didn't teach classes and they had offices.

"Bob? Bob Kass? Oh, yes, he's been here thirty, I believe. Do you want me to put you through to anyone?"

"Not today," I told her. I explained that I was just collecting names and that I'd call next week to set up interviews. I signed off with a big thank-you.

My treatment with Eric was in ten minutes. Before walking over to the salon, I used Danny's phone to check my voice mail in New York. There were a few return calls from feelers I'd put out for my next *Gloss* story and a message from Jack. He was looking forward to Saturday night, he said. Where could he take me for dinner that would be special? How would I feel about hopping into the sack with Jack on Saturday night now that I'd been French-kissed by the fetching Detective Beck? Was there a chance that my flirtation with Beck was my way of acting out my ambivalence toward Jack and my mistrust of him—because he'd behaved poorly? Could it even be *revenge?* Jack had a fling, and now I was going to have one, too?

The salon had a whole different feeling today. Whereas on the weekend it had been as chaotic as an airline gate when they've just announced they're awaiting the arrival of a plane part before they can begin boarding, today it was absolutely still. As far as I could tell, I was the only customer there. The person at the front desk, a woman with an Eastern European accent, checked me in and told me to change into a robe. Josh was nowhere in sight—but then no one else was, either.

I'd been sitting back in the waiting area for about ten minutes when Eric emerged and shook my hand. He led me back to the small room I'd been in before, though there weren't so many boxes against the wall. Things were obviously in the process of returning to their normal state here as the spa was readied for reopening.

"Do you know anything about Shirodhara massage?" he asked as we stood face-to-face in the pale glow of the room. There was a preternatural calmness about him that made you want to scream, "Look out for that falling boulder!" just to see how he'd react.

"*Shirodhara?*" I exclaimed. "No, I didn't even know that was what I was having."

"Danny obviously wanted to surprise you," he said with a wan smile. "It's a treatment with Indian roots.

You lie face up on the table and I give you a light massage all over, just really the front part of your body and your scalp. Then a stream of warm herbal oil is poured in the center of your forehead—on what's considered the third eye. It's very soothing."

"My *third eye?*"

"It's a window to your mind."

"Good to know. Perhaps you could explain more about it when we talk later."

When Eric massaged me, his hands were firm and certain in their movements. When he worked over my scalp, his fingers tangled in my hair, and I had to resist the urge to moan out loud. Yet as he had predicted, it wasn't a full massage, and it was over all too soon. After he adjusted the towel around me, I could hear him behind me, fiddling with some sort of equipment in that unhurried way of his. He placed another towel under my head and tilted my head back slightly. Then the stream of oil began to drip on my forehead.

It was a kind of weird sensation, almost hypnotic. After a few minutes I felt myself drifting off to sleep. I figured I would wake up either totally relaxed or fully programmed to be a presidential assassin.

I'm not sure how long I dozed for. When I came to, Eric was standing by my side announcing that I could get dressed now and that we would be meeting in the office. I put on my robe in the changing room and with a towel tried to sop some of the greasiness out of my hair. Glancing in the mirror, I saw that I looked as if I'd fallen headfirst into a vat of olive oil. When I stepped outside the room, Eric was waiting.

"That was . . . well, interesting," I said as we sat

down together in a tiny office off the reception area. He took the chair behind the desk, leaving me with the one on the other side. It was slightly discomfiting—as if I were on a job interview but decked out in only a robe.

"I'm glad you liked it," was all he said. Going out on a date with him would necessitate periodically taking his pulse.

"How many Shirodhara massages do you do here?" I asked. "Are people really interested in having them?"

He cocked his head and forced a polite smile, caught, I suspected, between the truth and the need to "sell" the spa.

"We don't do a *huge* amount of them," he admitted, "but if someone stays here for a few days and runs through most of the basic treatments, they'll try one. And it's good for us just to have them on the menu of services. It shows we offer a lot of variety."

I asked that he explain the point again, and he went through it, including some general information about Ayurveda, what he called the ancient Indian science of health and healing. His voice was as monotonous as the dripping oil had been. I supposed some people would find his placid manner relaxing, but to me it was totally disconcerting, almost unnatural—like genetically engineered food.

"So you're moving back into the spa today?" I asked when he'd finished his spiel.

"Yes, this afternoon."

"Are you dreading it?"

"What do you mean?" he asked, his face expressionless.

"Having to work in the same space where someone was killed."

He stared at me, and I felt myself shift slightly in my seat against my will.

"It's not going to be pleasant," he said finally. "But it will be good to get out of the salon."

"I know you said the other day that you hadn't been close to Anna, but you used to date her, right?"

For the first time, I saw something register in his face. I could see his mind working, measuring my words, trying to assess my motive.

"We only dated for a very brief time," he said. Back to the inscrutable face.

"Sorry to pry. I discovered her body that night, and it's been weighing on me. It's made me want to know more about her. I hear she was a . . . well, complicated person."

"Not really," he said coldly. "She was actually quite *simple* to understand—once you got to know her." They were innocuous words, but the icy tone in which he spoke them carried meaning, suggesting that what *he'd* come to understand about her wasn't very nice.

"Any theories on what might have happened that night?" I asked.

"None at all. She was standing in front of one of the treatment rooms when I left."

"Was she dating anyone else?"

"I wouldn't have any idea. Can I answer any—"

At that moment the office door was shoved open with one thrust, and I glanced up to find Cordelia standing there. Her smile for Eric morphed quickly into surprise at spotting me and then into the tiniest of frowns.

"Excuse me," she said, more to Eric than me. "I thought you were in here alone. Do you want to run down to the Anvil for lunch, Eric? Before the spa opens?"

"Thanks, but I have to take care of some things in my room."

"Just asking," she said. She reiterated her annoyance by pulling the door closed hard behind her. Piper had been right—Cordelia did seem to have the hots for Eric.

"I better be going," Eric said before I had a chance to toss out another question. "I have a brochure in the spa on Ayurveda treatments. I'll find it once we get back in there and leave it at the front desk of the inn for you."

"Thanks, I'd appreciate that," I said, rising along with him. He indicated with an outstretched hand that I should go first. Cordelia had vanished, and so had the woman who'd been working the desk.

After a survey of my room and a shower, I went down to Danny's office feeling frustrated. Eric had said nothing of significance, except that one charged comment about Anna. It had been difficult to know exactly what he was feeling, other than the fact that he'd not been president of the Anna Cole Fan Club.

Two people were leaving Danny's office as I arrived, both dressed in one of those white restaurant jackets. Neither one bothered making eye contact with me.

"Everything okay?" I asked as they headed down the corridor.

"Kitchen staff complaints," Danny said with a brave

smile. "But it's such a refreshing change from everything else that's been going on, I really don't mind."

"Any news about the mousetrap?"

There was. The head maintenance man had called just moments before to inform her that a trap actually *was* missing. He'd just assumed a mouse had gotten a leg caught and had limped off with it. I nearly gagged thinking of someone taking the dead mouse from the trap and wrapping it up to send me.

I was about to maneuver my way into a discussion about George's revelation, but before I had a chance, Danny took my arm.

"I was just about to come and find you, by the way. This would be a good time to go over to the spa. The first appointment there isn't until three, so the staff is still at the salon. Josh has been there for several hours, but he just ran out to get lunch."

"Perfect," I said. My conversation about George would have to wait.

I followed her out to reception and through the lobby, then along the corridor that ran to the side entrance of the spa, the one I had stood at the night of the murder, the same spot where I'd heard the thud. From the pocket of her mauve-colored sweater she pulled out her keys. She struggled for a moment with the lock, and as I glanced down I noticed that it was new. We stepped inside and I found myself experiencing a wave of déjà vu and then dread. This wasn't going to be any fun at all.

"I need you to give me a little tour, okay, Danny?" I said. "Let's start with the room I found her in. I can show you which one it is."

"It's room four," Danny said. "Piper told me."

Following behind her, I retraced the steps I'd taken Friday night, past the room where I'd had my own massage toward the room where Piper had discovered Anna. The curtains poofed silently as we walked by them, just as they had that night. But now there was no scent of green tea in the air.

I knew I wouldn't go to pieces when I saw the spot where Anna's body had lain, and I didn't, yet the knot that had begun to form in my stomach tightened. I stood in the doorway, with Danny right beside me, staring at the putty-colored tiles on the floor.

"I still can't believe she was murdered," Danny whispered.

"Can you show me the room that she did her last massage in?" I asked.

"Yes, it's this way," she said, leading me down the corridor in the direction opposite from where we'd come. It was eerily quiet, though I could hear what I thought was the sound of dripping water from another part of the spa. Danny reached the end of the hall, turned left, and proceeded a few feet to another corridor that ran parallel to the one we'd just come from. There were three treatment rooms on either side of this hallway. Danny pointed to the middle room on the north side of the hall.

"That one," she said. "It's treatment room eight."

"I keep wondering how Anna ended up in that other treatment room," I said. "I know she'd already left this room, because she walked her last client to the side door and unlocked it for her. So perhaps she was heading back to the front of the spa or was about to clean up when someone surprised her and dragged her into the other treatment room. That would mean it was someone with a key—because all the doors were locked after the last client left and there was no break-in."

Danny listened with a pained expression on her face but said nothing in reply. I wondered if her mind was taunting her with the possibility of George in the scenario I had painted.

"Another possibility," I continued, "was that she let the person in herself. He knocked on the door and she opened it, not expecting him to harm her. It may have been someone who worked here—like Eric—saying he'd forgotten something or that he wanted to talk to her. Or maybe a client who said he'd forgotten something—just like I had."

Even as I said it, though, I found it hard to believe Anna would have given after-hours entry to someone in her release massage club.

"Of course," I said, "there's a remote possibility she was killed by someone who'd been here for an appointment and hid out until everyone but Anna had gone. I take it the police looked at the schedule for the day," I said.

"Yes, I gave them a copy," said Danny. "And I looked it over, of course. There were several male clients around lunchtime, including one for Anna. But from four o'clock on, it was all women, and most of them were guests at the inn."

"It's definitely a long-shot idea. Let's walk over to the main reception area," I said.

There was still one other slim possibility—that Anna heard a knock at the door and let a total stranger in. But as soon as I saw the front door again and was reminded of its design, I realized it just couldn't have happened. Two narrow windows ran vertically on either side, and Anna would have seen anyone standing there. It was highly unlikely that she would have opened the door at night for someone she didn't know—despite how much she had liked living on the edge.

I asked Danny to show me around the rest of the spa quickly before Josh returned. I wanted to see the back door, as well as the closet where the Mylar paper was stored. Once again she led and I followed. I was struck again by how eerie it was here, how rooms that could seem relaxing and comforting when people were around were spooky when you had them all to yourself. That's more or less what the client Babs had told me. The empty spa had given her a creepy feeling. I flashed suddenly on something else she'd told me.

"Danny, before we continue, can I see the women's changing area?" I asked.

"Yes, it's right behind reception," she said.

I had just recalled the remark that Babs had made about finding Anna sitting in the locker room. It had always seemed odd to me, and I had wondered what she could have possibly been doing there.

The space was pitch dark, and my breathing quickened as Danny fumbled for the light switch.

I'd been in here only briefly last Friday night. There was a small anteroom and then a larger room lined on three walls with wooden lockers and another with the counter Babs had said she'd seen Anna sitting at. Adjoining the space was another area with sinks, changing rooms, toilet stalls, and a couple of showers. I turned to-

ward the counter. The wall above it was covered with a
large mirror, and stools were tucked under it. On the
countertop were a variety of complimentary toiletries—
brushes, combs, lotion.

Anna had been using the mirror, I suddenly realized.
She'd been primping, fixing herself up. Because Anna
had been expecting someone the night she was murdered.

CHAPTER 18

"BAILEY, IS EVERYTHING all right?" Danny asked, clearly worried.

"Yes, I'm just thinking," I said. "Does the employee locker room have a mirror in it?"

"No, I don't think so. At least not like the one in here, if that's what you mean. I think the girls keep small ones hanging in their lockers. I can show you if you want. It's near the back door."

"Yes, show me, will you?"

"What in the world are you thinking, Bailey? Please tell me."

"Something just occurred to me. I'm wondering if Anna might have been planning to meet someone the night she was killed. I had a chance when I was up here before to speak to Anna's last client, and she told me that before she left the spa that night, she found Anna sitting at the counter in the changing room, dressed in her street clothes. I just realized that it's the vanity counter here. And it seems odd that she would have checked herself out in a mirror and maybe fixed her hair or put on makeup if she was planning to go straight back to the barn."

"The therapists aren't supposed to use this room," Danny said, "unless they're helping to collect towels or something like that."

"Well, it was basically after hours, and—and she broke that little rule because she needed to use the mirror. Piper said she switched places with Anna because she had dinner plans and Anna was staying in. But that had been earlier in the week. Things could have changed. Someone might have called and made arrangements to see her. But since she was in charge of closing up the spa, she was forced to make it a late rendezvous: around ten-fifteen, ten-thirty."

"Who could it have been?"

"A guy would be my guess. I've tried to find out if she was seeing someone new, but I haven't had any luck. Yet I bet she was. That might have been why she blew off Eric." What I didn't mention was what Piper had told me this morning, that Anna had wanted to make another switch with Piper—in their final departure dates from the Cedar Inn and Spa. Maybe Anna had wanted to delay her departure because there was a new love interest.

"And you think that person could have killed her?"

"It's a possibility. I suppose she could have had a date that night and someone *else* killed her. If her date was around ten-thirty, he might have come by and found the place empty, just as I had. But it seems like an awfully big coincidence."

"And if that was the case, wouldn't the man have come forward by now?"

"Well, he might not want to once he found out she was dead. He'd be an automatic suspect."

"Shouldn't we tell this to the police?" Danny asked eagerly. "This could help them stop focusing on George."

"Not yet. There's not enough evidence, and they'd only scoff at my little theory. Besides, Beck would be pissed that I was butting in. Let me pursue it on my own for a bit."

"All right," she said with little enthusiasm. "If we're going to finish looking around, we'd better hurry. Josh will be back any second."

We headed down another corridor toward the back of the building. We passed the room with the famous *sento* baths and also a treatment room with a massage table and what appeared to be a large chrome hose on the wall.

"What's this for?" I asked.

"This is one of the two rooms we do wraps in. The hose is used to wash the mud off the client after the wrap is done."

"You mean the wrap the Mylar paper is used for?"

"Yes, that's right," Danny said solemnly.

"Are you really all wrapped up when you have it?"

"No, not exactly," she said. "You lie on the Mylar paper and they fold it over you."

As we walked I noted places someone could have hidden. Though I had just about talked myself into believing my theory about Anna having a date the night she was killed, I had no proof. There were still other possibilities, including that small one that she had been killed by someone hiding in the spa. I realized that a client or stranger could have slipped into a treatment room or one of several storage areas. Yet it was hard to imagine someone managing to pull that off for long with so many employees around.

As we reached the back of the spa, I saw that the entire addition was actually smaller than it seemed, designed so efficiently and with so many interesting twists and turns that it gave the illusion of going on forever.

The employee locker room was right next to the rear door, and there was no need for much inspection. It was a tiny room with a row of half lockers and a small wooden bench to sit on. There was a sink and above it a five-by-seven mirror hung with wire and a pushpin. It was clear why someone would choose to use the mirror in the guest changing area, especially if she was applying makeup.

I took a quick look at the back door before we left this part of the spa. There was a chain lock and two dead bolts, one new in bright, shiny brass. I asked Danny if the chain was new, and she explained that it had been on since the addition was built. So if someone had slipped in on Friday night with the help of a key, chances were he had used one of the two other entrances.

"Just one more stop, Danny," I said. "Show me where the Mylar paper is stored."

We wound our way back to the front of the building. At the end of the corridor where Anna had been killed,

Danny pulled open the door of a storage closet and pointed to what looked like a giant box of aluminum foil, still unopened.

"This is how it comes," she said. "One sheet is about as long as a body. According to Josh, there was a half-used box in here, but the police must have confiscated it."

"What about duct tape? Is that kept here, too?"

"Up there," she said, pointing to an upper shelf where two unopened boxes sat. "But Bailey, if Anna did have a date that night like you think she did, how would *he* have known about the closet—and the Mylar paper?"

"Well, he might be familiar with the spa. But also notice how close the closet is to the room Anna was killed in. Maybe he had an urge to cover her, and when he opened the closet looking for a blanket, he stumbled on this."

"Why *did* he wrap her that way? It's so horrifying."

"I have no idea. I spoke to a criminal profiler, and she said it was definitely significant. That it meant something to him. Look, Danny, I know this sounds crazy, but could I get one of those wraps today—when the spa reopens?"

"Why would you possibly want one, Bailey—considering everything that's happened?"

"Because it might spark an idea. It's been so helpful for me to be here today, to—"

The door slammed, and we both jerked in surprise. We heard sounds coming from the front reception area, footsteps and the swish of plastic bags. Josh had evidently returned.

Quickly and quietly I closed the closet door. As I was about to give Danny a suggestion that we walk toward reception, Josh appeared in the hallway. He was wearing dark denim jeans and a crisp white dress shirt, tucked in but no belt, and his hair was slightly damp and slicked back, as if he'd washed his hands and, without drying them, run them through his hair.

"What's going on?" he asked, glancing pointedly at me with a look that demanded an explanation.

"I wanted to look over everything one more time before the staff descended," Danny said hurriedly. "By the way, Bailey would love to try one of our wraps today. Is it possible to arrange?"

"A wrap? Goodness, aren't we feeling adventurous. Unfortunately, however, Hildaco is off today."

"What about tomorrow?"

"I gave her the whole week off, since there was no easy way to do the wraps in the salon. But—but Cordelia could do one. She does them sometimes as a backup."

I would have expected him to be annoyed by any request I'd made, but he seemed borderline enthusiastic about this one. Maybe he was enjoying the thought of the discomfort I'd feel with my entire body smeared in hot mud.

"Cordelia would be fine," I said.

"It's not going to be quite the same degree of expertise as one of our Eastern European specialists," he said, the sarcasm rising in his voice. "But then I assume you're just doing it for background research."

"We'd better be getting back to the office," Danny

said, obviously trying to hurry us out of there. "Josh, you can leave a message there for Bailey when you work out a time. Good luck with everything today. I'll stop back over later."

We both turned to go when Josh interrupted.

"Bailey, could you stay, please? There are a few things I wanted to add to what we'd talked about the other day."

Danny shot me a concerned glance, but I told Josh yes, fine. I didn't feel in any danger since Danny knew he was with me.

"So why don't you tell me what your game is?" he demanded as soon as we heard the faint *swoosh* of the side door closing behind Danny.

"I haven't a clue what you're talking about," I said.

"No?" he said snidely. "Well, I did a search on the collected writings of Bailey Weggins, and your travel oeuvre consists of exactly two articles, one of which is about a trek through the hills of the Equator. Not exactly the wide world of spas, is it?"

"That was just for last year. I've certainly covered spas in the past."

"What I *did* see was about a billion articles on Ted Bundy, the next generation. You're some kind of crime writer, aren't you?"

"I *also* write crime articles, yes," I said. "What of it?"

"I just find it very interesting that you're a crime writer who shows up at the spa under the guise of giving Danny feedback and four minutes later there's a dead body on the premises."

"So you're wondering if *I* killed Anna?"

"*Did* you?"

"Right. So what's your point, Josh?"

"I'm wondering why exactly you came here—and then why the hell you came back." As he tensed his jaw in anger, the snake scar began to writhe.

"It's actually none of your business, but I don't mind telling you—*again*. I'm helping Danny, just like I explained before. Because she's in a jam and she needs friends right now. Unfortunately, when you're a successful businesswoman like she is, you can't always be sure who you can count on—and who you can't."

As the implication of my words registered, I thought his head might explode off his body.

"What's *that* supposed to mean?" he asked, clearly furious.

"Just what I said. Danny needs to be around someone she can trust completely. Yes, I write crime stories. And you'd be surprised at all the unscrupulous things going on in this world. Now, since I take it you don't have anything to offer for my project for Danny, please excuse me."

I could sense him glaring at me as I walked down the corridor. I wouldn't have been surprised if he'd stepped into a treatment room, picked up one of the stools, and hurled it at the back of my head. As soon as I'd released the bolt on the door and stepped into the inn, I regretted my last comments to him. In a split second I'd decided to be provocative, try to flush him out. But all I'd accomplished was to make him as mad as a bull charging through the streets of Pamplona. He had learned I was a crime writer. He knew I liked to snoop. Now he knew I suspected him of something.

I wanted to catch up with Danny, but I was famished and I knew the only way to get lunch was to order room service or drive someplace. I selected option A. I went back to my room and ordered a box lunch with coffee. Since it would be a few minutes, I decided to return Jack's call. There was every chance he was in class, so I could leave a message at his office without having to go into detail about my whereabouts. I was surprised when he picked up.

"So you're alive," he said. Not in a testy way. Just an undercurrent of curiosity—like where had I *been?*

"Yes, alive and out of town, actually. That's why I've been hard to reach."

"You on a story?"

"Kind of. Well, no, not really. But it does involve a crime. I had wanted to tell you this whole saga Monday night, but you . . . well, you did such a beautiful job of taking my mind off it, I never got the chance."

"And what saga is that?" he asked in the even tones of a shrink.

I launched into it then. Most of the big details, but not all the little ones. I left out the part about me being chased in the woods and the mouse and my room being searched—just a few minor details—because I didn't want to alarm him. I felt oddly defensive, which I shouldn't have. I had every right to be here, helping Danny. I knew my guilt was all related to the Beck business.

"It sounds like a potentially dangerous situation,"

Jack said when I had finished. Still even toned, but I picked up an undercurrent of concern.

"I couldn't say no to Danny," I told him. "I really couldn't. I'm not going to be here all that long, anyway—and I'm being careful."

"You were careful last spring and look what happened. You ended up nearly getting killed."

"Jack, you're making me feel like a ten-year-old."

"I'm sorry. I'm just worried about you."

I felt the slightest urge to snap back with, "Like you were last summer?"

"I appreciate that," was what I said instead.

"So are we still on for Saturday night?" he asked.

"Yes, of course. I plan to be out of here by Saturday morning at the latest. I'm looking forward to seeing you."

After we'd signed off and I'd set the phone down, I imagined him in his office at Georgetown, analyzing our conversation just as I was about to do. I still *did* want to be with him this weekend, and I was glad I hadn't done anything to rock the boat. At least until I was sure what boat I was sailing on.

Before I rose from the chair, I saw that the message light was blinking. In the bright light of the afternoon, I hadn't noticed it before. I punched the code to retrieve the message. It was from Beck. Brief and almost curt. Please call him.

Oh boy. A man answered when I called with a brusque, "Warren Police." I asked for Beck and waited, my whole body tense in anticipation. Keep it light, I told myself. Don't be a smart-ass.

"It's Bailey—returning your call," I said when he picked up the phone.

"Everything okay over there?"

"Seems to be," I said, resisting the urge to announce that no dead bodies had surfaced today. "Any news on the mouse?"

"Not yet," he said. "Look, I was wondering if you were going to be around later."

"How later? There's one thing I was hoping to do this afternoon."

"Later later. I'm working tonight. I thought you might want to grab a drink after that."

"Sure. That—"

"Good. I'll meet you out front, then—at nine."

My heart went into the familiar canter. I was going to see him again. Maybe kiss him again. Maybe more. I felt a wave of guilt. I had just hung up from Jack, making promises about the weekend, and now here I was fantasizing about Beck. A guy would never feel this kind of guilt, I realized. Men thought nothing of having two, two, two lusts in one.

My box lunch arrived and I decided to eat it outside in the garden. After sticking it in my tote bag along with my composition book, I headed downstairs, planning to stop first in Danny's office. She was on the phone but motioned that she would be off in a second.

"What did Josh want?" she asked, setting down the phone. "I was concerned he might have some hidden agenda."

"Oh, yeah—he did. He was wondering what *my* real agenda was. He suspects, I think, that I'm playing amateur PI, and he's not happy about it."

"He called a few minutes ago to say he'd scheduled you for a wrap. We're closing the spa at seven tonight, but Cordelia can do it at six. Do you really want to go through with it, Bailey?"

I assured her I did, that it might give me a new perspective on what had happened. It was finally time to broach the subject of George's indiscretion. She could tell by the look on my face that I had something on my mind.

"What is it, dear?" she asked.

"There's something I want to discuss with you, Danny. When I asked you yesterday if you had ever had reason not to trust George, you—your answer sounded kind of funny to me. I've been wondering if—"

"*Funny?*" she asked, clearly perturbed. "I'm not following at all what you mean."

"I wondered whether there might actually have been some problem in the past." I didn't dare mention what George had told me for fear of creating further trouble between the two of them.

"Bailey, I would hope that you of all people would have some respect for my privacy in these matters."

In all the years I'd known her, Danny had never once expressed annoyance at me—until now. I felt my face turning red in discomfort.

"Danny, I'm so sorry if I offended you. I just thought there might be something you wanted to discuss but didn't know how."

She looked away, and an excruciatingly awkward pause followed.

"There isn't," she said, still not making eye contact.

"Now if you'll excuse me, there are some things I need to take care of."

I slunk out of her office like a dog who's been caught chewing the heels off a pair of shoes. I had now managed to get on just about everyone's shit list, including Danny's. But then what should I have expected? I was stirring things up, asking rude questions, withholding information. The only person who didn't seem miffed at me was Beck, and that was because he was clueless as to how much I was withholding from *him.*

Tote bag in hand, I left the inn and walked over to the gardens, taking a seat on one of the weathered wooden benches. It was slightly warmer than when I'd been out earlier, but still nippy, not the best of days for a picnic. But I needed the fresh air—and I certainly wasn't going back into the nature reserve for a hike. I ate my overstuffed sandwich without enjoyment, struggling all the time to keep the lettuce and tomato from slipping into my lap.

After I'd wadded the paper wrapper back into the box, I popped the lid on the coffee cup and opened my composition book. I began jotting down notes about the murder. George's remarks about his indiscretion, my conversations with Piper and Eric and Josh, my observations of the spa, especially the dressing area: I imagined Anna at the counter, combing her hair, not knowing that the only thing she was getting ready for was death. I needed to speak to Piper again before she took off. I sensed she'd been truthful when she'd told me she didn't know if Anna was seeing anyone, but maybe some odd, seemingly insignificant detail she knew of Anna's life might point me in the right direction.

What I *couldn't* imagine was how the Mylar paper fit into everything. I wrote down the words, followed by an equals sign. Parker Lyle, the profiler, had told me it was meaningful—but how? Had the murderer simply wanted to cover her, as homicidal maniacs sometimes do, and grabbed the closest thing he could find? Or did the Mylar have some special significance? I just couldn't imagine.

I thought about my trip to Wallingford. Now that I suspected Anna had been expecting someone the night she was killed, digging up her past in Wallingford seemed like a waste of time and energy. Yet I didn't want to leave any road unexplored.

Though the sun had managed to find a hole in a layer of clouds, there was a rawness to the day, and it became unpleasant to sit outdoors any longer. I returned to the inn. I was anxious to right things with Danny, but I needed to let the dust settle first—and give her a chance to reconsider coming clean with me. Her answer had sounded defensive, and I suspected that she wasn't so much annoyed at me as troubled by the information she was withholding.

I showed up for my wrap treatment ten minutes early, using the main entrance of the spa off the parking lot. The reception area was empty, except for a woman I didn't recognize behind the desk. She asked if I preferred a terry robe or a waffle one and then led me down the dim, hushed corridor to the changing area. There didn't appear to be any coordinators on duty.

The women's changing area was deserted, though I could hear the shower running. That meant at least one other client was on the premises. Since I was early, I took my time undressing, folding my clothes, placing them in a locker. The water kept running, but no one ever emerged from the shower.

Since the receptionist didn't come to collect me, I found my own way to the relaxation room. The curtains along the walls poofed out as I walked, ghostlike. I couldn't help but imagine Anna last Friday night in the spa, alone at first, then caught unawares by the murderer, the terror she must have felt when she realized what was going to happen to her.

I sat alone in the relaxation room for about ten minutes, not relaxing at all, with nothing for company but the endless gurgle of water over stones in the fountain. When Cordelia finally stepped into the room, she was pleasant but cool. What about me doesn't she like? was all I could wonder.

She led me to a room toward the very back of the spa. It was either the one with the hose that Danny had shown me earlier or an identical one—it was hard to tell because of all the twists and turns. A candle flickered on a small table in the corner, and music played faintly, something new age-y tonight rather than Asian. Cordelia informed me that while she stepped out of the room I should disrobe and lie face up on the table under the sheet. As soon as she was gone, I unbelted my robe and hung it on a hook on the back of the door. Climbing onto the table, I spotted the Mylar paper below the layers of towel and sheets, and the sight of it made my stomach lurch. A few minutes later Cordelia tapped on the door, and I called out quietly that she could enter.

"Have you ever had a wrap before?" she asked, turning back the very top part of the sheet and smoothing it down neatly.

"No, never."

"There are several steps in the process. First I give your skin a light brushing to exfoliate it. Then I use an actual exfoliating rub all over your body. Last I put on the sea mud and wrap you up like a cocoon. The mud feels cool at first, but once you're in the wrap it gets warm and bubbles a little. I'll massage your scalp during part of the time you're in the wrap, and then I'll put a cool cloth over your eyes while you rest. If anything becomes the slightest bit uncomfortable, just let me know."

"*Uncomfortable?*" I asked.

"Some people find the bubbling a little . . . well, it's just different."

For the brushing she used what appeared to be an ordinary hairbrush with natural bristles. Working in small circles, she covered almost my entire body, including my breasts. Next was the rub, which she explained was scented with eucalyptus. After rubbing it over my body, she turned on the hose, washing away every trace of the rub. After I'd dried off with a towel, I lay back down again, this time directly on the Mylar paper, and she began smearing the mud on me.

The smell was yucky, like something emanating from the Dumpster behind a sushi restaurant. And though the feel of it was refreshing at first, as soon as she folded the Mylar paper over my body and laid a towel on top, it turned hot and sticky, just as she'd said. I felt as if I'd fallen into a pan of bubbling marinara sauce.

"Sea mud is a natural purifier," Cordelia said, dimming the lights even more. "It rids the body of toxins."

She began to massage my scalp, working firmly and rhythmically. I was struck again by the strength of Cordelia's hands. They were like a man's, stronger, it seemed, than even Eric's. I wanted to just lie there and luxuriate in it, like a cat getting its head rubbed, but I couldn't ignore how yucky my body felt, trapped in primordial ooze.

After a few minutes she stepped aside, and I heard the sound of her wringing out something with her hands. Then she placed a cool, wet towel gently across my eyes.

"Relax now. I have to get a few supplies, but I'll be right back. You're going to love how your skin feels after you're done."

It had better end up as soft as a baby's butt, was all I could think, because the experience was ranking right up there with a pelvic exam in terms of enjoyability. I knew it would be easy enough for me to slip my arms out of my cocoon, but I felt claustrophobic nonetheless. It probably had as much to do with my memories of Anna in the Mylar as it did with the hot, gurgling mud. I saw her in my mind's eye, that horrible silver mummy. I took deep breaths and started counting backward from one hundred.

After a short time, I heard Cordelia slip quietly back into the room. Through the towel I saw the room darken completely, and I realized she'd turned off the lights. Next she placed a towel, or rather something heavier, a blanket, perhaps, over the top of my body.

I opened my mouth to tell her it was much too hot when I heard the breath someone expels when they blow out a candle. The room was now in total darkness.

"What's going on?" I called out. Suddenly there was another towel, heavy, being placed over my entire face. I heard a sound like tape being yanked off a roll and then something else pressing on my face. I felt a surge of panic. I could barely breathe.

CHAPTER 19

I TRIED TO yell from beneath the towel, but my mouth couldn't move enough to form words. I felt someone brush against my body, and then through the towels I heard the muffled sound of the door closing. There was no way I could catch a breath, and my heart began to beat wildly, as if it had lost all control.

As terror enveloped me, I tried to move my head, but something had locked it in place. Don't panic, I pleaded to myself. I concentrated instead on the blanket over my body. It lay there immovable, like a piece of heavy tarp covering a swimming pool. I wiggled my arms inside the cocoon, trying to free them. They felt heavy as stone. But I kept up the wiggling until I managed to pull my arms from my sides and stick both my hands through the opening in the Mylar. I could feel the blanket, and I began to punch it, harder and harder. When I'd created a pucker of material, I scrunched it up with my hand and shifted it to the left, piece by piece. Finally I felt the blanket slip to the ground.

I was nearly out of breath and frantic. My hands grabbed at the towel on my face, trying to tear it off, but there were strips of tape on it, and they seemed to go all the way around the table. I began to rock my head back and forth, loosening the grip of the towel and the tape until finally I was able to slither my body out from under it. My lungs felt ready to burst as I took my first breath of air.

The room was in complete darkness. For one terrifying second I thought I heard someone breathing near me, but I quickly realized it was my own breathing, working double time. I slithered off the table and carefully toed my way across the room. My hand felt for the light switch, and when I didn't find it in one second, I searched instead for the door. As soon as I touched the doorknob, I yanked it open. I stood in the entranceway, covered from head to toe in mud, as Cordelia, a shocked expression on her face, rushed toward me.

"What's the matter?" she exclaimed. "I was just gone for a minute."

"What's the *matter?*" I shouted. "I should ask *you* that question. Someone taped a towel over my face. I nearly suffocated."

"I—what do you mean over your face? I just put the one on your eyes."

"Well then, someone paid me a visit when you stepped away. Here, look."

I stepped back into the room and she followed, switching on the light and pushing the dimmer to high.

On the floor in a heap was a large white blanket. At the head of the massage table was a towel with what looked like two revolutions of duct tape going across the top of it and then along the underside of the table.

"I, I didn't put that stuff on you," she stammered.

"Well, *somebody* did. And I'm getting out of here."

"Let me wash you off first," Cordelia said. There was concern in her voice, though as far as I knew, she was faking it.

"No thanks," I said. "I'm not spending another second in this room."

I yanked my robe off the hook on the door, shoved my arms into the sleeves, and tramped toward the locker room like a swamp woman. For a split second I considered hopping into the shower there, but I didn't want to spend any more time in the spa. I hauled my clothes out of the locker and, wadding them up in a ball, stepped back outside again. Josh was standing there waiting, Cordelia by his side.

"What exactly happened?" he said in a clipped tone. His voice was lowered, however, suggesting that he wanted to be sure no other clients heard him.

"Someone came into the room when I was having a wrap and taped a towel over my face so I couldn't breathe."

"A wrap can be very intense. Once in a while someone has a—a sort of reaction to the confined conditions."

"Oh please," I said. "Next you're going to suggest I had an LSD flashback."

I turned to go.

"You're not leaving here like that, are you?"

"Don't worry," I said. "I'll use the *back* stairs."

I hurried down the corridor toward the smaller reception area, walking so quickly that the curtains along the walls stirred as they would if a thunderstorm were on its way. I didn't pass a single person on my way up the back stairs.

My heart was still beating hard when I closed the door to my room. I turned the dead bolt, put the chain on, and pulled the small table in front of the door. I waited until I got to the bathroom to peel off the robe. After giving the water a minute to turn warm enough, I stepped into the shower and watched the mud liquefy and run off my body. Then I lathered up and rinsed off.

I felt slightly calmer when I stepped out of the shower, but not much. As I was slipping a robe on, someone knocked at the door of my suite, making me jump.

"Who is it?" I yelled.

"Bailey, it's me, Danny."

I moved the table away, unlocked the door, and opened it. Danny stood there, her gray eyes wide in alarm.

"Are you all right? What happened?"

"What did they tell you?" I asked as I ushered her into the room and closed the door behind her. I was curious if Josh and company were spreading the "she went insane with claustrophobia" theory.

"Josh called and said that you thought someone had come into the room and put a towel over your head. Initially you accused Cordelia but then thought it might have been someone else."

"Not *put* a towel over my head. Someone *taped* a towel over my head."

I ran through the story quickly for her.

"Do you think it *could* have been Cordelia?"

"I don't know. I can't imagine what her motive could be. She doesn't seem to like me all that much, but that's hardly a reason to try to hurt me."

"I find it very odd that she left the room," Danny admitted. "The therapist is supposed to stay in there with the client in case they start to feel uncomfortable. Cordelia doesn't do wraps on a regular basis, but I would think she would know the correct procedure."

"She said something about needing to get some supplies. And someone could have slipped in when she was gone."

"Bailey, I'm honestly thinking it would be best if you left."

"I have no intention of leaving."

"But I'm worried about your safety."

"It's clear I've pushed someone's buttons, but I promise I'll be more careful. Besides, I'm planning to go to Wallingford tomorrow, so I won't even be around most of the day."

She gave each of my arms a squeeze, and as she pulled away I felt something wet on my hand. I glanced down and saw a tiny smudge of something brownish gray there and another on her sleeve.

"What's that?" I asked.

"It's mud, I guess," she said as she inspected it, holding a piece of her sleeve in her hand. "I went into the treatment room you'd been in once they called me down there. I must have gotten it on me then."

She said good-bye, and as she stepped into the corridor, she urged me to order something nourishing for dinner from room service. But I had little appetite. After changing into jeans and a turtleneck, I took an apple from the basket on the coffee table and lay down on the couch.

As I nibbled listlessly at the apple, I tried mentally to re-create my experience in the spa. My guess was that only a minute or two passed between the time Cordelia left the room and when the lights went off. It certainly could have been Cordelia who had scared me, but it might also have been someone who spotted her walking away and slipped in right after that. Josh had been around and could have done it. So could anyone else who was affiliated with the spa.

I tossed my half-eaten apple back into the basket, called the front desk to ask for a wake-up call at eight-thirty, and fell dead asleep. I knew as I was drifting off that I might regret my nap later, but I was too exhausted to keep my eyes open.

I was out in front of the inn by eight-fifty. I'd splashed cold water on my face after my nap, then applied lip gloss, blush, mascara, and a few smears of concealer to cover the pillow crease marks on my face.

Beck pulled up at one minute after nine, and rather than get out, he leaned across the front seat and opened the door for me. He gave me one of those smiles of his that seemed half smile, half grimace. He was wearing dark pants and a denim shirt under a sports coat. Since I knew he wasn't a fan of auto chitchat, I leaned back in my seat and watched the houses and trees zip by.

I was tempted to tell him what had happened. But I knew that if I spilled the story, it would only confirm that I was a snoop and someone wanted me out of there. So I said nothing. We drove out past the strip where Leo's was situated and then onto a rural road. We pulled up to a small bar/restaurant made of logs called the Trading Post.

Inside, it wasn't unlike the Bridge Street Tavern in atmosphere, though smaller, and tonight there was hardly anyone there. We sat at the bar. I ordered a beer. He asked for a Maker's Mark, straight.

"This is the kind of bar I wish they could just plunk down in New York City," I said. Ah, tonight I'd abandoned my smart-ass convo style and was going for something cuter, channeling Meg Ryan.

"You've got plenty of bars to choose from down there."

"But none like this. You've spent time in New York?"

"Not in a while. Look, I wanted to talk to you about last night."

I felt my cheeks redden. From his tone, I suddenly realized that this wasn't date two. This was the blow-off.

"Okay," was all I could manage.

"I enjoyed having dinner with you," Beck said. "But I stepped out of bounds, and I shouldn't have."

"You mean it's against some regulation? It's not as if I'm a witness to anything."

"No, but your account helps pinpoint the time of death. If there's a trial, you might have to testify. Besides, you're a friend of Mrs. Hubner's. And as you know, we've questioned her husband. I have to be careful with this case. It's very important."

"I understand," I said quietly. "I appreciate your being straight with me."

And I did. Beck was taking the rational path and his cooling things down solved my quandary over plunging back into a relationship with Jack while entertaining a yen for a country sheriff. Still, being rejected smarted.

There were a few silent, awkward moments, and then he began to tell a story about a brawl he'd broken up here, at the Trading Post, practically his first day on the force, and how he'd gotten a black eye. I chugged my beer, figuring since he'd taken me out to tell me he couldn't date me, he certainly didn't want to be sitting around with me all night.

We were in and out of the Trading Post in less than thirty minutes. He nodded good night to the bartender, and we walked silently across the parking lot. It was pitch black out, though the sky was scattered with a zillion stars and the filmy swath of the Milky Way. Beck walked over to my side of the car to unlock my door and stopped.

"Look, I'm sorry about all this," he said. "Maybe when the case is finished, our paths will cross again."

I glanced up at him in surprise.

"In fact, if you play your cards right, I'll take you to Leo's again," he said, smiling.

"I'd like that," I said.

"Would you?" he asked. Even in the darkness I could see that his eyes held a quizzical expression.

"Sure," I replied, not knowing what else to say. "And

look, don't feel bad about what happened. It was only a kiss. I won't tell if you don't."

To my total shock, he leaned forward and kissed me again, hard and deep. He leaned his body into mine, and I could feel his erection pushing into me. I let my tongue slip into his mouth, and as I did, his right hand slipped through my open jeans jacket and grabbed my breast so hard that it hurt. He pulled away almost as quickly as he'd kissed me.

"Deal," he said.

We drove in silence, except for a comment he made about Massachusetts drivers, and when we reached the inn he said good night and leaned across me to open the door. No kiss this time. But just as he had the other night, he waited until I was inside the inn before zooming away.

I practically ran to my room, the key poised in my hand. The inn seemed less than half-full this week, and as far as I knew, I was one of the few people staying along this corridor. Just as I reached my door, I heard a loud creak. My head shot to the right, in the direction of the back stairs that led to the spa. There was nothing there.

Once I was inside I went through the usual routine: flipping on the dead bolt, pulling the table up against the door, checking out the suite for signs of visitors. I felt the most nervous I'd felt since last Friday. It was clear from what had happened in the spa tonight that I was rattling someone's cage. One of any number of people could have slipped into the treatment room after Cordelia left. Yet I hadn't a clue who the culprit was.

As I lay in bed with one ear cocked to listen for weird sounds, I started ruminating about Beck—and Jack. Beck had pulled a strange double-take on me earlier, suggesting that we might get together in the future, and kissing me again. I hadn't wanted that kiss to end; I'd wanted to go further. But I didn't know if I wanted anything *more* than that from Beck. I had all these good feelings for Jack—when I wasn't pissed at him.

I was up by seven-thirty Friday morning, after a shortage of REM sleep so severe that it would have been illegal for me to operate heavy machinery. I made a small pot of coffee with the little machine in the bathroom and dressed in my black pants and a black turtleneck sweater. No one was at the front desk when I arrived downstairs, though I could hear music coming from the area of Danny's office. I walked behind the reception desk and down the corridor. Natalie was standing over Danny's desk, tidying stacks of papers as Céline Dion sang in the background. When she saw me out of the corner of her eye, she jumped so high that she was practically airborne.

"My God, you scared me," she exclaimed breathlessly.

"I'm sorry. I heard the music and wondered who it could be this early."

"I've got some filing to do, so I put the music on. It scares me to be back here alone."

"I thought you usually come in later. Where's the early morning guy?"

"He's having a break. I'm just here to get caught up, and then I'm coming back later."

"It must be hard for you—dealing with everything that's going on."

"My parents want me to quit," she said, her face filled with worry. "They get freaked every day I leave for work. They said I could only stay if my shift ended earlier. Danny's arranged for me to work until eight o'-clock every night, rather than midnight."

"I'm sure the police will catch the killer and you'll feel safe again."

"I guess. I mean, there was that other situation here just two months ago. That man dying. It just never seems normal here anymore."

"Are you thinking that the two incidents could be connected?"

"No, I didn't say that. It's just that it was awful when he died. There were police around for weeks, asking questions, and all these reporters and that guy's family was all upset and Danny was worried that the inn might get into some kind of trouble. And then we're barely done with it when Anna gets murdered, which is about a million times worse."

"Did you know Anna?"

"No. By sight, yes, but not to speak to. She hardly said two words to me the entire time she was here."

"You wouldn't happen to know if she'd been dating anyone lately—I mean, did you ever see her with a guy?"

She lowered her eyes, as if she felt awkward discussing Anna. "I know she used to date Eric—but that was quite a while ago. Since then I've only seen her alone. She didn't look like the settling-down type."

Before I left, I asked for a map of New England. All

she had was the office copy, but she offered to loan it to me.

I had lots to think about that morning, but the directions to Wallingford were tricky enough and the traffic heavy enough that I was forced to keep my mind mostly on the road. I picked up the Massachusetts Turnpike, this time going east, and took it for about thirty miles, where I got on I-91 and eventually something called the Wilbur Cross Parkway, and finally US-5. When I figured I was about twenty minutes from Wallingford, I pulled into a rest area, took out my notes from my phone call to the school, and called the main number again. I was pretty sure the woman who answered was the same perky chick I'd spoken to yesterday.

"Bob Kass," I said, trying to sound all nice and familiar, as if Bob and I went way back. I almost died when I heard her reply.

"Bob's not in today."

"You're kidding," I exclaimed. "I was supposed to speak with him."

"He's out sick."

Now what? I couldn't immediately ask her to put me through to one of the teachers on my list or she'd suspect something. I signed off and drove the last fifteen minutes to Wallingford.

It was a fairly good-size town, blue-collar in feel, with lots of industry on the outskirts and a sleepy little downtown. I found a place to park in town, bought a bagel and a cup of coffee, and called the school again. I tried to disguise my voice, and this time I asked for the math teacher.

"She's in class right now. Can I take a message for her?"

"What's the best time to reach her?"

"Around lunchtime, I'd say. She might be in the teachers room then. Can I help you with something?"

"Uh, no. Thanks."

It was going to be impossible to get by this babe. I called 411 and asked for a Bob Kass in Wallingford. There was a Robert Kass and a B. Kass, and I chose option one.

I knew I had the right number when a man answered sounding as if he had a towel stuffed up his nose.

"Bob Kass?"

"Speaking," he said, though he sounded half-dead.

"I'm so sorry to bother you at home when you're sick. But it's rather urgent. My name is Bailey Weggins. I don't know if you've heard, but a former student at the school, Anna Gianelli, was murdered while working for a friend of mine in Warren, Massachusetts. My friend is very anxious that the killer be found, but the police are moving at a snail's pace. I'm a professional journalist and I'm helping her. We've been told there may have been some kind of trouble in Anna's past, and we're trying to learn whatever we can about it—in case it's linked somehow to her death. I'm hoping I could speak to you."

There was a long pause before he replied, and I prayed he wouldn't blow me off.

"No, I hadn't heard," he said finally. "That's terrible. How was she murdered? When?"

"She was strangled. Just a few days ago. You knew her, then?"

"Not well. But I remember her."

"Would it be possible for me to talk to you? I've driven all the way to Wallingford today to try to learn whatever I can."

"I'm sick as a dog with this cold. But I could give you a couple of minutes if you want to drive over to my place."

"That's wonderful, thank you. Do you know if there *was* anything—I mean, any kind of incident in her past?"

"Yes," he said. "There was something."

CHAPTER 20

Whatever had happened to Anna Gianelli Cole, it was big enough that a man who hadn't known her well remembered it twenty years later.

He said his house wasn't far from downtown, but his directions were lousy. I found myself driving away from the center of town and suspected that I had taken a wrong turn. I asked for help from a man climbing into his car, and he told me to turn around and head back in the direction I'd come from. When I finally located the street, I realized Kass had said right once when he'd meant left.

His house was in an older development, maybe 1960s, which today, with so many fully grown trees, seemed almost quaint. He greeted me wearing Dockers and a plaid shirt, but I suspected he'd hastily changed from a bathrobe after my phone call. He was a pleasant-looking guy, mid-fifties, I guessed, with thinning, sandy-colored hair and hazel eyes that glistened from his cold. There was a dog with him, a golden retriever, white around the muzzle from age.

"Thanks again for seeing me," I said as Kass opened the screen door to let me in. "Especially when you're sick."

"It's just one of those early fall colds, but it's a doozer. Why don't you come in and have a seat. At the very least, it'll give the neighbors something to talk about. One of them is probably phoning my wife at work right now."

The house smelled of chicken soup and Vicks VapoRub. Kass led me past a formal-looking living room, through a kitchen, and into a family room/den with a brick fireplace, a hunter green sofa, and two matching recliners. The mantel of the fireplace was lined with family photos. Sliding doors looked out onto a redwood deck with an aboveground swimming pool, covered for the season. Kass motioned for me to take a seat, and as I did the dog waddled over and wedged her nose smack in the middle of my crotch.

"Peaches, get over here," Kass commanded. "Come on now." As Kass broke into a hacking cough, the dog begrudgingly skulked over toward the recliner his master had taken and flopped to the floor.

"I can't believe Anna was murdered," Kass said after his coughing had subsided. "Do they have a suspect?"

"They haven't arrested anyone yet. What concerns my friend, the owner of the inn, is that the police don't seem to be very thorough or imaginative in their efforts."

"The inn?" Kass asked, perplexed.

"Yes. Anna was working as a massage therapist at my friend's inn and spa in Warren. There was quite a bit of local press coverage on the murder up there, but Anna was still using her married name, Cole, and that probably explains why you hadn't heard about her death down here."

"As far as I know, she's got no family in town, so that's another reason we wouldn't have heard. She didn't finish high school here. She moved a few towns over and did her senior year there."

"So you said on the phone that there *was* an incident in Anna's past?"

"Yes," he said. "I won't bore you with a big preamble. She was baby-sitting one afternoon for a family named Ballard, and the little girl she was taking care of drowned in the swimming pool."

"It was a terrible tragedy," he continued after about thirty seconds, obviously interpreting my lack of response as shock at the horror of his revelation. But what I was really experiencing was total surprise. I'd never once considered anything like that.

"Do you know any specifics about the incident?" I asked.

"It was in the summer, late, if I remember. The mother was out for the day. She was a widow, by the way, though still quite young. I guess she'd had Anna baby-sit a few times before and felt comfortable with her. Anna was around sixteen at the time. The girl was just three or four. She could swim a little, but she fell into the deep end of the pool and apparently panicked."

He glanced out toward his own pool. "We didn't buy

ours until our youngest was seven just for that reason. All it takes is getting distracted for a second. . . ."

"Is that what happened with Anna—she got distracted?"

"That was the funny thing," he said. "She changed her story about what happened. At first she said she'd put the girl in her room for a nap and then gone into the living room to make a phone call. She said the girl must have slipped out of her room. But the police either obtained the phone records or said they were *going* to, and then Anna quickly offered up a new version. She said she had actually fallen asleep on the couch but had been too ashamed to say so earlier. In the end it didn't really matter how it happened. The family was devastated, especially the other kids."

"How many were there?"

"Two brothers—older. One, Carson, was sixteen at the time, and the other—Harold, I think—was just going into high school. He was maybe thirteen or fourteen."

"And Anna—how did she react?"

Kass took a minute to blow his nose on a big white handkerchief, making a sound like geese honking their way across an autumnal sky. "I assume she was pretty shaken up, but since I didn't really know her, I can't answer that. She wasn't on the college track, so our paths didn't cross much. Obviously her family felt pretty uncomfortable because they moved within a few months. I *did* know the Ballards, though—especially the older guy, Carson. He was a brilliant kid, a real math whiz, and he had his heart set on MIT or someplace like that.

His grades plummeted when he came back to school that fall."

"He was that distraught?"

"Yes, both boys were. But not just over the sister's death. The mother went into a deep depression after that."

Of course, I knew all about what could happen with a death in the family. And the Ballard boys had lost both a father and a sister.

"That's awful. Do you know where the boys are now?"

"They're not here anymore, that much I know. They left town, too, about a year later, moved to be near the mother's family somewhere. I heard she eventually remarried. Carson didn't end up at MIT, but someone told me he became a pilot out in California someplace. But you're not thinking that this could be connected to Anna's death, are you?"

"Not necessarily. I'm just trying to turn over every stone. Go back to the incident for a second, will you? Was there ever any suspicion that Anna had hurt the little girl?"

He looked surprised, then shook his head. "Gosh, I don't think that ever crossed my mind—or anybody else's, for that matter. But then this was before the days when nannies set their employers' houses on fire. It's a possibility, I suppose, but at the time the girl's death was all chalked up to carelessness."

"But why would Anna change her story?"

"The thought at the time—and there was never any proof, as far as I know—was that she had a boy with her. And that they were preoccupied, if you will. Anna had a reputation for being somewhat advanced as far as the boys were concerned. Now we call it girl power, but back then she was considered fast—or trampy or whatever name you want to give it."

He began to hack again and spat something into the hankie, almost triggering my gag reflex.

"I should let you get back to recuperating," I said. "I just wondered if you know what town Anna ended up moving to."

"Milford. My wife saw her there a year or so later."

"I hear she married young. You wouldn't know if her husband was from there?"

"No, haven't the foggiest."

I had just one more request. As we'd been talking, I noticed rows of high school yearbooks in the bookshelves that framed the fireplace. I asked him if there would be a picture of Anna in one of them. He hoisted himself out of a chair and pulled out a volume, flipped to a page with group shots of juniors, and pointed to Anna's picture. She didn't look that different from the way she did in the picture Danny had showed me—pretty, sensuous looking, her dark hair below her shoulders back then. She faced the camera smiling. The picture had been taken before the drowning and she appeared not to have a care in the world.

"And Carson Ballard?" I asked. "Would he be in here, too?"

Kass's eyes roamed the spread of group shots and lighted onto a caption. He pointed to a notation at the end. It stated that Carson T. Ballard had been absent the day the photo was taken.

Kass snapped the yearbook shut, as if that one addendum on the caption somehow summed up all he'd been trying to say. I thanked him, and he walked me to the front door. Peaches trailed behind us and, with the single-mindedness of a drug dog searching for contraband, made several more stabs at my crotch. Before I departed I asked Kass how far Milford was. He told me twenty minutes—to the east.

After finding my way back to the center of town, I bought a fresh cup of coffee and drank it in the car as I jotted down everything Kass had said during our conversation. I still felt stunned by what I had learned. Ever since Eve had told me there was something disturbing in Anna's past, I'd let my imagination run with it. I'd considered everything from abuse to pregnancy to vehicular manslaughter, but nothing close to what the incident actually was. I wondered how much it had tortured Anna. Was that the reason she had constantly been on the move and had enjoyed living on the edge? Eve had claimed Anna carried emotional pain in her body. On the other hand, though, people had described Anna as cold and distant. Maybe it had been years since she'd given the little girl's death another thought.

I was anxious to be on the road back to Warren, yet suddenly I found the town of Milford beckoning me. According to Anna's sister, she had married a guy she'd met her last year in high school. If I dropped into the school in Milford, I could look for a Cole in the yearbook and later try to track him down along with the Ballards. No sooner had the idea thrust itself into my head than I tried to talk myself out of it. Stopping in Milford would not only delay my return to Warren by at least an hour, but would all be for a long shot: the idea that Anna's husband might somehow be linked to her death. Connie had said Anna hadn't been in touch with him for years. But there was no letting go of the idea now that it was tugging so hard at my brain. If I didn't do it when I was this close, I might regret it later. An old reporter I'd worked with at the *Albany Times Union* had once told me that whenever you caught yourself trying to rationalize away the need to conduct a piece of research, it meant you damn well better do it. I picked up the map from the passenger's seat and attempted to figure out the best route to Milford.

Getting into the school library turned out to be easier than expected. I showed my *Gloss* business card to a woman at a desk in the lobby of the school and explained I needed to look at old yearbooks for background on a profile I was doing on a former student, and she called down to the library for me.

"It's fine," she said, putting down the phone. "You walk all the way down that hall there, take a left, and you can't miss it. Can I ask you something? Does *Gloss* still do makeovers? I could really use one of those."

That was for sure. She'd rimmed her eyes all the way around with jet-black eyeliner and her lipstick was the color of Pepto Bismol.

"Gosh, we don't really do those anymore. Sorry."

I actually had no idea whether *Gloss* did makeovers or not. The only part of the beauty pages I ever looked at was the weird "Beauty Q&A" column, where they printed questions like "Help, I shave my chin hair. Will it grow back like a beard?" But I had no time to spare for chatting.

The library was half-filled with students, most of them fidgety from hormone overload. I took a seat at a table in a corner near a shelf filled with decades' worth of yearbooks. I found Anna's year and went straight to the individual senior photos. There she was, preserved forever in a kind of tribute to *Charlie's Angels,* her hair now featuring wings along both sides of her face. This time she had a somber look on her face, far different from the previous picture. And though she was pretty—those dark, dark eyes and sensuous lips—there was something trampy about her this time. She looked like a girl who'd already clocked a lot of miles on a mattress.

After noting that her only activities had been girls soccer and senior prom committee, I flipped quickly back to the Cs. No Cole. I pulled down the previous three years' worth of books from the shelf and looked through them, but there was no one with that last name. I was just about to close the last one, three years ahead of Anna, when I caught my breath.

I almost didn't recognize him because he had a full head of hair. It was Rich Wyler. And if I'd had any doubts that it was one and the same, the caption would have swayed me: "Tennis 1, 2, 3, 4 (captain)."

He would have graduated from the school before Anna arrived, but he easily could have met her around town. He'd obviously recognized her when he started working at the inn. Maybe the "buzzing around her" that Danny had witnessed was him trying to form a connection again. But Anna hadn't liked him, Piper said. Had he been threatening to her in some way? Was that why he hadn't admitted to knowing her?

I made a few notes in my composition book before I left and then hurried to my Jeep. I was famished, but I wasn't going to take time to find a place to sit down and eat. Instead I pulled into a Burger King just before leaving town and ate my Junior Whopper while I found my way back toward the highway.

My mind was racing. I'd gone digging for information about Anna and hit the mother lode. What I'd found seemed so profound and significant: A child had died when she was under Anna's care. Yet I had to remind myself that it had happened twenty years ago and might have no significance whatsoever to Anna's murder. If Anna, as I suspected, had been planning to go on some kind of date last Friday night and that person had murdered her, her past didn't really matter in the scheme of things. I would try to find the whereabouts of the Ballard brothers, just so I could take them off my radar screen, but what I really needed to do now was put as much effort as possible into finding out if Anna had been dating someone new.

The trip back to Warren seemed to take far longer than the drive down, probably because I felt so antsy and anxious to get back. As soon as I was settled in my room at the inn—and had glanced around it to make sure no one had been snooping again—I phoned one of the interns at *Gloss* whom I used for research on stories. She had access to a special service that tracked people who had used credit at any point in their lives. If you typed in a name, it spat out a list of everyone with a match in the system, as well as each person's address. Then you could click on individual names to get more info—in most cases a birth date would be listed—and through a process of elimination, you could generally figure out where the person you were looking for was living. It was great for research and also a handy little tool when you found yourself fantasizing about some guy you'd had a carnal coupling with ten years before on a weekend in New Orleans and wondering if he still existed on this planet.

I took her quickly through what I needed, telling her to look for a Carson T. Ballard, around thirty-eight and possibly living in California, and a Harold Ballard, around thirty-six and living who knew where. And I told her I wanted to hear back by the end of the day.

After that I called the front desk and asked Natalie when Rich would next be on the premises.

"Do you want another lesson with him?" she asked.

"No, I just want to chat with him. I thought I could catch him at the end of a lesson."

"He was here this morning, and I think that's it for him. Lemme check. . . . Wait, no. He's back for a four-thirty. You could walk over right before then or afterwards, I guess."

"Thanks. Is Danny around, by the way?"

"I think she's been over at the spa most of the day. But she should be stopping by later."

"Would you tell her I'm back and would love to catch up with her at some point. Tell her I have some news."

Next, and most important of all, I needed to find Piper. She had said she was leaving this weekend, and I hoped she hadn't moved things up. I called down to the spa, praying Josh wouldn't answer. Some dude picked up and said that Piper was no longer employed at the Cedar Inn and Spa. I quickly changed into my blue jeans and, using the west end door of the inn, hurried to the barn.

As I pressed Piper's buzzer, I had a bad vibe. Standing in the vestibule, I could see through the glass door into the first floor of the barn, and everything looked so forlorn and empty. There was no answer to my first ring or my second or third. Maybe I had missed her.

As I turned to go, I heard a noise behind me. Cordelia had appeared out of nowhere inside and was pushing open the door to the vestibule.

She was out of her spa uniform, made up with red lipstick, and dressed in stretchy pants and a low-cut top that squished her breasts, giving her what I'd heard the fashion department at *Gloss* refer to as butt cleavage. She looked dangerously like Anna Nicole Smith. Her eyes widened when she realized it was me who was standing there.

"Can I help you?" she asked, her tone defensive.

"I was looking for Piper, actually," I said.

"I think she's gone. I mean, really gone. I saw her loading her car after lunch. She resigned from the spa, you know."

"Okay, thanks." I could have kicked myself. I should have gone looking for her *before* I left for Wallingford.

"You know, I hope you're not holding me responsible for what happened last night," Cordelia said in a snippy tone.

"Well, who do you think I *should* hold responsible?"

"I have no idea. If it's any consolation, Danny chewed my ass off for leaving you alone."

I was tempted to tell her you could hardly notice, but instead I pushed open the front door and stepped outside the barn, letting the door swing shut behind me.

Instead of returning to the inn, I made my way

around the back of the building toward the parking lot, on the fat chance that Piper was still loading her car. There was no sign of her. But as I walked by a short row of cars at the end, I spotted a yellow Volkswagen Beetle whose backseat was stuffed with wadded-up clothes, duffel bags, shopping bags, and junk that bore a striking similarity to the mess that had lain on Piper's floor earlier.

I jogged back to the front of the inn and entered the main entrance. Two guests were standing at the front desk, filling out a registration form under instruction from Natalie. I waited off to the side, trying not to tap my foot. After Natalie had called for the bellboy and he was leading the couple to the stairs, I stepped forward.

"Do you have any idea where Piper is?" I asked. "Cordelia said she left, but I think I spotted her car in the parking lot."

"She's here in the inn," Natalie said, "Danny arranged for her to have a spare room."

"Which one? I've got to talk to her."

"Twenty-seven. It's on the third floor."

I took the stairs two at a time. The third floor was laid out exactly like the second, but the ceilings seemed lower and there was a slightly oppressive feel up there. I found room 27 and knocked on the door. I recognized Piper's voice when she called out, "Who is it?"

"It's Bailey. I need to talk to you."

I heard a big sigh, followed by soft footsteps. When she flung open the door, she looked seriously pissed.

"What are you, some kind of stalker?" she asked. "Can't you just leave me alone?" She was dressed in blue jeans and an apple green jersey top, and her hair was spread out around her shoulders, brushfire style.

"It's important. And it will only take a minute."

"All right, but make it quick." She stepped aside for me to enter, glancing up and down the hall before she shut the door. The room was small, under the eaves, decorated in yellow and white. I assumed from the rumpled covers and Piper's bare feet that she had been lying on the bed before I arrived.

"What are you doing up here?"

"Danny said I could stay here since the room is empty. I'm leaving today, but I'm waiting for a girl I know in town to bring me some money she owes me. I didn't want to stay in that barn one more second."

"How come you're leaving today?"

"Maybe you haven't heard," she said, rocking back and forth with her arms across her chest. "There's a killer on the premises. And he prefers massage therapists."

"But you'd said you were leaving this weekend. Why move it up?"

She turned her face to the side, looking off at nothing in particular, then back to me, shaking her head.

"This place is freaking me out. I don't like the way Josh is acting toward me these days."

"Is he being nasty to you?"

"No. That I could deal with. He's being obnoxiously pleasant. I don't know if he's scared I might confess to the cops what Anna and I were doing or if he thinks I suspect him of killing Anna and he wants to convince me he's really the nicest guy in the universe."

"Are you thinking it *might* have been him?"

"I've told you a million times—I have no fucking idea who killed Anna." She threw her head back in frustration and let out a big sigh.

"All right, just calm down. I'm only trying to help Danny."

"I know, but you've been up my grill all week long."

"Well, then this probably won't thrill you, but I've got one more question."

"Oh, God," she said, running her hands through her hair. She seemed as wired as someone on crack. "Now what?"

"I have this hunch that Anna had a date scheduled Friday night. A date that she made *after* she swapped nights with you. I think someone was supposed to meet her at the spa. And that may be the person who killed her."

She started to wave her arm, rejecting my comment outright, but then her body went suddenly still, as if I'd shot her with a tranquilizer dart. I could see her begin to turn over what I'd said in her mind.

"She never said anything to me," Piper said softly.

"But you were just thinking something."

She walked slowly to the bed and sat on the very end of it. "Her top," she said finally, her voice flat.

"What do you mean?"

"I just now thought of it. She wore this new top to work that day. I saw her change out of it in the locker room. It was sort of pinky brown and it had a drawstring at the top and it was really sexy. And I realize now that I had this thought about it in the back of my head then, but it never really formed because she'd said earlier that she had no plans that night."

"You mean that it was awfully sexy for someone who wasn't planning to go out?"

"No. I mean, yes, but also that she had worn it to work. When she was just planning to go back to the barn at the end of the day, she usually wore her spa uniform to work."

"Okay," I said, starting to pace. "Let's say she had a date that night. A new guy—or a relatively new guy—was meeting her at the spa. I know you said you weren't aware of any new men in her life, but is there anything she said that might give us a clue?"

She thought, her brow wrinkled in worry.

"I can't think of anything," she said. "Though now it makes me wonder about her wanting to change dates with me—you know, dates for leaving the spa for good."

"Yeah, that's exactly what I've been thinking. Is there any chance she could have started seeing Eric again?"

"N-o. *That* I would have been aware of. Like I told you, he was still in his wounded puppy dog mode."

"One more name. Danny's husband."

"What?" she said incredulously. "You asked me that before and I told you no way. Have you seen that man's body? Anna only liked hard bodies. Whenever she had a flabby guy on the table, she called him a Poppin' Fresh."

"Okay. Look, I'll get out of your hair now. I appreciate all your help. If you mull this over and anything comes to you, will you call me at the inn and let me know?"

"Yeah, okay. Does this mean I shouldn't be so freaked out about Josh?"

"I don't have the answer to that."

I heard the clack of the dead bolt the minute the door closed behind me, so I obviously hadn't put her mind at ease. It was almost five. I decided to see if I'd heard from the *Gloss* researcher before I made my way courtside. I walked down the stairs to the second floor, my footsteps hushed because of the thick carpeting. As I turned to walk toward my room, I saw someone in a dark coat standing in front of my door. I stopped in my tracks, and the person turned toward me.

It was Danny. And she was crying.

CHAPTER 21

"DANNY, WHAT'S THE matter?" I called out, hurrying toward her.

"Can we go inside?" she said in a fractured whisper. "I don't want anyone to hear."

The irony of her words was lost on her—it felt in the silent corridor as if the inn had been shut down for the season—but I quickly fished my key out of my bag and opened the door for us. While I turned on the table lamp, Danny dabbed at her eyes with a sodden tissue.

"Here, come and sit," I said, taking her by the arm and leading her to the couch. "Tell me what's happened."

"It's George," she said, tears running down her eyes again. "Bailey, I'm beginning to wonder if he might actually have done it. Murdered Anna."

I caught my breath. "Why, what's happened?"

"I spoke to the lawyer. George has been so evasive

lately, I don't trust him to tell me everything. The lawyer let slip that there were *dozens* of calls to Anna—to her cell phone and her room in the barn. George led me to believe that it was just a few calls—to discuss these retreats he wanted to organize."

"That's odd. Piper mentioned to me that George had called Anna a few times. If he'd been really pestering her, I think she would have said that."

"It doesn't appear as if he were even talking to her. Some of these calls were made during the hours when she was working, and they may have just been hang-ups. It's as if he simply called to hear her voice on her answering machine."

"It sounds as if George might have been fixated on Anna. Does that seem possible to you?"

She lowered her head, bringing her two clenched hands to her mouth. It was at least thirty seconds before she pulled them down and spoke.

"I snapped at you yesterday when you asked me about George, and I shouldn't have. I was struggling with the fact that—that you had touched on the truth. Just before George and I came east, I suspected him of having an affair with a neighbor. I found some pictures of her in his desk. George denied the affair, but it was obvious something was wrong—he had the *pictures*. This woman was younger than me, more attractive, and I went to her home to talk to her. Not in an angry way. I don't believe anger ever accomplishes anything. I asked her to let him go, for the sake of my marriage. She denied the whole thing. She said she'd seen him watching her and that she thought he was obsessed with her. At the time, I assumed she was just covering up. Right after that, George confessed that he had spent some time with this woman but that it had never gone anywhere sexually and that he would never let anything like that happen again. I thought things might have progressed further than he said, but I wanted to save my marriage and so I let it go. Now, in light of this new development, I'm wondering if she was telling the truth all along. The pictures showed her looking off to the side, from a distance. I think George took them without her realization. He *was* obsessed with her. It's just like what went on with Anna."

"Did you ask George about the phone calls to Anna?"

"Yes, I confronted him right after I talked to the lawyer. He got all squirmy, just as he did in the other situation. He said he was calling her about these retreats but that he often had a hard time getting through, so he'd try again and again. I asked him to leave then. I told him to check into a motel and just stay away—from me and the inn. I don't want him anywhere near me."

"Gosh, Danny, I don't know what to say to make you feel better about this. It sounds as if he has some sort of problem. But that doesn't mean he killed Anna."

She rose from the couch and began to walk back and forth across the room, her arms clenched tightly around her.

"I know this sounds awful, but what difference does it make? I can't stay married to him one way or the other."

"Look, Danny, it *does* make a difference. He's still your husband, and if he's arrested and found guilty of murder, it could be extremely detrimental to you and your business. I'm not going to give up on trying to prove that it wasn't George who did it. I found out some fascinating information today, by the way."

She stopped pacing. "What?"

I urged her back to the couch, and over the next few minutes I shared with her the story about Anna that I had learned in Wallingford. I also told her about Rich and the fact that he had known Anna in a previous life.

"I can't even begin to digest all of this," she said, her face wrinkled in worry. "Do you think Anna's death might have been an act of *revenge?*"

"It's a long shot, but I still need to look into it. I'm trying to track down where the two brothers ended up. What I feel most strongly about, though, is what I realized yesterday over at the spa with you: that Anna probably had a date scheduled the night she was murdered. I just spoke to Piper, and she remembered that Anna had worn her street clothes rather than her uniform to work that day, something she wouldn't ordinarily do if she were going straight back to the barn."

"What about Rich—where does he fit into all of this?"

"I'm not sure. His being here might be just a coincidence."

"Shouldn't you tell the police what you know?"

"If they try to arrest George, absolutely. Until then I feel it's best to wait until I have something concrete. Otherwise I'd be spanked and banished back to New York for playing amateur sleuth."

"When *do* you have to go back to New York?"

"Tomorrow," I said, thinking of Jack. "I have something tomorrow night that I—that I really don't want to miss. But I'll keep at it until then. I feel like I'm inching closer to the truth."

Of course, as I'd been sharing all this new and fascinating information with Danny, I'd once again left out any mention of one of the juiciest tidbits of all: the release massage that had been added without her knowledge to the spa menu. I was going to tell her at some point, cross my heart and hope to die. But this wasn't the right moment. Not with her so distraught about George.

I glanced at my watch. I needed to find out why the intern at *Gloss* hadn't called me back, and I also didn't want to miss Rich. I told Danny I had a few more leads to follow up this afternoon but asked if we could spend time together later. She said that since it was Friday night, the dining room would be open and suggested we meet for dinner there at eight.

As soon as she'd repaired her makeup and left my room, I did a quick look around, checking again for evidence of snoopers. Then I phoned the intern. No answer. If she'd left for the day, I was going to throttle her on Monday. But as I was about to open the door of my room, she called back on my cell phone.

"Sorry, sorry," she said. "I was having some computer trouble. I found one of the guys you were looking for, but not the other."

"Let's hear what you've got."

"Okay, there's a Carson Ballard in Irvine, California. His birth year is one year off from what we talked about, but I figured this has got to be the guy. I also checked the whole U.S. and there's not another one anywhere else."

While she was speaking, I'd upended my purse in search of a notepad. I asked for Carson's number and scrawled it along with his name onto a piece of paper. I asked if she'd had any luck with Harold.

"There's just one Harold Ballard, but he's like a hundred or something. That's all I found."

I told her that I appreciated her efforts but I wasn't done. I'd need her to research one more name for me, which I hoped to have within an hour. I could practically hear her stifling a big fat groan.

As soon as I hung up, I tried the number for Carson Ballard. I got an answering machine and heard a message from one of those little men with the high voice that comes with the machine. I didn't leave a message.

I left the building a few minutes before Rich's lesson was due to end, just so there was no chance of missing him. It had grown colder outside, and the western half of the sky was churning with dark clouds. As I neared the court, I spotted Rich hurriedly popping balls into the hopper. I couldn't help but feel anxious about speaking with him. I was going to have to press him—to find out what his real connection had been to Anna and what he might know about her past. But there was a chance he might be the killer, and I didn't relish being alone with him. I was relieved when I saw a groundskeeper on the far side of the tennis court, chasing leaves away with one of those handheld blowers.

Rich glanced over when he saw me coming, but he didn't stop his efforts. By the time I reached the court, he was setting the hopper into a small storage shed just outside the gate. He looked up as I approached, but instead of one of those phony smiles, I was treated to a sour face, the kind he probably saved for when his students turned their backs.

"Lemme guess," he said sarcastically. "You liked my morning lesson so much you want another—even in the rain."

"No. I'm just wondering why you lied to me."

"You mean when I said you had a pretty good backhand?"

"When you said you only knew Anna in passing."

He rammed the hook of the padlock hard into the hole, holding the shed door closed with one hip as he did it. When he'd finished he spun around toward me. A big drop of rain plopped down onto my bangs.

"Who says otherwise?" he said.

"I do. I know you went to the same high school in Milford as Anna."

"What of it?" he said, his mouth in a snarl. "And why would I have owed *you* any kind of explanation?"

"I'm just curious as to why you would have gone to the trouble of lying about it."

"You're an awful little busybody, aren't you," he said, taking a step closer—too close. "Did the police deputize you? Are you trying to help them solve the case?"

I leaned my body back slightly so that he wasn't in my face. The rain had begun to fall harder now, dampening our clothes. Glancing over to where the groundskeeper had stood, I saw that he was no longer there. An alarm began to go off in my brain.

"Nobody *deputized* me," I said. "Someone just happened to tell me that Anna knew you a long time ago."

"Oh yeah, who?" His dark green eyes seemed to grab hold of me.

"One of the other therapists," I lied. I wasn't going to admit anything about my road trip.

"Yeah, I knew Anna, but like I said, so what? She was married to a friend of mine from Camden—Tommy Cole. It lasted about fifteen minutes."

"And you just happened to bump into her here?"

"That's right. I'm glad to see that you can think better than you hit a tennis ball."

The idea of him just bumping into Anna didn't seem so far-fetched. Anna had returned to the general area of the country she'd been raised in, and Rich had never left. But then why was he being so defensive?

"Where is this guy Tommy now?" I asked.

"What's it to you, anyway?" he snapped.

"Look, I'm just curious. I found Anna's body. I want to know what happened to her."

"Tommy? He's still in Germany. Army. He's been there for years. Now if you don't mind, I'm getting soaked."

He yanked off his baseball cap, shook some drops from the beak, and slid it back on his shiny bald head. He started to move past me, his wet sleeve brushing against my hand.

"Just one more thing," I said. "I heard Anna had some trouble in her past. Did you know anything about it?"

"The only trouble I ever heard about was that she couldn't keep her pants up."

He broke instantly into a sprint, leaving me standing there alone as fat raindrops splattered onto the asphalt court. I watched him disappear around the east end of the main building toward the parking lot, and then I broke into a jog myself, hurrying back to the inn.

By the time I reached my room, the rain was coming down hard. My windows were foggy and streaked, and I could hear the drum of water on the small roof outside my bedroom window. I pulled the little table against the door. Then I called the intern at *Gloss,* telling her I wouldn't need her help on that other name. I peeled off my sodden clothes and laid them to dry over several pieces of furniture. After slipping into the terry robe from my bathroom, I curled up on the bed with my composition book and jotted down notes from my afternoon conversations with Piper, Danny, and Rich.

I found Danny's revelation about George immensely troubling. Having an affair outside of your marriage was one thing, but surreptitiously taking pictures of women and then drooling over the prints put you in a whole different league. It was just plain creepy.

And I knew from experience how hard it must be for Danny to face the facts about her husband. Of course, I had no right to look down my nose at the situation. I'd been married for eighteen months to someone who was a closet gambler, who bet thousands of dollars on football games and horses without my ever knowing. I could envision what Danny would go through in the months ahead. After you find out someone you love and trust is not who you think he is, you spend hours replaying every memory, trying to spot the warnings with hindsight. You feel as if you ought to forfeit those years of your life because you had them all wrong. And you feel about as dumb as an eggplant for never having seen what was under your nose.

Yet as creepy as George now seemed, I really didn't believe he'd killed Anna. I'd had such a strong vibe when I stood in front of the vanity counter in the dressing room. Now that I'd talked to Piper, I could *see* Anna there in her new pink top, primping for her date.

And yet I'd been unable to dig up any evidence as to who the mystery man was. If Anna had snagged a new guy, wouldn't someone have seen her with him, wouldn't Piper have gotten wind of it? Maybe this was a first date. But then if the relationship was brand new, what reason would the guy have had to kill her and then gift-wrap her body?

As I glanced back over both the notes I'd written today and the earlier ones, I was struck by how often last summer turned up. William Litchauer had died then. It was in the summer that Anna had sensed she was being watched. Rich had started freelancing at the inn back then, bumping into Anna. Josh had learned about the release massage. I sensed that all the references to summer were pointing to *something,* but I didn't know what.

I'd told Danny earlier that I believed I was inching closer to the truth, and I *did* feel that way. But it was now almost seven o'clock on Friday night, the night before I was leaving, and I had no more leads to pursue. This might be as close as I would get before I pointed my Jeep toward New York.

I let the drumming of the rain lull me into another nap, knowing I'd regret it. But I felt suddenly weary from my trip this morning and my conversation with Rich and from everything else that had happened since

I'd been back at the Cedar Inn. I had also detected a slight, annoying tickle in my throat, a cold rearing its ugly head. For that I could probably thank Bob Kass, who'd been spreading germs around his den like a crop duster.

When I woke an hour later, I felt even worse. I found two loose and linty ibuprofen in the pocket of my purse and took them before changing into the one dress I'd brought, a light wool black number with a deep V neck. It was a little fancy, but I couldn't face my black pants one more minute. When I left the room I took a black wrap with me and stuffed my composition book in my purse for safekeeping.

I wasn't sure whether I was supposed to meet Danny in the dining room or the lobby, but as I paused on the second-floor landing to fix the strap of my shoe, I heard her voice from the lobby. And there was another voice I recognized: Beck's.

I descended to the ground floor slowly, trying to pick up the gist of what they were saying. I couldn't hear the words, but the tone sounded contentious.

"Is everything okay?" I called out as I stepped into the lobby. It was just the two of them standing there, Danny all in lavender and Beck towering over her in a black raincoat that gleamed with water. The lounge appeared empty, though from down the hall I could hear music and the murmur of conversation from the dining room. Beck took me in with his eyes, and I suddenly felt self-conscious with my boobs hanging out from the V of my dress.

"Detective Beck is looking for George," Danny said. She'd lowered her voice, but her agitation was apparent.

"I told him that George and I are not residing together at this moment and that I have no idea where he is. But he seems to think that I'm not being truthful."

"I wasn't suggesting that at all, Mrs. Hubner," Beck said, turning his eyes back to Danny. "I simply wanted to know if you had any suggestions where we might look."

"And I don't know, Detective," Danny said crisply.

I crossed the lobby, my heels clicking on the tiled floor. As I got closer, I saw that Natalie was at the front desk, moving papers around and trying to look busy.

"Are you planning to arrest George?" I asked, my voice low. "Should Danny be getting hold of the lawyer?"

"We just want to ask him a few more questions," Beck said. I'd looked him straight in the eye when I spoke, but he made his comment to Danny, not me. Something about that just annoyed me to death.

"Aren't there any *other* angles worth investigating in this case?" I blurted out. "Piper said that the night of the murder Anna was dressed up, like she had a date."

"Is that so?" Beck asked, glancing back at me. I'd shocked myself with my comment, but he looked even more surprised.

"Yes," I said, unable to stop. "And—and this summer Anna felt someone was spying on her. Shouldn't the police be looking into *that*?"

I started to turn away as I said the last part, flushed with embarrassment, ready to flee the dining room. Natalie had been pretending to mind her own business up until this point, but now I saw her head pop up.

She looked surprised, worried even, and her eyes shot toward Danny, who was standing just behind me.

"Should I send you a check for your consultation, Ms. Weggins?" Beck said. "Is that what you'd like?"

I turned back in his direction, fearful of what the look on his face would be. And it wasn't pretty. His eyes burned with anger.

"I'm just offering a suggestion," I said.

He ignored me and turned to Danny. "If you make contact with your husband, please ask him to get hold of me."

The front door burst open at that moment, and the three of us snapped our heads toward it simultaneously, as if we all expected something momentous. But it was just the night desk clerk, the one who'd started working late in Natalie's place. He glanced sheepishly at us, aware that he'd barged in at an awkward moment.

"Uh, sorry I'm a little late," he announced to Natalie. "Let me just get out of these wet clothes and then you can go." He slipped by us and disappeared down the corridor that ran behind the front desk.

Without saying another word, Beck turned away. He strode across the lobby and yanked open the door, then closed it quietly, as if he were working hard to control how pissed he was.

Danny let out a pent-up sigh as soon as he was gone. I felt as though it might be two days before the color left my cheeks.

"Natalie, I'm sorry you had to be in the thick of this," Danny said, turning to the desk.

"Uh, that's okay," she replied, though she looked funny, as though it really had unsettled her.

We said good night to her and made our way down the long front hallway of the inn to the dining room. As

I put one foot inside the room, I felt as if I'd just been beamed to another planet. Classical music played quietly in the background, a fire crackled in the fireplace, and several tables of diners chatted by candlelight.

We each ordered wine—I opted for Cabernet and Danny for Chardonnay—and we didn't begin to discuss what had just transpired in the lobby until each of us had taken a large sip. Danny's white wine glowed in the candlelight.

"I see now what you meant when you said the police might not be receptive to any theories from you," Danny said. "He was livid."

"I can hardly blame him," I admitted. "I came across as obnoxious and interfering. I wish I *did* have something more concrete I could use to convince him, but I don't. After I saw you this afternoon, I followed up on a few more leads, but they didn't go anywhere."

"I so appreciate all you've done, Bailey," Danny said.

"It hasn't amounted to *anything*. But who knows? Maybe something I said to Beck will spark something in *his* mind. Then he really *will* owe me a damn consulting fee."

I laughed sarcastically when I said it, but I felt crummy inside. Whatever attraction Beck once had toward me had undoubtedly fled, and although it was probably for the best, I didn't like how it had ended.

"Look, let's leave this miserable business behind us—at least for an hour," Danny said. "Talk to me about New York, about Greenwich Village, about *Gloss*. It will do me a world of good."

It did me good, too, to steer away from Anna, and the

spa, and Beck. I ricocheted all over the place in my stories, talking about Landon and the zany, eclectic dinner parties he gave and all my little rituals in the Village. As I spoke, I could sense my cold gathering steam, but the conversation, delicious food, and wine kept my mind off that as well.

"This has been so nice," Danny said when we were finished. "How about a brandy in the lounge before bed?"

"I'm going to say yes to that. I had a nap before dinner, and I desperately need something to knock me out or I'll be up for hours."

It was just after nine, and I expected that the lobby would be quiet now, but as we came down the hallway we saw a woman in a blue raincoat standing by the front desk. The clerk must have just spoken to her because I saw her shake her head in irritation.

"Is everything okay, Earl?" Danny asked as we reached the lobby.

"This woman is waiting for Piper, and I'm doing my best to find her, but I'm not having any luck," he announced.

She was about Piper's age, mid-thirties, and fairly attractive, though she had her hair pulled so tightly into a ponytail that it made her eyes appear permanently startled. She turned to Danny, having guessed that she was the one with the clout.

"I'm Lacey Cox, a friend of Piper's," she announced. "I've got money for her, and I can't leave till I give it to her. I'm later than I promised to be, but she said she'd wait."

"You know what room she's in, Earl?" Danny asked.

"She told me twenty-seven," Lacey said, not giving Earl a chance to answer. "He tried it and there's no answer."

"I talked to her earlier in the day up there," I said. "But I know she wanted to get an early start. Maybe she couldn't wait any longer."

"It's four hundred dollars," Lacey said. "She wouldn't leave without it."

"What about the barn?" I asked. "She may have gone back to her room there."

"I had the bellboy check," Earl said. "The room's empty and there's no sign of her."

Danny and I exchanged anxious glances. I felt a tiny tremor of fear beginning along the outer edges of my body.

"I know where her car is," I said. "why don't I check to see if it's still there."

I grabbed one of the complimentary umbrellas from the stand by the front door and headed outside. The rain had tapered off, and without bothering to open the umbrella, I ran so fast that my lungs pinched. As I reached the far end of the parking lot, I was flooded with an awful sense of déjà vu. It was one week ago tonight that I'd stood in this same place just before all hell broke loose.

I spotted Piper's car exactly where it had been parked before. Not good. I jogged back to the front entrance of the inn and found Danny nervously shifting from one leg to the other on the stoop.

"It's still there," I said. "We'd better check her room. But don't let on that we're alarmed."

Back in the lobby, Lacey was tapping her red nails on the counter and Earl had the phone to his ear.

"Still no answer," he said.

Danny announced to the two of them that Piper's car was still in the parking lot and that she and I would head up to her room in case she was asleep and hadn't heard the phone.

"Should I go, too?" Lacey asked annoyingly.

"Why don't you wait here," I suggested. "If Piper's there, we'll call down."

"I don't like this, Bailey," Danny said as we hurried up the stairs. "I don't like it at all."

"No, something's not right," I said. "Do you have the key ready?"

I rapped on the door four or five times and called out Piper's name. No answer. Taking a step backward, I let Danny unlock the door. We pushed it open together.

It took Danny a few seconds to find the light switch, and I held my breath until she did. When the two bed-side lights came on simultaneously, we saw that the room was empty. In fact, there was no sign Piper had ever been there. None of her belongings were scattered about and the duvet had been left perfectly smoothed.

"Are you sure this was the room she was in?" Danny asked.

"I think so—fourth on the left. Are all the rooms decorated the same way?"

"No, they're all different."

"This was definitely the room, then. Look, she might have gotten bored up here and gone to some other spot in the inn. Why don't we check the exercise room and the solarium. Anyplace else you can think of? A public space she might have decided to chill in."

"You've named them, other than the lounge. There's a small card room off the dining room, but no one ever uses it."

"Let's check everything floor by floor. Do you want to split up—or go together?"

"I don't think I could bear to do this alone," Danny said.

We began by first heading to the floor below, my floor, and taking a quick look up and down the corridor. The only people in sight were a couple letting themselves into a room at the very end. Next the ground floor. We glanced in the dining room, the card room, and the lounge. With each place we checked that we *didn't* find Piper, I grew more anxious. Next we headed to the west end of the inn, seeing no one as we moved along the maze of corridors. The solarium was dark and empty. Finally we went downstairs to the basement, taking a back staircase near the solarium that I had never seen before. This is where the mouse had come from, I thought, like something scavenged by a grave robber. Though the lower floor had been renovated with sparkling white walls, it was still the basement and it was eerie down there. The exercise room was empty. As we returned to the stairwell, the furnace came on with a large groan, making us both jump.

"Danny," I said, "I'm really worried. Her car is here, so it's clear she hasn't left. I think we should check the spa."

"The *spa? Why?*"

"I don't know. Because she may have left something

in the locker room there. Besides, it's the only place we haven't looked."

What I didn't reveal was the thought that had grabbed hold of me: That's where the first murder happened. If the killer was now after Piper, he may have taken her there.

We entered through the side door, Danny struggling again with the new lock. If I'd thought it had been spooky in the spa this afternoon, tonight it was terrifying. Danny and I practically clung to each other as we slunk down every corridor, pushing doors open, calling Piper's name. There was no sign of her.

"Now what?" Danny asked.

"I'm not sure. Maybe we should try the barn. I know the bellboy ran up there, but perhaps she's in one of the other rooms—saying good-bye to one of the therapists. And if we don't find her, we should call the police."

Danny suggested we leave by the main entrance of the spa—it would be faster. Before she opened the door, she reached into the bottom drawer of the desk in the reception area and withdrew a large flashlight.

"There are lights on the path to the barn. But I'll feel safer with this."

We exited the spa and walked in the dark along the edge of the parking lot toward the back of the building.

"Give me the flashlight for just a sec," I said. "I want to flash it in Piper's car."

We crossed the parking lot in the direction of the Beetle. It still sat there packed to the brim, ready for someone to take it somewhere. I flashed the light into the back, but there was nothing ominous, just gobs of junk in disarray. Stepping back from the car, I let the long beam bounce around the parking lot a few times and into the trees and a cluster of boulders that bordered it. On the blacktop, near the boulders, there was a scattering of wet leaves.

"Hold on," I said to Danny. "I just want to check this out."

With Danny close behind, I walked toward the area I'd noticed. It was just leaves, but there were more of them in that location than in any other area.

When we reached the rim of the parking lot, I directed the light beam into the woody area that bordered it and along the base of the boulders. An area of leaves appeared recently tossed. I glanced over at Danny.

"Do you want to wait here? I just want to explore a little farther."

"No, I'm staying with you."

We stepped off the blacktop and, holding the flashlight, I led us around the boulders, my high heels quickly becoming soaked. Suddenly there was a flash of tan ahead of us. Even though I'd begun to expect the worst, the shock walloped me.

It was Piper, covered partially with leaves and lying facedown in a tan raincoat, her long red hair wet and matted to her head and the side of her face.

CHAPTER 22

I**T SEEMED TO** take Danny forever to grasp the full meaning of what she was looking at. She kept staring at the body, trying to process it all.

"Oh, my God," she said finally, squeezing my arm so tightly that it hurt. "Is it—"

"Yes," I said, my voice hoarse. "Yes, it's Piper."

Danny started to move in that direction, but I pulled her back.

"Danny," I implored, "we can't go near there. We can't touch a thing." Last Friday night I'd disturbed the evidence because I'd had no choice, but I wasn't going to let anything happen in this situation.

"But what if she's still alive?"

"We need to call 911. We have to let the paramedics deal with it."

Part of me wondered if I *should* check for a pulse, to see if she might be alive. Yet it didn't seem possible that she could be. She was facedown, and there was an unnatural tilt to her head, as though she had turned it almost totally around like an owl. She had to be dead. And someone had killed her. It was clear that she couldn't have tripped and fallen, because leaves covered about half of her body, as if the killer had made a fast, incomplete attempt to hide it.

We rushed back into the inn, clinging to each other. Danny wasn't saying anything, though I could hear her breathing hard and shivering. With only my wrap around me, I should have been freezing, but the only thing I could feel right then was fear. And guilt. I should have told Beck about the release massage. If I had, Piper might not be dead.

Earl and Lacey were right where we'd left them in the lobby. Without explanation Danny grabbed the phone at the front desk and called 911. Her first words were an incoherent scramble, and I could tell the operator was asking her to slow down and repeat herself. I was about to offer to take over, but she took a deep breath, calmed down finally, and explained that she had found a woman dead on the grounds of the inn. When she set the phone back down, Earl just stood there with his mouth agape. Lacey erupted.

"Jesus fucking Christ!" she yelled. "It's Piper, isn't it? I should have known something like this would happen. She was terrified of this place. And now look what happened."

"Why don't you try to calm down," I told her. "Your screaming isn't going to help one bit."

"Earl, please go check the dining room," Danny said. "See who's there."

"There's nothing—there's no one in the dining room. The last people left when you went outside."

"Start rounding up people from the staff, then," I said. "No one should leave the inn."

I pulled Danny aside and suggested that I stand outside so I could direct the ambulance and police and that she remain indoors and keep an eye on the staff.

"All right," she said. Still not much of a reaction on her part. I wondered if she was in shock.

This time the ambulance arrived ahead of the cops. As I stood on the step, my shawl pulled tightly around me, they lurched to a stop in front of the inn. When the driver rolled down his window, I quickly explained what had happened. I jogged across the parking lot in front of them, and once the ambulance had stopped I used the flashlight to point the paramedics in the right direction. I waited a few minutes at a short distance, until I overheard one of them say she was dead. Then I hurried back to the inn. Ten or twelve inn personnel had gathered in the lobby, looking bug-eyed with terror. As Danny tried to comfort them, I watched out the window.

It was only a few minutes before two cop cars arrived in unison, one a cruiser, the other unmarked. From what I could tell, Beck wasn't with them. While most of the entourage headed around the building, two detectives, whom I recognized from last Friday night, came into the inn and spoke with Danny. She told them quickly about Piper being missing and us finding the body. One of the detectives walked over to the lounge doorway, glanced inside, and suggested we all sit there until the police had a chance to speak to us. Within two minutes Danny was called outside. I was left with Earl, Lacey, and a dozen other people I didn't know, all inn employees. I felt as though I were in one of those disaster movies where you find yourself in a grim situation with a bunch of strangers who by the second half of the film will be at one another's throats.

I realized suddenly that my body was chilled and achy, thanks to the cold that had been gaining ground all evening long. I found the remote control I'd seen Danny use, turned on the gas fire in the fireplace, and flopped into one of the armchairs directly in front of it. The flames performed the same monotonous dance over and over. I watched them anyway. My brain felt sodden with fear and guilt and anxiety, hindered from forming a coherent thought, but I tried nonetheless to piece together what might have happened to Piper.

She had obviously been going to her car when she was attacked. Maybe she had needed something from her belongings. Or maybe she was finally taking off, tired of waiting for loudmouth Lacey to arrive with her money. The killer had either spotted her unexpectedly in the parking lot or he may have lain in wait for her, knowing that she was heading out sometime tonight.

Had *Josh* done it? Piper had told me she was afraid of him. But what purpose would it have served for Josh? Piper was leaving town, going someplace, in her words, as far away from Warren as she could get. Besides, as Piper had told me, Josh didn't want to draw any attention to the sordid little situation at the spa.

Since Anna and Piper were both involved in release massage, it wasn't a big leap to assume that their deaths were connected *somehow* to that, rather than simply to their being employed by the spa. If there was one thing I'd learned as a crime writer, it was that bad things often led to other bad things. Maybe the killer was a client who'd been serviced by both girls. Or a sexual predator targeting them because they were prostitutes.

I should have spoken up. Yes, I'd wanted to protect Danny's business, and that was the main reason I hadn't come clean to Beck about the prostitution, but I had also been caught up in playing *Nancy Drew and the Case of the Cedar Inn Corpse.* Because of my pride and my ego, I was partly responsible for Piper's death.

And what a pathetic detective I was. I'd been on a wild-goose chase for the last few days, pursuing the "Anna's mystery date" angle and the "haunted by her past" scenario. And neither had turned out to be right.

The lounge began to receive new arrivals: five or six inn guests in their jammies and robes, looking either frightened and disoriented or totally put out. One guy still had one of those Breathe Right strips across his nose. I was anxious to know what was going on and what had happened to Danny, but when I walked over and tried to poke my head out the doorway, a patrol cop who had been stationed there asked me to step back inside.

Danny returned about ten minutes later. As shaken as she must have felt, she'd now moved into stay-in-control gear.

"They're going through the inn, room by room, asking people to come down here," she whispered.

"They're also trying to track down everybody who ate at the restaurant."

"Is there any guest who's registered tonight who was also here last weekend?"

She smiled ruefully. "Only you. I checked on the computer."

"Just watch," I said sarcastically. "Beck will probably arrest *me* when he realizes it."

"He's here, by the way—running the show. He asked if you were waiting in the lounge. I'm sure he's going to talk to you before long."

The mere thought of that made me nervous. And not just because of the contentiousness between Beck and me in the lobby earlier. I'd found another body and would have to confess everything I'd dug up on Anna so far, including the release massage. I didn't want to think about what the fallout would be. I could just imagine Beck bringing out cuffs and a red-hot poker.

The doors behind us slid open and we turned automatically to see who was entering the room. Danny and I stared in utter disbelief.

Piper had just walked through the door, alive, whole, her bright red hair pulled back in a ponytail. Danny and I looked at each other in utter disbelief, then rushed to her.

"How—how did you . . . ?" Danny fumbled, completely disoriented. "Wait, what's going on?"

"I have no idea," Piper said, looking both confused and scared. "The police knocked on the door of my room and told me to come downstairs. What's *happened?*"

"That wasn't you—in the—"

"But what room were you in?" I asked, interrupting Danny. "We looked for you in room twenty-seven, but there was no sign of you."

From the far end of the room, Lacey must have suddenly glanced up, because she let out a scream and practically flung herself in our direction. Everyone in the room stared at her.

"My God, Piper, they said you were *dead,*" she said, reaching us. "This place is insane."

"*What?*" Piper demanded. "Will someone please explain what's happening?"

"We will," I said, "but please just tell me first. Where *were* you all this time?"

"I moved to another room. Natalie asked me to switch because the room I was in is part of a suite and she said they needed to make sure it was ready for a guest checking in tomorrow morning. I asked her to tell Lacey when she got here. Then I fell asleep."

I knew as soon as she'd said the name what the truth was. I turned to Danny. Her face was wrinkled in confusion as she struggled to understand what had happened, to figure out who was actually lying dead in the leaves.

"Danny," I said, pulling her aside. "Danny, look at me."

"Bailey, what in the world is going on?"

"Danny," I whispered, trying not to show how distraught I was. "You've got to brace yourself. I think it's Natalie out there."

"*What?* Oh dear God, no."

"Yes," I said. "I just automatically assumed it was

Piper because of the red hair and because she was missing. Does Natalie have a tan raincoat?"

"Yes, yes, yes." Her eyes began to fill with tears.

"We better go out and tell the police. Though they probably know by now if they've found ID on her."

As we started to leave the room, Piper grabbed my arm.

"Aren't you going to tell me what's going on?" she asked desperately.

"Someone's been killed," I said. "We thought it was you because we couldn't find you. I'm just glad you're okay."

She looked freaked by the news and began peppering me with more questions, but I explained that Danny and I needed to speak to the police.

After I persuaded the patrol cop to let us out because we had new information, we were led to the suite of offices behind the front desk. As we reached the door to the small sitting room, we saw Beck standing inside, talking to a guy in plain clothes and a state trooper. The patrol cop indicated that we should go in.

Beck focused his attention on Danny, who, clearly shaken, blurted out the discovery we'd just made. I could tell from Beck's expression that we weren't offering him anything he didn't already know. He thanked Danny and told her that, yes, it *was* Natalie. Her parents' number had been in her wallet, and they had been contacted. That was all he was at liberty to reveal at the moment, he said, his eyes never leaving Danny's face. We turned to go, and he called out to me.

"Miss Weggins. Will you stay, please?" he said. "I have some questions for you."

I squeezed Danny's arm as she left the room, the state trooper trailing behind her. Beck took a seat, and, unbidden, I did the same, figuring that as miffed as he might be at me, he wasn't going to force me to stand through the questioning. The other cop busied himself with paperwork on the table.

"I'd like to hear your version of what happened tonight," Beck announced.

"Sure. Though I was with Danny the whole time, so I probably don't have much to offer beyond what she's already told you."

"Let me be the judge of that," he snapped.

Clearly I was still in the doghouse. As he took notes in that trusty little notebook of his, I went through the story pretty quickly: Lacey coming with money. My going to the parking lot. Danny and me searching the inn, etc., finding the body, and assuming it must be Piper.

"Trouble just loves following you around, doesn't it," he said harshly when I'd finished. "Why do you think that is?" The severity in his tone took me aback— and the other cop's head shot up in surprise.

"I have no idea," I said as coolly as I could. Maybe I'd been out of line earlier by implying he wasn't being thorough enough, but that was no reason for him to treat me like something nasty he'd just discovered on the bottom of his shoe. "I—"

"You need to come down to the station tomorrow to make a statement," he said, cutting me off.

"Fine," I said.

As I rose to go, so did the other cop. With papers gathered in one hand, he went out of the room ahead of me. I paused near the door, wondering if this was the right moment to tell Beck about the release massage. Since it was Natalie lying dead behind the boulders, not Piper, it meant that the murders probably had nothing to do with what had been going on at the spa—after all, Natalie wasn't even connected to the spa. But I knew that I still needed to come clean about my discovery. I'll wait till tomorrow, I thought. When I could grab Beck alone and the atmosphere might be less tense. I reached for the door handle.

"Miss Weggins," Beck called out.

I turned around and faced him, hoping that because we were now alone, he might say something to diffuse the tension between us.

"Don't talk to anyone out there, do you hear me?" he snapped. "To any guests or to anyone who works at the inn. This isn't your business—and you're to keep your nose out of it."

It felt like a slap. I turned quickly and left, yanking the door closed behind me. I realized that Beck no longer trusted me and I couldn't entirely blame him. But his behavior seemed out of line. I tried to put it down to the enormous pressure he was under with two murders on his hands—but that didn't make it bother me any less.

Back in the lounge, I scanned the room for Danny, but she was now missing in action. There were a few new faces in the room—massage therapists who I assumed were residents of the barn. Eric was with them. He stared at me from across the room, his expression never changing. I looked around for Josh, then remembered he lived in a town house in Warren.

Someone had taken my seat by the fire, and I was forced to settle for a straight-backed chair at a game table. My throat was really starting to throb. I sat down, resting my elbows on the table and my head in my hands, trying to shut out the noise. Pushing my confrontation with Beck from my mind, I focused on Natalie. Why *her?* She wasn't involved at the spa, she hardly knew Anna. Maybe there really *was* a serial killer at large, someone who worked at the inn or spa or who lived in the area and had simply targeted two victims at Danny's inn. None of it made any sense to me. But I also felt some of my guilt ebb away. When I'd thought Piper was the one lying dead, I'd felt partly responsible because I hadn't coughed up what I knew about the spa. But it didn't seem as if Natalie's death could possibly be connected to that.

After about ten minutes, Danny entered the room and walked directly across to the table where I stood. There was an odd brightness to her eyes, as if the strain of the night were finally getting to her.

"What's going on?" I asked.

"I'm shutting down the inn," she said resolutely. "There's a madman on the loose, and I'm not giving him another chance to hurt anyone here."

"But what about the guests?" I asked.

She explained that she and the inn manager, whom she'd called to the scene, had been given permission by the police to use one of the offices. They were going to call other hotels in the area and make arrangements for guests to stay there. I asked her if she needed help, and she said it would be best if they did it alone because they knew personnel at some of the hotels and could call in favors.

The next hour was awful. Danny went off to execute her evacuation plan, and I was left to ruminate and feel the fire spreading through my throat. I asked permission once to go to my room and was told no way by the patrol cop. Despite my body's aching from the cold, I was anxious to be doing something, anything, and I felt frustrated I couldn't.

Gradually the crowd in the lounge thinned. People were escorted away to be interviewed by the police. Eric left, moving by me without ever acknowledging my presence. Danny came into the room periodically, looking for guests in order to announce what their new accommodations would be. One woman had a hissy fit when she learned that she and her husband would be finishing up their romantic getaway at the Days Inn nine miles away. Danny, looking totally spent, made no attempt to mollify her.

It was midnight when Danny and I finally departed, with only the cops left behind. I was dressed in jeans by then, having been allowed to run upstairs to my room with a police escort and stuff my things into my bag. Danny and I agreed that I would follow her in my Jeep. As we stepped outside, we saw that the far end of the parking lot and the adjoining wooded area were cordoned off with yellow police tape and lit up like a movie set. Since both of our cars were in the front area, there was no trouble getting them. Danny pulled out first, creeping along at a snail's pace, and I followed behind her.

She had told me earlier that her place was secluded,

and she wasn't kidding. It was a one-story bungalow set back in some woods, about ten minutes farther from town. As we pulled in the driveway, a security light came on and she hit her brakes suddenly. A man was climbing from a car parked near her garage. My stomach started to knot. As he stepped out of the shadows, I saw that it was George.

CHAPTER 23

DANNY ROLLED DOWN her window as George approached her car. I just stayed where I was, my hand on the door handle, ready to do something if it was necessary. I couldn't hear what they were saying, but after a moment Danny shook her head adamantly and then George slunk off, climbed into his car, and backed out of the driveway. He looked over in my direction as he drove by—and glared at me.

I pulled my Jeep next to Danny's car and hurriedly joined her on the driveway. As she unlocked the door of the house, I stood with my back to her, scanning the dense foliage at the perimeter of the yard. I couldn't wait to get inside.

A light had been left on in the living room, and Danny quickly turned on others. Her house wasn't large, but it was charming, with lots of rustic antique pieces and Provence-style prints. There was a comfy living room and a large open kitchen and dining area with a fireplace. I guessed that down the hall were a couple of bedrooms.

"Do you want anything to drink, Bailey?" Danny's voice cracked as she spoke.

"Just some water. What did George want?"

"Not wine? I'm going to pour myself a big glass of white wine."

"Sure, that would be great." Though I felt so awful—from my cold and everything else—that I doubted it would help.

"You asked about George," she said as she opened the refrigerator. "He said he's been waiting here since he heard the news on the radio. He wanted to see what he could do to help."

"But you told him to go?"

"Yes, I can't trust him. Not after those phone calls to Anna. I need him so much right now, but—"

She was rummaging through the fridge, her back to me, and suddenly she stopped and her shoulders began to shake. As she pulled out the bottle of white wine, she was crying hard.

"I can't believe Natalie is dead," she said, sobbing. "I feel responsible. I should have closed the inn down earlier."

I went to her and put my arms around her.

"Danny, you can't blame yourself. It wouldn't have made any sense to close the inn down then. Life has to go on."

She managed to pour two glasses of white wine, her hands shaking so much that some of it splashed onto the counter. She wiped it up with a paper towel and then used the same towel to dab at her eyes.

"Natalie was so young and innocent and full of life," she said. "Why would someone do this to her?"

"I don't have an answer," I said. "Either there really *is* a homicidal maniac on the loose or else there's a connection between the two women that we just don't know about. Let me ask you a question. When we were talking about the case in the lobby with Beck, earlier in the evening, Natalie gave you a kind of worried look at one point. I couldn't tell exactly why."

"I'm not sure what you mean," Danny said.

"She shot you a look with her eyes. It was when I said something about Anna. I was asking Beck why he wasn't considering any other angles. At the time I thought she was just surprised by the contentiousness of the conversation, but now I'm wondering if something suddenly occurred to her."

She furrowed her brow in puzzlement. "I'm sorry— I don't remember anything like that."

I didn't push it. It was clear she couldn't recall the moment, and besides, I was a walking basket case. I asked her to show me to my room, and she led me down the hall to a guest room. I hugged her good night and crawled into bed without bothering to take off anything except my shoes and jeans.

Propped against the pillows, I nearly chugged the rest of the wine, hoping it would knock me out. But it didn't. I lay in bed with a pit in my stomach the size of a ham. My head was stuffed and my throat pulsed in pain. I wished I could sob like Danny, but nothing came out.

The next morning, I woke with a jolt to find Danny sitting on the edge of my bed. I knew it had to be late because the harsh light of an overcast day filled the room.

"What time is it?" I asked groggily. My throat felt raw and my head hurt a bit; but, surprisingly, my cold had not gotten any worse. It seemed to be idling, like a car at a red light.

"It's eleven."

"Oh God, sorry," I said. "I don't think I fell asleep until five. What's going on? Any news about Natalie?"

"I spoke to her father. He said that someone broke her neck. And wait till you hear this. He also told me that Natalie had been on several dates with Eric recently."

"*No!*" I exclaimed.

"Apparently the police have taken him downtown for questioning. Maybe he's some kind of a madman, Bailey."

"This sheds a new light on everything," I said. "I mean, I always wondered if Eric could have killed Anna, but I never once considered him a suspect in Natalie's death. Is this the first you've heard they were dating?"

"Yes. Natalie often chats about her personal life, but she never said anything about this. Maybe she thought I'd object because of the work connection."

"Could be. What's your plan for today, by the way? I'm supposed to show at the police station at some point."

She insisted that the first thing she wanted to do was fix me something to eat. After that she planned to make her own statement to the police and visit Natalie's parents. Later she would head to the inn. Her manager was there now, working with another staffer to cancel reservations for the next several weeks, and she wanted to assist him as well as work out a plan on what to do with the staff and everything else.

"Are you sure you want to shut down the inn this way?" I asked. "If Eric turns out to be the killer, you don't have to worry anymore."

"But we don't know for sure yet. And until we do, I can't risk anyone else's life."

When I entered the kitchen a few minutes later, I saw that Danny hadn't so much made me lunch as set out some things for me—fruit, a wedge of cheese, slices of salami. She was still pulling things from the fridge, dressed in her poncho.

"You go, Danny, and I'll deal with the food. And look, I want to help in some way today. What can I do? I don't want to just sit around here cooling my heels."

"But I thought you were planning to return to New York today."

"The police may tell me I'm not free to leave yet. Plus, I can't just abandon you in the middle of this. Why don't we play it by ear. If they end up arresting Eric, I can head back to New York first thing tomorrow."

She was grateful that I wasn't leaving yet. She said that once she arrived at the inn, she would determine if they could use my help making calls. She'd phone me to let me know.

After she'd gone, I did the one thing I was dreading most. I called the number of Jack's sublet in New York. Even if the police gave me clearance to leave later today, I couldn't just walk out on Danny in the middle of a second murder. And that meant I wouldn't be seeing Jack in New York tonight. Despite my confusion about him, I really had been eager to be with him again. I yearned for the thoughtful questions and wisdom Jack had such a knack for.

I was expecting I might get a machine at this hour, but to my surprise, he answered. I blurted out what had happened and explained that I would have to delay my return to New York.

"But I should be able to get back tomorrow," I said in a rush at the end. "You could come over and I'll make you an early dinner. I'll do spaghetti Vongole. It's my specialty."

What followed was not the sound of him licking his chops in anticipation of my cuisine, but rather utter silence.

"Jack?"

"I'm here. I'm sorry things are such a mess up there for your friend. Just be careful, okay? There's obviously someone very dangerous on the loose."

"But what about Sunday? Should we try for that?"

"Let's not make any firm plans right now—things are obviously complicated for you up there. Just call me if you make it back tomorrow."

"You sound kind of annoyed. I really have no choice, you know, but to stay here today."

"I'll have to take your word on that. It's just hard to know which part is obligation and which part is Bailey with cold feet."

"Oh please, Jack," I said. "You don't call me for a month and a half and then you sound put out because I have to change our plans once."

"You know me. I get paid to look at patterns." He said it in a light tone, as if he were trying to keep the conversation from getting testy, but all it did was annoy me even more.

"Well, maybe you ought to look at your own, Jack. I'll call you tomorrow."

I nearly slammed the phone down. First Beck, now him. They'd both been into me until the first second I wasn't behaving exactly as they wanted. In five days I'd managed to go from two hot romantic prospects to none.

After I hung up, I called police headquarters. The woman who answered put me on hold and then suggested I come down immediately. I was absolutely dreading seeing Beck again. But as it turned out, my statement was taken by an older cop named Davis in a hideous plaid sports jacket and a tie so wide, it could have doubled as a lobster bib. I kept glancing around surreptitiously, looking for both Eric and Beck, but I never got a glimpse of either one of them.

"Is Detective Beck around?" I asked as I was led back to the lobby. As much as I wasn't looking forward to face time with him, I needed to tell him about the release massage. Detective Davis informed me that Beck wasn't available—whatever that meant—but that if I called in the early evening, I might be able to reach him.

I let myself back into Danny's house using the set of keys she'd loaned me. I nibbled some more at the lunch platter, thinking about Eric. Something about him killing both women seemed off to me. Rejected suitors sometimes murdered the women they were obsessed with. But it was hard to imagine Eric being obsessed with Anna, killing her, and then quickly becoming just as obsessed with Natalie. Beyond that, there was still the matter of Anna's mystery date the night of the murder. It didn't seem as if she would have accepted a date with Eric, and even if she had, I doubted she'd be getting all decked out for it. The more I considered it, the tougher the time I had buying the idea of Eric as the killer.

At four Danny called to say that she was still at the inn, would be there for a while longer, and had several staffers working with her, so things were under control. She planned to be home by six and would pick up dinner on the way. Bored to death, I took a shower and changed clothes. As I rummaged through my overnight bag, I realized to my dismay that I'd left three or four pieces of clothing hanging in my closet at the inn. But it was just the excuse I was looking for. I decided to drive over to the inn and retrieve them. Before I could pick up the phone to call Danny, it rang. Cordelia was on the other line.

"Danny's at the inn," I told her.

"Actually, it was you I was hoping to speak to. Have you got a minute?"

"Sure," I said without enthusiasm, having nada interest in chatting with the queen of the menacing mud wrap.

"I could tell by the way you spoke to me yesterday that you still hold me responsible for what happened during the wrap."

"Give me a good reason not to," I said.

"That's what I intend to do."

I'd been moving about the kitchen with the phone in

my hand, pouring myself a glass of water, but as soon as I heard the words, I paused.

"Let's hear it," I told her.

"I think Josh did those things to you during the wrap," she said.

"Think?"

"I mean, I'm almost positive he did. I didn't actually see him go in the room, but from some information I pieced together from another therapist, it had to be him."

"Okay, well, take me through it, then."

"I can't right this second. But I thought if you wanted to meet me in a little while, maybe around seven, I could explain everything I found out."

I didn't like Cordelia much, and she'd never seemed to like me, particularly when she'd seen me in the office with Eric. I also had no reason to trust her. She might have something on Josh, but then again she might just be making trouble. Or she might be interested in learning what I knew about the case, particularly if she'd learned Eric was now a suspect. But I said yes, I would see her. I needed to learn what she was up to. She said she was staying at a friend's place and gave me directions.

I phoned Danny to let her know I was headed over there, but all I got was a recording announcing that the inn was temporarily closed. I tried again in five minutes. Still nothing. I felt a tiny swelling of anxiety. I threw on my jeans jacket, grabbed Danny's keys again, and made certain the door was locked behind me.

Set against the twilight sky with its darkened windows, the inn looked desolate, like a haunted house. If

Danny was here, her car would probably be parked out front, but there was no sign of it. Maybe she'd finished earlier than planned and was picking up dinner for us as discussed. Farther down the parking lot, I could see a small cluster of cars. It might mean some staff were still inside the inn. At the far end of the lot, near the trees, the yellow police tape flapped in the wind, but there no longer appeared to be any cops around.

As I stepped out of the Jeep, I was startled by the sound of an engine engaging. I glanced up and saw a car slide out from the small pack of cars in the middle of the lot. Even in the dusk I could see it was a silver Saab convertible.

With my heart beating harder, I watched the Saab drive alongside of where I stood and lurch to a stop. Josh lowered his window.

"You just love horning in on all the fun, don't you?" he said, nasty as a brand-new cold sore.

"Is anyone still here?" I asked.

"I'm afraid you've missed them all."

"Was Danny heading home?"

He was quiet for a moment, as if he knew the answer but was deciding whether or not to keep me in the dark.

"I haven't a clue," he said finally.

I turned on my heels and climbed back into my Jeep, going through the motions of searching through my bag for the keys. I had no intention of leaving—I needed to get my clothes. But I didn't want Josh to know I intended to hang around. As soon as I started the engine, he took off, his car screeching as it pulled out of the front gate.

Within a minute I was out of the Jeep again and on the top step of the inn, trying one key after another on

Danny's ring. I was beginning to think that the ring didn't hold an inn key when I found the one that fit. I turned it in the lock and pushed. The door opened with a mournful creak.

The first thing I noticed was the light coming from the hallway behind the front desk. Maybe Josh had lied about everyone being gone. I walked around the front desk and down the corridor.

"Anyone here?" I called out. The light, it turned out, was coming from the small sitting room. The table was covered with computer printouts, and there were half a dozen half-empty coffee cups. The room had the forlorn look of a place that had been used for a time at full force and then abandoned.

I heard the sound just as I was turning to leave the room. It was that mournful creak again, of the front door opening. My first thought was Josh. He'd come back. I felt the urge to hide, to duck behind a desk in one of the offices, but this area would be the first he would check. Instead I strode out to the front, trying to look cocksure of myself.

But it wasn't Josh. It was Beck standing there in the dusky light of the lobby. I felt relieved, but at the same time uncomfortable. I had no idea how things would play out with him after the dressing down he'd given me last night.

"What are you doing here?" he asked, sounding more perplexed than angry. He took a couple of steps closer to me.

"I'm going back to New York, and I forgot half my clothes in my room last night. I thought Danny would be here."

"How did you get in?"

"Danny loaned me a set of keys."

"Don't you realize that someone very dangerous is on the loose? He's killed two women already. You shouldn't be here alone."

"I thought you had a suspect," I said. "Plus, even if Eric didn't do it, the killer would hardly be hanging around the inn. It's closed. There's nobody left here to kill."

He half smirked, half smiled. I was reminded of why I had found him so utterly attractive.

"Thanks, though," I added. "Thanks for your concern. It's . . . well, unexpected."

"And why is that? Because of the way I spoke to you last night?"

"Yeah. I've had bear bites that hurt less."

"I hope you can see how much pressure I've got on me right now. Plus, when we talked in the lobby last night, I realized that you'd been poking around in the case—when I'd told you not to."

"I'm sorry," I said. "I've just been so worried about Danny."

This was finally the time to tell him about the prostitution. He wasn't going to like the fact that I'd hid it from him, and I needed to steel myself for another blast of anger. I realized, in fact, that we were standing in almost the exact same spot we'd been in last night when I'd first made him so mad. Maybe I'd suggest we have coffee someplace and I would tell him there.

Something about the déjà vu of the moment, of being there in the lobby with him again, made me turn around instinctively and look at the front desk. Then I turned back again to Beck. His deep blue eyes gazed into mine and held them so hard, I couldn't pull away.

And suddenly the realization hit me. Last night when we had stood in the lobby and Natalie had glanced up, a worried expression on her face, I'd assumed she'd caught Danny's eye. But Danny had told me later that she had no memory of such a moment. It was because she had never looked at Danny.

Natalie had been looking at Beck.

CHAPTER 24

"WHAT'S THE MATTER?" he asked gravely.

I realized that my face had instantly betrayed my bewilderment.

"Um, nothing. It's just . . . everything all of a sudden. You know, Natalie, Anna, it's all so horrible. I should leave. It's really hard to be here."

"I thought you said you needed to get your clothes." He crossed his arms over his chest and looked at me warily.

"Right. I do. They're in my room." I was doing everything in my power to sound normal, but it wasn't working.

"Do you want me to come up with you?"

"No. No, I'll be okay."

"I'll wait down here for you, then. Are you sure you're okay?"

"I'm fine." Thanks to my anxiety, I'd sounded cryptic, almost dismissive.

I turned and hurried up the front stairs, trying to appear as if I were in a bit of a rush, but not frantic, which was how I felt inside. My mind was a total jumble. Something was wrong, but I wasn't sure what.

It took me over a minute to get the door to my room unlocked because my hands were trembling. Once inside, I turned the dead bolt. Then, after flinging open the closet door, I yanked my clothes off hangers and gathered them into my arms. Finally I sat on the bed and tried to think.

If Natalie had looked up at Beck last night, not Danny, the question was *why?* I was pretty sure it was right after I'd made the comment about how Anna had thought she was being followed. Had my comment triggered a revelation on Natalie's part, caused her to realize that some piece of information she was privy to—and had up until that moment dismissed—was significant after all? Why look at Beck in particular?

I saw her in my mind. The glance she'd given had been one of more than surprise. It was worry, even alarm. Had she been looking at Beck for reassurance? Or because the revelation had something to do with him? All I knew for certain was that soon afterward, Natalie's shift had ended and she had been murdered on her way to her car.

I didn't know what to do. I couldn't very well barricade myself in my room and demand that the police come over and rescue me from their chief detective. For one thing, I had no proof that Beck had done anything. He had no motive, no connection with Anna or Natalie. He was a cop, for God's sake. Yet I knew that Natalie had looked at Beck last night, and I knew, with all the instincts I possessed, that it had meant something. And he had acted so strangely when he had questioned me after Natalie's body was found. I didn't have time to figure it all out now, alone in a deserted hotel, with a potentially homicidal police detective. What I would have to do was go back downstairs, seem perfectly normal. But I didn't know how to do that.

Quickly I dug through my purse for my cell phone and punched Jack's New York number.

Please be there, I pleaded to myself. He picked up on the second ring.

"Jack, I need your help," I said urgently. "I'm back at the inn and it's all shut down and there's a cop here and there's something funny. I think he might be connected to at least one of the deaths, but I'm not sure how. I'm all alone with him. And I think he suspects now that I'm feeling weird about it. And I need to seem normal, but I don't know how."

"Wait, slow down, Bailey," he urged.

"I can't slow down. I'm up in a room and he's gonna wonder what's taking me so long."

"Shouldn't you call the police?"

"I wouldn't know what to say. I don't have anything specific to go on. Just tell me how to play the situation. How do I stay in control?"

"How old is he? Is he a macho kind of guy?"

"Mid-thirties, and yes, macho. But not over the top. Not a redneck."

"Listen to me then, Bailey. The *last* thing you want to do is look like you're trying to control the situation. You can't be tough or threatening to him. You have to be an actress. Be girlish and compliant. Act vulnerable, like you need him."

"*Vulnerable?* But won't that just make it worse? If I seem scared, he'll be sure I know something. And there's no way he'd have any mercy."

"Don't seem scared of *him.* Because yes, that makes you a potential threat to him. Make it seem like you're scared of something else and that you need his help."

"Okay, I better go. I'm going to head back to Danny's house and I'll call you from there."

"Bailey, don't hang up. Leave your cell phone on, okay, so I can hear what's going on?"

I agreed and hurriedly said good-bye. Not bothering to slam the door, I raced down the hallway toward the stairs. As I stepped off the landing above the first floor, I saw that Beck had already started to ascend the stairs. He'd been coming to find me.

"Everything okay?" he asked. There was a tiny edge to his voice.

"Yeah, I guess," I said.

He knew for sure that something was up, and I needed a story—to distract him from realizing that what was weighing on me was him. And I had to use Jack's advice.

"Actually, there *is* something I have to talk to you about," I added. "I need your help."

I kept descending the stairs until I was on the same step as him.

"What is it?" he asked. His voice sounded cold and flat, barely curious.

"Something weird happened in the spa yesterday," I

said, catching my breath. "I should have told you about it earlier, but there was so much going on."

I thought I saw him relax the tiniest bit. We descended the last steps of the staircase together and stood face-to-face. There was only one light on in the lobby and with the tiled floor, it felt like a mausoleum. I launched into my tale about the wrap and the towel over my face, describing every detail. He listened silently, his face without expression.

"I feel so relieved that I finally told you," I said when I'd finished. Vulnerable chick, just as Jack had told me.

"Was Eric on duty?" he asked.

"I assume he was, but I didn't see him. Do you think it could have been him?"

"It's possible."

I glanced surreptitiously at the door. I needed to get out of there somehow.

"You don't have time for a cup of coffee, do you?" I asked, forcing a smile. "I mean, just to talk about this."

"I don't have time—at least right now," he said. "I've got to be someplace. I just came by to pick up something I left here last night. Maybe later, though. In the meantime, you need to be careful. We haven't actually charged anyone yet with the murders."

The edginess was gone from his voice. He seemed normal Beck again. Had I let my imagination run away?

"I'll be careful," I said, inching toward the door. "Thanks."

He stayed behind in the inn. As soon as I was in the Jeep, I locked the doors and fished my cell phone out of my bag. "Jack," I said, "are you there?"

The connection was dead. I hit redial and heard a

busy signal. I would try again later. All I wanted to do was get out of there.

I barely took my eyes off the rearview mirror the whole way back to Danny's, but there was no one behind me. As I pulled into Danny's driveway, I was surprised to see that her car wasn't there. She'd left the inn over an hour ago, so where was she? I opened the door, trying to keep the key from jumping out of my hand. Once inside, I made sure I'd locked the door.

The answering machine indicated there were four messages, and without bothering to take off my jacket, I quickly hit play. The very first one was from Danny. She was calling from her car, probably shortly after I'd left the house. She said she had shut down work at the inn earlier than planned because Natalie's parents had asked for her help in making funeral arrangements. She suggested that I fix myself something for dinner using whatever I could find in the fridge. There was a frantic call from an inn staffer, anxious to know what was going on. The last two calls were from George, begging for Danny to talk to him tonight.

I yanked off my jacket and put a kettle of water on the stove. While I waited I poured myself what was left from the white wine bottle. My cold seemed to be gaining ground again, and I wanted to dull its force. After taking a large swig, I began to pace the kitchen, trying to think through the Beck situation. I was almost positive that something I'd said about Anna in the lobby last night had provoked a reaction in Natalie: a memory, or a certain realization. But I had no idea what it all had to do with Beck. Natalie had mentioned that police had been around a lot in the summer, and surely she'd crossed paths with Beck then, as well as on the night of Anna's death. But that kind of intersection alone didn't add up to much. I needed to know if it went beyond that. What I wanted most was to rule *out* any deeper connection. I couldn't bear the idea that Beck might be a killer.

I had been busy focusing on Natalie, but I also needed to consider the possibility of a connection between Beck and Anna. Because whoever had killed Natalie had probably killed Anna. Certainly Beck knew Anna from the Litchauer investigation. He had interviewed her back then, probably had her walk him through the spa. Had he become infatuated with her? Was he the date Anna had been waiting for that night? Had Natalie seen the two of them together? But why would Beck *kill* Anna? Or had I gotten totally off-track? Maybe Natalie had realized something else entirely—that Eric or even another man, a stranger, might have been stalking Anna once I raised the topic. A thought wiggled its way through my brain, and I held my breath.

I walked over to the countertop where I'd dropped my purse and rummaged through it. What I was looking for was the scrap of paper I'd written Carson Ballard's phone number on. It was at the bottom, already crumpled. I sat at the kitchen table with Danny's cordless phone and pushed the buttons. This time a woman answered.

"Who is this?" she demanded after I'd asked to speak to Carson. She obviously assumed I was either a female predator or someone wanting to upgrade her long-distance calling plan.

"It's an old friend calling with some news."

"Just a minute." I heard her lay the phone down. Thirty seconds passed.

"Yes?" It was a man, and he sounded wary.

"Hello, I'm Bailey Weggins," I said. "Are you the Carson Ballard who grew up in Wallingford?"

"Why do you want to know?"

"I'm helping to put together a retirement party for Bob Kass, the guidance counselor from the high school. You were on the list of students he wanted to invite."

"Yeah, I remember him," he said, his voice more relaxed. "He was a good guy. How'd you find me, anyway?" Okay. Carson Ballard was definitely in California. Three thousand miles away and clearly not wreaking havoc in the Berkshires.

"Your name and number were on a list someone gave me. I'm not sure how they tracked you down. Does your brother live in California, too? We'd like to reach him as well."

"Jeff? No, he's back east. I'm not really in touch much with him."

Fear rushed through me like water through a hose. My eyes pricked with tears.

"J-Jeff?" I stammered. "I thought his name was Harold."

"No one ever calls him that anymore. Jeffrey's his middle name—that's what he uses."

"So his name is Jeff Ballard?"

"No, Beck. He took my stepfather's name."

I put down the phone without even saying good-bye. The whistle on the teakettle blew shrilly, and I reached to turn off the stove. I could feel my hands beginning to shake, and I knew there was no way to stop them.

Anna Cole had been responsible for the death of Beck's sister. Then, over twenty years later, she had turned up in the town where he lived. He'd arrived at the spa to investigate William Litchauer's heart attack and had recognized her. A few months later she was dead. Was it Beck who'd been watching and following her last summer? Was it Beck she had primped for at the mirror? Clearly she had never recognized him, but then, when she'd known him previously he'd been only thirteen or fourteen and going by a different name.

My mind blundered back to the night of the murder. Beck had seemed so focused on the fact that I might have seen something of significance in the parking lot. What he might have been worried about was that I had seen *him*. And then there was that day in the woods. If he was actually the killer, he might have parked his car on the back road the night of the murder and hiked through the woods to the spa. When I'd seen him that day, he wasn't out looking for evidence. He'd probably been retracing his steps, making certain he hadn't dropped anything. He was the one who had probably followed me that day, tracking me like a deer in order to learn what I was up to.

And what about the mouse? And the incident in the spa? And my room being searched? My money was on Josh for those, his way of keeping me out of his territory. Cordelia suspected him of the towel stunt. And Beck had seemed genuinely surprised about the mouse. Besides, Beck preferred subtler methods for dealing with me, like long, hard kisses, I thought with chagrin.

I realized, too, how delighted Beck must have been to discover that George had been calling Anna. And that

Eric had dated both Anna and Natalie. It gave him two viable suspects.

But how did Natalie fit into everything? Clearly she had seen something or known something, information about Beck that tied him somehow to Anna. I had sparked the connection for her with what I had said last night in the lobby. Whatever it was, it offered enough of a threat to Beck that he'd moved quickly to silence her.

My stomach was churning. I could feel the taste of bile. I had kissed Beck. I had fantasized about making love to him. And he was a murderer. Or was there a chance that despite his connection to Anna, a connection he felt prudent to conceal, that he hadn't killed her, that the link between Anna and Natalie's deaths came from some other person, like Eric, or the slick, trick-playing Josh?

Out of nowhere, I heard a small rapping sound. It was the front door. The first thought that flashed through my mind was George. On the answering machine he had sounded desperate to connect with Danny. Great, just what I needed. I walked from the kitchen into the living room. I could see the form of someone through the sheer white fabric over the window in the door. The person knocked again. I moved closer. To my total surprise it was Cordelia.

I glanced at my watch instinctively. It was seven-thirty. I had told her I would meet her half an hour ago.

"I'm sorry," I said, opening the door. "I—Something urgent came up and I lost all track of the time."

"I thought something like that happened. I decided just to drive by. Is Danny here?"

She was wearing a faux-fur-lined jeans jacket that

with her large breasts made it appear as if she had a bulletproof vest on underneath. No heavy-duty makeup tonight, however. I guess she hadn't felt the need to knock my socks off.

"No, she's helping Natalie's family. Why don't you come in."

She stepped inside, rubbing her arms. A blast of cold air shoved its way in with her.

"I'd love something hot to drink," she announced. "It's freezing out there."

"There doesn't seem to be any fresh coffee, but I could make you tea."

I was still reeling from my discovery about Beck, and the last thing I wanted to do was play tea party with Cordelia. But she'd told me earlier that there was something important to share about Josh, and I needed to know how it all fit together.

I led her to the kitchen, and as I turned on the kettle again, she unbuttoned her coat and sat in one of the chairs around the table. It was only a second before the kettle, already heated, let out a scream. I was so on edge already that the noise made me want to jump out of my skin.

"So who told you that Josh put the towel over my face?" I asked, skipping the chitchat.

"One of the other therapists."

"Yeah, but which therapist?"

"What difference does it make?"

"I'm not interested in playing games, Cordelia."

"All right, it was Eric. He saw Josh go into your room. If Josh tried to hurt you, maybe he did that to Anna."

As we'd been talking, I'd found two English Breakfast teabags in the cupboard. I slipped the bags into a pair of mugs and poured the steaming water over them, then set the mugs on the table. Cordelia grasped one in a hand that seemed as large as the end of a boat oar.

"You know they brought Eric down for questioning, don't you?" I informed her. "He apparently dated Natalie as well as Anna."

"Eric?" she asked, almost in a shriek. She'd clearly *not* known. She rose from the table as if she were about to go into a tailspin. "What do you *mean?*"

"I mean that Eric is being questioned about Anna's murder—and Natalie's, too."

She grabbed my arm, pinching it. She was strong, strong as a man, really. I didn't like what was happening.

"Let go of my arm, Cordelia," I said. "You're hurting me."

"Tell me what you know!" she demanded.

She still had my arm, and I snapped it away as if I were yanking a curtain down from a window. She reached out, trying to grab me again, and when I stepped back, she staggered forward. An alarm bell went off in my head. What was going on with her? I thought suddenly of how jealous she'd seemed when she'd found me with Eric the other day. I thought of her insistence on meeting me tonight. And I thought of her hands.

Suddenly, from the other room, we heard the sound of the door opening. We turned in unison to the doorway. Danny, I thought in relief.

Jeffrey Beck walked into the kitchen and stared at us.

The sight of him made the bones seem to fall away from my legs, so that they felt instantly rubbery. Cordelia regarded him dumbfounded, as if he were an actor who'd just entered the wrong scene in a play.

"What are you doing here?" I asked feebly.

"You should lock your doors," he said. "It's dangerous out there." I realized then that I'd never put the lock back on after I'd let Cordelia into the house.

I glanced from Beck to Cordelia and then back to Beck. I wasn't sure whom I should be more afraid of.

"I just told Cordelia about Eric being arrested," I said. I needed to force the attention onto something other than me. "She's very upset."

"Are you out of your mind?" Cordelia screeched at him. "He couldn't harm anyone."

"Just calm down," Beck told her, moving closer to her slowly, like you would with a nervous horse. "Eric is simply helping us with our investigation."

As I stood there, frozen in place, my eye fell onto the kitchen table. The paper with Beck's brother's name and number was lying there in clear view. Beck caught the slight movement of my head and turned toward me. I tried to hold his eyes with mine, but they slid toward the table and I saw his body tense.

He raised his head and chuckled oddly. "I *knew* something was the matter," he said. "I knew back at the inn that you'd figured something out—but I wasn't sure what, or how."

"What are you talking about?"

"Don't be coy with me, Bailey."

"I—"

"I said don't be coy," he snapped, his voice filled with quiet wrath.

"I want to know about Eric," Cordelia interjected shrilly, oblivious to his rage, to the danger we both were in. "What are you doing with him?"

Beck pivoted sideways and in one swift movement smashed his fist into the side of her head. She toppled over, crashing onto the kitchen floor and lying there motionless.

"Look," I said to Beck, attempting to hold my panic at bay, "I know what happened in Wallingford. I can understand why you hated Anna."

"Oh yeah? You think so?" he asked mockingly.

I tried desperately to think of a plan, but fear was flooding my brain, short-circuiting everything. Just keep talking, I told myself.

"My father died when I was young—so I can imagine what the loss was like for you. Was it just a coincidence—meeting up with Anna again?"

"I'd say it was more like *destiny*," he said. He glanced absentmindedly down at Cordelia's unconscious body, as if he were looking at a trail of mud on the floor. "I walk into the spa this summer and there she is. She didn't even recognize me, but I knew it had to be her. The person who let my sister die. You don't have any idea what it was like to know that she just went on with her life all these years. She never had to face up to what she did. There were people back then who actually felt *sorry* for the bitch. And then it all fell into my lap. I had the chance to finally bring her to justice."

"So you asked her out on a date?"

"Not right away. That would have been against the

rules—right, Bailey? Just like I had to talk to you about. So I waited a few months. And she was more than game. You women all respond to the same things—did you know that? You're all so easy, really."

"All I know is that I really liked you from the moment I met you. I thought we had a connection."

"Oh please, don't play that game with me," he barked. "I know what you've been up to. You've been digging at this thing like a dog in a hole. That Natalie was a busybody, too, you know?"

"But how—"

"She couldn't mind her own business, either. She was just like you."

"Natalie discovered something?"

"She saw me one night last summer, a few weeks after we investigated that body in the spa. I nearly made her jump out of her panties."

"You'd been watching Anna that night?"

He did that half-smile, half-grimace of his. "There's a spot in a cluster of trees where you can look right into her window. I wanted to check up on her, get an idea of her routine. She was still dating Mr. Exotic then, but I could tell it wasn't serious by the way she'd flirted with me at the spa. The same old Anna. He's lucky he got away."

"Natalie caught you looking in the window?"

"No. You think I'd make that kind of mistake? But she saw me coming down the path from the barn when she was getting into her car. It looked funny, me being there so late, but I told her I'd been checking out the property, making sure everything was okay. She *seemed* to believe me. I don't think she'd have ever remembered it until you opened your big fat mouth about Anna being stalked." He started to edge around the kitchen table toward me.

"But that didn't mean she automatically assumed you had . . . hurt Anna," I said, trying desperately to think what to do.

"Oh, but she knew something was funny—and I couldn't take the chance. I waited for her out in the parking lot, and asked her what was wrong. She was agitated and I could tell she didn't entirely trust me. I couldn't risk her yapping about that night to anyone—including you. All it would take is someone asking a few questions and before long they'd piece together the connection between me and Anna."

"Beck, I don't blame you, I really don't. What Anna did to your sister was horrible."

"What she did to my *sister?* Oh, that's just the half of it."

"What do you mean?"

"Why do you think Anna wasn't watching my sister? She had me in my bedroom, fucking my brains out."

I gasped.

"After it happened, I panicked. Anna told me it was *my* fault, that I better keep my damn mouth shut or she'd tell my mother what I'd done with her. I wasn't even fourteen yet. I was just a dumb kid. She got me out of the house, made up this whole story. It was like another game to her. She didn't care. She didn't dream at night the way I did about what it was like to be under eight feet of water and not be able to breathe."

"Look, Beck—"

"Don't 'Look Beck' me. You and Anna have a lot in

common. You like to flirt, you like to play games. And you didn't realize I was the one playing with you. You're smarter than her, but it isn't going to do you much good, I'm afraid."

He was shaking his head back and forth as he talked, losing it, and I knew any second he was going to reach out and knock me down as he had Cordelia or he was going to put his arms around my neck and squeeze.

I stared into his eyes and reached slowly behind me with one hand, feeling for the tea mug I'd set on the table behind me. As fast as I could, I picked it up and flung the hot tea in his face.

He cried out and stumbled backward, grabbing at his face with both hands. He stood between me and the front door so I tore down the hallway toward the bedrooms, careened into the bathroom, and slammed the door shut, locking it.

With one glance around the room, I saw that I'd bought myself only a few minutes. The door was made of old wood, and he could probably knock it down easily.

There was one window, on the small side but wide enough for me to slip through. But by the time I escaped he'd probably be able to catch up with me on the other side. I glanced around for anything to defend myself with. There was nothing more threatening that an electric toothbrush. Suddenly Beck rammed his body—or something else hard—against the door. It made a sound like a crack of thunder.

"Beck, please," I called out. "I care about you. Don't hurt me."

He struck the door again, and this time it jumped on its hinges.

My only choice was to go through the window and make a run for it. I turned the lock and raised the window as quietly as possible. Cold air forced its way fast through the first crack of an opening and then surged through as soon as I had the window all the way up. I stepped back to the door and once again pleaded with Beck not to hurt me. I needed him to think I was just standing there with my fingers hopelessly crossed.

I snuck back to the window and shimmied halfway through, peering into the frigid darkness. Frantically I pulled the rest of my body through and dropped to the ground. A small security light on the back of the house cast an eerie puddle of light. I could make out that there was a small backyard, a toolshed of some kind, and nothing behind that but woods and blackness.

My car keys were in my purse on the kitchen counter. It seemed like my only option was to run through the woods. But Beck would realize soon enough that I'd slipped out the window, and then he'd come after me. He was faster and stronger, and I knew he'd catch up with me. I had to think of something else. I had to *do* something.

I raced toward the toolshed. With my eyes now partly adjusted to the darkness, I saw that there were rakes leaning against it and a shovel. I picked up the shovel and buried myself in the shadows behind the shed.

I heard one loud bang from within the house, and I realized that he had finally knocked the door off. In my mind's eye I could see him rush to the window. Then there was the sound of his feet hitting the dirt below the window. He was coming this way, thinking I might be hiding behind the shed. I tightened my grip on the shovel.

Suddenly he was there, right in front of me. His face was tight with rage. Before he could even react to the sight of me, I slammed the shovel onto his head. There was a cracking sound and then a *ping* as it bounced off his skull. He staggered back and collapsed to the ground.

I dropped the shovel and began to run toward the house, to the right side of it where the driveway was situated. I knew it was crazy cold outside, but I could barely feel it. There was nothing but silence behind me, and I hoped I had knocked Beck out cold. Without stopping I twisted my head to look in the yard as I ran. I could see only the outlines of Beck's body. He had raised himself to a sitting position. In a minute, he'd be after me again.

CHAPTER 25

I RAN HARDER, the cold air resisting me like water. I had to fight off the urge to cry in despair. I knew if I locked myself back in the house, Beck would break a window, find his way in somehow. What I needed to do was retrieve my keys and get in my Jeep—before he caught up with me.

As I rounded the corner to the front of the house, I lurched to a stop. Blue lights flickered like fairies through the trees at the far end of Danny's road. Then I heard sirens. As I gaped in disbelief and relief, two cop cars came careening down the road toward the house.

I began to run again, and by the time I'd reached the end of the driveway, the cars had screeched to a halt. I shouted, waving my arms. The first car was unmarked, with one of those temporary lights the cops throw on the top. Two men in plain clothes jumped out of the first car, including Davis, the one with the wide tie who'd interviewed me earlier in the day. Pointing to the back-yard, I blurted out that Beck was chasing me, trying to kill me, that he had killed Anna and Natalie.

They made certain I wasn't injured and then drew guns. So did the two cops who had jumped out from the patrol car. One of the detectives shouted for a uniform officer to stay behind with me, and then he took off with the other two cops toward the back of the house.

I spun around to watch them. I still felt terrified, as if somehow Beck would take them all down and I would still not be safe—like one of those nightmares in which no matter where you find to hide, you realize they will find you.

From where I stood I had a view of a sliver of the backyard, but it was too dark to tell if Beck had gotten fully up. Suddenly I saw a man duck through the small square of yard lit by the security light. One of the cops yelled, "Halt!" and then yelled it again. I steeled myself for gunshots, but none came. Instead there was a crash-ing noise in the trees near the house. The patrol cop next to me, young with a mustache, checked on his radio to see if backup was on the way. "Hurry, hurry," I wanted to scream at whoever was at the other end. A body erupted from the woods and a cry tore out of me. Beck seemed to fly toward me, but the next second, one of the detectives tackled him from behind and he landed hard on his side. The other detective stood over them with his gun pointed at Beck's head. The patrol cop shoved me in back of him, blocking my vision, though I could hear the low murmur of voices. After a minute came the tramp of footsteps on the cold earth. The two detectives surrounded a now upright Beck whose hands were cuffed behind him. The look he gave me as they passed was empty of any emotion.

One of the patrol cops and the second detective led Beck to the patrol car and guided him into the backseat. As the three of them took off in the car, another patrol car sped down the road in the direction of the house. Both cars slowed down as they eased by each other on the road.

Beck was gone. I was safe. I realized for the first time that I was shaking hard, like a loose hubcap. Detective Davis asked me again if I was all right. I told him I was just shivering from the cold. And from being friggin' terrified, I wanted to add. Suddenly I remembered Cordelia.

"There's someone injured inside," I said, my teeth chattering as I spoke. "He punched her in the head and knocked her out."

"All right. You better come inside, too." He waited a split second for the reinforcements to jump out of their car, told one of them to call for an ambulance, and then led me into the house with several cops in tow.

Cordelia was still on the floor of the kitchen, but she was in a sitting position, holding her head in her hands. While Davis stooped to help her, a patrol cop guided me to the living room. Someone would be in momentarily to question me, he said.

I waited on the couch, willing myself to stop trembling—without any luck at first. But eventually, as I got warmer, the shaking began to subside. I could hear murmuring from the kitchen, the cops talking to Cordelia and trying to find out what shape she was in. The reinforcement cops fanned out through the house, and before long the ambulance arrived. Cordelia was taken out on a stretcher, though from my vantage point she seemed conscious and lucid.

I saw a few of the cops consult with one of the paramedics and she immediately walked over to me. She took my pulse and asked me a few questions to make sure I was really okay.

No sooner had they finished with me than Danny burst into the house and rushed to my side. Before I had a chance to say anything, Davis asked that she wait in another room and he'd speak to her shortly. He took a chair across from me and pulled out a notebook. He was joined a minute later by a guy who introduced himself as Detective O'Rourke. I realized he was one of the cops who'd been first on the scene the night of Anna's murder.

I took them through everything, admitting that I'd wanted to help Danny and had snooped around. I described my trip to Wallingford and how I'd found out Beck's true identity. At one point I saw them shoot each other knowing looks.

"What is it?" I asked. "You didn't know, did you?"

"No," Davis said, "but some of Detective Beck's behavior lately had started to worry us."

"Is that why you came here?" I asked. "How did you know Beck would be here?"

"We got a call from a friend of yours in New York. He was concerned, based on a few things you'd said. He didn't know where Mrs. Hubner lived, but he told us you had been headed to her house and might be in danger."

I could hardly believe it. Jack had called the police. He had saved my life.

"Does he know I'm okay?" I asked.

"Yeah," Davis said. "Somebody spoke to him. We told him you'd had a close call but that you were fine."

It was just before ten when the police finally left. Before they departed they explained the drill to me: I would have to go downtown the next day and make an official statement.

Danny said she would put out a plate of food for me, and while she fussed in the kitchen, I called Jack. I thanked him, told him that if he hadn't called the police, I would surely have been killed. We agreed that we would meet at my place the next night at six. My voice was full of things I didn't want to fully express until I was face-to-face with him.

The meal turned out to be more cheese and salami and olives. I wasn't really in the mood for another European picnic–style lunch, so I just picked at it and decided to concentrate on the wine. I needed something to calm me. My hands weren't shaking anymore, but it felt as if it were taking a force of will to keep them from doing so.

The only thing Danny knew by this point was that Beck was the killer, so as soon as I'd had a little bit to eat, I told her the whole story, including how I had pieced together the Beck connection—and what Beck had revealed to me.

"So what was the Mylar paper all about?" she asked.

"I'm not sure. He'd already strangled Anna, so he didn't use it to kill her. I think it might have been a symbol—of water, of suffocation."

"He must have been shocked when he ran into Anna this summer at the spa," she said.

"I know. Of course, it wasn't a *total* coincidence. It seems as if they were both drawn back to the same part of the world. You know, Matt Litchauer said something to me about how the police hadn't given a damn about his case, and yet you'd told me that Beck had been very conscientious. Probably the reason Beck gave so much attention to the spa was Anna."

"I can't believe *she* didn't recognize *him.*"

"He probably looks totally different now than he did at fourteen, especially with the gray hair. Besides, I'm sure she barely gave him a second thought back then. For her it must have been all about the kick that came from seducing him. The fact that his name isn't the same practically guaranteed that she wouldn't put two and two together.

"I just thought of something," I added. "Beck didn't interview Anna's sister when she was here. He probably didn't want to take the chance that *she* might recognize him."

"Why did he take so long to kill Anna? Why not do it last summer?"

"I think he felt that Anna would have been wary if the investigating cop asked her out on a date. So he waited a few months. Maybe he found a way to bump into her. By then the Litchauer case was closed and there'd be no reason for her to be suspicious. He also probably wanted to put some distance between the case and when he killed Anna—especially after having bumped into Natalie that one night. That would reduce the chance of anyone connecting him to things."

"Poor Natalie," Danny said. "She was murdered simply because she was at the wrong place at the wrong time. If she hadn't bumped into him in the parking lot that night, she would still be alive."

"It wasn't just that," I said. "It was because of what I said in the lobby. Natalie had obviously forgotten about the night she'd seen Beck, but as soon as I made that remark about Anna thinking someone was watching her, Natalie flashed on it. It could be that she'd always found Beck's explanation for being on the property kind of odd, but she had no real reason not to buy it. But as soon as she heard my comment, it clearly disturbed her. Maybe she would have ended up dismissing it, but Beck couldn't risk it."

"What about Rich?" Danny asked. "You said he'd lied to you about knowing Anna. Does this mean he had nothing to do with her death?"

"My guess is that he only lied about knowing Anna because he didn't want the police breathing down his neck. The more of a connection you have with someone, the greater your chance of being considered a suspect."

"Does this mean that Eric will be released—and that they'll leave George alone?"

"I assume so. They're both totally in the clear now."

She set her wineglass on the coffee table and leaned back into the couch, frowning.

"There's one thing I still can't figure out. You said Cordelia came by to tell you that Josh had put the towels over your head. If he didn't kill Anna, why would he do something like that?"

It was finally time to tell Danny about the release massage. I confessed everything I knew, including

Josh's decision to deal with the situation without letting her know. Her shock at the news quickly turned to anguish—and then dismay because I hadn't been forthcoming.

"Danny, I had to make a judgment call," I said. "Initially you'd put a premium on finding out what had gone on at the spa, but when I came *back* to Warren, it was to help prove George hadn't murdered Anna. I got Piper to talk to me by convincing her she could trust me, so for the time being, I just didn't want to say anything. Plus, I was afraid that if you knew, you'd feel forced to tell the police—and that would have certainly killed your business."

"And do you think I should tell them now?" she asked, wringing her hands.

"Is there any point? The three women involved are all gone now. There's nothing to report. So I'd say no, let it go, protect your business. There are still plenty of their former clients out there, but my guess is that because of Anna's murder, they're not going to come skulking around to see if you're still open for that kind of business."

What about Josh? she wanted to know.

I told her that it was up to her, but personally, I'd send him packing as fast as I could. He'd tried to deal with the crisis at the spa without telling her, so she could never really trust him again. Besides, I thought he was dangerous. He'd not only put those towels over my head, but he'd probably sent the mouse to me. *And* searched my room at the inn. Granted, he was trying to keep me away from the spa to protect it, but that was for his sake, not hers.

Danny got up to refill our wineglasses and used the opportunity to call the hospital and check on Cordelia. It turned out that she had been examined in the ER but was never admitted to the hospital. Danny found Cordelia's cell phone number on a card in her purse and tried that. Cordelia answered and explained that she had been released after the doctor had determined that all she had sustained was a black eye. She was spending the night at a friend's.

As much as I dreaded lying in bed alone in the dark, I couldn't hold my head up any longer. I took one more sip of wine, hugged Danny good night, and trudged down to the guest room. Thanks to pure exhaustion, I ended up falling asleep almost instantly. I was out cold for the night and didn't wake up until eight. Forget about hypnosis, I thought as I stirred in bed Sunday morning. Being terrorized by a homicidal maniac had turned out to be the real cure for my insomnia.

I got my trip to the police station over as soon as I could. As I drove downtown I felt wired, anxious, but I wasn't prepared for my reaction when I stepped out of the Jeep. A wave of fear almost pulled my legs out from under me. I wondered where Beck was. What if they had him locked up in a jail right on the premises? Would he know I was there? I gulped large breaths of air, trying to make myself calm down.

Detective Davis took my statement, but several detectives gathered around as he did. I guess everyone was anxious to hear the Beck story, to learn about the secret, murderous side of the guy they had worked with for years. I almost had a heart attack when someone said something about talking to me again tomorrow. I explained that I had to get back to New York and that I would be glad to speak at length to anyone by phone. They didn't fight me on it—though they reminded me that when Beck's trial got under way, I would have to come back to testify.

Danny was waiting for me with homemade muffins. I devoured two of them along with a huge cup of coffee. She had changed into a white blouse topped with a velvet, plum-colored jacket that played off her gray eyes. She looked tired but spunky, like the Danny I'd always known. Last night I'd done all the talking. Now I was anxious to hear what was going on in her mind.

"It may be a totally uphill battle, but I've decided I'm going to reopen the inn next week," she announced. "There's no danger to anyone. So hopefully over time, the guests will return. I'll run the spa until I find someone who can replace Josh."

"Oh, Danny, that's the right decision, it really is. And what about George?"

She looked off to the side, gathering her thoughts from someplace unknown, and I was fearful that she was about to proclaim that she was giving him the proverbial one more chance.

"I can't take him back, Bailey," she said resolutely. "I just can't. I should have broken things off after the other incident. Thank God the inn is all in my name."

I left for New York around noon. I drove most of the way on automatic pilot, my brain buzzing with thoughts like an overturned beehive. My feelings were just as wacky. Some moments I would feel flushed with pride for having solved the crime all by my lonesome. At one point I think I even got this goofy, "my mommy is gonna be so pleased with me" grin on my face. I felt relieved, too, that Danny was safe—and that I was finally going home. But then periodically I'd slip into a funk: about Anna, about Natalie, and of course about Beck. There was no way to rewrite history. I'd been infatuated with him, and he'd been a murderer. He would have killed *me*.

And what about Jack? I wondered as I barreled down the New York State Thruway, the Catskill Mountains rising in all their glorious colors along my right. I was yearning to see him, yet I felt hopelessly confused. Had I mistaken gratitude for desire? Had I talked myself into being happy with the consolation prize? Oops, potential boyfriend number one turned out to be a psychopath, so let's call in backup Jack.

I had planned to leave my bags off at my apartment and then hightail it to the fish market to pick up some clams. After all, I had promised spaghetti Vongole. But as soon as I threw my bags on my living room floor, I realized I was too mentally fried even to boil water. I ordered roast chicken and salad from a restaurant on University Place. Maybe Jack would think I'd made it all myself if I served it on cute place mats—and didn't put out the packets of premoistened towelettes.

I straightened up my place, fluffing the pillows and turning the lights on low. What I *didn't* do was light any scented candles. I figured I'd dry-heave if I smelled anything made with green tea, frankincense, or something else Marco Polo had lugged home with him.

Jack showed up exactly at six, a bottle of Châteaux Beychevelle in hand. He looked good, so good. His brown hair looked silky, as if he'd just showered and his cheeks were a little bit red from the cold. He was wearing jeans, a white T-shirt, and a navy V-necked cashmere sweater, a bit more relaxed than I usually saw him. It felt delicious when he folded his arms around me.

"God, Bailey," he said, pulling back and staring into my eyes. "You scared me to death yesterday."

"Well, I *would* be dead if it weren't for you. How did you explain it all to the police? Tell me what happened."

"I could only hear bits and pieces of your conversation with that guy, but I didn't like his tone. There was an edge to it. Then I lost you. I couldn't tell whether your phone had just died or he'd done something. I had no way of tracking you down, so I called the police and I told them just what you'd told me. That you were worried the cop might be the murderer. I was afraid they would just blow me off—he was one of them, after all. But they seemed to take me seriously."

"From what I've picked up," I explained, "they had started to find his behavior a little irrational lately."

"And what about you? What made you suspect him?"

There was a hint of something in the way he asked it, that perhaps his curiosity had been aroused about my connection to Beck.

"I *didn't* suspect him," I said. "At least not until four minutes before I called you. Why don't I tell you the whole story before we eat."

We opened the wine and sat on the couch, where I told him the horrible tale. Except I left out the part about my lusting after Beck. For one second I considered confessing and getting it off my chest, just the way Jack had gotten his little fling with Miss Pittsburgh off *his* chest, but I knew that it might spoil the mood, and I didn't want to do that.

First of all, it felt too good to be sitting there next to him. And it felt even better when he kissed me, tenderly at first and then hard and urgently. I'd had a hellacious weekend, and I was looking forward to the kind of sex that would make me forget everything for a while—including my own name.

Besides, on the drive home, I'd sort of figured some things out. Yes, I'd had a strong physical attraction to Beck, but what helped sustain it, I suspected, really *was* the resentment I'd been harboring toward Jack. For his not calling me during the summer, for his sleeping with that other chick. Yet I also realized that I had to finally accept part of the blame. I *had* been emotionally aloof with Jack, and I couldn't fault him for being drawn to someone else when he'd felt needy. Hell, I'd just done the same thing with Beck.

In the car I'd also thought a lot about what Cat had said earlier in the week—about leaving the past in the past, like a pair of last year's Jimmy Choo shoes. Sometimes that makes perfect sense. In fact, if Beck had done it, the whole horrible nightmare would never have unfolded. But sometimes what's in the past is a good thing, and you shouldn't move on just for the sake of the new. Jack was worth going back for, I decided—and I was going to give it one more try with an open mind and heart.

Besides, I can't even afford Jimmy Choo shoes.

More
Kate White!

Please turn this page
for a preview of

'TIL DEATH DO US PART

available
wherever books are sold.

CHAPTER 1

THE FIRST TIME she said her name on the phone that January night, I couldn't place her—though there was something vaguely familiar about the voice. It had a snooty, trust-fundy tone, as if she were announcing, "I own a Marc Jacobs bag and you don't."

"Ashley Hanes," she said once more, this time with exaggerated emphasis and irritation, the way American tourists sometimes speak to foreigners who don't understand them. "We met at Peyton Cross's wedding. I was a bridesmaid, remember?"

Oh, right. We had been introduced late last April in Greenwich, Connecticut, during the infamous Cross-Slavin wedding weekend. Ashley had graduated from the same exclusive private high school as the bride and was now working, if my memory was correct, as an interior decorator in Greenwich—though working was apparently something she chose rather than had to do. An image of her began to loosen from my memory: long, chestnut-colored hair, slim as a French baguette, and haughty as hell, just like the voice. She was the kind of woman who would meet you at a party and look right through you, as if you were a potted palm.

"Oh, right, I'm so sorry," I said. "I'm in a little bit of a fog at the moment. How are you anyway?"

I was pretty sure what was coming next. Since I'm a contributing writer for *Gloss* magazine, I often get phone calls from people I've met asking for fashion or publishing-related favors. But I write true-crime and human-interest stories for the magazine and I'm not connected to the glittery, glossy stuff. Just for the record, I am categorically unable to help someone become a Ford model, gain admittance to a Chanel sample sale, or publish a confessional article on how a liposuction procedure left ugly scars along her buttocks.

"I need your help," she said.

"Okay," I said. "Though if it's—"

"There's a very serious situation, and I have to talk to you about it."

Serious to someone like Ashley could mean her hairdresser was out of town for the week, but the alarm in her voice sounded real enough that I was concerned.

"Is it about Peyton?" I asked. Though I had spoken to Peyton on the phone once last summer, I had not laid eyes on her in nine months—not since she had dazzled a room of five hundred guests in a satin Vera Wang wedding dress with a low-cut, crumb-catcher bodice. From there she had headed off for a cruise of the Greek islands with her new husband, David, who'd made a fortune in the world of finance—whatever that means.

"No. Well, *indirectly,* yes. Look, it's not something I want to get into on the phone. Can you meet me to talk about this?"

"All right. Tell me when—and where. Are you still living up in Greenwich?"

"Yes, but I'm in New York tonight. At the Four Seasons Hotel. Could you come by here for a drink?"

"Tonight?" I exclaimed. It had started to snow a few hours earlier, and as I glanced across the room toward the window of my fourteenth-story apartment, I could see it was coming down harder now—in big, crazy swirls. I live at the very eastern end of Greenwich Village, on the corner of 9th Street and Broadway, and it would be a bitch getting a cab up to 57th Street in this weather—and an even bigger bitch getting one back.

"It's urgent," she said. "When you hear what I have to say, you'll understand why I need to see you immediately."

It didn't seem like I had much choice but to acquiesce. She sounded about as eager to hear me say no as she would to travel by Greyhound, and besides, if the situation really did involve Peyton Cross, even indirectly, I was curious to know what it was. I explained to Ashley that it might take me forty-five minutes to get there. We agreed that I would ring her on the hotel house phone when I arrived and she'd come down to the bar in the lobby.

I'd been reading a book when she called, dressed in bagged-out sweatpants and drinking a cup of instant hot cocoa in honor of the snowstorm, and now I was going to have to head out into the mess. Several months ago I'd moved into a steady relationship with a guy named Jack Herlihy, but because he taught psychology at Georgetown University in Washington, D.C., we only saw each other on weekends. Some nights I'd see a movie or have dinner out with friends, but more weeknights than not, I was holed up in my apartment, either alone or chatting with my seventy-year-old next door neighbor, Landon. Though I looked forward to my weekends with Jack, the rest of my nights had become about as scintillating as C-SPAN. Landon had told me lately that he was worried that I might start adopting stray cats.

I changed into a pair of tight dark jeans, a black turtleneck sweater, silver hoop earrings (in an attempt to look a little dressier), and my snow boots, which I found after foraging in my closet for five minutes. It was actually the first time that winter that we'd had more than flurries in Manhattan.

I was surprised when I stepped outside to see that about two inches of snow had already stuck to the ground, and you could tell by the swollen look of the sky that more was on the way. I opted for the subway, the IRT at Astor Place. It would be faster than hunting for a cab—and it would take me to within two blocks of the hotel.

As the train hurled through the tunnel, its floor sopping wet with melted snow, I had time to consider what trouble might be brewing for the captivating Peyton Cross. From all reports, her life couldn't have been going better. In her early thirties like me, she'd been dubbed the next Martha Stewart—or "Martha Stewart wannabe" in the eyes of the people who envied her so much they couldn't stand it. She ran a combination cooking school, catering business, and gourmet kitchen and food shop out of an old farmhouse and barn on the outskirts of Greenwich. Her first cookbook was due out sometime this year, and she was a frequent guest on the Food Network. A television show of her own was probably already in the offing.

As they say, I knew her when—she was my roommate freshman year at Brown. She was extremely vivacious, pretty in that kind of scrubbed face, not-overly-sophisticated preppy way, and from what I could tell, afraid of absolutely nothing. Though some guys were totally intimidated by her, the majority was mesmerized, and she always had a pack of them mooning over her. Life as her roommate was entertaining but also exasperating. That's because she could be selfish and rude. She'd ask me to meet her at dinner and then make me wait for an hour in the cafeteria, or she'd borrow my best shirt and then leave it balled up with the dust bunnies under her bed. Over time I figured out how to avoid situations with her that could end in me cursing under my breath. The trick for surviving, I learned, was to keep my expectations low and enjoy the show.

We both got singles sophomore year, and though we were friendly and occasionally grabbed a beer together, we didn't see a huge amount of each other. I bonded with several women who, unlike Peyton, seemed to carry the good-girlfriend gene. After college Peyton and I stayed in touch by e-mail, though infrequently. When I left my gig as a reporter at the *Albany Times Union* and headed for Manhattan, hoping to break into magazines, I called her for some insight. At the time she was working for *Food & Wine*, developing recipes. She promised to introduce me to a few people in the business, and to my surprise she actually came through. She also invited me to Greenwich several times for parties she was throwing as part of her burgeoning catering and event-planning business. That was the thing about Peyton—just when you were ready to strangle her, she could charm the pants off you.

Her wedding had been one of the more lavish I'd ever attended but also breathtakingly original. It was held in a historic house on the outskirts of Greenwich, and Peyton arranged for her own company to do the catering. That was partly because she didn't trust anyone else to do the job with her degree of genius, but also for the PR value for her business. Friends of mine had sworn I'd bag some rich guest that day, but David Slavin was almost twenty years older than Peyton and his business associates and friends were paunchy and pathetically boorish. I'd spent a good chunk of the day flirting with one of the bartenders.

The snow was coming down even harder when I emerged from the underground at 59th and Lexington. I felt relieved when I finally stomped into the marble, two-story-high lobby of the Four Seasons. I rang Ashley's room to tell her I'd arrived and then headed over to the lobby bar, requesting the most private table they could manage. Like the lobby, the entire area—the marble walls, the Roman shades, and the furniture—was done in shimmering beige. A little too mausoleum-like for my taste.

Though I hadn't recalled Ashley's name when she'd first said it on the phone, I had no trouble recognizing her as soon as she strode purposefully in my direction. She had a rich girl's air of self-importance and entitlement, the kind that many A-list actresses try for years to acquire but never do.

As she got closer I realized that the dark green thing she was wearing was actually a fur coat. Either she was planning on going out afterward or she'd been reluctant to leave it in the room. It was, I suspected, sheared beaver or mink, lush and plush and worth at least twenty thousand dollars. I wondered if her car sported a bumper sticker that read, "I *don't* brake for small animals."

She slid into the chair to my left without bothering with a perfunctory air kiss or even a hello. I guess she figured we'd gotten our pleasantries out of the way on the house phone. She wore her chestnut hair pinned back tonight, accentuating the slenderness of her tanned face. Her cheekbones were so high and sharp, you'd risk a paper cut if you got too close to them.

"Did you order yet?" she asked briskly, shaking off her coat to reveal a sleeveless orange dress and thin buff arms. She glanced at my turtleneck and jeans with a soupçon of disapproval, as if I were wearing one of those plastic lobster bibs that says, "I'm a piggy."

"No, I was waiting for you," I told her.

She jerked her head around toward the center of the room and signaled for the waitress. She appeared on edge, and I assumed it had to do with the news she was about to divulge. There didn't seem to be any reason to spend five minutes on small talk, so as soon as she had ordered a dirty martini and I'd ask for a glass of cabernet, I jumped in.

"So tell me, what's going on?" I asked.

"When was the last time you spoke to Peyton?"

"It's been a while. Last summer, I guess."

"Do you remember the bridesmaid with the short black hair? Jamie Howe?"

Jamie. She was the bridesmaid I'd spent the most time talking to, mainly because she was also in the magazine business. She'd met Peyton during her tenure at *Food & Wine* and had since become an editor at another food magazine. I hadn't particularly liked her. She was sullen and, I suspected, jealous of Peyton's success. She kept talking about how lucky

Peyton was to have David to foot the bill for all of her ventures.

"Sure. She lives here in New York, right?"

"Lived," she said, almost defiantly. "She's dead now."

"You're kidding," I exclaimed. The news took me totally by surprise. *"How?"*

"She was electrocuted in her apartment—down on the Lower East Side. It happened in September."

I sat there momentarily speechless while Ashley took a fortifying sip of her martini. As she swallowed, she laid her French-manicured hand flat against the front of her dress, as if it helped the vodka go down more easily. When she set the glass on the table again, I caught the cloying scent of olives.

"Gosh, I vaguely remember hearing that someone in the business died like that," I said finally. "But I had no idea it was her. What happened exactly?"

"She was taking a bath and a CD player slipped into the tub," Ashley said.

"That's horrible."

"I know. And hard to believe someone wouldn't know better than to set it so close to the tub."

"What do you mean?" I asked. "Are you thinking—"

"Until last week I didn't think much about it at all," she said, suddenly sounding frantic. "I'd never even met Jamie before the wedding. But—wait till you hear this. Two weeks ago another of the bridesmaids died. My roommate, Robin Lolly."

I let out a gasp so loud that a media mogul type at

the next table turned his head in our direction. She was right. I could barely believe what I was hearing.

"How?" I asked.

"She was taking antidepressants, and she had some kind of fatal reaction. It was from mixing them with the wrong kind of food." Her eyes filled with tears as she spoke, but they seemed to come as much from nervous tension as from sadness.

"Robin?" I said. "Is she the one who worked at the farm with Peyton?"

"Yes, yes," Ashley said impatiently. "She was the very pretty one—with the long blond hair. She managed the shop at the farm."

"That's terrible," I said. "Were you two very close?"

"We weren't what you'd call best friends," she said, shaking her head quickly, "but we'd known each other since high school. Robin, Peyton, Prudence—she was the maid of honor, remember?—and I all went to Greenwich Academy together. Robin and I started sharing a town house last March. My roommate had moved out and Robin had just gotten divorced. She needed someplace to live."

"Was she at home when she died?"

"No, she was up in Vermont—all alone—at a ski house her parents left her. She'd driven up on Friday and the coroner said she must have died shortly after she arrived, though her body wasn't discovered until a cleaning person came in Monday morning." Her voice choked as she spoke the last sentence.

"I'm so sorry," I said. "This must be awful for you—and for Peyton, too."

"Look," she said, suddenly grasping my arm so hard it would have taken the Jaws of Life to remove it. "Don't you find it odd that two perfectly healthy young women who were in a wedding together would die within a few months of each other in such bizarre circumstances?"

"Are you saying you think someone *killed* the two of them?" I asked. "Because they were *bridesmaids*?"

"All I know is that something's not right about it, and I'm going out of my mind. Robin and Jamie hadn't even met until the wedding. But they became friends after that. And now suddenly they're both dead as a result of these strange accidents. I'm terrified something could happen to *me*."

"I know how upsetting this must be, but it really sounds like nothing more than an awful coincidence."

She shook her head agitatedly.

"That's what *everyone* says—Peyton and everyone else."

"Well, do you have anything else to go on?" I asked.

"To begin with, I find this whole food and drug mixing thing preposterous. Robin was very clear about the foods she wasn't supposed to eat. She told me what they were so that if I ever cooked for us, I wouldn't include any of them."

It was hard to imagine Ashley doing anything with food other than calling the Zone hotline.

"But sometimes people cheat with food, no matter how religious they say they're going to be about their diets," I told her.

She glanced nervously around the room, as if she was afraid of eavesdroppers, then leaned closer to me.

"That's not all. After Jamie's death, Robin got really weird. She seemed nervous and tense."

"But that was probably just normal grieving," I suggested.

She let out a ragged sigh.

"I can't believe this," she said. "I thought you of all people would take it more seriously. I guess if my life is in danger, I'm going to have to take care of myself."

There was a manic edge to her voice, and the media mogul glanced over again. It probably appeared as if I was trying to talk her down from a coke high.

"Ashley, look, you need to chill on this. Even if the worst happened and someone killed both of them, it may have to do with their being *friends,* not being in the wedding together."

"No, no," she said, shaking her head. "I thought that too for about forty seconds, but then I remembered something. Right after Jamie died, Robin started asking me about the wedding. She wanted to know if anything had seemed strange to me that day."

I felt the hairs on the back of my neck shoot up, as

if they'd been lollygaging around, half-listening, and now something had finally caught their attention.

"What do you mean *strange*?" I asked.

"I don't know. Nothing occurred to me when she asked other than the fact that the damn bridesmaid dresses made us look like giant balls of butter—and when I asked her to be more specific, she told me to never mind. At the time I didn't associate her question with Jamie's death, but now I see it has to be connected."

I asked if she'd pointed any of this out to the police and she said she'd told the officer in charge of the investigation of Robin's death about Jamie but he had dismissed it. The out-of-state factor had clearly deterred the police from seeing any kind of connection.

"So what exactly is it that you want from me?" I asked finally.

"Come to Greenwich. Just look into this. Isn't that what you *do*?"

A woman like Ashley wouldn't care that it wasn't *really* what I did. Yes, I'd gotten involved in a couple of murder cases, and yet basically I'm just a reporter. But trust-fund chicks like her were only interested in locating the spot where their needs intersected with what you had to give.

I thought for a moment, sipping my wine. It sounded on the surface as if the situation really *was* nothing more than a dreadful coincidence. But the question Robin had asked about the wedding disturbed me. At the very least I wanted to talk to Peyton. She must be reeling from it all.

I told Ashley okay, that I would visit Greenwich to talk to Peyton and possibly make some other inquiries. The next day, Wednesday, would actually be the best day for me to make the one-hour drive because I needed to be at *Gloss* on Thursday for a meeting with the deputy editor. Ashley seemed instantly relieved. I took down her number and told her that I would be in contact with her tomorrow, after I figured out what time I'd be leaving.

We asked for the check and she paid it, though there was a moment when I thought she was going to ask me to split it. Typical. After walking her to the elevator, I slipped out of the rear entrance of the hotel on 58th Street. The snow was still coming down hard and cars crawled along the street, their wheels sometimes spinning and whining. Miraculously a yellow taxi appeared and no one tried to bulldoze me for it. As I nestled into the warmth of the cab, I realized that a knot had formed in my stomach. The conversation with Ashley had rattled me.

Back in my apartment I pulled off my coat and boots and, without turning the lights on, flopped down on the couch. Lit by a blanket of snow on the terrace, my living room was practically aglow. I sank back into the cushions and tried to conjure up Peyton's wedding day. Much of it was a blur by now, thought I could recall the big details. The ceremony, in a Protestant church in Greenwich, had taken all of fifteen minutes. The reception, on the other hand, had gone on for hours, starting with a cocktail hour that had featured a vodka and caviar station among other extravagances. Dinner was five courses long, including a cheese course before dessert.

The phone rang suddenly, startling me. I picked it up from the side table next to the couch. It was Jack, just calling to say good night.

"I tried earlier," he said. "I didn't think you were going out tonight." Not accusatory, just curious. I blurted out the whole story.

"That's definitely weird," he said. "But I wouldn't let it alarm you. In all likelihood, it's just a coincidence."

"Doesn't it defy some natural law of probability?" I asked, knowing that because of his training as a shrink, he might be up on such things.

"Not really. It's known as a cluster. It's a set of random events that seem significant because there is more than an average amount of them. But they're just that—random. They really don't mean anything."

He told me again not to be alarmed, and then we moved on to a discussion about the upcoming weekend. It was momentarily distracting, but no sooner was I off the phone than I felt a new wave of disquietude. The two deaths could be random, sure, but then there was that odd question Robin had asked of Ashley: *Did anything about the wedding seem strange?* I couldn't imagine, though, what occurrence that April day could possibly have led someone to murder two women who had just met.

I turned the lights on finally, and after traipsing down the hall to my tiny office—which had once been a walk-in closet—I rummaged through my desk drawer until I found a photo of the wedding party that Peyton had sent me last summer as a souvenir. There was Peyton and David in the center and off to David's left, the best man, Trip, one of his business associates, and several older groomsmen I'd barely spoken to that weekend. Off to Peyton's right were the maid of honor and the five bridesmaids. And there I was among them, my short blondish brown hair shellacked into a Doris Day style and all five feet six inches of me entombed in yards and yards of yellow taffeta.

You see, that's why Ashley's story troubled me so much. I'd been a bridesmaid in Peyton Cross's wedding, too.

BAILEY'S BACK
AND BETTER THAN EVER . . .

In Kate White's new mystery
'TIL DEATH DO US PART

AVAILABLE IN HARDCOVER FROM WARNER BOOKS
ISBN: 0446-53175-8

ALTHOUGH PEYTON CROSS'S WEDDING WAS THE WEDDING OF THE YEAR LAST YEAR, SHE'S BACK IN THE NEWS...AND FOR ALL THE WRONG REASONS. THE MARTHA STEWART-WANNABE'S FORMER BRIDESMAIDS ARE DROPPING LIKE FLIES, AND THE INTREPID BAILEY WEGGINS IS CALLED INTO SERVICE TO INVESTIGATE. THERE ARE SO MANY SUSPECTS BAILEY'S HEAD IS SPINNING, AND AS A FORMER BRIDESMAID HERSELF, BAILEY MUST WATCH EVERY STEP SHE MAKES IN THOSE STILETTO HEELS . . .

AND IF YOU MISSED IT BEFORE . . .

. . . PICK UP KATE WHITE'S FIRST NOVEL,
IF LOOKS COULD KILL

THIS IS THE NOVEL THAT INTRODUCED THE INDOMITABLE SLEUTH BAILEY WEGGINS. WHEN A POISONED BOX OF CHOCOLATES CLAIMS THE LIFE OF HER BOSS'S NANNY, BAILEY'S ON THE CASE, TRACKING DOWN CLUES ALL OVER THE NORTHEAST AND REALIZING THAT WORKING AT A FASHION MAGAZINE CAN BE KILLER . . .

AVAILABLE IN MASS MARKET FROM WARNER BOOKS
ISBN: 0446-61257-X

Carnival Elation

7 Day Exotic Western Caribbean Itinerary

DAY	PORT	ARRIVE	DEPART
Sun	Galveston		4:00 P.M.
Mon	"Fun Day" at Sea		
Tue	Progreso/Merida	8:00 A.M.	4:00 P.M.
Wed	Cozumel	9:00 A.M.	5:00 P.M.
Thu	Belize	8:00 A.M.	6:00 P.M.
Fri	"Fun Day" at Sea		
Sat	"Fun Day" at Sea		
Sun	Galveston	8:00 A.M.	

For booking form and complete information
go to **www.getcaughtreadingatsea.com** or call **1-877-ADV-NTGE**

Complete coupon and booking form and mail both to:
**Advantage International, LLC,
195 North Harbor Drive, Suite 4206, Chicago, IL 60601**